Vote fo

CW00969375

By the same author:

English through Literature
    (a five book series)
The World in Stories
    (with J.H.Adcock}
Your Early Years in Teaching
Your CV in Teaching
Your Application for a Teaching Post
Your Interview in Teaching
In Place of Schools
Teaching Tomorrow

Acknowledgements:

Thanks are due to June Adcock for her editorial
work, to those who commented on the original
manuscript, and to those many journalists whose
work has been drawn on and without whose
diligence, perseverance and courage serious
failings in our society would pass unnoticed.

Vote for Terry Park!

The Common Sense Man

John Adcock

Deacon & Roberts, Publishers

2009

Copyright: John Adcock, 2009.

ISBN: 978-0-9564061-0-1

A CIP record for this book is available
from the British Library.

Published by:
Deacon & Roberts, Publishers,
The Old School,
Village Green,
Ruddington,
NG11 6HH.

Cover design by:
Clare Brayshaw

Text set in 10/11 New Times Roman and printed on
80gsm paper produced from sustainable forests.

Printed, bound & distributed in the UK by:
York Publishing Services Ltd.,
Hatfield Road,
Layerthorpe,
York, YO31 7

Contents

'Politics is the art of preventing
people from taking part in affairs
which properly concern them.'

Paul Valery (1871-1945),
Quel 2 (1943).

'The great majority of mankind are
satisfied with appearances, as though
they are realities, and are often even
more influenced by the things that
seem than by those that are.'

Nicole Machiavelli (1469-1527).
The Discourses (1517).

Week One

For one dreadful moment the accumulation of dirty dishes reminded Terry of depressing summers spent in seaside hotels as a temporary, assistant washer-up. Being a cash-strapped student on a minimum grant he had needed the money but hated the work, and his already frail self-confidence had not been strengthened by the discovery that his menial job and impecunious state held little attraction for the hotels' younger and more attractive guests.

But it was not happy holidaymakers of the late 1970s who had deposited today's unwashed crockery in his kitchen. Noisy guests from his fortieth birthday party had departed in the early hours oblivious both of his neighbours' need for sleep and of the debris they had left behind.

Now, with the eight o'clock news bulletin well under way, only the thought of the pile sitting there when he returned from school made him tackle the job there and then. He used gallons of steaming water and long squirts of scented soap as he scraped, scrubbed, washed and rinsed. He heaped cups, dishes, plates and glasses high on the draining board until they resembled a badly built pyramid after an earthquake.

'And there they'll stay,' he said to himself, 'until they're dry!'

Terry Park, a champion of common sense, saw no point in using time and energy on a job that would do itself. While he had regarded that as a sensible practice, his wife had not, and it had been a long-running bone of contention; she had wanted each piece washed, dried and stored away in its designated place. Further altercation had arisen over the installation of a dishwasher. Terry's wife had long argued in favour and scorned his assertion that it was an indefensible extravagance in a household of two. Such differences, while not major factors in their recent divorce, were ones which, when added to a myriad others, made the couple wonder why they had married in the first place.

But more significant reasons for their separation had been his wife's unwillingness to support her civil service union in militant action over pay and pensions and her total indifference to the wider political arena.

'Give over,' she had said, 'waste your own time if you want to, but don't waste mine. It makes no difference what you think, nothing will change. Politicians are the same the whole world over: they'll do what suits them, when it suits them, in a way that suits them, full stop. I see their nauseating machinations in the Town Hall every working day!'

To avoid a row Terry would not respond and, exasperated, she would add, 'Good grief, Terry, open your eyes! Don't you see the millions who never bother to vote? The millions who never make it to the polling booths? Don't you ever wonder why? I'll tell you why: they don't vote because they see how pointless it is and they sussed that out decades ago. With more common sense than you'll ever have they press on with their lives and do the best they can with what they've got. It's high time you did the same and stopped fighting other people's battles. Most of them don't give a hoot about politics anyway and even if they did you couldn't stand up for them all on your own! Even Terry Park can't take on the whole damned Establishment!'

While Terry had conceded such views were widespread and that her conclusion was more or less accurate, it had not been enough to save the relationship. After efforts at reconciliation and thirteen childless years they had drifted apart.

Although the separation had been received badly by her Baptist parents it had been foreseen. They had always regarded Terry Park as a trouble-making hothead unworthy of their daughter. He never went to church or read the Bible, had no time for organised religion, and had introduced left-wing politics on his first visit to their home. They well remembered the occasion when, in an era of winter strikes that had deprived them of gas, coal and electricity, he had asserted that militant trade unionists were testimony to the maxim: "God helps them that help themselves." Thankfully the couple had seen little of him after the marriage but they had missed their daughter greatly.

Yet when the divorce came they could say little. They knew their girl was the transgressor when she abandoned Terry to live with a faithful old flame of university years. But to their relief the divorce was settled amicably: both Terry and his wife agreed to let common sense prevail and no lingering lawyer made his fortune out of them.

*

As usual Terry listened to the current affairs programme that followed the news and by the time he had swilled clean water round the sink and draped the dripping dishcloth over the taps – another "horrible habit" his wife had abhorred – the presenters had reached their review of the daily papers. All agreed that the main topic was the strongly rumoured general election, and Thursday 2nd May was the commonly forecast date.

Speculation had started when the Third Assistant to the Principal Deputy Minister of Homeland Information had twice stated that the government would not call a surprise or 'snap' election. Such denials were seen as the clearest possible indication that a general election was imminent and all parties had swung into campaign mode.

Terry had to turn up the volume as the overweight and yellow helmeted youth next door revved repeatedly his motorbike engine before departing for Mansworth Liberal Arts college and his lengthy course in community well being. Thinking again that noise abatement laws needed tightening and that some aspects of higher education were ill named and overdone, Terry craned to hear his radio. There was general agreement that if an election were called immediately no party would be pleased; all had problems needing further time for resolution.

But Terry knew this unpopular government was unlikely to run its full term. Although difficult to imagine things could get worse and then a last minute election in November would mean the government's demise.

Yet that was their worry, he had one of his own – that of surviving the start-of-term staff meeting without becoming unduly depressed. There he would have to switch from the excitement of national politics to the dreary issues confronting an inward looking and wholly uninspiring suburban comprehensive school where he would witness backbiting, hidden agendas, scrambling for resources and blatant jockeying for better positions in the staff hierarchy. His patience would be tested. But, he mused, as he silenced the radio and reached for his car keys, the school's shenanigans would be little different from the high jinks he would face in the Palace of Westminster if he became a Member of Parliament.

*

To clear his head Terry would have preferred to walk the mile and a half to school but inclement weather made him use his car. He knew that in rush hour traffic the short distance might take forty minutes and make him late for the meeting, but that did not worry him for, despite teachers' sensible pleas for a later start, the head teacher, always fearful of disapproval from on high, adhered to the customary hour of nine o'clock.

His car radio was tuned to a local station and already interviews were taking place with constituency bigwigs and, occasionally, rank and file voters. He learned that, as with the national parties, the local parties had their difficulties. Constituency chairpersons were flustered, prospective candidates were apprehensive and party agents were distraught. All had banked on more time and complained they had been dropped in it from a great height.

The traffic got heavier and Terry's car came to a halt at road works whose start had coincided with the Monday morning rush hour. 'May Heaven help us,' he murmured as the rain came down on the fluorescent jacketed, hard-hatted workmen. 'What a time to start!'

As the radio programme moved to local candidates Terry forgot the road works as he strained to hear. It seemed the sitting member for Mansworth South-West, Modern Labour's Dr. Audrey Anderson, whose majority at the last election was miniscule, was in trouble again. Hetty Hopkins, a young reporter from the local daily, *The Mansworth Evening Messenger and Times*, was claiming that the Mod Lab MP had lost favour by allying herself closely with the unpopular government and had been overheard saying, "too many idle people want everything done for them." But her worst gaffe had been to question the role of a hereditary monarchy in a modern democracy without making it perfectly clear she was talking about the institution generally and not the Queen personally. Those constituents unable or unwilling to distinguish between the two, of whom the MP claimed there were many, had given her a rough ride and Hetty Hopkins' newspaper had benefited from a stream of angry letters. While the regrettable episode had strengthened the party chairman's doubts about the lady's prudence, this was no time to replace her.

There was comparable unhappiness in the Tolerant Democrats' camp. For months the party had been trying to smooth over February's rumpus when the same Miss Hetty Hopkins had disclosed that their prospective parliamentary candidate had befriended a local, landowning, pink-coated master of baying hounds and been given rent-free use of a weekend cottage on his estate. Well-chosen photos of rural vistas, country houses, stables, paddocks, hunt servants, sleek mounts and milling hounds accompanied her article. That the party had regained little ground was shown at a meeting called to protest the closing of an old people's home. Cries of *Tally Ho!* had greeted the candidate and the blowing of hunting horns had interrupted his indifferent speech.

But the local caucus of Today's Tories had nothing to laugh about. Their candidate's divorce from his constituency-popular wife of thirty years in favour of a voluptuous French actress from Nice, plus reports that he had invested heavily in the American armaments industry, had

4

done nothing to help. Only narrowly had his candidature been endorsed.

As the programme moved to the possibility of fringe candidates attracting vital votes, the traffic thinned and Terry moved cautiously off the Sir Quentin Reynolds Ring Road onto a quiet suburban avenue. Soon he turned into the curving, tree-lined drive of his school.

The weather worsened as, switching off his radio, he eased his elderly Rover between the nearly-new Volvo estate car of a deputy head teacher and the long-obsolete but immaculately kept Ford Escort saloon of the school's meticulous teacher-librarian. Chuntering to himself as the wind-driven rain lashed his car roof Terry grabbed his brief case and made a dash for the school's imposing main entrance.

The summer term had begun.

*

Terry Park's well-used leather brief case was a farewell gift from fellow teachers in Newcastle upon Tyne and reminded him daily of friendly, reliable colleagues who shared his belief in the value of common sense. Today, glad to escape the late March winds and early April showers, he clasped the case to his chest as he shouldered apart the heavy glass doors of his current school.

Lying in wait was the fifty-one-year-old caretaker, Arthur Hull. The man waved meaningfully from the far side of a space-wasting foyer while, shaking rain from his jacket, Terry smiled back warily. Hull had a nose for trouble.

'That girl's coming back, Mr Park. Be here Thursday.'

Terry stared at Hull in disbelief. 'They're letting her in?'

'Thursday morning, sharp.'

Terry's face clouded over.

'I see,' he said. 'Thanks, Mr Hull, I'll remember that,' and he turned away. But then, changing his mind, he stepped forward to scrutinise Hull. This news, if true, meant open warfare.

'Thursday? How d'you know?' With some relief he placed his case on a terrazzo-tile floor that was shinier now than it would be for the next three months. 'Who told you?'

'Mrs Eastman. There's been a phone call, an E-mail and a letter.'

His earlier thoughts of how a general election would make a welcome distraction from the term's dull routine had prevented Terry's spirits from sinking to an all-time low, but now, as if encased in lead, they plummeted to unfathomable depths. Such news, reaching him via caretaker via school secretary, was not only disturbing in itself but was typical of the way things were done here. Sensible, union-minded staff in Newcastle upon Tyne would not have tolerated it for a moment.

So, he thought, the sensual Mrs Ingrid Eastman, senior of the school's two secretaries, was yet again revealing secrets, among other things, to all who crossed her path, and Arthur Hull, womaniser supreme, crossed her path frequently.

The firmly ensconced, come-hither Mrs Eastman was a mature, well-built woman of forty-four on whose comely figure Hull liked to dwell. In fact he lusted over it and begrudged her husband his marital pleasures. Mrs Eastman, well aware of Hull's desires, would lead him on and, with a nod and a wink, slip him many a piece of gossip. She knew the whole staff would learn of anything leaked to Hull long before the day was out and then she could sit back and watch the fun.

But simmering sexual jealousy was not the sole reason for Hull's aversion to Fergus Eastman. According to the caretaker the odious man was a fascist in all but name - far to the right of General Franco.

'No doubt we'll hear more at the meeting,' Terry replied, trying to appear unconcerned, 'along with all the other good news!'

He pretended to laugh, but he was not amused: he was dismayed. Hull rarely got information wrong, especially on such worthy topics as fights, suspensions, expulsions, appeals, readmissions, police enquiries, loitering with or without intent, disturbing the peace, drug dealing, shop-lifting, bullying, common assault, car-theft, threatening behaviour, arson, graffiti, gangs, vandalism, blackmail, illicit liaisons, Peeping Toms, prostitution, pornography, under-age pregnancy and verbal or physical abuse. All were grist to Arthur Hull's mill.

'And the staff meeting will start late,' said Hull as he walked away. 'Mrs Olde rang in. The head's had another of his turns.'

'May Heaven help us all!' Terry said to himself. 'Olde's caving in already! Why in hell's name doesn't the man retire?'

His frustration increased as he realised that instead of fighting rush hour traffic he could have had a decent breakfast and heard more of the news. It could be today that the date of the general election would be announced and here he was wasting time because a head teacher who should have departed years ago was again indisposed. So, with an hour to spare and a disinclination to wait in an ill-tempered staff room in which the coming election would rouse little interest, he decided to go to his class base, make tea, and examine the summer term's lists of pupils to see how many extra bodies the weak and ailing, "Never-Say-No" head teacher, Adrian Olde, had admitted during the Easter break.

*

For his forty years and one day Terry Edgar Park was a fit man. With shoulders back and head held high he was of average height and weight. He registered five feet ten and a half inches and, on rising and before eating breakfast, weighed eleven stones, thirteen-and-three-quarter pounds: he liked to keep below twelve stones. He drank modestly, smoked not at all, paid little to his dentist and was rarely ill. He used a pair of off-the-rack reading glasses only when light was poor and print was small, and he could hear the faintest of whispered remarks in any classroom. He had a pleasant, roundish face and a full head of almost black hair, which was greying only slightly over the ears, while its length would be of considerable interest to any regimental sergeant major.

Apart from opening days of term and first lessons on Monday mornings he gave warm smiles to friend and foe alike. He was one of a diminishing number who, in the closing decade of the Twentieth Century, could claim fair contentment as a teacher – someone who, when left to get on with it, took pleasure in his classroom work. He liked young people, was keen on his specialisms of social studies and English literature, and enjoyed the skilled and varied arts of teaching. But over the past few years he had found that factors beyond his control had impeded such practice and reduced his satisfaction. He thought the worst of these, as in the country generally, was the demise of common sense.

Later, with a mug of strong tea in his hand, he stood by the window of his first floor classroom and took in a scene which, while attractive in itself, it was becoming worryingly familiar. As did his Newcastle brief case it reminded him of the years spent at this school and of the need to decide whether to stay put or move on. But move on where? There were, as he knew well, far worse places than this. And therein lay the rub: this school might be OK if its objectives were thought out and consistently worked at, but there was little sign of that happening any time soon. Indeed, as Hull had revealed, there would be no more common sense on display this term than last. Terry knew that when a once good school was in deadly decline his own prospects, if he stayed, would not be bright.

Reflecting on the term just past he knew trouble had started in January, when, on the morning a posse of intrusive inspectors was to begin its fleeting assessment of sixty-six teachers' long-term achievements, four centimetres of snow had drifted gently against walls, hedges, fences and gates. It had coated already icy roads and made a carelessly driven truck skid into a low brick wall and shed its cargo of potato chips with the result that, by eight-thirty, the school's main driveway was blocked. From his classroom window Terry could see that very spot and recall events as if they were happening today.

*

As the shaken driver was treated for bruises a no-nonsense policeman directed all comers, including the inspection team's indignant lady leader, to a narrow side entrance a hundred yards away. The constable, unaware of the leader's outstanding importance in the world of education, insisted she and her colleagues park well clear of the school gate and then join jostling pupils as they squeezed excitedly through a narrow opening fifty yards away. Her displeasure was apparent.

Expensively dressed as they were, the team of assorted assessors lacked the solid footwear needed for a dignified walk on icy pavements. They slipped and slithered as, dodging snowballs, they approached the foyer where an uneasy head teacher practised his words of welcome.

That light snowfall, picturesque in itself and welcomed by children young and old, caused the usual disruption in an ill-prepared nation. School buses were late and three teachers had car problems. Some children were kept at home while those compelled to attend made the most of the confusion. Doorways, corridors and stairways were awash, cloakrooms were indescribable and, outside in the cold, a blaspheming Hull struggled with shovel, salt and sand. Morning assembly was late, the first lesson was cancelled, lesson two became one, three became two and so on through that awful day.

The chief inspector, a shapeless lady who, if she were honest, knew she had been uninspiring as a classroom teacher, had to rearrange her team's schedules. She was then unimpressed by the school's depleted assembly which necessitated a reluctant stand-in pianist, an unprepared reading from *Matthew 7*: "Judge not, that ye be not judged" and a half-hearted singing of Thomas Ken's hymn, carefully selected by Terry's musical colleague, Dafydd Hughes, "Redeem thy misspent time that's past, and live this day as if thy last." But wholly abandoned was The Head Girl's scheduled rendering of Handel's aria, "Art thou troubled?"

The inspector found further changes necessary when two teachers called in sick and a smell of gas in the chemistry laboratory closed that facility. But the final straw came when Inspector Number Seven, a nervous novice in the inspection stakes, sat in on what he thought was to be a full-bloodied enactment of the Luddite riots only to find himself viewing a colourful video on the breeding cycle of emperor penguins. Because of the rearrangements the disorientated adjudicator had gone to the biology department's Mrs Pauline Edwards' natural history lesson instead of the social history department's Mrs Patricia Edwards' dramatisation of Ned Ludd's response to industrial progress. It was the embarrassed man's first and last duty in the inspection set up and, to his credit, he admitted he was "not a little relieved to be leaving."

The inspectors' report was not the best ever recorded but few teachers bothered about that. Some carefree souls thought the laughs on the first day were worth the mediocre assessment received while others hoped for better luck next time round. Some simply shrugged their shoulders: what did the views of these itinerant busybodies matter anyway? In only three and a half days what had they really learned about Outer Mansworth Comprehensive School and its deep, intricate, long-standing problems? The sooner they got lost the better!

*

But Terry was not easily daunted and always tried to look on the bright side; last term had been and gone and the one coming might be better. Perhaps, he thought hopefully as he ran a finger round the rim of his empty tea mug, perhaps the local education authority would be more generous, the governors more helpful, the inspectors more constructive, the advisors more credible, the head teacher more decisive, the staff more co-operative, the pupils more amenable, the caretaker more accommodating, the unions more determined, the resources more plentiful, the politicians more thoughtful – but there was a laugh! The very idea of meddlesome, publicity-seeking, career-conscious, seat-savvy politicians being "more" thoughtful was good for a laugh any day! "More" implied they had a modicum of thoughtfulness in the first place and, even at the start of another term, that idea would bring a smile to many a teacher's face!

But was that being fair to politicians? If that picture was correct why was he, Terry Park, so interested in politics? Why did he hope, one day, to join the politicians' ranks? Why was he so interested in the coming general election? Why had he let politics come between his wife and himself? He considered carefully and, as usual, tried to see both sides of the case. He knew many politicians gave unstintingly of their own time, could earn more if they had stayed in their original professions, helped constituents beyond the call of duty, and, behind the scenes, supported worthwhile causes.

But that was just the point. Too much of their work was "behind the scenes" and unappreciated by a public aware only of the scandals, the bungling, the empty Commons benches seen on TV, the point-scoring, the trotting out of the party line, the ridiculous and incomprehensible parliamentary ritual, the sickening public-schoolboy rowdiness, the unwillingness to admit errors, the evasive answers, the fulsome self-determined salaries, the generous pensions and lavish expenses and, most of all, what was seen as a lack of common sense in decision making. But, he mused, whether or not this dark description was correct, it might as well be if it was the one fixed firmly in the public's mind. Ask any marketing man and he would soon tell you: 'Perception is everything.' Couldn't politicians see that for themselves?

He needed to think that one through. If he became a politician could he live with that unflattering image? Could he face having his own views distorted, his weaknesses exposed, his good work ignored, his private life revealed? Could he? Could he call on people to *"Vote for Terry Park!"* and, subsequently, take the flak that would surely come if they did just that and he was returned to Parliament? Could he?

These doubts had been building steadily. When only thirteen he had looked forward eagerly to elections both local and general; stood for the radical left in his grammar school mock-elections; had stuffed campaign envelopes for the local Labour Party when he should have been doing his homework; delivered leaflets, and written vitriolic letters about grasping capitalists to left-wing newspapers. He thought those times had been times of excitement, times that had meaning. People had been interested in politics then: they had voted in larger numbers, heckled at meetings and watched developments keenly. His father had told him people once sat through the night beside smoky coal fires listening eagerly to election results on crackling radios. But today, despite central heating and broadcasts perfect in sound and vision, many didn't bother to tune in. They didn't give a damn! To them the whole arena was a murky one where untrustworthy and grasping people practised sleaze.

Had his wife been right?

"They press on with their lives and do the best they can with what they've got. It's high time you did the same....!"

Should he still be a politician?

However, he told himself, he needn't answer that question today. He was not forced to go into politics and that, at least, was a consolation. If he stayed where he was he wouldn't starve and was unlikely to be thrown out of his job; he didn't depend on the votes of fickle parents and their children to keep him in work. Also consoling was the thought that this term couldn't be worse than the last. Or could it?

*

The unfortunate week with the roving inspectors had set the mood for the rest of the spring term. The weather was atrocious and outdoor activities were cancelled; the heating system proved inadequate; mutterings about poor pay came from kitchen staff; a weekend break-in deprived the school of twenty-one computers; bickering governors argued about introducing rugby football for boys and soccer for girls; the music room roof leaked and two elderly pianos went out of tune; a recently-established and rapidly-growing teachers' union threatened militant approaches to age-old grievances; daily disputes between departmental heads intensified; the performance of the school's worst teacher worsened; the head master's nervous disorders called for more frequent absences, and, after weeks of procrastination and amid deliberately engineered and adverse local publicity, the most difficult, objectionable, scheming, trouble-making, untrustworthy, anti-school pupil Terry had ever set eyes on was suspended in the penultimate week of term. Never had an Easter break been so warmly welcomed by the teachers of Outer Mansworth Comprehensive School (Mixed).

*

Terry ruminated as he sat at his desk and tapped his fingertips rhythmically on a pile of papers. Looking ahead realistically he knew little in the school would have changed and certainly nothing would have changed for the better. Unresolved problems would be carried forward and added to those in the pipeline and so *ad infinitum.* As with present-day politics education was not what it was when he had left school twenty-two years ago.

But the rumours of a general election intrigued him. He wished he had been able to hear what the radio commentator had said about fringe candidates. While there would be the usual crackpots he had particularly wanted to hear of any reference to the ultra right-wing People's Patriotic

11

Party (PPP).

While Terry saw the PPP as a collection of bigots, fewer and fewer people seemed to share his opinion. Like it or not, the PPP had been gaining ground both in local elections and in opinion polls and he had wanted to know if they would be marching with banners held high in Mansworth South-West. He knew they had gained support with their strong, clear-cut stands on law and order, taxation, benefit-fraud, mass immigration and outright opposition to the European Union - all linked inextricably and deliberately to the notion of national pride. And he regretted that the main parties, during debilitating decades of political correctness, had played right into the hands of the opportunity grasping "Thank you very much" People's Patriotic Party.

But was that a disinterested view of the PPP? If a party emerged with policies that appealed to people – policies the main parties would not pursue – why shouldn't the PPP or any other group come along and offer those policies, and, if that's what people wanted, win their freely-given votes? That, after all, was part of a democracy and it was the main parties who, deliberately or not, had ignored issues which were of understandable public concern. It was their fault things had got to this sorry state. What short-sighted, arrogant fools they had been not to listen to the people and what a mess they had made! And in the end, he thought, it came back to the ousting of common sense.

*

It was at frustrating times like these that Terry thought of his robust but amicable exchange with Jenny Jean Jones, an attractive, auburn-haired twenty-one year-old teacher-in-training. But recalling that year-old conversation did nothing to lighten his mood.

'Doesn't anyone question it?' Jenny had asked. 'Doesn't anyone suggest a different way of teaching children? Not *anyone*?'

'Not really. Those who do are put off by establishment indifference and give up. The fortunate souls who can change jobs do so, smartly.'

'And don't come back?'

'And don't come back.'

As well as being an imaginative teacher, an inveterate writer of unpublishable novels and a fledgling politician, Terry Park was a talented amateur actor. He could recite verbatim both sides of that conversation and, as would any seasoned player, knew the lines of his leading lady as well as his own. He was relating the facts of modern teaching life to Jenny, the tall, lively, university post-graduate student who was undertaking five days' classroom observation in the school where Terry worked. He had been made her short-term mentor and Jenny, while liking Terry, had disliked the school's impersonal regime. Further, unlike many young people in her position, she made her views known.

'I heard rumours' she said, 'but didn't believe them.'

'What did you hear?'

'Well, I heard that here, for instance, over sixty teachers have many meetings, concoct reports, anticipate inspections, conduct tests, check key stages, meet targets and prepare for exams, every term.'

'Every term.'

'And people who do less teaching, chair meetings, work from offices, they are the ones who've been promoted? The ones who might have been the best teachers and who are lost to the classroom?'

'Afraid so.'

'And they're the highest paid? The teachers who don't teach?'

'Yes,' Terry hesitated, 'generally speaking.'

'It's ridiculous.'

'It is.'

'And you accept it?'

Terry shrugged his shoulders.

'I see,' Jenny said thoughtfully. 'You do. You go along with it as you do with the National Curriculum. You don't work out what's best for each child and offer appropriate tuition with personalised study programmes knowing children are all so different from each other, and that individualist means of working in that way exist already?'

'You put it remarkably well,' Terry said. 'But there's not the time. We don't *like* the system: we tolerate it. And remember, *teachers* are all different, they have their strengths, weaknesses, interests, just as children do. They'd like to plan for themselves, they'd like to develop things they do best, but they don't; they follow the politically devised state curriculum *en masse*. And, I'm sorry to say, they do so without much meaningful protest, without the fight to the finish that's so badly needed. They shrug their shoulders and say it's all laid down.'

'By whom?'

'Ministers, MPs, education officers, councillors, governors, inspectors, examiners, advisors, administrators, and accountants: the whole wretched system is awash with them.'

'But what do those people know about real schools, real children?'

'You tell me.'

'And what's it got to do with *real* education?'

'Nothing.'

'*Nothing*?'

'Nothing at all.' He tried not to laugh at her incredulity.

'Yet all those children are compelled to attend school?'

'Yes. Truants are rounded up like stray sheep on a mountain.'

'By attendance officers?'

'And police.'

'*Police*?'

'Yes. Parents can be cautioned, fined, imprisoned.'

'Imprisoned? At the end of the 20th century? *Imprisoned*?'

Jenny's face was lit by her anger. Terry had not met a student- teacher like this before: he approved.

'Yes. Parliament makes the laws,' he said. 'We just go on …'

'It's so despotic,' she persisted, 'cruel, futile. Some children aren't suited to school: some resent it and get little out of it, others fear it! And you can't *force* a child to learn, we all know that! You can strap him to a seat, stick textbooks or handouts in front of him, shove a pen in his hand, make him look at you, make him take notes, slap worksheets on his desk, stand over him, but you *can't make him learn*! Not learn anything worthwhile? Can you?'

'Of course not. But keeping him there reduces the national truancy rate and provides party politicians with a few positive statistics.'

'But you might turn him off education for life?'

'Yes.'

'While his anti-school attitudes upset others?'

'Yes.'

'So it's counter-productive: a waste of money?'

'A frightening waste. Billions and billions of pounds.'

'Every year?'

'Every year, and rising. Politicians think "more money" is the only answer because they've no other ideas. "Look how good we are: we've put *millions* more into education!" No, it's the ideas they lack.'

'But there are thousands of capable teachers. What of them? They must have ideas - and votes. Why don't they make a song and dance at general elections? They've got the power to do something.'

'Have they?' mused Terry. 'Have they got power? They can't even organise themselves into one strong trade union and speak with a single voice. They're pathetic the way they allow themselves to be divided, weakened and ruled. You'll find out. Just look round this place.'

'So, do you think schooling's a waste of time as well as money?'

'A lot of it is.'

'A tutor at university told us about this – he'd been a head teacher. But I took it with a pinch of salt. I thought he was exaggerating.'

'He wasn't.'

'No, he wasn't: I see that now. But it defies common sense!'

'*Common sense?*' This time Terry laughed aloud, quite unable to contain himself. 'Common sense is at a premium, young lady! This country lacks common sense more than anything else – and not just in education! So don't, please, talk to me about common sense!'

Then he was sorry for laughing and wished he had not said: "young lady." It was patronising, ageist, sexist, in every way politically incorrect. Today everything had to be politically correct, especially in education. He tried to assess her reaction but he needn't have worried; she hadn't even noticed. Jenny Jean Jones had far more important things on her mind than political correctness. She was pondering on her future: *forty years* of this?

*

The next term Jenny returned for an eight-weeks' period of teaching practice. Her assessment was so high she was persuaded to apply for a permanent post in the school and now worked well, if questioningly, in Terry's humanities department. Her critical outlook suited Terry Park but, although he remembered their earlier conversation, it had not been referred to again.

*

Before the staff meeting Terry visited the men's room. There he switched his thoughts from Jenny Jean Jones to Arthur Hull and his unwelcome news. Although he could be contrary and irritating, Terry liked Hull. While he had all the "find-me-if-you-can" characteristics of many a school caretaker and knew more about working to rule than any President of the TUC, he was an affable oddity. His left wing views were well argued and Terry sympathised. He was a fountain of information in many areas and sometimes Terry took his racing tips and won. Then he would buy Hull a pint at *The Standing Oak*.

15

It was there he had learned how well-read Hull was. He suspected Hull read novels as he sat behind the slightly open door of his retreat - a stuffy room tucked away at the far end of the school foyer. Bulldog clips held a calendar of race meetings, *The Sun's* sports pages, and timesheets for the school's six part-time cleaners. The hideaway was a prime observation post and little escaped Hull's gaze - especially the arrival and departure of visitors.

The half-glazed door still had '*Caretaker'* painted on it: Hull refused to be known as a porter, school janitor, building supervisor, site manager, school keeper, custodian, or any other fancy name.

'No sense in it,' he said. 'Job's the same, so's the pay!'

As he zipped up his fly Terry nodded to himself as if rerunning the conversation. Just as Hull's job was basically the same as it had always been, so, in Terry's mind, was the job of a teacher. Education was, or should be, a simple, warm, humane, caring process, a matter of developing trusting relationships between teacher, child and parent, of reading widely and discussing as deeply as each child could all that was in that literature. And what they read could be the entire world: its history and geography and people. It would make a whole curriculum in itself... Then he found himself drying already dried hands.

*

Terry's mum and dad had been delighted when he passed the eleven-plus exam and moved to a boys' grammar school. They rewarded him with the many-geared bike they could ill afford, and uncles and aunts sent congratulations and postal orders. His parents, hiding their views on snobbery and elitism, provided the uniform, books and equipment the new school demanded. Then for seven years they watched Terry, in his learning and his developing attitudes, move away from them and their lifestyle. Nevertheless they were pleased to see him excel in the sixth form and, along with his literature, history and social studies, retain the family's interest in left wing politics. His acceptance by London University to read sociology was applauded even when the couple discovered that sociology was not wholly synonymous with socialism.

Terry, who had hoped for an upper second, was exuberant when he gained a first. Within weeks, and without his acquiescence, he learned that his previously almost-forgotten name had appeared in bold gold lettering on the honours board of his old school, *and* that a gowned and smiling headmaster had mentioned him in morning assembly!

Despite being advised by the university appointments board to apply for civil service entry at top level, Terry still remembered his failed, confidence-sapping Oxford University entrance interview and saw little likelihood of a man of his social background reaching the higher echelons of the civil service. Rightly or wrongly he saw that as an august body populated by public schoolboys and Oxbridge men – with a few girls from good homes thrown in for appearance's sake.

His mother died suddenly only months after his graduation and he felt compelled to stay within easy reach of home until his father had adjusted to his loss. So Terry stuck to his original plan of teaching social studies and spent an argumentative year studying for a post graduate teaching certificate at the university in the city where he now lived and taught. After the demands of his degree studies he found the teaching course easy and that, he thought, was wrong.

He then taught in a grammar school and at an adult education centre and spent two thought-provoking years with VSO in Africa. Back in England he taught in a "challenging" school in Newcastle upon Tyne. There he had liked the city, made friends, and met his future wife.

*

Despite doubts about the country's antiquated education system, Terry was an excellent teacher. He was popular with pupils and respected by colleagues. For eight years he had headed the humanities department of Outer Mansworth Comprehensive School and was supposed to be contemplating an overdue career move.

But Terry was reluctant to seek promotion. He was taking longer than expected to settle after his divorce and knew he could find even worse schools than this. He was interested in his subject and had no real wish to be promoted to deputy or head teacher. Further, as he knew well, he was a political animal. He could not decide whether to accept what he had in this fairly secure job or venture full-time into radical writing or left-wing politics. With teaching's steady decline in attractiveness those last two interests had become his real loves and if they could be combined he would be ecstatic.

He had been writing stories since he was eleven and had had several included in his school magazine. But he had neglected his stories as politics took hold. Then his radical contributions to the local press and his university's student newspaper won him few friends of influence.

'Park's politics won't do him any good at all,' his sixth form history master had said. His head-nodding colleagues had agreed: politics wouldn't do Park any good.

'Become involved in politics after you've taken your degree,' his university tutor warned, 'no party will select non-graduates now and without a party you're stymied. So get stuck into your work here!'

His interest in politics had been revived by Jenny Jones' four words, "it defies common sense," and by the rumoured proximity of the general election. In the past year he had begun to write a satirical novel in which Britain's main parties were driven into the wilderness by the emergence of a new, free-thinking, invigorating, Common Sense Party: a party whose rise to popularity he based on the simple philosophy of asking people what they wanted and making an effort to provide it. And, he claimed, what voters wanted most was more common sense. He was developing the novel's main character gradually and, unsurprisingly, it was taking the shape of a trade union supporting teacher who was head of sociology in a large comprehensive school. But he was having problems with the narrative: it would not work out.

*

The school's long, wide drive was entered through wrought iron gates and offered a seductive approach to the mid-1960's building. Its landscaped grounds complemented the desirable suburb of the one-time manufacturing city of Greater Mansworth. The district housed liberal and conservative voters and, as if by magic, yellow and blue posters would be displayed in windows and pinned to garden gates on the very day an election was announced.

Now unashamedly trading on its past reputation, the school was oversubscribed even though it accommodated eleven hundred pupils instead of its statistically concocted establishment of nine hundred and eighty-two. The building had been designed by that worthy architect Rudolph M.R.R.Charte, whose own teaching experience was limited to two uninspiring years of part-time lecturing in a dreary polytechnic on the theme of lightweight, but heavy load-bearing, roof beams.

To all those who taught in Rudolph Charte's school such limited teaching experience was apparent in the impractical size and shape of its classrooms, the strange layout of its corridors and assembly areas, and its stadium-like foyer. The man's heady design lacked the foresight that could have been supplied, fee-free, by any experienced teacher.

But the mellow brick-built, large-windowed school in its tree-rich grounds was outwardly attractive. From its imposing appearance and semi-rural setting parents thought, in their sweet innocence, that it must be "a good school". Some poor souls struggled to buy over-priced houses in its catchment area – choosing a book by its cover.

The suburb was lower middle class although most parents would have omitted "lower." The four hundred houses were built, despite robust objections, on a green field site and planned by the same Rudolph M.R.R. Charte. He included the *Standing Oak Inn* – a pub named in memory of the century-old tree felled before preservation orders began to bite. Elderly residents told of firemen removing banner-waving and shrieking protesters from the oak's highest branches and of patrolling policemen with straining dogs surveying, closely, crowds of irate onlookers. But law and brute force prevailed: the noble tree fell.

'There goes our past,' said one old man. 'It's all over!'

The school was only half a mile from the Little Mansworth Campus of the highly regarded, pre-World War Two, redbrick University of Greater Mansworth. There, like Jenny Jean Jones, Terry Park had taken the one-year Post Graduate Certificate of Education, the course which would turn him, hopefully, into a conventional schoolteacher.

Today the school's inner workings belied its high, popular esteem and inspectors' reports were lukewarm. Terry attached no importance to that. 'If the inspectors didn't like what we're doing that must be a good sign,' he stated in a follow-up staff meeting. 'We must be developing along the right lines.'

At the anxiety-ridden head teacher's request his remarks were not minuted, but were well remembered. Each year discontent among staff heightened. Factions formed, fought, reformed and fought again, while individuals were increasingly irritated by the iniquitous salary system, the time and money wasted on a combination of meetings, red tape, new rules, ever-changing plans, statements of intent, curriculum amendments, loss of respect, deteriorating pupil behaviour, paucity of sanctions, the growth of health and safety legislation, the ever-soaring cost of administration, and, of course, the immeasurable price of stress.

*

Terry Park entered the crowded, rowdy staff room reluctantly. Some teachers, making coffee, were in a small kitchen which adjoined the room on the far side and which lay directly opposite the staff room's other entrance: that door, usually closed, led to a peaceful passage known, significantly, as "The Executive Corridor".

It was here that the head teacher, deputy heads, head of careers, head of sixth form, heads without portfolio, and five heads of other years had their rooms. Office apportionment was all-important as it displayed levels of managerial status, as did the positioning of an office: those at the corridor's quiet end, near the library and away from pupils, were most favoured. As cynics remarked, the further you were from pupils, chalk and classrooms the higher your standing and pay.

At the foyer end of the corridor, well away from but diagonally opposite Hull's hideout, was the secretaries' room. Originally it had housed one secretary and catered for only a fifth of the work now undertaken. The need for two secretaries and the inadequacies of their accommodation said much about the expansion of bureaucracy throughout education. Once, in a reaction without precedent, teachers had united to resist attempts to take "a small portion" of their staff room for "temporary" secretarial use. Even they weren't having that!

*

Terry looked round the staff room despondently. Already Ursula Irving, the senior deputy head teacher, had checked that all was in order and was nodding impatiently to the hesitant headmaster.

Adrian Olde, now in his third headship, saw her signal. 'Thank you, thank you,' he said nervously to the staff. It was as if the ever-worried man wondered what he would do if they all ignored him and chatted on, but today, mercifully, silence soon prevailed.

Olde was sixty-three and looked older. Thirty years earlier he had secured the headship of a small school in competition with ninety-nine other candidates. The Director of Education had told the six short-listed men they had done well to be selected against such opposition. That number of candidates for the headship of an unremarkable school was normal for those times, and common sense, Terry thought, should make politicians ask why so few teachers applied for headships today. Were they *so* fearful of the likely answers?

In the spirit of the age Olde had done a sound job and was promoted to a larger school. While that assignment had gone well, he sensed that the role of the conscientious head teacher was becoming annually more onerous. He attributed this to the increasing size of his second school, demographic changes in its catchment area, ever-increasing demands of administration, and his less than perfect health.

Nevertheless, a decade later, he had obtained his present headship. The compilation of a suitable short-list from a paucity of applicants had presented the governors with problems but, to their relief, an acceptable candidate had been found in the prematurely balding, tall, skeletally thin Mr Adrian Mark Olde with his externally taken degree of London University, and he proved to be the agreeable, unassuming, trouble-avoiding traditionalist they sought.

Today the short-skirted, fulsome and firmly bosomed Mrs Ingrid Eastman, on whom Olde relied, took the minutes. Uncharacteristically Olde dealt with preliminaries quickly and moved to *Item One* at which juncture he seemed particularly uneasy.

With eyes downcast, he said, 'I propose to readmit the unfortunate girl excluded late last term. I'm sure you will recall the case.'

The teachers did recall the case: collectively they blanched.

'It was, I must confess, an unhappy time, but over the holiday I have given the matter serious thought.'

'So have I,' interrupted Sheila Tipping, the school's sole teacher of German language and literature who offered also subsidiary French and Spanish, and who was a member of the newly formed teachers' trade union, or "professional association" as some preferred to call it, Teachers For Radical Action (TFRA). She, too, had been given news of the imminent readmission by that staunch upholder of free speech and open government, school caretaker Arthur Hull.

'I am opposed to her re-admittance to any year, or any class or any group, for any subject, at any time, under any circumstances, for any reason, at anyone's behest. I trust that makes the position clear.'

Supportive voices were heard. Mrs Eastman pencilled in names.

'If you will hear me out Mrs Tipping,' said Adrian Olde, 'I will try to show that the case is not quite as clear-cut as would ... ...'

'Bullying, extortion, spreading malicious gossip, aggression, gross impertinence, influencing weaker girls, refusal to wear school uniform in favour of scanty blouses and disgustingly tight jeans, open plagiarism, incomplete or late assignments, smoking in the toilets, persistent truancy despite numerous "final warnings" would seem fairly clear cut to me,' argued Sheila Tipping.

'But ...' began Olde.

'Culminating in forcing, I repeat, Mr Olde, *forcing,* four frightened children to surrender their dinner money to her or her cronies. And, don't forget, there were rumours of drug use.'

Middle-aged Sheila Tipping, the comfortably-housed wife of a dental surgeon, mother of a son working abroad and two daughters at different Oxford colleges, well-dressed, skilfully made-up, regular client of an expensive city centre hair stylist, knew there was a shortage of teachers of German language and literature who could also offer sixth form Spanish. Her employment was secure.

Olde vacillated. He had expected opposition, but not put so soon or so vehemently. His hesitation allowed Mrs Tipping to continue.

'Isn't this the third school from which this wretched girl has been excluded?' she pressed. 'Perhaps one of those would take her back? Doesn't the local education authority encourage schools to assist each other in these matters? Is no head teacher amenable?'

'I am obliged to agree with Mrs Tipping,' said Ursula Irving. 'And I say *'obliged'* deliberately because I detest exclusion; often it is not the child who is to blame but the parents or peer group – or both. But today I must take issue with the head teacher for I see no alternative to continued exclusion, and, remember, I had most dealings with her last term. I had to support staff and check the negative influence she was having on other girls – and boys! I want no repetition of that.'

Terry thought the deputy head's case was inalienable.

'And the education authority has an obligation towards permanently excluded pupils,' said Dafydd Hughes, a TFRA member.

Ursula Irving nodded agreement although she had little time for Hughes. He was far too union minded and, like the militant, recently appointed, Teachers For Radical Action local union official, that truly awful man Eddie 'Bloody' Collins, a real barrack room lawyer. And Ursula had not forgotten Hughes' verbal attack on her in a crowded staff room late last year. Knowing Ursula was involved with one of the teachers' unions which discouraged any militant action, Hughes had accused its members of undermining other teachers' interests.

'When you say you'll never fight no matter what happens you give the bosses a free hand to drop us in it!' he had stormed, 'then you let us all down. Things get worse and worse, the profession sinks lower and lower, and you pacifists end up hurting the very children your pathetic policy is supposed to help!' Then he had marched out giving Ursula no time to reply, but a more moderate man had supported her.

'Forget him, Ursula,' the man had said, 'your lot does more to raise the teachers' image than all his rowdy reds. That's what matters.'

Terry had not joined in, but he knew a man like Hughes would never accept that a softly, softly approach might, occasionally, do more good then driving snorting bulls at every gate in sight. But, if he had to choose, he would be on Dafydd Hughes' side.

Ursula had been senior deputy head since shortly before Olde's arrival. A smart, young-looking forty-nine, she had decided she would not be applying for headships. She had seen what being a head had done to well-meaning people. The struggling Olde was one and she envied him not. She had a light timetable, her own office with fresh flowers, pictures, kettle, coffee maker, fitted carpet, bookcase, armchair, and, with this weak boss, such authority as she chose to take without the buck landing on her desk. She was content to wait for her index-linked pension and worthwhile lump sum; then she would travel.

She was also in the unusual position, for a deputy, of being school representative for a moderate teachers' union which was increasingly at odds with Teachers For Radical Action and she found her peaceful union work interesting. Reluctantly, because she seemed to be allying with Dafydd Hughes, she had today donned her union hat. She was angry that Mr Olde had not consulted her about the readmission and knew that even her own her tolerant union would not countenance bullying, extortion or violence. No union would approve the stance being taken by Mr Olde, not even his own tiny elitist educational union, the General Association of School Managing Executives, (GASME).

'The police should have been called in about the extortion,' said Sheila Tipping. 'It would have been a lesson to her and others like her and a load off our backs. But the opportunity was missed – again.'

'Now, Mrs Tipping, be fair. The parents of the bullied girls were unwilling to go to court,' Olde said. He ignored a derisory snort from a distant seat. 'Whereas the mother of the excluded girl is now contrite and, I understand, prefers not to go to the excluded students' appeals panel to seek re-instatement, even now.'

'*Even now*? What does that mean?' rasped Dafydd Hughes. Hughes was twenty-nine, good-looking, as Welsh as they come, and built for the forward line of a rugby team, but, as he had made known, he did not play rugby: he hated the game.

'Even now?' he repeated. '*Even now*? Are we to write and thank this contrite mother? Send her a *Welcome Back* card with roses? Are we?' His "are we?" was Welsh, very Welsh. The 'we' ended on a distinctly rising note. And his tenor voice was fine enough for the most selective of Welsh male voice choirs.

In his seven years of teaching Hughes had made his name as a talented teacher of music and drama. In the city's cathedral the school's senior choir had sung, with vigour, variations on one of his own themes and was now rehearsing his sensitive transcription of a recently unearthed early-nineteenth-century hymn believed by knowledgeable local historians to have originated in a long extinct circuit of eight South Wales Valleys Primitive Methodist Chapels. Dafydd Hughes was a strange mixture: painstaking and delicate with his music but impatient, rebellious and coarse in other walks of life. As with Terry, politics meant a lot to him and he relished thoughts of the coming general election. But today the school's politics ruled.

Dafydd, with the accentuated and shortened 'a' pronunciation he preferred, was as strong a trade unionist as his brother and sister, both of whom were now teachers. Their prematurely retired father still talked disconsolately of the miners' 1980s defeat by "That Woman" and urged his children always to support their union and vote Modern Labour. 'No one will look after you but your own class,' he had drilled into them. 'Don't you forget that.'

Many times Dafydd had told colleagues that he wished all teachers could have heard his sick father's words; they would then show more interest in teachers' unions and politics. Terry saw him looking round at the bodies packed into the staff room and guessed what he was thinking: that on the whole they were a spineless shower who wouldn't know a full-blown strike from a Quaker meeting. And he could only agree. Many, for instance, couldn't give a damn about the coming election – yet electing a government that meant business about education was their one hope of more satisfying work and a richer life.

'I must report all expulsions to the governors,' said Olde, ignoring Hughes; such interventions from Hughes were predictable. 'And, in view of the mother's letter, they will be minded to re-admit. Also, she has written to the Chief Education Officer, so, while you may vent your feelings in here, I must respond to the world as it is.'

'And we must teach in this school as it is.'

'I am aware of that, Mrs Tipping.'

Olde leaned past his scribbling secretary to view Mrs Tipping clearly. 'But remind me, Mrs Tipping, does this unfortunate girl study mid-nineteenth century European literature? Does she attend your classes?' There was the glimmer of a smile on the tired man's face.

'That is irrelevant. The "unfortunate girl" will be taught directly by many of my colleagues and, in the school's daily life, will affect us all. The staff is at one in this.'

How I'd like to believe that, thought Terry, but what a hope!

Miss Jenny Jean Jones, coming from the same South Wales region as Hughes and an admirer of his manly physique, sat watching and listening intently. She was making good progress in her work even though Terry had given her a difficult group of fourteen-year-olds for three lessons a week. She seemed to be coping although he guessed their prolonged special study of *Prominent Changes in Teenage and Parental Attitudes to Human Sexual Behaviour Since World War Two* had assisted her in retaining pupils' interest. He was not too sure what was being learned but at least there had been no disturbances. Were boys entranced by her figure and vivacity, and girls by her trendy clothes and skilfully applied makeup? They all seemed absorbed by the intimacies of the topic.

From what she had told him earlier Terry knew that Jenny was astonished to witness such acrimony at staff meetings and to see the head of a large school subjected to such opposition from a fairly small but vociferous group of teachers. She had not realised that head teachers were prone to this kind of treatment especially on such critical matters as discipline and exclusion and she had not been surprised to see this head teacher, whom she had come to regard as quiet, kind and considerate, looking so weary. Terry feared her already expressed doubts about remaining in teaching would deepen.

'On a further point,' said Olde, 'of which I talked last term, this girl is only fourteen and is, I know, something of a problem to you and to me, as she is, I am sure, to her mother and neighbours. But, despite that, do we, because she is, as one of you remarked last term I am sad to say, "a pain in the … in the neck," do we wash our hands of her and consign her to a human recycle bin? Do our joint responsibilities end once we have given the girl her due allocation of English and mathematics? Do we then go home and forget all about her?'

'If only!' came from the far side of the room.

Olde was angered by that and briefly showed it, but he made no reply. Instead he sat on the edge of his chair. All were listening. 'Do we say that the end of a school day is the end of education, the end of our collective care, concern, compassion? Is *that* what we say?' He paused. ' I do hope not, and I ask you to think again.'

'They're not fair questions,' said Sarah Graham.

Olde looked sadly at Mrs Graham. Although she was an intelligent woman with a respectable classics degree she was one of the world's worst teachers and was to receive follow-up visits from unhappy inspectors. Olde knew Mrs Graham was not insensitive to her own unsuitability and realised other teachers were affected by her inability to interest pupils in anything except fooling around. He knew, too, that she was as eager to keep her teaching job as others were for her to lose it. Now thirty-seven, with a work-shy husband, three young children, an irresponsible mortgage, two credit-bought cars and a hankering after holidays abroad, she needed every penny teaching could give her. Year after year she struggled to do a job she disliked because she thought any other work she could find with her lack-lustre personality and little-in-demand academic qualifications would not attract her current salary or offer the same family-amenable hours of work. She knew she was not liked, made little impression on her pupils and had been written off by her colleagues as a teaching liability.

'Could the girl be taught at home?' It was Jenny Jean Jones' first contribution to a staff meeting. She looked round nervously. She wondered if anyone had heard and, if they had, whether they would ignore her as they had Sarah Graham.

'At home?' asked Terry. He was pleased to see Jenny summon up the courage to speak. It was only in staff meetings she seemed reticent; did that say something about staff meetings? 'At home?' he repeated, 'that sounds promising. In what way?'

'A friend at university was home educated until she went on to a sixth form college. She and her brothers were taught at home by their mother and, at times, by other parents alongside their children. The families worked together and used public libraries, museums, art galleries, parks, youth and community centres, the Internet, radio and TV. They constructed their own curriculum and programmes. She said it was a wonderful way of learning and later discovered she had no problems with her chosen 'A' levels and got really good grades.'

'Home-based teaching needs determined, educated, enterprising parents or grandparents, expensive resources and able children,' said Sarah Graham dismissively. 'That's not the situation with this girl.'

'But the resources needn't be expensive ...'

'The principal resource is the sacrificial input of the family. It wouldn't work in this case,' Mrs Graham insisted, and was then amazed to see several teachers nodding in agreement at her words.

'Yes,' said one. 'This girl's home is appalling. There were five or six

26

children at the last count - some of whom she's supposed to look after - her mother's weak, her father's a fly-by-night known to the constabulary, and the whole bunch is a burden on social services.'

'Quite,' murmured Olde, 'so isn't that exactly why she needs us?

'Yes, and home-based teaching is now widespread,' insisted Terry. 'Many families are beginning to realise how well they can provide for their children and ...' but he was not allowed to finish.

'I appreciate all that,' Ursula interrupted brusquely. 'Education of children without the use of traditional schools may be the way forward eventually, but on an all-embracing national scale it is far, far into the future and *we* have a problem *here* that needs a solution *now.*'

'Let us take the girl back,' Olde urged.

'Let us pray,' murmured Hughes.

Although provoked again, Olde bit his lip and gave the impression he had not heard. Jenny Jones looked let down, but Terry was pleased she had spoken and smiled encouragingly. At the very least he wanted her to give her teaching career a fair try.

'Mr Olde, are you asking us to vote on this?' he asked. 'I appreciate what you say about the girl, and have sympathy with the view that we are not here merely to instruct children in a motley collection of externally imposed subjects ...'

'We don't all go along with that,' said Hughes.

'And I can't see why we ...'

But Hughes would not yield. 'With respect, we're not attending a seminar on the moral philosophy behind state schooling.' He glanced at Olde. 'Although that would be better than some of the topics we spend fruitless hours discussing. We're here to decide whether a disruptive, dishonest, repeatedly-warned girl is to be allowed back into *this* school for *us* to teach, on *Thursday* of this week.' He emphasised the three words and for good measure, repeated "*Thursday*". 'And I'd have liked more notice of this. We're being unprofessionally rushed and have insufficient information to consider things dispassionately. But if it's being put to the vote mine is a resounding '*No!*'

'So is mine,' said Sheila Tipping.

Sarah Graham nodded but this time was ignored. Ingrid Eastman struggled to keep up with her minute taking.

'I feel it is not really a matter for a vote,' argued Olde, fearing the outcome. 'I have to make a decision and report to the Chairperson of Governors: she has to be informed. I regret you were not given more notice, I did not intend to spring it on you. But it is not a new matter and you know as much about it as I do. I am inclined to readmit and give the girl one more chance. She is too young to be cast adrift and I believe her mother will be co-operative.'

'Maybe,' said Ursula Irving, 'but will the other parents be so co-operative, especially those whose own children have been traumatised?'

'Traumatised'? Is 'traumatised' the right word?'

'Yes, Mr Olde, it is. We're talking about the bullying of children by this girl and her associates – and we have not yet discussed *them* – bullying that has gone on too long. It is well known that a child who is bullied at school, and, remember, forced to attend school, and who is too frightened to tell others – even his or her own parents or teachers - is traumatised in any possible meaning of the word.'

Olde was silent. He looked more wretched every moment.

'And,' added Mrs Tipping, 'we are not putting her outside our care in the arbitrary way you suggest. That is not a fair description of our attitude and it is unjust to appeal to us in that way. If I may say so it is a particularly nasty form of arm-twisting. As we all know there are other sources of paid, professional help open to this mother, and there are expensively maintained centres for such pupils here in this city and those should be involved now, and not left until Thursday.'

'Hear, hear!' said Dafydd Hughes. 'When it gets to this stage it is not our job. It's over to the ...' he grinned, 'the experts.'

There was much fidgeting. Large as the staff room was it became hot when crowded and group tension was high. Everyone felt tetchy; clearly this term would see as much procrastination as the last, but, although many were aggrieved, few were willing to fight. They let the militant minority man the machine guns while they kept their heads well below the parapets. And also there was a small number who sympathised with the head teacher's sentiments but they were silent in case they seemed to be "sucking up to the boss."

Terry had mixed feelings, yet his treasured common sense said that a thousand children in the school should not be exposed to one girl's subversive influences or disruptive behaviour. Common sense said the right to learn of those who wanted to learn should not be jeopardised by those who did not. Common sense said that gifted teachers' work was nullified if a pupil openly refused to learn. Common sense said that detaining in school by force those who did not wish to be in school and who made those feelings known was wasting millions of pounds a year.

But common sense had been thrown out of British schools years ago – and of other places. His gaze moved from Olde to the pupil-free playing fields. He thought about his often-started novel, *The Common Sense Party*. What he had been witnessing this morning was further justification for writing about an imaginary, newly-formed party free of the hindrances of hidebound ideologies, 19th century institutions, stifling sentiments, vested interests and outmoded practices.

He would work his CSP into his novel by giving priority to problems facing schools, problems of which he had knowledge. He would make the CSP view the future of education from an alternative perspective. It would question the relevance of the anachronistic 1870s school-based system and ask whether personalised, tutor-aided, home-centred teaching and learning, supported by radio, television and other free, readily available teaching technologies, could replace it. That could be linked to his idea of replacing the country's bickering political parties with smaller, simpler groupings. His imagination raced ahead. In that scenario teams of independent parliamentarians, selected for knowledge and expertise rather than political prejudices and party allegiances, would work together in different areas of the nation's life. But a new political system had to go hand in hand with a new education system. So which came first: chicken or egg? That really was the question he would have to answer. But then he heard Adrian Olde giving his standard response to a contentious matter.

'Let me think about it,' he was saying. 'Let's leave things as they are for the moment. I'll see the Chairperson of Governors shortly.'

'Mr Olde, the well-meaning Reverend Lena Napier will be firmly of your mind and will sway the other governors. She will want this girl back in school for the same reasons as you do and will be encouraged in that by the wishes of the local education authority. There is no point in delay. We simply do not want her back.' Sheila Tipping sat erect, arms folded. There was no need to talk further.

'Nevertheless, I will leave it there for now. So, *Item Number Two: Library requisitions*. Mr Jenkins, you wanted a word?'

Mr Jenkins, owner of the showroom condition but aging Ford Escort saloon, wanted many words. He spoke at length while few listened. Sixty-six teachers were only two hours into the new term and were already back with the delaying tactics that had, since Adrian Olde's arrival, become part of their daily working life. Like Terry, most appreciated that Olde tried his best but knew that in attempting to please everyone, he pleased no one. They knew that he made himself ill, was a benevolent liberal of the old genre, was, in his way, an irresponsible idealist who attributed his romantic beliefs to undergraduate studies of the later works of Rousseau, that he was a man who would deny that his well-intentioned actions were practised in order to provide him with what one cynic had called "the will of the wisp self-satisfaction of the smiling, unthinking, long-term, disaster-causing, do-gooder."

Most teachers were now gazing disconsolately out of the tall, floor to ceiling windows on the southeastern side of the room. Rudolph M.R.R.Charte had designed those perfectly proportioned windows for their external visual appeal - windows which made the room cold in winter, hot in summer. They looked out onto the deep-green, rain-watered expanse of playing field with its close cut grass and twenty-four tall, still bare poplar trees planted strategically on its far boundary to hide from view the east-west truck-laden dual carriageway. Spring-cleaned seagulls circled the field looking for food scraps tossed aside by feckless children. They screeched as they scoured the empty turf angry that their flight leader had again got the opening day of term wrong and that there would be no discarded crisps or crusts until tomorrow lunchtime. Terry turned his attention to the busy secretary, Ingrid Eastman; she would have plenty to tell her husband, Fergus.

Hull, too, had studied the Eastmans carefully and from him Terry had learned that Fergus was an outspoken and extreme right-winger, an independent financial advisor, and an active member of the school's governing body. Eastman, Hull had been told, remained in the Outer Mansworth Conservative Club even though he claimed the party – and the club - was lurching to the left. But, again according to Hull, Ingrid was proud of her man and apart from her work as senior school secretary helped Fergus in his political life. The coming general election would involve them both and, Hull claimed, as few events of any consequence in the Mansworth South West constituency escaped them, they would use that information to party advantage.

As Jenkins droned on the teachers ignored him and studied Olde. Why didn't he retire? He was unwell and could leave with a hefty lump sum and a sizeable index-linked pension. What *was* he waiting for? Dozens of head teachers in the county had retired early - which said much for their foresight and the unattractiveness of the job. Given such a golden opportunity many staff here would, without a backward glance, be heading fast for the foyer, car keys at the ready, petrol tanks full, houses locked, destinations determined, routes checked, passports to hand, foreign currency purchased, joy overflowing.

Mr Jenkins distributed his library request slips. 'By the end of April, please, and authors, publishers, prices, ISBN's, are so helpful. And do prioritise your preferences, funds remain limited.'

'Thank you, Mr Jenkins, thank you. So, may I take it there's no other business?' Olde had noticed Mr Hughes slipping off to the staff kitchen – no doubt to turn the urn to "high".

'So, no other business?' Olde looked round like a practised auctioneer anxious to end a disappointing sale. 'No questions on the library for Mr Jenkins?'

There were no questions on the library for Mr Jenkins.

'Is the school likely to be used as a polling station at the general election?' came from a voice at the rear. 'I think the town hall is still out of use - still being refurbished – for a few more weeks?'

'A day of unavoidable closure?' chimed in another hopefully.

'Shall we wait until an election is announced?' asked Olde.

'That can't be put off much longer,' said the first voice.

'Nevertheless ...' began Olde, but Terry Park moved things on.

'A temporary replacement for Mrs Wilkinson, perhaps?'

Mrs Wilkinson, when she was in school, taught English literature, and she had now begun maternity leave. It was the curvaceous lady's fourth pregnancy in a little over six years.

There was a long, drawn-out moan. Not Mrs Wilkinson again!

'Reads too much D.H.Lawrence,' muttered Sarah Graham, 'thinks she's Lady Chatterley revisited! Or she's sex mad!'

'Or her husband is. Built like a breeding stallion!' grinned a neighbour.

Mr Olde frowned. 'Ah, yes,' he said. 'Of course, Mrs Wilkinson. I imagine she will return after her baby is born, in mid-October.'

'And until then?' questioned Terry relentlessly. 'She has, I believe, a full teaching timetable?'

A full teaching timetable! Now all members of staff were attentive and those who had half-risen to fetch coffee and biscuits paused. It was as if their soccer team had had a penalty awarded against it in the closing seconds of a close-fought, goalless game. And, as if packed on the terraces, they turned as one body to watch the vital kick.

There were groans: Park had scored! Non-teaching time *was* at risk! Mrs Wilkinson *did* have a full timetable: over twenty lessons to be covered. That was fifty minutes per lesson multiplied by twenty every week for thirteen weeks. Then there was the marking! There was so much marking in English literature. And who had read the set books? What *were* the set books for God's sake?

'I am not hopeful of finding a suitable supply teacher to cover for her in the short term,' said the worried Olde. 'It is not just the expense, although that is a factor given the school's tenuous finances, but there is such great difficulty in tracing supply teachers who have examination-preparation experience and a sound knowledge not only of the syllabus, but of examination techniques and likely questions based on previous years' papers. As you know, there is a national shortage of good teachers of English, a shortage not fully recognised.'

'So term starts tomorrow,' said Terry, 'with no cover?'

'That is likely.'

'But, Mr Olde, you know there is a limit to the cover teachers must give,' pressed Mrs Tipping. 'Teachers For Radical Action is firm on this. It's another matter that cannot be allowed to drag on and on.'

Olde looked anxiously at his senior deputy, but Ursula Irving was unhelpful. While she had little patience with the TFRA, which she considered militant, left wing and unprofessional, she knew it meant business. The steadily growing TFRA could cause trouble over this and attract more members. Also she knew that the union's newly appointed, part-time district secretary, Mr Eddie "Bloody" Collins – a none-too-competent teacher of mathematics at another of the county's failing schools - was aching for his first fight. That fight could start here because little aroused teachers more than loss of non-teaching time. What did that say about the job?

Also, like Adrian Olde, Ursula could not stand Collins and she had warned Terry repeatedly about associating with him too closely, but Terry's friendship with Collins went back a long way. The moderate Ursula claimed Collins was self-opinionated, ruthless, ambitious and dangerously determined to make the TFRA an unstoppable power on the educational scene. She knew, too, that he supported the Equal Shares Party, (ESP), an ultra left-wing group that had broken from the Modern Labour Party - or the 'Mod Labs' as they were now called. To Eddie Collins and his crowd, she guessed, Mod Lab was a re-jigged bourgeois clique to be treated with disdain. No doubt Collins labelled them "traitorous revisionists" - invoking the revolutionary language of the 1917 early Soviets. But, while he was an outspoken supporter of the ESP and was, no doubt, licking his lips at thoughts of double trouble at a general election *and* at a large school in his union district, she felt sure he would put the needs of the TFRA first.

'No,' Ursula had told a friend, 'that headstrong man is a born rebel and his links with the ESP will do the teaching profession no good.'

Many others were afraid of the party's intolerant attitudes and its merciless programme of radical reform based on a redistribution of other peoples' hard-earned, carefully saved cash.

'This is urgent, Mr Olde,' she said. 'Mr Park is correct to remind us of union policy. Something must be done'.

'Very well,' said Olde wearily, 'Tell me what.'

Good grief, thought Terry. He's the boss, on more than twice our salary, does no teaching from one week's end to the next, often phones in ill, delegates all he can, has deputies and secretaries running round like blue-arsed flies and then has the nerve to ask *us* what to do!

'Find a supply teacher within two or three days – or let's say by the weekend,' Mrs Tipping offered generously. 'That's all you can do, *find* someone. I realise exam classes are difficult to cover but there must be somebody. Try a job-share, re-advertise, ask around, phone agencies, call acquaintances, re-organise schedules within the school.'

There was alarm shown at that, particularly by Mrs Graham.

'Warn the Education Officer and the governors of the seriousness of the situation,' continued Mrs Tipping. 'Tell them parents will not take kindly to their children's exam work being neglected – that there have already been numerous complaints about last year's appalling results and about the lack of staff continuity. Surely that will wake them up?'

'And the money?' remonstrated Olde.

'Money? An effective supply teacher for one term might cost ten thousand pounds,' said Mrs Tipping angrily. 'The money spent by this school in one year is millions and rising. The most important use for that money is to pay teachers to do as good a job as they can in the conditions that exist for the children who are here. If that isn't done, can't be done, or won't be done, then close the wretched school this very morning because its very *raison d'etre* disappears.'

'Really ...'

'Yes, Mr Olde, "really." That really is the position. One that needs resolving before the children return tomorrow. It really does!'

'I'll speak to Mrs Irving after the meeting.'

That was seconds away, and Mrs Eastman concluded her minuting with, "The meeting closed at 11.35."

Ursula Irving did not hide her frustration. Terry exchanged despairing glances with Dafydd Hughes. Mrs Graham showed alarm and Miss Jones displayed amazement. Mrs Tipping was first to claim coffee, which, in a show of disgust, she took to her language lab. Mr Hull noted the teachers' varied expressions of disquiet, apprehension, dismay, irritation, resignation or feigned indifference as they trooped out of their stuffy staff room where condensation clouded every window.

Hull shrugged his shoulders as he set out for a pint of the best and a quiet read of his newspaper at *The Standing Oak* He grinned as he glimpsed the low-priced airline's calendar hanging in the secretaries' office, *Monday, April the First!*

Tuesday 2 April.   **A Rectory Meeting**

Adrian Olde was the only child of a couple who managed a store in a Devon village for thirty years. The two were ardent members of the Anglican Church and raised their only son in that denomination. Adrian was grateful for this as the faith strengthened and comforted him. Later he played an active part in the Anglican parishes where he worked as a teacher. He attended a Church of England teacher training college and, disappointed by the academic level of the two year course, read for an external degree of London University with the help of books traced for him by a young librarian at the nearby university. He made friends with the young librarian, and, as did Adrian's parish priest, she supported him when he felt like abandoning his studies. She admired his tenacity and was interested in his subject. She stayed with him until he gained his degree in moral philosophy and was as disappointed as he when he gained only third class honours. But six months later Olde married the young librarian from the nearby university and the low class of the bridegroom's degree was temporarily forgotten.

Forty years on, yesterday's cantankerous staff meeting disturbed him, but he was sad rather than angry. Once he had looked forward to his work but now, in the privacy of his office, he counted the weeks to the summer holiday. Thirteen! And so much to endure before then!

After the meeting he had talked to Ursula Irving and she had agreed to concentrate on finding a fill-in English literature teacher while he dealt with the excluded girl.

That issue worried him deeply. To him the exclusion of any child signified both his school's defeat and the rejection of a young and vulnerable human being. Continued exclusion would worsen the child's social relationships and her employment prospects, and could lead to more trouble - a person whose life had barely begun! And some of those teachers who were among the first to claim education was about strengthening human affinities rather than passing examinations were ones who cried the loudest for her rejection. Nobody, during the whole of that dismal meeting, had referred to the girl by name; it had been *"that girl!"* which reeked of hypocrisy. Olde hated hypocrisy.

But he had to act, and so, to begin the lengthy permanent exclusion process, he drove to the rectory to see the Chairperson of Governors, the Rev. Lena Napier, to tell her of the staff's negative response and to seek her help. As chairperson of governors at several schools for over ten years she would have faced such problems before.

Adrian liked the rectory. It stood on a plot of land wider and deeper than the average for the estate. The lawned garden was bounded on one side by a high, hawthorn hedge - the remains of one that had once divided home farm fields. The entrance hall was wide and light and Lena's study was off to one side. That, too, was bright with ample window space, white Venetian blinds, plain, pale green curtains, white painted sills and tastefully arranged flowers. All was in keeping.

Little could be seen of the garden because the ground dipped gently away from the rear of the house although more could be seen from Lena's desk which was placed close to the larger window. The nearby bird feeders and baths attracted, according to Lena, at least twelve species including greenfinches, siskins, blue tits, coal tits, great tits, and sparrows. 'And blackcaps and chaffinches on the bird table and collared doves and wood pigeons strutting around beneath.'

But today Olde had little interest in Lena's feathered flock; it would have taken a full flight of bald eagles to excite him.

*

Usually Adrian Olde and Lena Napier talked together easily. They had similar social backgrounds and the same compassionate Christian outlook. They supported four church charities, donated to pacific civil liberty groups, helped the homeless, and signed petitions relating to prison reform. Sceptical antagonists called them "the wholly holies".

Lena, sixty-one, had read English history at university with special reference to the early industrial revolution in England but in her final year had rejected the teaching career she fancied in favour of social work and a move to the probation service.

Her parents were lifelong Methodists and, with them, she had been influenced by a young and handsome local lay preacher who spoke spiritedly of the support given by the prominent Methodist, Dr.Donald Soper, to pacifism, current social causes and other controversial, establishment-challenging policies. Her parents had often provided the visiting minister with lunch and the young man had been a regular guest. But Lena's easily aroused teenage romanticism had died a quick death when the man announced his engagement to, according to an indignant Lena, the plainest, dullest, most straight-laced Sunday school teacher ever drawn to World Wide Methodism.

Later, when she had moved from home, unhappy experiences with resolutely traditional members of a Methodist church in a market town sent her temporarily, and later permanently, to nearby Anglicans. There she had made friends, become an active church member, and met her husband. Mrs Napier, as she became, proved to be a hard working, widely read woman of high intelligence, firm beliefs and outspoken views. The Methodists' loss had been the Anglicans' gain.

She worked for a higher degree in her spare time paying her own fees. She used disguised material from her professional practice to provide case studies which she subjected to skilled 'cause and effect' analysis. Her perceptive tutor suggested she move above M.A. studies so that by studying for a further year she could expand her thesis to make it suitable for a Ph.D. She worked so diligently and presented so clearly that her work was accepted for a doctorate on first submission.

Over the years Lena's work in the soulless homes of despondent teenagers and later in courts and juvenile detention centres troubled her conscience. She was unable to reconcile the purposeful and settled life of her husband, children and herself with the marginal existence suffered by her unfavoured clients.

Supported by her husband she developed her professional work in tandem with her voluntary work and, in her Anglican church, found information and resources she could add to that of the probation service and courts. After talks with her persuasive parish priest and an equally determined bishop she was encouraged to apply for entry to church ministry. After further study and the occasional difficulty in digesting some of her tutors' theology, she became, at forty-eight, The Rev. Dr.

Lena Napier. On giving up her probation work she became a full-time parish priest and was now the highly regarded leader of a team of three Anglican clergy working in diverse parishes in Outer Mansworth.

She retained her interest in the wellbeing of young people through voluntary service on probation boards and school governing bodies, including the Chair of Outer Mansworth Comprehensive (Mixed).

*

Today Adrian Olde had phoned ahead and mentioned his need to discuss the exclusion, and his secretary, Ingrid Eastman, had listened in to the conversation. As did her husband, Fergus, she knew of Lena Napier's intellectual ability and of her spheres of influence and realised that with this current problem Mr Olde could not hope for better advice or firmer moral support.

Olde never had qualms about leaving Ursula Irving in charge of the school. She was respected, fair, competent and methodical. During his longer absences, when she became acting head teacher, he thought it would be a good experience for her when she came to apply for headships. But this line of thought was quashed when Ursula assured him that she did not want a headship, would not apply for a headship, and would not accept a headship. Olde knew of other capable teachers with the same, determined "no thank you" attitude. And, he thought, the powers that be still did not ask: "Why don't some of our very best teachers want to be head teachers? What has gone wrong?"'

Today Adrian Olde could be ten years older than his true age. He was unnaturally pale, had a hangdog look, and was in no way like a man who had enjoyed two weeks' holiday.

'I have not met the girl's father,' he began, 'nobody seems to know where he is, but I have talked to her mother and have notes of the meetings. At first I thought she was untruthful, aggressive and uncooperative; so did my deputy.'

'Unity Irving?'

'*Ursula*. She's most able. But what we thought was aggression was a way of hiding fear: fear she had lost control of the girl while she, as her mother, had years of legal parental responsibility ahead of her - the girl is barely fourteen. At the second meeting she seemed more reasonable – in my opinion - but not Mrs Irving's. The mother agreed the bullying had to stop and I made it quite clear we needed a firm commitment before we could even consider re-instatement and she accepted that. About the

37

extortion – the girl was bullying younger children to hand over their dinner money - she tried to deny it and said the "supposed" victims had made it up and she didn't trust either them or their parents. I said I had witnesses and she withdrew her denials so I did not need to mention the police. She accepted, too, that there was a history of truancy in the family and that her daughter refused to wear our simple, inexpensive school uniform.'

'Inexpensive to you,' Lena smiled.

She wondered how many precious hours had been spent arguing about the stripes, colours and crests on school ties, blazers and badges and how many pounds had been spent on their acquisition. And, for Heaven's sake, what impression did a uniform give of the educational system: that all children were the same and must be dressed the same? Uniformity before individuality? Was *that* the message?'

'Inexpensive to you,' she repeated.

'Maybe.' Olde conceded. 'But at the third meeting the mother cried and said she didn't know what to do. She said her husband washed his hands of the girl. On the fourth visit she brought a friend and both said they'd got 'good behaviour' promises from the girl and thought she could make a go of it if allowed back. I made no promises but said I'd see what could be done.'

'And you would have her back?'

'Yes.'

'But the teachers won't?'

'No.'

'None of them?'

'I'm not sure. Some who will not have her back are resolute ones and members of the new, militant union Teachers For Radical Action, and they are among the best teachers I've got. If TFRA supported a walkout I couldn't keep the school open.'

'Is TFRA that strong?'

'Yes,' said Olde, 'and growing. It's not just the numbers but also the quality of the teachers who've joined.'

'And can they do that? Just walk out?'

'Legally? Yes, if they are balloted, give notice and make it official. And they've got a new district secretary, Eddie Collins, known by many as Bloody Collins because "bloody" is his favourite adjective. He's longing to flex his muscles.'

'I've heard of Mr Collins,' said Lena, 'and I wouldn't call *him* a "quality" member! Any school would be better off without him! He's an out-and-out leftie isn't he? A real Marxist?'

'That's the one. And he's in a with a new extreme group, the ...'

'Equal Shares Party. They're threatening to make a noise at the General Election. But people aren't fools. They all know what *that* party's a resurrection of.'

'*Think* they know,' said Olde nervously. 'Neither they nor we must say so openly, but, yes, I fear Mr Collins is an unpleasant man. He'd sue the Pope if he had the chance.'

Lena Napier laughed for that conjured up a jolly picture: surely the court case of the decade! But the caution was so typical of Olde. No wonder people said he had never risked anything in his life.

But her laughter was short-lived for, in all the years she had known him, she had not seen him looking so unhealthy. He could be cracking up. His job seemed beyond him. Perhaps beyond anyone? She poured strong tea which Olde drank quickly.

'Isn't someone else on your staff in that party?'

'I don't think so, but there are ten or more in his union including Sheila Tipping, Terry Park, Dafydd Hughes, young Jenny Jones – and I'm sorry they've enrolled her - but they're not in the Equal Shares Party. In fact Mr Park seems to be dreaming up a party of his own: some Common Sense Party, but he'd get meagre support.'

'Meagre for now, maybe, but perhaps he's onto a future vote winner? Perhaps common sense could be the saviour of us all?'

'Saviour?' Olde scrutinised his dog-collared friend.

'Figuratively speaking,' she said, nodding good-humouredly as she passed him his second cup of tea. 'Figuratively speaking.'

Olde accepted the qualification with the cup.

'We're losing a whole generation of voters,' Lena said, 'the young ones just don't want to know. They're tired of the old parties and can't see any differences between them, but they might take to a 'new look' party that's not a party, where MP's vote on issues as common sense directs them? Yes, that's what I was thinking about,' she continued, 'but, saviour or not, common sense *is* lacking. And, as with our current problem, common sense says that someone else should teach the girl and teach her something else, somewhere else. There's always home tutoring? Wouldn't that meet legal requirements?'

'Possibly. There's a woman at the university working on home-based education by making use of modern technology, multimedia, personal tuition, and phasing out the schools. Susan Mansfield's her name, a published Ph.D. She comes into our school with her teaching practice students – trainee teachers. She's pleasant, perceptive and full of wide-ranging and,' he very nearly smiled, 'impractical ideas.'

'I don't mean universal home-based teaching,' said Lena Napier. 'That's years away. I mean the sort of home tutoring that's here in this city now, the tutoring provided for disabled or seriously ill children in their homes or in hospitals, where individual tutoring is appropriate.'

'This girl isn't disabled or ill.'

'Not ill?'

'Not the kind of illness that would persuade the local authority to home tutor. It's expensive and could upset other parents, they'd think the best way to get one-to-one teaching was to be uncooperative and disruptive. They'd see it as rewarding bad behaviour!'

'It wouldn't make sense?'

'Not as they'd see it,' said Olde. 'Besides, whatever option is used to deal with her – transfer, referral unit, special school, sin bin, home teaching or whatever - the indisputable fact would remain that my school had rejected her, washed its hands of her, told her she wasn't wanted, to go away, to go somewhere else. *That's* what I find so hard to accept.'

'I would feel the same.'

'And there's another worry. Some parents would support teachers in militant action. They'd remove their children the day the girl was re-admitted. I've heard from some who argue it's not sensible to let a whole school be disrupted by one unruly pupil. They're calm about it, there's no malice. They say, quietly, simply, that either common sense prevails or they remove their children and complain through every avenue, and there are plenty of avenues to explore and plenty of knowledgeable parents round here ready and able to utilise every one.'

'With a general election close,' said Lena pensively.

'Exactly. We've got nervous political councillors on our governing body, and we've got Audrey Anderson, M.P. She's probably been on tenterhooks for weeks.'

At the last general election Dr. Anderson had won the seat for Modern Labour just ahead of the party known as Today's Tories. Her majority had been confirmed at 222 after three ill-tempered recounts followed by ten minutes of booing, whistling, jeering, catcalling and foot stamping that was heard far beyond the Old Town Hall.

Lena had met Anderson and did not like her. She knew the MP, who was short, stocky and normally brimming with self-confidence, was in her mid-fifties and married to an unpopular, high-ranking hospital administrator. She had been a medical doctor and having worked as a general practitioner had no wish to return to "that under-resourced, soul-destroying, legal minefield of a job." Now, with an MP's salary, fully-claimed expenses and sundry add-ons her spendable income exceeded what she had received from medicine. Equally important, she had told Lena, an MP's lifestyle was more varied, enjoyable and influential than anything encountered in a doctor's office.

But her life was not all roses. Both Lena and Adrian knew she had ongoing trouble with her two secondary school sons. Neighbours - and not only her political opponents - regarded them as delinquent, and the family situation was not helped by the MP's frequent absences from home. However, with their combined salaries and unearned income she and her husband lived well and had secured places for the boys at an all-inclusive boarding school. With a level of cynicism normally reserved for lawyers and estate agents, Anderson's more critical constituents noted the boys' despatch to the elitist institution. '*Labour*!' stuttered one, 'what an utter farce!'

'With her tiny majority Anderson won't want trouble with teachers and parents at a time like this,' agreed Lena, 'especially if the local press gets wind of it. It's the sort of tale journalists savour. And, as you say, some governors will be on the campaign trail already and two are Mod. Lab. They'll have no inclination to sort out messy school exclusion problems. They'll resent the publicity and blame it on us.'

'So what do we do? The situation worsens by the hour,' said Olde. And so did his appearance. 'We've now got to cope with parents, the unions, the press, the local MP, the governors ...'

'And the Church. Don't forget the Church!'

'The Church?'

'The bishop is showing an interest in excluded teenagers. He thinks there's too much exclusion and sees it as an indefensible rejection of the young by older educated people who should know better. He's to see if the Church can provide counselling and safe meeting places for the expelled vulnerable. He's to involve the Diocesan Education Officer.'

'Not that dreadful man Count?'

'I'm afraid so.'

'Cecil Count!' groaned Olde. 'Dear Lord, that's all I need!'

Now he was beyond help: he must retire. He should have gone years ago because there was a limit to what any head teacher could stand and the Reverend Cecil C. Count, M.A. (Cantab), was beyond even the most liberal teacher's range of tolerance.

'He's pompous, insensitive, interfering and ill informed! Even loyal C of E teachers can't stand him. He does more harm than good.'

'I can't comment on that, but I'd like to,' replied Lena gloomily. 'It all becomes so difficult. Why does the education of our children become such an expensive, complex, frustrating, stressful and almost debilitating activity? It should be simple, enjoyable and rewarding. It's not a cold scientific process or an exercise in macroeconomics, but a slow, gentle, humane activity. What so many children need in this cold, impersonal, competitive, computerised and target-obsessed world are kind words, a pat on the head, a cuddle, a warm hug, an arm round the shoulder, a loving squeeze: they're better than all your white papers, green papers, enquiries, surveys, report findings and key stages.'

Horrified, Adrian Olde turned even paler. 'A warm hug? *A loving squeeze*? You can't do that! There must be no physical contact with schoolchildren: *none*! It's not on. I've had to warn staff about that.'

'Warn staff? On whose say-so?'

'Anonymous officialdom. I know it's wrong, you know it's wrong, anyone with an ounce of common sense knows it's wrong - but there it is. Yes, I agree that a fond, warm hug would work wonders, give reassurance, consolation and encouragement to a child, a satisfying feeling of inclusion, and the knowledge that someone cares. But it's not on!'

'Ridiculous! Over three hundred thousand decent, dedicated, well-meaning teachers and millions of needy children deprived of the God-given chance to give and receive tokens of love, comfort and support because frightened authorities can't or won't sort out a tiny minority of potential abusers? Who's supposed to be governing this country, the decent majority or a tiny minority of perverts? Once again it's anything for a quiet life, the easy way out! It's on a par with the weak teacher who punishes a whole class because she can't or won't identify the real culprit. It's cruel, cowardly and counter-productive!'

For several seconds Olde did not answer. 'I know,' he said. 'My school has just had thousands of pounds spent on surrounding its grounds with steel fencing two metres high to keep out vandals and loiterers. At least that's what I'm told it's for, although it might be to keep children in who want to escape. The fence is repugnant and its presence, to my mind, is a physical representation of the failure of our educational system. It makes the whole school look like a besieged army camp in alien territory and isolates it from the community it's supposed to serve, and it's cruelly off-putting to all who see it. It says: we'll *make* you stay in, or we'll *make* you stay out.'

'Or both?' added Lena.

'Or both. And it says that to the very citizens whose taxes paid for the school to be built and later maintained. It's indefensible.'

She waited. It was not only the exclusion that was worrying him; this man was facing a personal crisis.

'And always eating away at the back of my mind,' he said, 'is the awful thought that we've got everything wrong. Do you know, Lena, I look round at the condition of society after 120 years of compulsory state education and wonder what we've done? What have been the benefits? Is society more moral or kinder or more compassionate or industrious? Are people more content? Are families stronger? Do people value simple, worthwhile pleasures? Do they see how little is needed for a fulfilling life? Do they appreciate that fouling the environment to achieve so-called prosperity is suicidal? Is education nothing more than passing exams to get a well-paid job - blatant self-interest? Well, *is* it? Are schools doing enough to emphasise far-sightedness or are they adding to the nation's competitive urges and furthering a consumerism that will finish us off? Worst of all, do they send some young people out into the world feeling they are failures? Young people asking, after eleven years of schooling, just what have they achieved? If some children feel they are failures, then that is wicked: *wicked*! No Christian should countenance that.' He paused. 'After over a century has state education, on which we have spent so much, done so little? Indeed has it, with some children, done harm?'

'It probably has,' said Lena. She looked outside: two sparrows were busily gathering materials for their nest. She and Olde were quiet until Lena continued, 'but don't blame it all on the schools. That would be unjust. Never do that. Never blame it all on just one party.'

'I don't, but there's now no other institution left that can change the way we live. Only education can do that - and it isn't working. Some older pupils *sense* that schools aren't working – that schools are irrelevant to them. So fifty thousand play truant every day and many more would do so if they dared! Is that "education"? And every day over one thousand are excluded – some of infant school age! Is *that* "education"? Of course it isn't. It isn't even common sense because it's building up more trouble for the future. Real, real trouble.'

'All right, but don't you realise I often feel the same about the church? People don't play truant, they just don't come! Since 1945 we've had a catastrophic fall in the size of congregations yet our services remain much the same with the rituals, ornate clerical garb, old-fashioned language, and strange, archaic titles like "canon" or "rural dean" or "suffragan bishop." And what does "the venerable archdeacon" mean to the average person in downtown Liverpool, Leeds or Leicester? Nothing! Like the legal system – and, possibly, medicine - it's part of an ancient set-up intended to keep people mystified – and, with us, it keeps them away - separates church from people. Those rites might mean something to a minority, but that's preaching to the converted. Aren't we being selfish if we keep those customs for our own comfort and reassurance because we like them and they are familiar? Aren't we selfish if, knowingly, we persevere with them and repel some who might otherwise join us in worship?'

'Those who can't summon up the courage to step inside a church?'

'Yes. Those people. People who, if they peep inside a church, don't like what they see and hear, or don't understand what's going on.'

'This does nothing to cheer me.'

'It isn't meant to! But you got me thinking about our churches' predicament when you were talking about schools although, as I hinted, it's not just us, it applies to lots of other British institutions: the law, parliament, medicine, even our banks. Think how many people won't open accounts and take advantage of bank services because they feel uneasy or don't understand what they have to do or how the banks work or because they think – *think* – mind you, the counter staff, managers and clientele are of a superior and standoffish social order.'

'Banks have tried to address that and have better opening hours.'

'Those that stay open. And in many people's estimation the banks still have a social pecking order. How many barons, noble lords, knights of the garter, ladies of the bedchamber or assorted social climbers are members of the ethically motivated Co-op Bank?'

'Not many, I suppose.' Olde paused. 'So we change our approach? We move worship out of churches, politics out of an outdated parliament, judges out of stuffy, alienating courts and childhood education out of schools - out altogether.'

'Altogether?'

'Altogether. If the school is the stumbling block which prevents many children getting the education they want and need, why keep it?'

'But altogether? As drastic as that? You're serious? *Altogether*? '

'I think I am, because if I view my own school dispassionately I see that not only do lots of children not want to be there, but that many teachers don't want to be there either. If that's the case, what on earth's the point of it? What are we doing? There's no common sense in that, and making frequent and time-wasting minor changes on the periphery will never cope with that level of disenchantment. No worthwhile education can thrive forever on compulsory, regulated and unpopular attendance at schools which have become too big – that have outgrown the localities in which they are situated, that bus children around the county, denude villages of their young and exacerbate the difficulties of giving individual care and attention. It's ludicrous.'

'I agree, but other institutions are too big, it's not just in education. Politicians seem determined to push the notion that bigger is better.'

'Perhaps better for the nation's economy, but not for humanity?'

'It is not,' said Lena. 'Just think of big banks, big companies, big airports, big hospitals, big supermarkets.'

'Yes, but the closing of small village schools is the example I'd stress. Think how much has been lost there. Then ask yourself how many teachers now live in the locality of their school and really get to know the environment or circumstances in which their pupils and families live? How many villages see their children taken to some giant complex which is supposed to be better?' He paused, 'to say nothing of adding to the rush hour and the all-polluting school run.'

'I see.' Now Lena hesitated. 'Have you told others how you feel?'

'Only you. But I don't see things improving. I become increasingly attracted to alternative approaches – to non-school-based approaches - though that's too late to matter much now.'

'Too late? Too late for you, or too late for anyone?'

'Let's say for me!' He gave a wry smile. 'Too late for me.'

'All right, let's say that,' she said gently and thoughtfully. She bided her time before trying again to face the immediate problem.

'I understand what you say,' she said, 'I do. But now, you know, we really must deal with today and the girl. Is there no way of persuading staff to rethink? They are the obstacle – or some of them. If they agree to take the girl back we can promise them an overhaul – to which they will all contribute – of the whole expulsion system. Then they would have something different to come back to after the summer holiday.'

'They've heard all that before, "Buying time" they'll say, "pie in the sky." No, she can't come back on Thursday, I couldn't face it. If there's nothing else we can do, it must be referred to the local authority until the end of term.'

'But they won't act until she's been excluded for some time.'

'So we sit it out. But we must begin the process now.'

Lena shrugged her shoulders; she had expected this. She looked intently at the disconsolate Olde. There was no question the man should retire. Not only was he unwell, he was getting strange ideas. Expulsion, or permanent exclusion - this latest can of worms - could finish him. But, concerned as she was, she did not want him to retire yet. The upset would be horrendous and she would be assailed from all quarters. It was already April and if Olde gave notice now they could not, without a mad, reckless and unheard of rush, fill his post by September. Any suitable candidate prepared to accept the job – should one be found – could not take up post until January because of the contractual requirements of giving notice unless, of course, the person was already employed in this county. Or, could she allay her concern for Olde by offering him greater support if he stayed another term or, if that was inadequate and it seemed he would be made seriously ill, by angling for a candidate from within this education authority? A few strings pulled or favours returned?'

'Adrian,' she said, and this was unusual for it was 'Mr Olde' when they met officially, 'let's keep calm and view our options.'

'That won't take long.'

Lena smiled as Olde looked up from the small, neatly laid tea table and prepared to speak. He had thought of something else.

'How about the Chief Education Officer or "The Director of Child Services" or whatever he's labelled now? Can't he do something? The girl will become his responsibility and, after all, he's paid enough!'

'Matthew Zing? What earthly use is he? He'd pass the buck back to me. "Internal matter, Chairperson," he'd say. "Not within my remit, but do, please, keep me appraised of developments."'

She paused, then said, 'I can hear him saying it. He would size up the situation and realise he doesn't have to do anything until we permanently exclude the girl. Zing's certainly not one to grasp nettles for the hell of it. He'll wait until the very last minute - *and that's not yet.*' The words were rapped out. 'Our Dr Zing still has career ambitions.'

'Yes, he wrote to me, "Please keep me informed."'

Efficient and businesslike as she was, Lena Napier was a kind woman. Foremost in her Christian beliefs, underlying all her work, was a loving care for the individual parishioner whether a member of her church or not. The sickly look of Adrian Olde troubled her. She wondered about the role of the head teacher in today's schools. Was it fair to expect one person to have such responsibility with so little authority? Was the role a vital one? Couldn't intelligent, experienced, university-educated teachers organise their school without "a boss"? Wouldn't it add to their professional standing to do just that? Why did they need someone – someone they hadn't chosen – to oversee their work, to represent them to parents and governors, to tell them who to teach, where to teach, when to teach, even what to teach? It was different when schools had *teaching* head teachers, when each head had a class and was paid a little extra for essential management duties. But today? Nowadays most heads seem to wrestle with school-created problems and take on more and more work outside the classroom - the place where they could do *really* valuable work. And where does that get them? Head teachers cost vast sums and, one supposes, deprive children of ongoing contact with able and practised mentors. Even worse, the service finishes up with people enduring such stress that hundreds, like Adrian Olde, were made ill and ready to quit. Indeed many had quit. It was devoid of sense.

She gazed out of her study window. Distant daffodils would soon be over, but the tulips were early and the primroses promising. Most garden birds had finished nest building and were preparing to rear their young – all on their own without a secretary or computer in sight.

'I've a friend who was a head teacher,' Olde said quietly.

'Was?'

'He retired - very early, nine years ago. Never been into a school since except to see his grandchildren's work – and that out of loyalty to them. He asks me what it's like now and I tell him.'

'What do you tell him?'

'That it's worse, and he says: *"That's* what I've heard, Adrian."'

Olde was standing now, ready to leave.

But why is it like this, Lena thought, who's behind it? Who are the powerful, nameless, faceless, untraceable people responsible for this sad state of affairs? Where are they? What are their phone numbers and E-mail addresses? Where do they live? Where are their offices? Why do they do it? Why aren't they called to account? Why can't they appear regularly in public to answer basic questions about education from the worried parents who pay them so handsomely?

'I'm sorry?' he asked.

'Never mind,' she smiled, 'I was talking to myself.'

'I often do that! Sometimes in a school that's the only person a head teacher can talk to! But we'd better try to be realistic; our school needs a new person at the top. I've been a head teacher long enough, I really have. It would be better for me to step down now so that someone else, someone fresh, can start in September right at the beginning of the school year. There's still time for me to give notice.'

'But not to be replaced by September,' protested Lena.

'There's a month.'

'*A month*? A month to appoint a head teacher to an oversubscribed school with trouble brewing and a general election in the offing?'

Reluctantly Olde sat down again on the edge of the settee, his brief case on his lap, his car keys hanging, loosely, from one finger.

'Lena,' he said quietly, 'please listen. It's not three years since I was really ill. I thought it was a nervous breakdown, so did my wife, but my doctor did not. Whatever it was I don't want a repetition because that would be of no use to anyone and, above all, it would be unfair to my wife. I'm sure I should retire now. In fact I have a duty to go. While sitting here I've been thinking and I've made up my mind that retirement would be the better course.'

'A course that would leave us without a head teacher.'

'Without a sick head teacher.'

'And we'll have Unity Irving in charge for a whole term.'

'*Ursula*. She'd manage. I'm sure she would.'

'I don't like her, nor do some of the other governors. And, as you must have noticed, at some of our meetings she comes over as a hard woman.'

'She's a conscientious teacher-governor representing the staff.'

'No doubt, but I'm sure she won't be placed on any short list formed to appoint your successor. You yourself said she doesn't want to run a school – which several governors think strange - and others find her union links too strong. Isn't she a school rep for one union?'

'Yes, but for a pacific union – there'll be no trouble from that quarter. The governors needn't worry about that.'

'Even so, I doubt if they'd have her, even for one term. They'd hire a locum using money we can't afford. So please stay for just one more term. We can arrange more secretarial help and Ursula can be relieved of her teaching and do more administration. We'll fix the funding.'

'No. I couldn't face it. I shall go'.

'You won't sleep on it?'

'I don't sleep: that's half the trouble. Nor does my wife.'

For once in his life Olde was adamant. Lena faced defeat. Quietly she moved the tea table to one side and sat down beside him. They were silent for a moment and then she took his hands between hers and looked him fully in the face. 'Shall I say a prayer, Adrian?' she asked gently. 'Shall we seek God's guidance and blessing?'

They bowed their heads. Lena prayed. Then, sadly, the Rev. Dr. Lena May Napier saw her troubled guest to the door. She did not look forward to the next two terms.

Wednesday   3 April.   *The Standing Oak*

The pub's gently swinging sign, a little faded, was fixed to a tall, stout wooden post set firmly in the forecourt of *The Standing Oak.* Sceptics said the post came from the healthy tree felled to clear the ground for the horrible hostelry. The sign showed a fully-grown oak tree beneath which a chestnut-coloured mare grazed contentedly.

The pub itself, built in mock Tudor style, was out of keeping with surrounding houses or anything else within five miles. It was eight hundred yards from the secondary school gates and less than a mile from a pedestrians' entrance to the University of Mansworth campus. In the early evening the pub's bar took on an academic flavour - one that became less discernible as the night wore on.

The saloon bar had its early evening flavour today. At a narrow table in a bow window overlooking a potholed, almost empty car park, were Terry Park, Sheila Tipping, Dafydd Hughes and Eddie "Bloody" Collins. Collins had come to hear the latest on both the excluded girl confrontation and the maternity case with its likely re-distribution of teaching duties. This was bread and butter work to Collins and gave rise to threats of union action and a welcome increase in membership.

But that was not the current topic. Dafydd Hughes was laughingly dismissing suggestions that the pretty, superbly shaped, friendly assistant school secretary, Louie Anne Lee, fancied him.

'Rubbish! Where've you been looking? It's not me she's after, it's you,' he said pointing to Terry. 'She creates any excuse to talk to you.

You're too slow, mate, that's your trouble, you should follow it up – she's yours on a nice warm plate. Stir your lazy self! Get cracking!'

'I'm old enough to be her father! And married.'

'And divorced,' murmured Sheila. 'And plenty of young women like experience in a man, Terry, not some fumbling novice who's not sure where to start. Dafydd's right: you could be in clover.'

'There's a song about clover,' tittered Hughes. *'Roll me over in…'*

'We all know the song,' said Sheila. 'Several versions. But crude schoolboy humour's not what we're here for. We've two serious matters: a supply teacher and a troublesome teenager. We need the first but not the second. What do we do?'

'Get more beer,' said Hughes as he headed for the bar.

'We take the two together,' said the chubby-faced Collins, still on his first half-pint. He regarded this gathering as a business meeting with high potential and so chose to drink little even if others were paying. 'From what Terry says the girl's readmission is postponed until Monday, but it's still an issue. But you say less than half the staff would walk out over the girl, mainly those who teach her?'

'Tolerate her,' corrected Sheila. 'No one teaches her!'

'Yet still less than half,' Collins argued. 'But it's likely more would be affected by having to cover if no supply comes in for the frequently pregnant piece.'

'Which it won't,' offered Hughes on his return. 'The procrastinating Olde can't or won't get cover.'

'Same bloody thing, same bloody chance!' said Collins. 'Some who wouldn't come out over the girl might come out over all the extra teaching and they needn't be the same ones. When would Olde have known about the need for cover?'

'Weeks ago if Mrs Wilkinson had told him early.'

'So he's done bugger-all about it since before Easter? He's brought this on himself. He should have had it sewn up by now. He knows the legalities. Unions fought for years about their members giving unpaid, unlimited, unappreciated cover.' Collins was thinking aloud. 'So, suppose he can't get his cover – especially for the exam classes – we could put the two groups together and get more support?'

'Exactly,' said Hughes, 'but would it be enough to close the school? How many do we need to close the school - with health and safety and all that jazz?' He pretended to play a trumpet.

'Give over!' said Sheila. 'This is serious.'

50

She had long been impatient with Hughes. Although the man was likeable he was also flippant, unreliable, and too heavy a drinker.

'Exactly. Would we have enough to close the school?' persisted Collins. 'That's what I need to know. *How many*? And would they really come out if it came to the crunch? How difficult could we make it if there were not enough to close the bloody school but the original ones still came out? How many blacklegs and scabs would defy the pickets and crawl in to work?'

'Scabs?' his listeners chorused.

'Yes, *scabs!* Bloody strike-breakers! Don't you lot know anything? The bastards who'd supervise the classes of the strikers! How many strikebreakers would there be? How many good little boys and girls would do anything to please their bloody boss and get another feather in their crappy caps and to hell with their mates?'

'Very few,' said Terry, scowling. He thought Collins was overdoing things. Arrivals nearby had overheard him.

'Watch your language,' Sheila said. 'And don't assume all teachers are as union-mad as you. They're not.'

'More's the pity,' said Hughes who had behind him four generations of "union-mad" family members. 'But, don't worry, we'd sort the sods out afterwards!' Gleefully he rubbed his hands together.

Collins beamed: he liked them young and eager.

'And "the boss", as you put it, worries me,' Terry said. 'He's ill. I hold no brief for him, but a strike could make him worse.'

'Finish him off?' asked Sheila who, like Collins, had little patience with Olde. 'So what? It's his own fault he's still stuck in his job.'

'Dead right,' agreed Collins. 'Have no sympathy there. No one makes them become head teachers and, when they do, they themselves choose to be different. Most don't even belong to class teachers' unions; they set up their own "head teacher" cliques to look after their own interests. If they deliberately choose to cut themselves adrift that's their bloody funeral. Look, mate, they're mini-bosses on the big boss's side. Shed no tears for them!'

He paused as if sensing he had perhaps gone too far and too fast. He began to speak quietly and more persuasively. 'Look, your boss can either stay and face the music or shove off. It's his choice: it's entirely his choice. Don't feel sorry for him – he's lucky to *have* the bloody choice – his pension will be worth more than you're earning for doing a full time teaching job in a dump like that.'

His listeners were still unhappy.

'OK,' Collins said, trying again, 'I respect some head teachers - the ones who've remained in an ordinary assistant teachers' union and who've backed militant action and helped union power grow. They've got guts. They're a special bunch and they get our support every time. But even they have to ask themselves: '*why* am I a head teacher? Was I lucky? Did I know someone? Was there a shortage of applicants? And what's my bloody job now I've got it? Is it to wear a smart suit, slick tie, sit in a plush office behind a big desk with a row of telephones, hire secretaries, look important and dish out orders while the riff-raff teach? If that's it, we don't need them. Let's not be mealy-mouthed, let's say it straight, we don't bloody well need them! Let's be kind, if you like and say they themselves would be happier back in the classroom teaching children while some eighteen-year-old clerk with 'O' level English and some passable maths sits in the office and does the basic admin. Teachers could run a policy-making committee on a yearly-rota basis. We don't need head teachers and we won't be a real profession until we've kicked them out, every bloody one - kind, compassionate, efficient, hard working or not. OK,' he paused, 'let's say it's the role we're against, not the individual, but,' and he could not resist one final dig, 'it can be the individual as well!'

'And the inspectors?' prompted Dafydd fondling his tankard. He really relished all this. Bloody Collins was in fine fettle today.

'Those bootlickers should never have been admitted in the first place. It should have been made clear fifty bloody years ago by all the unions – including the head teachers' outfits - that when school inspectors walked in, teachers walked out, and that they'd walk out every bloody time until the bloody government got the bloody message! The country would have saved billions of pounds, thousands of wasted hours and avoided dozens of nervous breakdowns. The interfering, clueless politicians and their inspector lackeys would have been put in their place. Then we could have built ourselves up and earned public respect and self-respect, but now the creeps have such a foothold it'll take a ton of dynamite to shift them.'

'That's union policy? Blow them up?'

'Common sense, Mrs Tipping. 'A common sense policy. It's needed if teachers ever want to get anywhere and become a full profession. But we'd need massive support.'

'Which we won't get,' said Terry.

'We can try.'

There were now more people in the pub, and more noise.

Sheila slipped Terry a ten-pound note. 'Terry, I don't like the look of that lecherous slob leaning on the bar examining every short skirt in sight and imagining what's underneath. You go and get my round - and only a half for me.'

When he had gone Sheila turned to Eddie Collins. 'Look,' she said, directly, 'I'm with you on most of what you say although I don't think you help the cause by putting it so offensively. You've got a good case and needn't put it so crudely. But, that aside, you'd better know that Terry has been thinking about applying for headships and you could upset him by talking like that. He's the sort of man who'd be torn apart by his conscience. He won't know where he stands and, if you ask me – which you won't - I think he'd make a different sort of head teacher.'

Collins grimaced, then shook his head wearily. 'You don't get it, do you? You just don't get it. You still don't bloody well get it!'

He paused and then went on to speak in staccato mode. 'He'd *still* be a head teacher! Don't you see that? He could be as nice as you like, as industrious as you like, as conscientious as you like, as fair as you like, as all-seeing as you like, as considerate and sympathetic and kind as you like, turn twenty bloody cartwheels in school assembly while strumming a guitar and togged out in the latest gear, but he'd *still be a bloody head teacher!* Do you understand? We don't need them and, most important, we don't want what they symbolise!'

'That's your view. But there's another thing.' Sheila Tipping leaned forward as if to avoid Dafydd hearing her. 'I suspect Terry is well disposed towards our own head teacher. He doesn't like to see a man getting into the pitiful state Olde is in. Nor do I. I know Olde's weak, doesn't grasp whose side he's on, galls people, sees too much of that governors' chairperson the holier-than-thou Napier, lets parents take him for a ride and gets the school round his neck. But beyond all that, he's a sick man. So if you're going to initiate strike action – which I'd go along with – and don't get me wrong on that because I'm with you all the way there - he should be given fair warning and time to quit. Argue as you like - and I know how strong the case is - but I'm telling you here and now, Mr Collins, I'll not be party to killing a man either directly or indirectly, whatever the cause.'

Her voice had risen and Dafydd had overheard her last sentence.

'You're wrong there, Sheila,' he said. 'We can't allow sentiment to stop us. Olde can't stay on in his job preventing us from acting in the profession's best interests. You're saying that if he stays put and if we like him and don't want to hurt him, we don't take action. Well, that's another form of establishment blackmail, the same as the insidious "teachers or nurses mustn't go on strike because they'll hurt the kids or patients." It's boss's crap and I'm not buying it. Nor should you.'

Sheila knew what he meant and, in the long term, thought him right. It was the old story: in winning a righteous war innocent people would get hurt. But was Olde an innocent party in this particular battle?

Terry returned, dispensed the beer, and soon caught up with the conversation. Eventually they decided that if the girl was readmitted or if no supply teacher was found, they would consult staff and report to Collins by Friday noon and he would notify head office and have ballot papers ready by Monday morning. Sheila, meanwhile, would talk to the deputy head Ursula Irving, inform her of their concerns and see if she could persuade Olde either to change course or retire.

The pub was filling fast.

'Now let's change the subject,' Sheila said.

O.K., what's the name of that lovely tutor piece who comes into school from the university bringing droves of luscious trainee teachers?' Dafydd Hughes asked. 'That's the sort of job I'd like: homely working conditions, tiny personal groups, cosy tutorials, six or seven sexy, eager students, good pay plus expenses, plan your own courses, come and go as you like, eight week vacations, and, on top of all that, influence without responsibility! I'll tell you what, comrades, you can stuff your headships if there are jobs like that on offer!'

'Her name is Susan Mansfield,' said Terry. '*Doctor* Mansfield to you, Hughes, and she's conducting valuable and radical research into the feasibility of alternative forms of childhood education.'

'Fancy that! So that's what she does!' Hughes grinned and drank.

'It is. She wonders whether we have to go on teaching as we do when it's obvious we've had enough. She says the school, like many other social institutions in this country, has outlived its usefulness and that for some children it might be doing more harm than good. She wants schooling replaced by other arrangements and holds that conditions are now ripe for change. She's hoping to get a book published on it. And,' he said looking at Hughes, 'her job isn't such a cushy number.'

'Went to Oxford or Cambridge, I suppose?' asked Collins.

'Oxford. She went on merit - on an exhibition from an old grammar school,' snapped Terry, 'she was active in the students' union and got a good degree. Is that a crime? She takes *The Guardian*, reads widely, usually votes Mod Lab, plays bridge and the violin, likes Mozart concertos, appreciates water colours, swims, hikes, shares a small holiday home in Italy, and has a sister working in Lebanon.'

'So there, Mr Collins!' grinned Dafydd, mockingly. 'You can stuff that in your pipe and smoke it!'

'Terry seems to know a lot about her,' smiled Sheila Tipping, ignoring Hughes, 'please tell us more! I've only seen this virtuoso in passing.' She drank deeply. 'How old is she? Forty-five? Fifty?'

'Thirty-seven last month. And it was my birthday three days ago, and thank you for your many cards!' Terry tried introducing sarcasm to fend off their interest in Susan, but they persisted.

'She taught in several secondary schools in the city,' he added.

'Was a bit of a rebel, too,' said Collins approvingly. 'But she got people's backs up when she sided with delinquent kids.'

'She had her reasons.'

'And she gave the union rep problems,' continued Collins. 'That was in the school where she was acting head teacher for a term.'

'She has a mind of her own,' agreed Terry, 'and likes fair play.'

Still they waited.

'She has a tutor's flat in the university, comes from a working class family in Scunthorpe, has a twin sister, many friends in the United States and, not that it's any business of yours, she's single.'

'Lesbian?' enquired Dafydd.

'No, you damn stupid git, she's not!' retorted Terry Park angrily, thumping the table until the glasses jumped. Dafydd hooted and pretended to slide off his stool with mirth. Collins guffawed, Sheila shrieked. People nearby turned, shocked at the language, noise and general carry on. And this lot were teachers?

'Temper, temper!' reproved Sheila.

'Do I see prejudice rearing its ugly head?' asked Collins.

'No, but I'm interested in her work. There's a lot in it. In many ways our schools *have* shot their bolt, you've only to look round with eyes half open to see that, or read the papers or listen to the radio or watch TV if you find reading difficult. The head teacher issue is only one of many and it's unfair to blame head teachers alone for the mess education is in. Politicians are the main culprits - can't stop interfering. 'M.P.' should stand for Meddling Person! The teachers who are on the ground and in the know should be making the decisions and exploring the alternatives and be doing so without preconceived ideas.'

'What preconceived ideas?' queried Sheila.

'Thinking that 'the school' as we know it is a vital part of a child's education. It isn't. If we were to re-plan children's education from scratch, with no prior assumptions, nothing on the drawing board, effacing all that has gone before and putting it from our minds, we wouldn't even *think* about creating the system we've got now. That's what Susan says. She says we should sweep everything aside, start afresh and see what can be done with the wonderful teaching resources we'll have in an exciting 21st century that's almost here. Our standardised, enclosed, time-serving schools wouldn't get a look in.'

He hesitated. The others stared at him.

'If we were starting from scratch, people would be horrified if it were proposed that 'children-only' buildings like those we use now be erected to provide, or deliver, an education, and that children be packed into them by the hundred, compulsorily, for six hours a day, five days a week, for eleven or more years, and that those places be fenced-in like some low-security prison. They wouldn't believe it was a serious suggestion. They'd say it was some pervert's idea of a joke.' He hesitated again. 'If, eventually, they realised that the building of such schools *was* a serious proposal, they'd arrest the proposers, charge them with child cruelty, put them on the prohibited list and, if they still persisted, give them five years inside without parole.'

Still they waited. 'I often talk to her about it. We talk about it a lot.' Then, as an afterthought, said, 'that's when she's in school, of course.'

'Of course! But even so, I'm beginning to think the eye-catching Louie Anne Lee can look elsewhere,' Hughes taunted.

'Don't be so damn childish, Hughes. 'Don't you take anything seriously? Try to make yourself useful for once, go and get some more beer and bring some peanuts or crisps or hula-hoops.'

'And bring another change of subject,' demanded Sheila. 'This one's as bad as the last'. She wafted away cigarette smoke coming from two distant tables as it curled dreamily overhead. 'Filthy habit!' she exclaimed as the smoke drifted further. 'Time it was banned.'

Collins gazed at Terry wondering if he was still the reliable rebel of the past. He seemed soft on Adrian Olde and now there was this adulation of some head-in-the-clouds fancy piece from the university.

'OK' he said, 'a different topic. How's the book going?'

Terry did not answer.

Eddie Collins had been a friend of Terry's for twelve years. For three of those they had taught in the same school, made things tough for the management and exchanged ideas for radicalising the teaching profession. But now Collins could see that Terry was upset and, it seemed, vacillating. Was he really smitten with this university bint? Not like the Park of old to fall for a blue stocking? And where was Park the mutineer – the man whose great-grandfather led factory strikes, was blacklisted, lost jobs, supported Ramsay MacDonald in his campaigning, and then, in disgust at being let down by workmates, went over to the Communist Party and nearly wrecked his marriage doing so? Was this shilly-shallying Park that brave man's progeny?

'You know what I mean,' Collins said, 'your novel about some common sense party. Sounds good: we're short on common sense!'

'I've made a start. Early stages. Ideas, thoughts, references, notes, jottings, newspaper cuttings.' Terry didn't like this topic, either.

'A start? Well, write in that your pretend party's got two million members and that it wins a general election. That would get the buggers worried – even if it's only a story!'

Although they shared similar views on teachers' unions and their function, and the urgent need for teachers to take militant action as a determined single body, the men's broader political interests differed.

'Which is more than can be said of your Equal Shares Party,' said Terry. 'The ideas behind your party - and we know where they come from - were tried, found wanting and scrapped long ago – or should have been! And, if you don't mind, the Common Sense Party would not be *my* party; it would belong to its members. And it would not be a party in the accepted sense of the word – not like the present parties.'

'So what would it be? What *would* the CSP stand for?' asked Sheila.

'In here?' Terry looked around. The smoke was denser, irate words came from the bar, and the noise level had risen.

'Yes, why not?' asked Collins. 'You've a fair cross section of the electorate in here. Just look round! My God, what a bloody sight!'

Terry hesitated, but drink had loosened his tongue 'All right.' He thought for a moment and then looked hard to see if they were goading him, but they seemed serious.

'The CSP would do away with the traditional parties altogether: Labour, Conservative, Liberal, they've all been tried for ages and have made the country the shambles it is today. It would point out that our elections are farcical because you have to choose from three similar outfits – three outfits that you probably don't like anyway - then you have no more say for another five years while those three "parties" pretend to squabble with each other and get nowhere.'

'Worse than that,' said Collins, 'the outcome of a general election is usually decided by voters in forty or fifty marginal constituencies so that the millions of voters in the other six hundred count for bugger all – and they're beginning to realise that – at last!'

'I'd never seen it that way,' murmured Hughes.

'Then the saints preserve us, it's obvious enough!'

'In my novel the men and women comprising the Common Sense Party would claim that people have had more than enough of that pathetic three-party pretence. They'd show that millions don't vote because it's a waste of time, or scribble rude messages on their ballot papers. They don't give a damn who wins because it makes no difference and they don't believe a word politicians say anyway. CSP leaders would argue it's time to jettison the whole derisory, wretched, damaging, obsolete, ineffective, parliamentary set-up and start again.'

'That's remarkably similar to Dr Mansfield's view of our education system,' said Sheila Tipping coolly. 'Doesn't she see that as derisory, wretched, damaging, obsolete and ineffective, and want to start again?'

Terry was silent.

'Perhaps our party political system and our electoral system need to be updated as urgently and as radically as our school system?' suggested Dafydd. 'Tackle the two together. I'm serious,' he added.

'Maybe,' said Terry.

'*Maybe*? Hell's bloody bells, Terry,' snapped Collins, 'you won't get one without the other. You won't, or rather your girlfriend won't, get the changes she's after in education while you've got this useless three-party "all pals together" circus and the old school tie brigade along with a bevy of do-gooders and feel-gooders who won't change the things that really matter in a hundred bloody years!'

'Watch your language,' hissed Terry 'and she is not my girlfriend. She's a university lecturer and a researcher and a teacher-colleague. Got that, mate? Sure? Shall I say it again for you? A *colleague*! Anyway, I'm off, I've had enough.'

'Sit down and calm down Terry,' said Sheila. 'And yes, watch your language Collins. *Eddie* Collins isn't it?'

'You know bloody well it is!' snorted Collins.

'Thank you, *Eddie*. Now just listen, Terry,' Sheila repeated. 'I'm interested in this CSP and I bet I'm not the only one. So fill us in.'

Terry sat down, but did not speak. He sulked.

'What you've said is clear in principle, but what would the party do? What would it *do*? What will the Common Sense Party stand for in your novel, Terry?' persisted Sheila. 'Can't you tell us that?'

'Of course I can. I've worked it all out, but only as a starting point. It would press for a one party state, or rather a "non-party" state. That one "non-party" would be a group of elected MPs motivated by common sense. From them would be selected such ministers or chairpersons as are needed to run essential departments. The decisions those ministers made would be based on the party's over-riding rule of acting on clearly observed common sense lines. Where there was dispute in the country on a really major issue a national referendum would be held with the electorate voting electronically from home with foolproof ID. The technology's already there. The result would be known within hours. The voters' wishes would be binding on the government for three years. In that time they would either meet those wishes or be replaced and banned from standing again.'

'How long's it taken to put all this together?' asked Hughes.

'Ages.'

'With help, of course!' Hughes smiled.

'Yes: with help. But to continue,' he would not be ruffled by Hughes again, 'constituencies would remain the same as now, perhaps a few less – say 400 or 500 - and members of parliament, or rather representative members in an advisory council, would continue to care for their constituents and be judged individually at each five-yearly election on how well they did that job – and judged on *that job* alone. Then everything – literally everything - would be modernised. The ridiculous wigs, gowns, silks, ermine and other nonsensical, expensive, time-wasting, egotistical dressing up, Queen's Speeches, Black Rods, woolsacks, whips, bells, divisions, "ayes to the right," rubbish, "honourable members," "noble lords and baronesses," would all go to a downtown charity shop or the city dump.'

'And the knights of the bloody garter!' guffawed Collins thumping the table. 'Keepers of the Privy Purse! What a fund wasting, time wasting, farting fiasco it all is! So sod the bloody lot! And how about "The Stewardship of the Chiltern Hundreds" for another belly laugh?'

'What's that?' asked Hughes.

'Exactly!' grinned Collins. 'You don't know and fifty million other poor sods don't know either.'

'Or care,' said Sheila. 'And that's the real problem.'

'It means an MP jacks it in before his time's up,' said Terry.

'Or wants to spend more time with his family.' chortled Collins.

'Or might be ill?' Sheila suggested. 'Genuinely ill?'

'Never mind all that, I've not finished,' stressed Terry. 'All the other off-putting, elitist, traditional, centuries old, suffocating public school and Westminster hide-bound clap-trap would disappear as would the House of Lords. Then Parliament's, or the *Council's*, hours would be standardised at nine till six, five days a week, and it would sit throughout the year – no more obscenely long vacations - no more cynically saying that there's no time for an important bill only a day before they pack up for an all-paid ten-week vacation. They'd get four weeks' annual leave without bank holidays because bank holidays would go. Bank holidays are a glaring example of the past ruling the present and they pass no 'common sense' test: they are inconvenient, no longer needed, cause congestion and road accidents, hike up prices, are costly to businesses and a throwback to a different social age – a time when workers had no paid holiday entitlement.'

Collins nodded and was about to speak, but Sheila got in first. For once Collins was too slow.

'I agree bank holidays no longer make sense,' Sheila said, 'but their abandonment would hardly be earth shattering? And, really, no one gives a toss whether Black Rod falls on his backside. Fill us in on vital issues. People care about important things and want to see something positive done. What about referenda? Would there be referenda on new motorway systems, capital punishment, abortion, compulsory school attendance, examinations, green belts, new housing developments, climate change, taxation, retirement age? Would aloof high court judges, coroners, police chiefs, top civil servants and magistrates be elected by and be answerable to the *common* people? You must stress that it's *Common* Sense for *Common* People. Would the CSP bring sanity into our over-the-top, Brussels-led health and safety legislation? People care about *those* things and get fed up of politicians squabbling like mardy infants while the years fly by and practically nothing of significance to ordinary voters ever gets done.'

The listeners drank up. Even Collins was quiet.

'Of course it would,' said Terry. 'Each major issue would be examined by and voted on by the people at the time it was current. At present you have to accept or reject a whole pack of measures bundled together by one particular party trying to win popularity. That's not common sense because you may support some of the measures proposed by Mod Lab or Today's Tories or the Tolerant Democrats, but not support the other measures in their manifesto. You then find yourself voting for something you don't agree with in order to support something you do. It's ridiculous and makes people say: 'Scrap the lot!' Or they end up trying to guess which will be least harmful. That's negative voting and if that's common sense, then heaven help us all!'

There was interest in what he said and the force with which he said it. Hughes nodded, looking thoughtful.

'And there's no common sense in allowing institutions to grow so big that individuals are lost in the crowd.'

'Like prisons?' offered Collins.

'I was thinking of schools.'

'But prisons,' persisted Eddie Collins. 'Don't you remember Keith Jackson's dad? Six bloody months for a piffling benefits fraud.'

'No fraud is piffling,' objected Sheila.

'Six months for sixty quid? While the blasted judge who sentenced him would spend that on his dinner and charge it to the taxpayer!'

'Your blasted judge didn't steal the sixty pounds!'

'But he could have washed his hands, had a coffee, a cheeseburger, French fries and all the sauces on offer at the nearest Mc Donald's for only six quid,' scoffed Hughes, 'and saved us the other fifty-four.'

Terry smiled. Then said, 'Yes, I remember Jackson, and the case. We both taught him at Derby Road East – a right shambles that was.'

'Well,' said Collins, 'I told the boy I'd visit his dad in jail and I did, six times, and it was a bloody eye opener. A thousand men with real problems jammed into a bloody great pile of bricks and mortar which offered well-meaning staff little chance of treating them like human beings or finding out what's wrong with them and how they might be helped to go straight. If you'd wanted to devise a system where hope was abandoned you couldn't have done better than build a place like that and fill it with resentful prisoners - strengthening their feelings of isolation and their understandable belief that nobody gives two fucks about them. A place where for years they're cut off from all that's good in society so that many come out worse than when they went in.'

'So you'd let them all out,' scoffed Hughes.

'Of course not! That's the sort of stupid, ignorant, contemptuous and controversial remark that rouses the right-wingers and makes sure nothing ever gets done. Instead of one jail with a thousand prisoners we need twenty secure bases with fifty men or women in each with a stress-free staff who know the prisoners as *people* and where prisoners feel they matter and can be prepared to do some good when they get out. And the smaller the group the better.'

'Minimalisation?' suggested Terry thoughtfully. 'Minimalisation?'

'Yes,' agreed Collins.

'Push for minimalisation instead of nationalisation?'

'But minimalisation is such an ugly word,' said Sheila.

'But what it stands for is not ugly – the very opposite. Yes, we'll have common sense *and* minimalisation.'

'Could be the same thing?' said Sheila quietly.

'Could be. I'll think about that.'

'So you're making policy as you go along,' objected Hughes. 'And I thought you told me it was to be called the Ordinary People's Party?'

'It was, at first, but I think Common Sense Party is better. It brings home the primary need for common sense.'

'It does,' said Sheila.

'I was going to leave out 'party' to show my idea is totally different and owes nothing to the old system. Then it was to be "The Common Sense Group" but that was limiting, and, despite hours of thesaurus-hunting, I found nothing better than party.'

Their table was now the only reasonably quiet one. They looked round wondering what to say next. Had Terry hit on something big? Would his idea have popular appeal and be worth following up?

They pondered further until Dafydd Hughes, with a smile, leaned forward and touched Terry's sleeve. 'Terry, old chap,' he murmured seductively, 'try out your idea by standing as an independent candidate at the general election, then sit back and see what happens.'

Terry was astounded, but Sheila almost leapt to her feet.

'Yes, of course!' she urged excitedly. 'That's it! Of course it is! Why didn't I think of that? Go on, Terry, lots of people would support you! They would! They really would! Lots and lots and lots!' And she clutched his sleeve as she spoke. 'Lots and ...'

'Yes! Yes !"*Vote for Terry Park!*'" shouted Hughes. 'I can see it on the hoardings all over town. "*Vote for Terry Park! The Common Sense Man!*" Wonderful! Marvellous! Just what the country needs!'

They gazed, eagerly waiting for a response, but Terry was aghast.

'Go on man, have a go: put yourself forward,' exhorted Hughes.

'We'll all back you,' urged Sheila, 'and we'll call you *The Common Sense Man with a Common Sense Party … Vote for Terry Park!*'

'Yes! And I've heard that all the big parties have got real problems locally,' pressed Hughes relentlessly. 'Some really big problems with prospective candidates toadying to ministers, messy divorces, French floosies, American shares, hunting lodges, mounted masters of baying hounds, and stupid statements that have upset thousands.'

Now Sheila was leaning forward fervently, her face close to Terry's. 'You'd be in with a chance! You'd be far better than that lot.'

'A *candidate*? A real live candidate? You're all mad! This is *fiction*, for God's sake,' rapped Terry. 'I'm writing *fiction*! I'm writing a novel! There's no such party as the Common Sense Party – haven't you grasped that yet?' He saw another pint placed before him and downed half of it in one gulp. 'Thanks,' he said to Collins and went on: 'but there *is no party*! Don't you know the difference between fact and fiction? The Common Sense Party is all in my head!' He tapped his brow. 'Here. Right here. Right here in my head!'

'That's where all parties start, in someone's head,' offered Sheila.

'Too bloody true!' confirmed Collins, now favourably impressed by Sheila Tipping. 'Bring the idea out of your head and into the open. Do what they say and stand as a CPS candidate. You don't need a whole party to do that, just a few signatures, a decent printer, a loud voice, a thick skin, a sickening smile and five hundred quid.'

'Thank you, Mr Collins,' said Sheila. 'We all know the conditions and that anyone can stand even in our bloody awful democracy.'

'That's what I was getting at to begin with,' said Dafydd moodily.

'It's not on,' Terry said in an undertone.

'Why?'

'It takes money. And not just for a dead-cert lost deposit. It would be pointless. I'd get nowhere and look a fool. It's make-believe! I'm writing a story, a novel, and haven't even got *that* started properly.'

'Damn the bloody book, just get out there and *do* something!'

'But think for a minute,' said Dafydd recovering, 'this is a marginal constituency, only two hundred votes in it – just the sort where you'd make a mark, and it's right here on your doorstep - no expensive and time consuming travelling, no monkey suits, no hotel flunkies in the gear with hands out for their tip! People round here know you and you know them. Lots don't like the present MP – especially the women. Apart from her gaffes they think she's a well-off bitch trying to be Modern Labour.'

'Not *trying* to be Modern Labour, she *is* Modern Labour, scoffed Collins, 'that's the whole bloody trouble…'

'Think about it,' insisted Sheila excitedly: Mr. Terence Park, MP!'

'No big deal these days,' said Collins scornfully.

'But think of the money, Boyo!' enthused Hughes. 'Self-awarded pay rises after every election, boosted pensions while they clobber other's people's pittances, expenses that make your mouth water, two homes, directorships, consultancies, articles, TV interviews - all cash-making add-ons. Go on, man: you'd mint it. Stick your nose in the trough! "All aboard the gravy train,"' he chortled, '"calling at The Bank, The Stock Exchange, The Ritz, Oxford Street, Heathrow and first-class to Barbados!" Who knows, you could even slip the odd fifty smackers to your poor pals in the pub before you fly!'

'Forget all that!' said Collins. 'You'd have to put an end to their outside jobs. The bastards should be content with their full-time salaries for part-time work; after all, the House is in session for only 128 days a year! Just like the Oxford colleges so many of them come from. You'd think 60,000 constituents would be enough …'

'Don't be so negative,' snapped Sheila. 'We're trying to get Terry to stand – not put him off.'

'Exactly,' said Hughes, beginning to side with her.

Terry gazed at the drink-stained tabletop.

'Terry,' Sheila continued slowly, 'we don't say you'd get in – but you would give the others something to think about. I bet you'd get five hundred votes and that could tip the balance in this constituency and you'd have got your party off to a real headline-grabbing start!'

'But I haven't got a party! Can't you grasp that? How many more times have I got to say it? There is no Common Sense Party!'

'Then make one,' ordered Dafydd Hughes. 'Someone's got to start something new, and start soon. Why not you?'

Four muscular shaven-headed men whose evening did not start until the first three pints were downed had replaced the easily shocked people at the nearby table. They talked heatedly and knowledgeably about a pub-based darts league on the far side of town.

Terry sat, slowly shaking his head. Collins was right about the other jobs. Didn't a few greedy MPs set a terrible example and ruin the image of them all? And Sheila was right about a fringe party making a difference, he'd thought of that himself, and Hughes was right about the need for a new party. He was *really* right about that.

'You're still not interested? Won't give it a try? Won't take a risk?' Collins drained his glass. 'Well, never mind, but I'm off. And the best of British luck with the book. Sounds OK to me – but you're probably right - you won't get far with your Common Sense Party in the UK. We're too bloody conventional. Think, we'll soon have a moribund 18th century parliament in a 21st century country – and ordinary people know it! It's a lousy system full of archaic practices, mumbo-jumbo language, stupid dressing up and vested bloody interests! It's the most selective club in town: free to members and bugger all to do with the man in the street. Try your idea in the USA, you'll get nowhere here.'

'And you won't help with the novel?'

'Not on your Nelly, but I'm flattered - thanks for asking! The union work's enough for me - and my teaching - such as it is.'

Collins said no more, Hughes fetched more beer, Sheila waited for Collins to leave, Terry changed the subject.

'OK, let's look at something else,' he said. 'I'm worried about the PPP – the People's Patriotic Party. They're picking up votes, winning seats in local elections, getting loads of money, spreading propaganda, instilling fear and getting away with it.'

'Getting away with it? It's a free country,' countered Collins.

'Free country? *Free country?* You amaze me!' rasped Terry. 'You really do! You know the PPP's ultra right wing and covers it up by posing as the people's party, spouting patriotism, singing *Rule Britannia* and waving the Union Jack. They scare voters by choosing emotive issues and get support from those who can't see what they really stand for. It's been done before with terrible consequences.'

'A passing phenomenon,' said Sheila. 'Don't get so worked up.'

Terry was scathing: 'And where does your son work?'

Sheila did not answer.

'Won't you tell us?' urged Terry. 'He works in Germany doesn't he, and before that in Italy? Where next: sunny Spain? Don't those names ring a bell? And you talk to me about a passing phenomenon?'

'Stop living in the past. Those countries are democracies now.'

'So's this country, for the moment,' uttered Terry. 'But look at PPP views on immigration. Don't say you go along with those?'

'Not altogether, no, but a lot of people are worried by immigration and they think it's not talked about enough. And there's a lot of sense in wanting a five year ban on all immigration as long as it's regardless of race, colour or creed so that we can get ourselves sorted out and get some sort of population policy in place.'

Collins and Hughes nodded. Terry was shocked at their silence and puzzled by Collins' indifference. Didn't he loathe the PPP?

'Their so-called population policy is whitewash and in my view is very much about race and colour and creed. Well, isn't it? And there's a general election coming,' Terry continued turning to Collins. 'Aren't you afraid they'll cream off votes, get decent MPs thrown out – even win themselves seats?'

'No, I'm not. Sheila's right: you're getting far too worked up. And anyway, so what? If the PPP puts forward policies that appeal and people want to vote for them that's their right: they don't need your permission. But sod the PPP. They're nothing.'

Collins rose to leave. 'And don't you forget, people might vote PPP because they're sick to bloody death of the other useless shower. Perhaps the main parties ignore people's fears while the PPP listens! So you ask yourself, mate, if you don't want the PPP to grow, what is there about your Common Sense Party that will help win votes from the disillusioned multitude who might be turning to the PPP? Ask what will make the poor buggers say: "Yes, the CSP's a possibility – it's different – let's give *that* a try." Stick something like that in your manifesto – such as our ever-growing population – controlling that's common sense by any bloody definition.'

'You mean because we're overcrowded?' put in Hughes.

'Of course I do,' Collins growled. 'So get thinking, Terry old boy. If you're worried about the PPP gaining ground don't sit there running it down, ask *why* it's growing.' He smiled at a near ashen Terry. 'That's shaken you hasn't it? And so it should! But never mind, I'll give you a hand with your novel, throw in a few ideas - but no more. And I'm not getting involved in the general election, that's really kidding people! Teachers for Radical Action takes my time and is more worthwhile. And stop agonising about the PPP. Our politically correct media will make damn sure the only publicity the PPP gets will be negative - or they'll sideline them like they do the other ventures they don't like.'

'You astound me Collins, you really do: that's just what people said about Hitler, Mussolini and Franco! Fascists the lot of them – but they went on to rule most of Europe for over five years.'

'Are you so sure the PPP is fascist?' asked Sheila.

'Yes, aren't you?'

'No.'

'I'm staggered. I really am.' Then he swung round on Collins. 'Don't you know, Collins, that here, in this city, in this very district, we've got PPP men, and that two are on our school's governing body?'

'There are? Name them!'

'No!" shouted Sheila banging the table, 'not in here for God's sake!'

'I *will* name them! That nauseating creature Fergus Eastman and his pathetic lackey Giles Townsend, and the ...'

'Townsend?' cried the astounded Hughes, '*Townsend*?'

'... yes, and that snotty-nosed vice-chairman Wally Walker-West is a fellow traveller!'

'Keep your bloody voices down!' warned Collins suddenly. 'Right down. Keep them down, *right now*,' he urged. 'Look who's walked in: a flypaper after flies – and not flies in flaming flight either!'

*

Hetty Hopkins had arrived with her latest boy friend. At what some regarded as the tender age of twenty-four, Hetty was the youngest and most successful reporter on *The Mansworth Evening Messenger and Times*. She had used her training, her bubbling sexual attraction, her intelligence, her guile, her wit, her charm, her pretended little girl innocence to capture many a juicy story. More than one Mansworth citizen had been fooled by her implied confidentiality or her claim that she was acting in the public interest, or by her sexy insinuations that she wouldn't mind reporting a hotter topic than the Women's Institute's Cross-Stitch Competition. After viewing the published results of a session with Hetty Hopkins several gentlemen had sworn they would never speak to the press again. Tonight, dressed provocatively and sporting more than adequate make-up, she could be taken for one of the more expensive ladies of the town.

But Hetty's personal life was less of a success. A string of partners had come and gone as she wended her way through the sixth form of Terry's school, then through her undemanding course in journalism at one of the old polytechnics-cum-universities, and then through three thrusting years at *The Messenger*. It was rumoured she had used her range of talents to persuade the newspaper's aging editor to employ her full-time. But that susceptible executive had soon been replaced by a hard headed, emotion-free, go-getting, trouble-shooting female who knew not only the tricks of the newspaper trade but was exempt from Hetty's machinations. Life had been tough for Hetty Hopkins since the arrival of her sexually immune and envious editor.

In contrast, Hetty's current larger than life boyfriend, known by the more vulgar elements as "Hetty's Hulk", was a bruising, eighteen and a half stones of bone and muscle. He would enhance any shot-putting team at the Olympic Games, dominate a rugby scrum, ensure victory for his side in a tug-of-war, or find lucrative employment as a nightclub bouncer. Now he secured preferential treatment at the bar and seemed *au fait* with Hetty's wish to have a rum and coke with limejuice and crushed ice served in a tall glass without a straw.

Hetty looked round and saw Terry Park and also Sheila Tipping whom she knew from dreary *Messenger* assignments at the school. But she wondered about the other men. The older, red-faced one was familiar and she could identify him later from her paper's library of mug shots, but the younger one was new – and not bad-looking.

She gave the four a wave but would not join them. Professionally she preferred to talk to people singly when it was easier to elicit information, not when they were bunched formidably in a drinking group of three or four. Anyway, she thought, this was supposed to be a social occasion with her boyfriend.

Her professional contact with Outer Mansworth Comprehensive was ongoing. Although the school had undergone changes since she was a pupil she still knew it well. She had covered - in addition to unbelievably boring prizegivings, barely recognisable Shakespearean productions and painfully discordant orchestral concerts – several headline-grabbing stories involving bullying, extortion, drug dealing and, in one memorable year, a shoplifting sortie by a well-led team of fifth-form girls from affluent homes. She had interviewed their mothers and her sympathetic reporting of parents' growing lack of confidence in the school had shown in her writing. Such partiality had angered governors and alarmed her new editor, but the correspondence it had attracted and the consequent increase in circulation had banished thoughts of censorship.

Lately Hetty had, despite her customary lack of feeling for others, noted the stressed state of head teacher, Adrian Olde. As a pupil she had thought him a timorous man who allowed pupils to transgress too easily, even though she had been one of the transgressors.

*

school? What is it this time? Yet more bullying? Resignations? Is Park involved? He's supposed to be writing a book about some embryonic common sense party? A new party? Is that it? Can't be flying a kite with Eddie Collins in the election can he? Or is it Olde? The man's obviously ill - is it about a replacement to be made by those bickering governors? That would stir things up! Any appointment now would be seen as political. Boy, there are some promising lines there!

As the Hulk's hand returned to her knee and eased itself higher and higher, contentment spread across his scarred and stubbly face. God, it didn't take much to please a man! But her thoughts were still on the earnest talkers. She *had* seen the younger man somewhere, some choir concert? Was that it? Maybe. But what was going on? Was it the school or the general election? Either would make a story, but, she wondered, now professionally aroused, if I could link them and run them as one I could fill the front page and make a name for myself!

Thursday   4 April.   **A Persistent Reporter**

'All you've got is tittle-tattle. Get the facts. Get them to talk – that shouldn't be difficult with teachers. Gyrate your behind at the men and flatter the women – make them feel important. But get me a story, and get it soon! We can't keep filling the paper with rumours of an election – we need stories based on facts,' rapped the editor.

'OK,' agreed Hetty grudgingly, again ruing the day this granite-faced woman took command. 'But don't badger me. I'll get some.'

She thought again of Mr Park who'd joined the teaching staff during her final years at the school. She thought he'd liked the shape of her rear end once, and, from what she'd now found out about Hughes – ah well – one woman's behind in the hand was worth ten in the bush to him! And if they wouldn't talk one of the other men would - she needed only one to succumb. It would be easy to get a staff list from that talkative, soft-touch secretary, Ingrid Eastman.

But Ingrid seemed edgy and anxious to ring off. That was unusual, and the weak excuse that she was expecting important calls furthered Hetty's interest. Hetty joked about the school facing imminent closure and, while Ingrid would normally have laughed and thrown back stories about nosey reporters, today she shied away promising only to let Hetty have a staff list. She seemed extra nervous when asked for the Chairperson of Governor's name and number saying Hetty must have those already.

'It's just that these things change from time to time,' Hetty had explained, 'like head teachers come and go?' But that was the end of the conversation. Ingrid did not rise. Her caginess was noted.

Hetty's next phone call was to the rectory to learn that Lena Napier was working in the parish church. Although Hetty was there in less than ten minutes there was no sign of Lena. The church was open for cleaning and a lady walked over to speak. Hetty said she wanted *The Parish Magazine* for its local news - and to view the "Coming Events" board, and was surprised when the woman addressed her by name. It transpired Hetty had been at school with her eldest son, and that now her youngest child, Karen, was there ready to take final year exams. The mother remembered how smitten her boy had been with Hetty and had been grateful that Hetty, who had a string of eager boyfriends, had let him down lightly.

'But I'm beginning to think the place is not nearly as good as when you and Paul were there. I'll be quite glad when Karen's out of it'

Hetty noted the 'Paul' and remembered Paul Blake, who had had a pathetic crush on her. The ninny had been seventeen and hadn't a clue: he didn't know where to start! So this was Mrs Blake - the lady renowned for fine flower arrangements. Hetty remembered writing a pretty humdrum piece about the local flower-arranging group.

'So I've heard, Mrs Blake,' she said. Why d'you think that is?'

'The head teacher's not very well and hasn't been for some time, and some teachers there I don't like - and they seem to run the place.'

'Is Mr Olde still the head teacher?' asked Hetty innocently as she flicked through the *Magazine*. So, she read, Mrs Megan Morgan was still making her marmalade but had had to raise the price, the plant sale was a success, the Easter collection was rather disappointing, Mr. Philpott ran the weekly raffle, Captain Walter Walker-West (Rtd) was due to open the July garden party, and there was an appeal for another bell ringer.

'Mr Olde's been there a while?'

'Yes. But Karen thinks he might be leaving soon. She says there's some gossip about that. And the rough behaviour needs sorting out.'

'Your priest is a governor there?' prompted Hetty, still not looking up. 'At the school, I mean.'

'The Chairperson, actually,' said a different voice. Lena Napier held out her hand. Her quiet walk from the sanctuary had gone unnoticed.

Hetty, although startled, was skilled in the arts of covering up and the regaining of composure. 'Of course,' she said, ' and I'm Hetty Hopkins from *The Messenger*, and I was ...'

'I know who you are, Miss Hopkins, and that you've called for a copy of *The Parish Magazine*. Not in your league, surely?'

'It alerts us to Church events we might need to cover.'

'Which are few in number, I recall?'

'Demands on space ...'

'Of course. And you already know Mrs Blake, I see.'

'I was at school with her son.'

Mrs Blake had stepped back, embarrassed, wondering what had been overheard, and was preparing to resume her cleaning.

'No, no, don't leave, Beryl, I don't want to stop your conversation, and I must go anyway. Goodbye, Miss Hopkins.'

'Just let me say I'm sorry to hear Mr Olde is not very well,' said Hetty before Lena could leave. 'But he must be near retirement? And quite soon? His job can't be getting any easier?'

Lena waited.

'This term?' pressed Hetty. 'There are rumours.'

Lena hesitated, but only for a moment. 'Which for now, Miss Hopkins, must remain rumours.'

Mrs Blake looked carefully at the priest. Hetty noticed both the priest's hesitation and the cleaner's look.

'But he can't be going this July, surely?' asked Hetty looking directly at the minister and holding her gaze.

Lena smiled: she could deal with Hetty Hopkins and her ilk. 'I must be off, but it's been good to see you in church,' she said to the young reporter, 'I hope we'll see you here regularly and not necessarily on newspaper business. The times of our services are in the magazine. You might find Evensong appealing, it begins at four-fifteen now.'

Lena left as quietly as she had come.

'Well, well. I've a feeling Mr Olde will be retiring shortly,' Hetty said to Mrs Blake. 'Did you get that impression?'

Mrs Blake's only reply was to say she had the pews to dust and needed to make a start on the brass before lunch - in less than an hour's time. To herself she said, 'I'm so glad the Minister didn't tell a lie. That would have been awful.'

*

The Rev. Lena Napier was annoyed at having exposed herself to Hetty Hopkins. She guessed what the reporter would make of their exchange, but had been determined not to hide in the vestry of her own church. But those thoughts had to be cast aside as she began to phone the governors to tell them their head teacher was leaving. She explained, patiently but firmly, that if they were to appoint a new person for September they had only twenty-six days in which to do it. Although all were annoyed, and several were sceptical of the timing, they agreed to try.

An argument persisted as to whether they were to use the four-person plus chairman panel they used when interviewing for assistant teacher posts or whether it should be enlarged. Lena made twenty phone calls before it was agreed that Captain Walker-West, as vice-chairperson, should join the panel and, on the insistence of Fergus Eastman, that Giles Townsend should make a sixth member.

Lena contacted Dr Matthew Zing - a man who, she knew, set great store on being addressed as 'Doctor'. But the wary Zing maintained that, as he had received no formal notice of Olde's retirement, any meeting would be premature. Nevertheless, Lena asked the Chief Education Officer to check on Olde's position and was later invited to his office.

Lena hoped Zing's estimate of her was higher than hers of him. She saw Zing as a non-controversial man who held strong opinions on nothing and shunned all risk-taking. As a politician he would make an ideal candidate for the Stand-for-Nothing Party. The colourless man devoted what efforts he made in life to achieving a peaceful existence punctuated by unspectacular and routine promotions. He was, at forty-nine, a member of a very high Anglo Catholic church, played a fair hand of bridge, collected pre-1952 British postage stamps (fine-used) and specialised in elusive shades of the Jubilee issue of 1897.

Lena stressed that time was of the essence. That worried Dr Matthew Zing who did not like things rushed. But Lena emphasised that the governors did not want to face the long autumn term without a head teacher. She did not mention that she had no wish to deal with Ursula Irving, as an acting head teacher, for any length of time at all.

Zing chose to regard their meeting as a formality. While he stressed his acquiescence was not required, he listened, made occasional notes, and insisted Napier's programme for advertising, short listing and interviewing were matters for the governors. He noted that Tuesday, 30 April would be the day for interviews and that the governors would offer, as an aid to recruitment, periodic study-leave and a marginally higher salary. Zing said either he or his deputy would attend the interviews if invited. The meeting lasted barely fifteen minutes.

Then the CEO sat deep in thought. He saw more problems at Olde's school, but would not get involved; there was nothing there to further his ambitions. He was surprised no governor had objected strongly to the timing of the appointment, but, as none had, the smoothest of transitions was required with, preferably, a biddable candidate of his own choice installed.

He called his secretary: 'Mrs Jackson, bring in Sonia Smith's file, please – Sonia Smith, head teacher at All Saints.'

*

Later, and long after most teachers had gone home, a brief statement appeared on the staff room notice board at Outer Mansworth Comprehensive School informing the staff that, on the retirement of Mr Adrian Olde, B.A. (Hons), London, the governing body would appoint a new head teacher for September.

Friday 5 April.   **A Puzzled Probationer**

Pique emerged during morning break at the proposed rise in the new head teacher's salary, the promise of sabbaticals, and the haste with which the appointment was being made. While the teachers knew they would not be widely consulted on a change that would affect their work and the well being of their pupils for years to come, they did feel they might have received more than an A5 memo pinned to the bottom edge of the notice board.

Probationer teacher Jenny Jean Jones watched as teachers came and went. Most were merely irritated by such off-hand treatment and she was surprised to see how readily they accepted their low, non-consultative status and how little thought they gave as to how that status might be raised. She suspected many were products of the system in which they now worked. Most were able to become teachers because they had done relatively well at school, had worked hard, passed exams, behaved sensibly, and rarely questioned what they were taught or how they were taught it for they assumed it was the norm. Now they expected their own pupils to see schooling in the same dismal light so that some of those pupils would, in their turn, become equally compliant teachers. And so it went on – a worrying system of self-perpetuation. The result was, she felt, that many teachers had too low an opinion of themselves and of their profession.

Jenny hoped she was wrong for she did not want to subscribe to such an interpretation of teachers' work and recruitment, but already she could see how easy it was to let each day come and go. The tiredness that modern class teaching brought left teachers with little energy for converse thinking, protestation, or ameliorating action. Could the ensuring of 'apathy through exhaustion' be an employers' callous policy? Surely not! But, for example, few teachers mentioned the rumours of the general election now headlined in every paper.

She knew teachers grumbled about the hierarchical staff structure, the curriculum, the testing imposed on their pupils, and the stressful, periodic inspections to which they were subjected. But, being an intelligent young woman and more politically aware than many of her colleagues, she realised already that while many would moan to each other in private, as a body they were unlikely to do much to raise their semi-professional status. The more venturesome might find another job but others would take the salary, look forward to the holidays and the pension and, in the meantime, tolerate the *status quo*. If so the outlook was unattractive for an enterprising person. She wanted to ask Terry what he thought about her prospects and the profession's future but did not want him to think she was considering quitting already.

*

'Do you know what's going on, Jenny?' Terry asked.

He was sitting with Dafydd Hughes and Ursula Irving sipping his second cup of weak tea. He preferred strong tea and usually made his own in his room, but not today. 'Come and sit here with us, we're chewing the fat. Move over, Hughes, show some manners!'

During Jenny's two terms at the school Terry and Dafydd had noticed the girl's interest in teacher politics and had recruited her to Teachers For Radical Action. If she stayed in teaching – both men had detected signs of disillusionment – she might become a TFRA school representative and then move on from there.

'We're going to alert Eddie Collins as to what's happening,' he said. 'Eddie is district representative for the TFRA. He'll keep an eye open to see if employment legislation is breached - such as the job description. It will be scrutinised, so will the position of the teaching staff-members of the governing body and the part they're to play in the appointment, which, directly, will probably be none - especially if there's an internal candidate. Ursula, here, is a staff representative, but not with Teachers for Radical Action.'

Jenny nodded. She felt disadvantaged sitting here with Ursula Irving whose substantive rank as the senior deputy was way above her own. She was also wary of Hughes, but for different reasons.

'So even if ...' she began.

'Yes?' prompted Hughes.

'If Mr Collins does all he can, it won't make any real difference?'

'Make no difference?'

'No. The system will be the same whoever's appointed. There will be a head teacher and deputies and assistants and school buildings and classes and set hours and terms and a National Curriculum and tests and league tables. And ...' but then she hesitated. Ursula was looking at her intently.

'Go on,' said. Ursula, 'don't mind me.'

'There'll be the same staff pecking order?'

Dafydd laughed out loud. 'You're damn right there will! It would take a revolution to alter that and you won't get a revolution in this forelock-touching tip! We're in feudal times here!'

He took Jenny's hand and squeezed it affectionately: here was a girl after his own heart. But Jenny removed her hand. Dafydd looked to see how the deputy was reacting and Jenny glanced at her warily, too. But the deputy was giving nothing away, she simply suggested more coffee, but did not offer to fetch it.

'What will happen in the next few weeks, Jenny,' said Ursula, 'is that the governors will appoint a new head teacher. Like it or not, that is what is called 'the procedure'. Then, after peering round as if to see who was listening, she lowered her voice as if to give the impression her next words were for Jenny alone, 'and I'm not very fond of that procedure either, but there's not much one rep from one union on one governing body in one school in one county can do about that.'

'But changes will never be made. ...' began Jenny.

'Until some one makes a first move,' finished Dafydd.

'Thank you, Mr Hughes. But, Jenny, it's wrong to suppose no changes have been made or no initiatives tried,' said Ursula, 'because they have. Terry is not alone in wanting something different.'

'But no one's got very far,' said Hughes. 'Common sense tells us that teachers who know this school, with all its good points and bad points, who know the children and many of the parents and the district in which they live, are the ones who should be appointing the new head teacher - that is if we need a head teacher at all!'

'You're right about common sense,' said Terry, 'but what you don't say, and what I think Jenny was hinting at is that it's the school itself – the school as an institution - that's the real stumbling block.'

'Maybe,' said Hughes, 'but I don't buy all that "no-schools" lark. But, just think, if they don't get their skates on and appoint some character for next term we'll be headless! Headless chuffing chickens! But if that were to happen, and we really *were* headless, then a brave, imaginative, farsighted governing body could say to the teaching staff, "There you are folk, try organising *yourselves* for a term; let's see how you get on."'

'That's hoping for a miracle!' said Ursula smiling wryly. 'The very thought would scare them silly! Imagine if such a 'try' succeeded! Think of the consequences for other schools and for the Educational Establishment generally. They'd never wear it. They'd never risk it.'

'You've hit the nail on the head,' said Terry. 'It's not on, but it's a wonderful thought.'

'And the bell's gone,' stated Ursula emphatically, 'and, getting back to procedure, the procedure here is that when the school bell rings we proceed to our assigned classes. The pupils' learning resumes and continues until the next bell says it ceases and the procedure is repeated. Formal learning ends at noon but continues, I suspect, informally but more effectively, on the school field or in the dining room or the cloakrooms. That is the procedure and that, after all, is education today.'

So they proceeded to proceed - except for the thoughtful Ursula. She sought Hull to tell him of developments. She knew what a vital post Hull held and realised how important it was to keep the site manager amenable, and so, as far as possible, she took him into her confidence. She felt sure, however, that Hull knew about the retirement already because he read the staff notice board and got further information from the loose-tongued Ingrid Eastman. The deputy had long suspected Hull fancied Ingrid for he seemed to grasp any opportunity to chat with her, and more than once she had seen him eying the voluptuous secretary from his well-placed cubby-hole.

*

But Mrs Eastman did not command all Hull's attention. He had observed Susan Mansfield and come to regard her as an amenable, lively woman with an excellent figure who was a cut above most of the other women in the school. Often he had watched her in the foyer talking to Terry Park and, knowing of Terry's recent divorce and womanless state, wondered whether the deprived schoolmaster was making a pass at the university lecturer. Often the two had a laugh together and that was always a promising sign, as was the way they lightly touched each other as if to raise themselves a rung or two on the intimacy ladder. And further, from what he overheard, they were not always discussing the latest student teacher's classroom performance.

Sometimes he transposed the couple and they became a pair of 1880 lovers meeting near a remote and weatherworn rural church in the setting of a Thomas Hardy novel. But he checked himself there for the fate of many Hardy couples was of romance ending in disappointment - even tragedy - and Hull, a kindly man at heart, would not want to see this couple ending like that. He respected Terry because there was no side to him. He liked Dr Mansfield too, not just for her looks, but because she was friendly and passed the time of day. With her, as with Terry Park and Ursula Irving, he felt he had a recognised place in the school and that his work was appreciated.

That brought Hull to the Eastmans. Fergus Eastman sometimes called to collect his wife after school, but even if he had to wait Eastman never spoke because he, Hull, might never have existed. He doubted whether Eastman had the slightest suspicion he fancied his wife. To Eastman he would be a colourless man, just 'one of the cleaners'. No, Eastman was a condescending, lip-curling snob, one who did not parley with the lower social classes.

But that was not all. He thought Fergus, who was an influential, long-serving school governor, was sufficiently right wing to support, secretly no doubt, the ultra-right wing People's Patriotic Party – the party hated by Hull. He would watch Eastman carefully in the coming weeks. He would see whether the PPP made noises locally at the general election and whether Eastman became involved. The man might be tempted to show his cards openly and then lose the game. At this stage Hull would drift off feeling the world would be a better place without Fergus Eastman. A firing squad at dawn? Fifteen years' hard labour without parole? An unfortunate accident? Bankruptcy? But damn the man, it was time for a pint and a one-way bet on the four-fifteen at Folkestone – on the field's favourite filly, Fatima the Fourth.

*

Hetty Hopkins re-read what she had discovered about Outer Mansworth Comprehensive School. Beginning life in the early Sixties as a secondary modern school for girls it had been enlarged in order to rescue a boys' school from their 'temporary' accommodation in a depressing array of eight ex-army huts, two tatty canteens and an ablutions block.

While the merging of the sexes did little to raise academic standards it had made life more interesting for the older pupils. The newly constituted school was enlarged both when the school leaving age was raised in 1972 and when architect Charte's housing estate was further developed. Then, in its joined state, the school had established its own fifth and sixth forms, greatly improved its local reputation and became oversubscribed. But influential left-wingers on the county education committee, backed by an old and embittered backbench member of parliament, had disliked the school's growing emphasis on academic work and its comfortable middle class sixth form. They disagreed with the school creating its own 'A' level groups instead of using the authority's sixth form colleges. Then, in what some saw as blatant retaliation, funds for the school were kept to the legal minimum. After that, and year by year, standards and morale had declined.

The first head of the combined school was disappointed with her inheritance and left before the school was rehoused on its present site. The decline continued and her successor lasted even less time.

Hetty checked the newspaper's cuttings library, school magazines, minutes of governors' meetings, newsletters, education committee sessions, inspectors' reports and Internet pages. Soon she knew more about the school than did most of its own teaching staff.

She gained data on Teachers for Radical Action from its web site and saw how quickly the union had grown. Its down-to-earth agenda included a pledge to examine alternative ways of educating children and to support pilot schemes aimed at evaluating revolutionary approaches - one of which entailed the replacement of the school-based system by a more humane way of working – provided, of course, that union members' personal and professional interests were not compromised.

She had nearly completed her Internet search on the TFRA when a link, *'Members' Requests'* appeared. A founder union member, Terence Park, sought examples of how the use of common sense in education could improve the lot of teachers and, subsequently, their pupils. That, in turn, he claimed, would lead to the greater use of common sense in society as a whole. The link confirmed that Park was writing a novel called *The Common Sense Party* which had a much wider remit than education alone, and that Park sought ideas from other members. Hetty followed two further links relating to alternative teaching systems, and one referred to current work being done at The University of Greater Mansworth by a Dr Susan Margaret Mansfield.

Hetty knew the name.

Saturday 6 April.   **Teacher and Lecturer**

But Hetty was not satisfied. From the school's assistant secretary, Louie Anne Lee, she learned that Mr Olde often spent Saturday mornings in his office catching up on paper work. She stored this information knowing that such an hour might be one in which she could get the head teacher alone for a talk on the school's affairs - she smiled at "affairs" - by trading on her status as "an old girl" – another smile! But for now she would concentrate on gleaning information from dissatisfied parents.

The excluded pupil issue came up frequently. The references to the girl's readmission "not making common sense" impressed her. The use of more common sense in school matters seemed to be what most parents wanted and Hetty began to think that if its field were extended Terry's make-believe CSP would not be so very way out.

Other complaints were about overcrowding from parents whose children were already there and of the lack of places from parents whose children were not. But when Hetty contacted the Chief Education Officer, Dr Matthew Zing, and the local MP, Dr Audrey Anderson, neither was helpful. Both adopted the stance: "beware of the press unless it ensures favourable publicity" and both parried danger-laden questions by saying they had, of course, "noted the concerns of some parents" and that "these were, of course, being looked into most carefully." Neither told Hetty that the growing interest in the school, with its high potential for ill-timed political trouble, both angered and alarmed them.

*

That same morning, by accident, Terry Park met Susan Mansfield in the

80

university bookshop on the Little Mansworth Campus. They chatted easily before Susan led Terry to a small stand given over to a display of books on alternatives in education.

'I persuaded the manager to fix this,' she said, smiling. 'And that's not difficult if students are buying my recommended course-books from his shop. But years ago there would have been no point in pressing him because there wouldn't have been enough titles for a good display. Now there's a wide selection.'

'Most are from the USA,' said Terry, leaning over the table.

'So?' questioned Susan. 'So? It's the ideas in them that matter not the country they come from. Anyway, what the United States does today we do tomorrow and millions home-educate there and the number's growing every year.'

'This is not America. Americans frequently forge ahead ignoring problems. To them a straight line is the shortest distance between two points regardless of what's in between. We don't do that. We see the obstacles – and, admittedly, they're often imaginary.'

'Absolutely! We see so many that we end up doing nothing! But, I agree, in this field many British people have fears which need to be allayed. I accept, too, that the absurd notion "education means school" is set so deeply in our culture it will take some shifting. But it can be shifted. It *will* be shifted! There may be, at this very moment, some education authority, perhaps a small one, planning a system without using schools – planning a scheme based on my ideas – may even be considering a pilot scheme to test the water.'

'I don't think so. Nor do you.'

'But we don't *know*, do we? But we do know that nothing, *nothing*, lasts forever. The school-based system of education is no exception. It will die and be replaced by something else either because authorities become desperate and *have* to find something different or because some brave councillors or high-up officials or name-making MPs see the advantages and persuade an authority to give it a try.'

'A dream world!'

'But it isn't! A start will be made somewhere. And we can start that – we ourselves - by questioning candidates at the general election.'

'And they'd run a mile. They know voters would see that as a crazy scheme to close schools and that would be the surest vote loser you could come up with. Parents need schools.'

'But not necessarily for reasons to do with education? More to do with child care – even babysitting?'

'I won't argue with that.'

'Good. So when you've looked at these books I'll show you that this shop has a coffee bar where we can argue comfortably.'

'Coffee bars in book shops – another transatlantic import!'

'But one worth taking,' she smiled.

She looked at Terry closely. He came alive when he argued; then he was quite attractive. She would pay for coffee, and, maybe, a small cake.

*

Hetty phoned just as Terry, can of beer in hand and several others lined up, switched on the radio to hear a commentary on his team's away match against Little Scoring's second eleven.

'I won't keep you,' Hetty said, 'But I'm doing a piece on your school and its teachers for *The Messenger* and I'm really interested in you and your book and your Common Sense Party ideas, they're just what the country needs! So can you let me have a …'

'Where d'you get all that from? Who've you been talking to?'

'Now, Terry, don't be like that!'

'Come on Hetty, name names!' A suspicious Terry was now doubly annoyed. 'Who's been shouting his mouth off?'

'No one. I downloaded it from the TFRA's web site: it's all there in the public domain. You asked members for examples of how common sense could help our schools because you're writing a new book about it. Remember? So let me come round and talk.'

'No,' said Terry hastily, 'just tell me what you want to know.'

'Well, if the CSP got into power, what would it do?'

'First, Hetty Hopkins, it would lock up journalists like you and lose the key. OK? Now, I'm going to listen to a soccer match which starts in exactly two and a half minutes.'

'Plenty of time. What would the party do about transport, that's a pet peeve round here.'

'Transport? Road transport? Well, all street parking would be banned,' said Terry, now angry at giving this woman - ex-pupil or not - any time at all. 'People would have to park their cars off the roads to keep roads clear for moving traffic – which is what they were built for in the first place and for which they're now maintained out of public funds – right? No permanent street parking. No using the road as your garage or as a free car park: that's common sense.'

'Lots of people haven't got garages.'

'Too bad! If you can't show where you're going to keep your car you don't get a licence. You can't keep a horse without a stable, a plane without a hangar, a boat without a mooring, so you won't keep a car without a parking lot. That's more common sense! Next question.'

'None. On that answer alone your party's dead.'

'Don't you believe it!'

'It is!'

'Never! People will soon come to their senses. The same with traffic offences: first offence - *any* offence - five years' ban. Second: ten years. Third: a life ban, and that *means* life! They join the UTD group.'

'UTD?'

'"Unfit To Drive". And that will be a mighty big group! We need as many people off the roads as we can - there's too much traffic on them already, so – *common sense* - those who don't drive safely, off they go, and good riddance! Common sense – two birds with one stone – *fewer* drivers, fewer *bad* drivers. Result? Less aggro, fewer accidents, less call on hospitals, cheaper insurance, easier driving, better traffic flow, less pollution. Everyone gains except the selfish, reckless types who won't obey the rules.'

'You're too easily logical, Terry. You wouldn't survive your first public meeting - you'd be lynched! So what about schools and truancy? Truancy's a growing problem here in Mansworth.'

'There wouldn't be any.'

'No schools?' she asked eagerly.

'No *truancy*. School would be voluntary. School is an expensive public service so there's no point in offering it to people who don't want it and who wreck it for others – common sense! Now, the match is on and we nearly scored!'

'But … …'

'Sorry, Hetty, no "buts". Meet me in the pub some time and buy me a few drinks – you can claim them on expenses - which is more than I can! So cheers now – and be a good girl!'

Later he would check the TFRA web site. What *was* on there? He needed to know. But in stoppage time his team scored their fifth goal so he opened his fifth can. After all, five-nil away from home wasn't bad, even against a managerless Little Scoring Reserves who'd had two men sent off in the first ten minutes!

But Hetty will want a replay, he thought. She's not that easily beaten!

Every Sunday at lunchtime Terry enjoyed two pints of Ruddles best bitter - but not at *The Standing Oak*, that was too near his school and might house beer-drinking sixth formers. He frequented an older town centre hostelry, *The King of Morocco*, an easy walk from home.

He flicked through his newspaper: more about the election, yet still this awful government hadn't named the day! People would lose patience and the dithering government would lose votes. Inside was a colourful account of a wife-collecting, fast-living, overpaid film star's romance with a millionaire's sixteen-year-old daughter. That made Terry wonder, as he had on Friday, whether, despite the age gap, there was something going on between Hughes and Jenny Jean Jones: they seemed to be together plenty. Was the randy Hughes leading poor Jenny astray?

He moved on to a million pound libel case involving *The Daily Slur* and an MP's claims for expenses during her month-long fact-finding mission, by private jet, on the protection of pandas in Outer Mongolia. She claimed caring constituents had expressed considerable concern about the rare animals' welfare. Terry was finishing his first pint when a man approached, uninvited, and sat down.

'Think I know you,' the man said. 'What are you drinking?'

Terry was annoyed. He came to this pub for a quiet drink and a read of the Sunday paper, not for company.

'Ruddles?' the man asked noting the beer's colour. He fetched Bass for himself and Ruddles for Terry. The donor was a thickset man, short, balding, with a thin moustache and narrowing but long, uncut eyebrows. His face was rough and red, had two scars on the left cheek, and a small brown mole, with hairs, on the lower right. He wore jeans, a creased check shirt, dark grey socks, and once-white trainers.

'You're a teacher at the Comp. I've seen you there. I'm a governor – Vic Sneade.' He offered his hand and grinned as his grip made the teacher wince. 'Problems up there, aren't there?'

Terry did not like the look of Vic Sneade. 'Are there?'

'You know there are! Plenty!' He chuckled. 'Don't worry, I'm not snooping, and you can't tell me anything I don't know. My grandson's there – Tim Sneade, fifteen, bright kid, bored out of his bloody mind.'

Terry could not recall the boy but accepted he could be bored out of his mind, "bloody" or not. 'And I'm Terry Park,' he said, folding his paper. 'I don't think I teach your grandson.'

'Don't *think* you do? Don't you know?'

'I teach ten different classes a week with thirty pupils in each.'

'And you can't know them all! And that, mate,' the man almost snarled, 'is where the trouble lies. Though the kids are all different, they're only names on a list to you. Just like the factory where I work - the school is too big. Every bugger knows it, but sod all is done.'

'Look, I don't want to be rude,' said Terry tetchily, 'but ...'

'You're here for a quiet drink. Well, calm down. You can have your drink – on me – and the next, but before you get all het up you might like to know I'm on your side. You soppy teachers are asked to do the impossible. If we workers were crapped on like you lot we'd walk out and the factory would shut – pronto!'

He waited while Terry drank. 'I'm the colour-match foreman at Williams, Evans, Jones & Roberts - that bunch of penny-pinching paint makers. Been there thirty years - that's where I learned to stir things up!' He laughed and took another swig - half a pint in one go. 'You teach humanities - whatever that is.'

'How do you know?'

'Governors have staff lists with subjects taught. You're on it.'

'That's a relief!'

'And you work your arses off.'

'There's a lot to get through.'

'And not much time?'

'No.'

'So why d'you waste it?'

'Waste it?'

'How many meetings were held last year to decide on the new school uniform? Guess the number of man-hours squandered on that.'

'Hundreds. But we didn't all go along with it.'

'But you put up with it, like good little boys and girls.'

'This isn't really ...'

'You teachers are a bit like the kids you teach, aren't you? You know nothing but school. Those who ...'

'If you're going to give me Bernard Shaw's wisecrack, don't bother: I heard it years ago – before you did.'

'OK, but what's it for – this uniform?'

'I don't know. All the old reasons, I suppose. *Esprit de corps ...*'

'*Esprit de bloody corps*! What the hell are you running? A French regiment of foot?'

'We have to keep up with other schools.'

'Well you're not doing. You're dropping down the league tables and you'll be relegated – two divisions in one go! And if you ask me ...'

'I don't ask you.'

'Well take my word for it, you're for the drop. And you need a new boss? And by September? That stupid old fart's finally jacking it in?'

'Now look ...'

'I shouldn't talk like that? Why not? He's well off, and he's on a hiding to nothing up there. He's ill, he's old, he's incompetent, he's got his balls in a twist, he's behind the times and the parents are fed up with him. He should have gone years ago. Why mince words? The school's a shambles and needs somebody new and nifty and right now. Will you apply?'

'*Me*? Me apply? I wouldn't stand a chance. I'm not even a deputy head or a head of year. You know the rank order. If I was in the army I'd still be a two pip lieutenant. Anyway it's not my line. I wouldn't want it.'

'That's why you're in with a chance. Not many will.'

'Including me.'

'Pity. Another drink?'

The conversation continued until Terry had had enough. As he stood up to leave, Vic Sneade leaned forward.

'Look mate, don't rule it out. The governors might want someone local, someone familiar, someone who knows the score, knows the school, knows the district, keeps the kids quiet and the school out of the headlines. Could be you! The salary's good – over sixty-five grand and rising - and a cast-iron pension! More than I can ever dream of!'

As Terry departed, Sneade chortled, waved to someone across the smoke-laden room and switched his drink to another table taking Terry's half-read newspaper with him. Poor twit, he thought, for he knew Terry had no chance of the headship and that had nothing to do with rank or experience or how good a teacher he was. It was politics, all politics - especially now. Still, there was no harm in stirring things up – and after a lifetime of practice he was pretty good at that!

*

Terry did not like Sundays. Since his divorce Sundays had become lonely days. He thought one of the days of the week should be called 'Loneday' and Sunday would be as good as any. The lack of someone to talk to hit home when he had things of importance on his mind. He thought of Susan Mansfield, but did he know her well enough to impose on her at short notice? While he liked to think he did, he was not sure. So he talked to himself.

Although he had told Vic Sneade he was not interested in a headship that was not entirely true. He had kept his options open by maintaining his interest in writing and politics, and by studying spasmodically for the qualification that all aspiring head teachers need: the National Professional Qualification for Headship {NPQH), the qualification that could make him the worthy head teacher of some lucky school!

Checks would be made on him and his referees, of course, but he knew that apart from his TFRA membership he and they would be clear. What was discouraging was the fact he was not the type to appeal to education officers, school governors or any of the august souls who appointed head teachers and if it became known he was writing a book about some Common Sense Party he would be damned further. Worryingly, he himself had leaked news of that and by the time Hetty Hopkins had finished with it the leak would be a torrent. If he added his growing interest in alternative education he might as well forget about becoming a head teacher anywhere – certainly not head teacher of a large school like Outer Mansworth Comprehensive (Mixed). But did that matter? There was nothing to stop him having a shot - except his own doubts – and he could deal with them.

So, his mind made up, he checked there was beer in the fridge and picked up *The Radio Times*. What was on TV tonight?

Good grief! *The Sunday Service* from an unknown village church near Macclesfield, then Round One of an amateur song contest *Down on the Pier with Rosie* from Bognor Regis, followed by highlights from *The Week in Westminster* and, believe it or not, the repeat of an extended party political broadcast on behalf of Today's Tories presented by a well-known City banker!

He reopened the fridge with alacrity.

Week Two

Grinning widely, Dafydd Hughes brought in the early edition of *The Mansworth Evening Messenger and Times* and slapped it on the staff room table where a dozen teachers were tucking into cheese and onion sandwiches brought in by Hull. The Co-op had done well today.

'Penultimate page,' he said. 'Dictionary here for the ignoramuses who don't know the meaning of penultimate. And a big advert for Olde's job. They're not wasting time! Salary's boosted and the lucky winner gets Sabbaticals. He'll need them!'

'Or she,' said Sheila Tipping.

'Or she? Are *you* applying?' cried Hughes with a guffaw.

Sheila glowered as she grabbed the paper and turned to the advert. 'Why's it in this rag and not the *Times Educational Supplement?* Are they after someone local?'

'Maybe,' said Terry nonchalantly. 'Perhaps the local rag is all we're worth? But it'll probably be in the *TES* on Friday.'

The staff was angry at the perks offered for a job they thought was overpaid already and which some said was both surplus to requirements and a waste of teaching expertise. Three thought the school's description was misleading and if applicants believed all that was in the advert they were in for a shock.

'I'll get the full job description from Ingrid,' said Hughes. 'A nice smile and an appreciative gawp at her gaping front should do it, then we can read what it really says and have another laugh!'

Several more curious teachers joined them as they ate and drank and the conversation turned to the anti-school group playing up in Year Nine. Soon it shifted to Olde's worse than usual morning assembly, then to the litter on the field, chipped cups in the kitchen, lack of safe parking spaces for staff cars, the latest TV soap about six sex-crazed teachers, late deals on Algarve apartments, special offers on some supermarket's "British sherry", and Ingrid Eastman's eye-catching split skirt. Jenny Jean Jones listened thoughtfully.

Terry picked up *The Messenger* and flipped through the pages. He found no feature article by Hetty Hopkins - so she'd missed Monday's deadline. He was half pleased, half sorry. Then, sliding the paper back across the table, his thoughts turned to the hopelessness of the situation. Much as they grumbled individually, teachers would never get together as one determined body to make things better. Unlike the East and West Germans they seemed incapable of knocking down the barriers that prevented their unification. And so, for Terry Park and many others, afternoon school could not end quickly enough.

*

'I've visited my students and thought Joyce Farrell was doing well. Have you seen her teach?' Susan was talking to Terry in the foyer before leaving school. She smiled sweetly at the hovering Hull.

'Could I have a word somewhere else, Terry?' she asked quietly, 'after I've signed out.'

Could she have a word? She could have a thousand!

All visitors signed in and out in the secretary's room. Terry went with Susan and soon wished he hadn't. Ingrid's glance was a knowing one while Louie Anne Lee turned to avoid seeing him with Susan.

'Everything OK?' queried Ingrid, passing Susan the visitors' book. They'd make a fine pair she thought, as if she was a percipient partner in a profitable stud farm: healthy, free and on the market!

'Fine, thank you,' replied Susan. 'I'll be in again next week.'

She did not speak further until she and Terry reached the end of the Executive Corridor and stood again in the foyer. 'Not keen on her,' said Susan, 'that secretary.' Then, looking to the far side, added, 'that man doesn't miss much, either.'

Terry had seen the overalled Hull retreating to his cubicle, but after a friendly, curious glance, Hull had closed the door.

'Considering you don't come here too often, you don't miss much yourself, but they're both harmless, they just want to know what's going on.'

'Exactly,' said Susan. 'And what is going on? Is something wrong? No one seems happy today.'

As they walked to Susan's car Terry related the day's events and hinted, as if hints were necessary, that he found it all depressing. 'So many teachers just accept things as they are.'

Susan turned to him. 'Let me put this lot in the boot,' she said, 'and sort out these other books for return to the university library, then you can come with me and we'll have a cup of tea and some chocolate cake.

89

Put your things on the back seat. Afterwards I can either run you back for your car or you can walk.'

Terry Park concurred readily and was quiet as they drove the short distance to the campus. There were few students in the modern, thickly-carpeted, multi-storied library and Susan soon returned her books and brought tea and cakes to the corner where Terry sat. He had watched her admiringly and thought again how attractive she was. It was strange she had not married, but then, he was being macho, why should she marry? If she wanted male company she could get it in abundance without licences, rings, churches, bells, choirs, parsons and troublesome legal commitment. He knew the pitfalls of ecclesiastical or state-authenticated partnerships - they could be draining and costly.

'The staff didn't really expect to be consulted in depth, did they?' she asked. 'The teachers in the school to which a new head teacher is being appointed are the last people to be asked what they think. And they're surely not envious of whoever gets it?'

Terry described the haste to appoint and the inducements on offer.

Susan nodded.

'But you had a taste of being a head teacher?' Terry prompted.

'Only for two terms as an acting head in a school I was already teaching in and because nobody else wanted it. It wasn't much like the real thing – you're already friends with many of the staff and you know you're giving up the job soon and will be reverting to type – or role – so there's little you can do to change things permanently. It's fleeting and artificial but, if you don't take it too seriously, it's fun – and you learn a lot.'

'You'd have wanted to change things?'

'Maybe,' said Susan. 'But my heart wasn't in it. Whatever a head teacher does he's still working in a school; the walls and fences are still there and so is the increasingly complex set of expectations of what a head teacher is supposed to do. So, unless he's a true revolutionary and doesn't give a damn about what other people think he's terribly limited as to what he *can* change. He's tied by a set of role expectations that are firmly in place before he steps into the job.'

'You could say the same about newly-elected MPs.'

'Easily. They're tied by tradition and protocol as well.'

Terry considered for a moment. 'But I still think you'd make a good head teacher. You'd have fresh ideas. People would like you and you'd carry them along with you whatever you wanted to do.'

Susan smiled. 'You don't know me well enough, and fresh ideas are not what most people want – certainly not people in power.'

She regarded him carefully. She knew his background because this was not the first time they had talked. She guessed he had been friendly with few girls before marriage and had then stayed with his wife for many years. They had had no children and the divorce was not wholly of Terry's making, whereas she had been acquainted with countless men of different incomes and classes, and in different situations, for different reasons. She saw Terry as a trusting but vulnerable man. Also she could see he was becoming fond of her and that had to be stopped before he got hurt. She would start now.

'I left my last school because of an affair,' she said. 'It began while I was acting as head teacher. A local education authority inspector, "a friendly advisor" he called himself, seemed to take an inordinate interest in the school. It became noticeable to others that I was the principal reason for his frequent and extended visits. He was pleasant at first and interesting to talk to. He was good-looking and fit and had been a spin bowler with the town cricket club. I suppose I was a bit flattered and perhaps led him on. We went out for a while and he was excellent company. He said he was married but I knew that and it didn't bother me because I've little enthusiasm for marriage as a social institution and he said he was on the verge of leaving his wife – the old story! But I guessed he wasn't, it would have damaged his career prospects!' She laughed out loud and a nearby student looked up. 'But I was wrong in not putting him off at the start.'

'But you liked him?' Terry hesitated. 'You were in love with him?'

'In love? Heavens, no! Not a chance.' She laughed again. Another student passing by, who knew her, smiled and considered asking for a notice to be posted: *All Laughter Forbidden in the University Library.*

'I don't "fall in love" as you put it and won't let myself. I like men, I like being with men; to me they are usually more interesting and exciting than women and I'm drawn to the ones I like – I really am. But I'm not going to settle down with any one of them, that's not what I want of life. I'm not a one-man woman and never will be.'

'As far as you know.'

'As far as I know – yes.'

Terry finished his tea and with a damp finger picked the cake crumbs off his paper plate one by one. His depression was worse now than it had been at the end of school, and it showed. But Susan was determined to make things clear.

'The inspector pretended he wanted marriage – said he was ready to divorce. He made pass after pass: wouldn't take 'No' for an answer. He was obsessed. What was going on became common knowledge, but he was the instigator and *his* job was on the line, not mine; he had more to lose. I began to think he meant what he had said about leaving his wife and so I told him I wouldn't marry him even if he got a divorce. Then he got nasty and it rubbed off on some of the staff and that continued even after the new head was appointed. I was pig in the middle. I didn't need that, and it wasn't fair to the others.'

'Go on,' said Terry, wretchedly. 'Then what?'

'I had some money so I left the school, and the town and had a gap year – a gap year aged thirty-one! But I finished my doctorate, at least most of it, and was able to get a temporary job here supervising postgraduate students on teaching practice. It was a wonderful job after what I'd experienced in schools. Eventually I did some lecturing and took a few seminars and three years ago got a full time post. Lucky old me - paid to do work I love! And look at this wonderful library and its facilities for research: it's all mine!'

'I use it too,' muttered Terry. 'As a post-grad ex-student I have an external reader's card.'

He looked crestfallen. She had upset him. She toyed with the idea of inviting him to her apartment, but decided against. One night she would, but not until he'd got used to the idea she would never belong to one man and getting that over to Terry Park would take time.

'Of course, and I hope you make good use of it! Look, let's go over to the senior common room. We can get something to eat there even if it's only a snack, and we can talk in comfort without disturbing anyone. You can tell me more about your job, what it's *really* like and I can tell you more about mine. But I must warn you, I've then got some serious marking to do, three extended essays of five thousand words each and I like to put lots of notes in the margins to try to get my students to think.'

'Think?'

'Yes, Terry, *think*! One of the biggest binds university lecturers have these days, apart from pay and cuts in resources and the awful English of some of their students, is that so many students will not think for themselves, will not question current practices or assess, objectively, alternative and radical ideas. Too many are so used to being spoon-fed to make sure they get the "right" answers to intellectually undemanding questions and win 'A' Level Brownie points for their schools that much natural and necessary curiosity has not been developed by the time they get to us. Despite that, I try to make them think, but it makes my marking a long process. So, although I can't finish the essays tonight, I can't put off starting them, either.'

Terry understood what she meant.

Tuesday 9 April.   **A Poor Response**

Hetty's feature article appeared in the *Messenger* in truncated form. Her 1,200 words had been cut to 1,000 to make room for a last-minute story about the arrival of boy triplets to a single mother with seven children already, and an advert for the world's most nourishing cat food. Both, according to the pragmatic editor, had to be squeezed in.

Hetty's anger was wasted. She was told the giving of free publicity to Park and his romantic speculation about some frivolous fringe party was not the paper's job and that her piece would have been cut even without the need for space.

'But there's a general election in the offing!' stormed Hetty.

'And that's not a fact. No date's been announced. And your copy on Park's venture wasn't fact either, just hearsay on what he *might* be doing. Don't you understand, I want facts, facts and more facts, so go out and get them and write something *factual* and attributable.'

And, as the editor shut her office door, Hetty seethed.

*

Terry was relieved to find there was little in Hetty's piece about himself. He had worried that in his annoyance at her call he had been indiscreet with an intrusive journalist. He should have put the phone down much sooner but he hated to appear rude. He had not been concentrating and could not remember what was said.

But why had she phoned? Had governor Sneade been talking? Or Eastman, via his wife? His mind kept going back to the vacant headship. How serious was Vic Sneade about going for Olde's job? Why had he raised it? Who else had he talked to? Hetty Hopkins?

Eventually he confirmed he had nothing to lose by applying. He would not get the job, but he might get an interview, and that would be useful experience if only for his long-gestating book and give the impression, should it come to a crunch, that he was not completely without ambition within the traditional teaching orbit.

'After all,' he said to himself, 'only a madman would give up teaching and gamble on making a living from writing.' He had to acknowledge, too, that he hadn't written a tenth of the book, let alone found a publisher. And as for the CSP – well, as he had been told – no one would get anywhere with that in this tradition-bound country. How he wished he had applied years ago for American citizenship. He could see now why so many men and women of ambition, intelligence and thrust had moved permanently to the USA or Canada, or Australia or New Zealand. And how about the five million Brits who lived abroad? Why had they moved away? Not for the climate alone!

That longing for America had been another source of friction between himself and his wife. She had enjoyed their long holidays in the United States and had liked their many American friends, but she had drawn the line at living there.

'Not everyone shares your blind adoration of all things American,' she had altercated during a late night dispute. 'You need to remember the Ku Klux Klan, the McCarthy era, Death Row, the gun lobby, Vietnam, Watergate and the number of their own presidents they've murdered!'

Today he waited near the school office for most of the afternoon break until Hot Pants Ingrid was called away. Then he nipped in: 'Quick, Louie Anne, give me an application form for Olde's job, and the job description. And don't tell Ingrid or anyone else!'

Louie Anne handed him the papers and whispered, 'but the closing date's on Thursday, and,' looking at him with concern, 'you wouldn't want that awful job, would you?'

'Don't worry, I'm not likely to get it, and I'm not sure I'll apply. Give me some envelopes, too. Thanks Louie Anne!' He smiled at her gratefully. 'Now, remember, not a word to anyone!'

Terry set his last class of the afternoon a piece of silent reading and encouraged them to settle down by saying: 'Then you can finish the reading for homework.' That meant, as he knew, that every child would make sure the prescribed chapters had been read before the end of school. Terry sat in front of the pleasant set of twelve year olds and read the lengthy job form and its accompanying details. What a load of codswallop! Do I really want this? Hell's bells, does *anyone*?

His hopes of nipping home early were wrecked when Fergus Eastman hailed him a shade too heartily. The tubby, balding man was wearing his "I've come to collect my wife" chauffeur's hat. In that case Eastman had time to spare.

'Ah, Mr Park,' he said cordially. 'Just the man! You must have some influence here. Can't you persuade your head teacher to stay on a bit? This is not the best of times to swap pilots. He thinks a lot of you so you might have some clout.'

'Me? Clout?' said Terry. 'Not a hope, Mr Eastman.'

'But you'd like him to stay? Better the devil you know, eh?'

He steered Terry along the Executive Corridor to the library. Only a prefect librarian, a tiny homework group, two absorbed chess players and a spotty youth seeking nudes in the art magazines, were in there.

'Speaking for the governors,' confided Eastman quietly, 'they'd be happy for the old boy to stay another term. Then, if there's the expected general election, we can get that out of the way without a lot of head teacher enquiries and meetings and interviews jamming the works. The election could be over in a month.'

'By which time it will be too late to appoint a head for September.'

'So?' asked Eastman.

'Mr Olde's not well. Staying on longer would make him worse. He's had a good innings and should be allowed to go, and go now, if that's what he wants.'

This annoyed Eastman who picked up a well-thumbed newspaper and, adjusting his expensive bifocals, glared at the front page. 'More election rumours. More crime and light sentences. More taxes and price hikes. More scroungers, more villains on the loose. Five million for a soccer player, million for a barrister. Golden handshakes for failed executives. More big bonuses. More moaning Minnies. Huh! This country's had it!'

He threw the paper onto the library table in disgust and then turned to Terry, and, at close range, fired a question.

'Is being head teacher such a rotten job? We used to get scores of applications for headships like this. What's changed? Go on, tell me!'

All right, thought Terry, recovering quickly, you've asked for it!

'There's growing stress, lack of support, uncertainty about what they can and cannot do, red tape, changing legislation, bureaucracy, fears of legal action, militant unions, angry parents, dissatisfied staff, worrying and time wasting tests for everything that doesn't matter, meddlesome governors and self-seeking politicians, league tables, inspections, too little secretarial help, social isolation, responsibility without power, not knowing who your friends are … '

'All right, I get the message,' said Eastman, hiding his annoyance. He even managed a smirk and exhibited a full set of well-cared-for teeth that were only just beginning to thin and yellow. 'So, the job doesn't appeal to you, then? Won't see your application in the pile?'

'Pile? Is there a pile?' asked Terry, cautiously. He'd given this man information, so he'd get some in return.

The homework children walked past on their way out.

'Ah, that would be telling,' said Eastman, alert. 'But,' after looking round at the librarian, the chess players and the spotty youth, who were all a safe distance away, he closed in. 'Between ourselves, you're right to question it. There's been a rotten response! A pathetic shower of time-wasting unappointables. It's worse than for the headship at Lower Point Middle School and, good God, that was bad enough.'

The door opened and Jenny Jean Jones and Dafydd Hughes came in chatting easily. They acknowledged Terry and Eastman although the latter was a stranger to Jenny. They moved towards the chess players as the spotty youth sidled out, and stood together closely leaning over a low, central bookcase to share the local paper.

Terry and Eastman moved to the door exchanging more words. Then they saw Ingrid leaving the ladies' cloakroom. She greeted them warmly after noting, through the open library door, the two earnest newspaper readers. She had changed into a tightly fitting, low cut dress which oozed sex from top to bottom. With that to go home to, thought Terry, why does this stupid man worry about governors' meetings and vacant posts? Doesn't the fool know what life's all about? Good grief, what a voluptuous figure that woman has! His imagination ran riot as Ingrid moved ahead of him all too conscious of his gaze. Perhaps he'd been womanless for too long. Far too long?

Through the foyer windows he watched the Eastmans walk to their year old Audi and clamber in. Ingrid's skirt was so tight she had to wriggle for several seconds to secure her seat. 'Ye gods, I'd settle for that behind any day or night,' Terry muttered, 'and how!'

Jenny and Dafydd saw where he was looking but, fortunately for him, could not make out what he was saying.

*

Terry took in little of the early evening TV news and even less of the national weather forecast even though his favourite female presenter, casually dressed and smiling sweetly, was in colourful close up for nearly a minute. Fergus Eastman's disclosure of the poor response meant that he, Terry Park, was likely to be short-listed. Should he still apply knowing that? He had to see what Susan thought.

*

They met at the University Staff Club. It stood high on Main Site and was warm, comfortable, spacious, expensively furnished, tastefully decorated and unashamedly select. It overlooked an undulating, tree-favoured campus, the fruit of a landscape-designer's work of decades ago. It would now gladden the hearts of any National Trust gardener.

'Beer?' asked Susan. 'Shall I get two pints?'

'Let me ... ...'

'You can't. You're not a member. Sit there and think about what you're going to do.' She went to the small but well-stocked bar and gave the barman her order. He would bring it to their table. For a moment Terry thought only Oxford and Cambridge colleges offered such luxury to their privileged faculty, but he was not really interested in the waiter or the furnishings or the landscape or even the snacks under glass covers on the bar. Susan was all he wanted. Even Eastman's wanton wife could take a flying leap, interesting as that would be. Dr Susan Mansfield had class.

'The drinks will soon be here,' she said, 'he's tapping a new keg. Tell me again what Eastman said.'

Terry retraced the events of the past days and arrived at his own dilemma. 'So, from what Eastman hinted, I could be in with a chance. Strange things are happening in teaching appointments.'

'That's nothing new.'

'I agree, so I'd probably get onto the short list and that could be both intriguing and embarrassing.'

'Because you wouldn't want the job?'

'I'm not sure. But the thing is, if I got it, I could use the position to try out ideas and introduce a bit of common sense. I know a few on the staff who'd be willing to do something different – something *really* different. But I'd need advice, union advice.'

'About what?'

The drinks arrived and Susan asked for wholemeal ham and turkey sandwiches with side salad and crisps. Terry drank eagerly.

'About turning it into a democratically run school. I would stand aside.

I would cease to be the traditional head teacher. I would turn it into a school where an openly elected staff committee took decisions, but only after the fundamental issues had been debated and put to the whole teaching staff by referendum.'

'No input from pupils?'

'Fifth and sixth formers would debate most issues and give an opinion to be taken into consideration by the teaching staff.'

'I see. Rather like your Common Sense Party set up? Bring in the rank and file – cut out the differentials – give the common man a say?'

'Yes, I'm not sure about "set up" but yes, the school could become a micro CSP, a sort of model.'

'It's been tried before and not got far. Usually the attempts have come to grief, and sometimes acrimoniously. There are examples on record. So in these days you'd really have to watch it. As head teacher, you would still be legally responsible for what went on in the school - including what went wrong. Could be nasty. Lawyers are more active now and are quick to cash in.' Susan did not like lawyers.

'That's why I'd need legal advice – from the TFRA.'

Susan was silent. Now, his spirits raised slightly by the conversation and the beer, he looked about with interest. As there were few people in the spacious room he felt able to walk around freely examining paintings which hung on three of the walls. This can't be a bad life, he thought, enviously. Not bad at all. Then one particular work, a small landscape, attracted him.

'I presented that,' Susan said. 'It's on permanent loan. It was a great uncle's work although the house was my grandmother's, in Shropshire. We spent holidays there when I was small; it was very different from the Scunthorpe where we lived! Do you like it?'

Susan had moved to stand behind him and after a while moved nearer. Terry was aware of her closeness, her bodily warmth and the allure of her perfume. He became more conscious of that than the beauty of the wooded hillside scene with the low-roofed and white stone cottage perfectly placed to the left and on the thirds. He peered at the date and saw it was a work that had been delicately painted and tastefully framed fifty-five years ago.

He did not reply.

'Do you like it?' she repeated.

'Very much. I'd have kept it. It's a lovely picture, but to have those associations as well, I couldn't have parted with it.'

'I'm not a sentimental soul. And anyway, as I said, the painting's on loan. I can take it back when I leave – if I leave,' she added hastily. 'Have you looked at the other artefacts?' She escorted him round the other walls pointing out pieces donated, mainly, by several generations of the university's fine arts students.

'What do you think?'

'It's a wonderful room.'

'It is. This staff club was once the house of a wealthy city merchant and is much older than the university. It was requisitioned in both world wars and used as a convalescent home for officers. It was retained along with the trees and the high brick wall that runs round the grounds when the university acquired extra land in the late 1940s.'

She placed a hand on Terry's arm and led him back to their corner seats. The food had arrived.

'So, now, what have you decided?' she enquired. Susan's tone had changed. She was no longer the relaxed niece looking at the painting of her grandmother's cottage. She had become sharp in a businesslike way. 'Will you apply for Olde's job?'

'I've not decided.'

'But the closing date's only two days away.'

'OK. I'm thinking about it and I'll decide tomorrow – by mid-day.'

' But I need to know now.'

'Probably I will, if only for the experience.'

'Is that "yes" or "no"? Be quite sure, because if it's "no" then I shall apply. I've been thinking about it for days as well.'

'You!' Terry gasped. 'Apply for Olde's job? *You*? For a thankless job in a declining, has-been comprehensive when you're comfortably fixed here doing worthwhile work that interests you in surroundings that are wonderful? Hell's bloody bells, Susan, you're joking!'

'I'm not joking.'

'Then you're mad.'

'And I'm not mad.'

Terry gazed at her in disbelief. 'You can't mean it! Not really?'

'I do.'

He shook his head again.

'But Susan, look round. Look at this room, look at what's in it. Just look outside and see what's there, the trees, the park, the gardens, the library, the lake, the peace and quiet, and think about your valuable work here, your research, your students, your access to schools whenever you

99

like, your free time, and all the resources you so enthuse about! You're not saying you'd give all that up? Are you?'

She did not respond.

'Are you?'

'You're surprised at what I've told you – about applying. But believe me I was equally surprised when you said you would apply for a job you don't want, don't agree with, in a hierarchical system you loath and for reasons that don't convince me one tiny little bit.'

'But you are … …'

'My turn, Terry.' She leaned towards him. 'You said you'd take the job in order to introduce a bit of common sense and to experiment.'

'And …'

'Listen! Those experiments would be nothing but a tinkering with a system that should have been consigned to the scrap heap forty years ago. Anybody with only two grams of intelligence and one gram of imagination could see that when personal computers, laptops, TV, cable, videos, compact discs, DVDs, mobile phones and cameras, desktop publishing, the Internet and all the rest were in place, any need for our nineteenth century, autocratic, compulsory, standardised, mass-attended, restrictive, prison-like schools had gone for ever!'

She took a bite from her sandwich and a drink from her glass.

'What you're proposing, Terry, if you become a head teacher, is to change a little bit of this, a little bit of that but, basically, to keep the present set up. Your "democracy" – how magnanimous of you to offer a modicum of democracy to "your" staff – your so-called "democracy" would still exist between solid brick and glass retaining walls. You wouldn't merely fail, you would delay the exciting, personalised, parent-involved education we could have right now. If you did that it would, in my mind, be a gross dereliction of duty, a duty to do the best we can for coming generations of British children, to clear the air and start again. That's putting it bluntly, but I mean it. And I say just what I mean.'

Terry was stunned. For a time he was silent. First he looked at her, then turned away. He looked towards her great uncle's painting but did not see it, at the room's artefacts but did not see them, at the barman but did not see him, at the trees and lawns outside but did not see them either. Only Susan's flushed intensity registered. She had depths of political passion he had not suspected. 'All right,' he said eventually, his voice full of resignation, 'but you'd do no better. You'd have the same problems. So why do *you* want to apply? Tell me that!'

'Because I would turn the whole school into a community resource centre, open it to everyone, twenty-four hours a day, ask parents to come in, give ongoing child-rearing advice to those who sought it, promote teachers into being professional personal tutors and give them the freedom to use their initiative and their skills to do their very best with a small group of children, and, with parents' co-operation, give each child an individualised study programme in accordance with his or her own needs. Parents, children and tutors would meet in many different places, not just in the resource centres, and not always in the same size groups or at the same times or for the same purposes. The tired old structure – the National Curriculum, school hours, weeks, terms, years, exams, could all go – and fast. Self-seeking politicians and nosy inspectors wouldn't be allowed within smelling distance of where the real, absorbing studies were being done. They'd be told to go away and stay away - for ever!'

'And you'd be thrown out in a month!'

'Not so. Don't you see, that by the time this frightened, law-abiding, minutes of the last meeting, committee-bound shower had decided what, if anything, they were going to do about it, my scheme would be up and running and would be so popular, so humane, so warm, so effective, so all-embracing that the fools who thought of opposing it would back away. Then they'd craftily switch over and say how simply wonderful it all was and that it was just, *just* what they'd been thinking of doing themselves. That's how it works and how change comes about.'

'I'm staggered.'

'So you should be.'

Terry was agitated and, without thinking, moved to the bar to get more drinks. The barman looked across to Susan, uncertain.

'It's all right, John. Charge them to me.'

'I'm sorry,' murmured Terry. 'I forgot.'

'Don't worry. Come and sit down.'

By the time the drinks came, Terry was calmer.

'And, you suppose,' he said, 'that if I went ahead and applied for Olde's job, it would lessen your chances? You want me to drop out?'

'Not necessarily,' said Susan. 'I've been thinking about that.' She ran a knuckle round the rim of her glass: she had not wanted another pint. 'I've had another idea. Perhaps we could work as a team.'

'A team? How?'

'First, by being realistic. The chances of either of us getting the job are miniscule, so let's face up to that. We know there's probably someone lined up for it - some smooth, obedient, unimaginative, risk-avoiding, time serving nonentity. So, if the truth were known, they don't give a damn whether there's a huge response or not, it makes no difference to them. They're only worried because it *looks* bad.'

'But Eastman said ...'

'Don't trust him: he's putting up a smoke screen. Don't trust his buxom, come-and-get-it, can't-wait-for-it wife, either. I bet they both know who'll be appointed. So, if, by both applying, we provide them with convenient short list makeweights they can pretend it's all open and above board, and we'll have helped them. So, in return, we need have no compunction in making use of them.'

'Use? What use?'

'As publicists. Once we get to the interview room we can say what we like, be as outrageous as we like, and put forward our scandalous ideas. The more they're taken aback the better. They won't be able to keep things under wraps because it will all be minuted. With a bit of crafty manipulating it will – surprise, surprise - leak out and be picked up by the local press - by a well-known young reporter! - and then, hopefully, by the nationals. Our ideas will be let loose. Things will never be the same again. Never will they be able to say, "There's no alternative" because they will have been shown one. The whole panel will have been shown one, and the groups each member represents will have been shown one. They can't deny it. They will have to contend with your common sense politics scenario and with my ideas for teaching their children without using old-fashioned schools.'

'The cat will be out of the bag.'

'*Two* cats! Exactly! That's how it will be. What do you think?'

Terry experienced excitement and doubt. To be in a team with her would be exhilarating, but what would be the team's chances?

'Suppose the general election's called while all this is going on?'

'Marvellous! It will add to the furore! Then people can '*Vote for Terry Park!*' twice. So come on, double candidate Park, what do you think?'

Susan had no need to ask. She had guessed what he would think: his misgivings would disappear. He would be with her. She had seen men attracted to her like this before. If she'd suggested a swim to the North Pole in mid March he'd have rushed home for his kit.

'Well? Are you on? Do we grasp the opportunity?'

'You needn't ask. Of course we do!

'No regrets afterwards – even if it all goes horribly wrong?'

'No. And anyway,' he asked nervously, trying to reassure himself as she brought him down to earth, 'what can go horribly wrong?'

'You'd be surprised! If the Establishment got too scared they'd make damn sure all sorts of things went wrong - wrong for both of us. We'd be finished career wise and any otherwise. And that would be for starters! They're really, really nasty when they're up against it, and believe me, they never yield anything easily. So, think, and think carefully. Are you still on?'

'I'm still on.'

'Right, so finish the beer, and have some of mine.' She tipped half a pint into his glass. 'We've no time to lose. We've forms to complete, supporting letters to write, testimonials and referees to find, answers to interview questions to prepare – and a dry-clean for your interview suit. We'll go to my flat and you can see what it's like. We can work out what we're going to do and when we're going to do it. OK?'

'Yes,' said Terry, brightening. 'It sounds wonderful.'

Susan smiled. She'd thought that's what he'd say.

Wednesday 10 April.   **Words of Advice**

'Ingrid, is Mr Olde free?' asked Terry. 'I'd like a word.'

'Sorry, two governors with him.'

'Which ones? Do I know them?' He had been hoping to hand in his application personally thus avoiding the inquisitive Ingrid Eastman.

'The Rev Lena Napier and Captain Wally Walker-West,' said the pretty, pouting Louie Anne Lee as she looked up from the photocopier. She was an intelligent young woman who had left school eagerly at sixteen and now, some three years later, regretted not staying on to prepare for university entrance. '*Wally Walker-West*! What a stupid name – but at least 'Wally's' appropriate. The stuck-up piece! And he dyes his hair – what's left of it,' she muttered, 'and still calls himself "Captain!" Didn't even make major! Can't stand the man!'

'That won't worry him twopence,' said Ingrid as she turned to face Terry. 'Can I do anything? Something to give him?' She had seen the A4 envelope. 'Leave it here,' she said with a smile, 'I'll see he gets it.'

'Thanks. But I'd like a word with him as well. I'll come back.'

'Top secret? That makes a change. Not many "top" secrets in this place! Not your resignation, is it?'

Terry was saved by Louie Anne Lee.

'Listen, they're coming out. Nip in now and dodge the Captain.'

Ingrid looked daggers. The girl interfered too much and would do anything to please a man she fancied. Dafydd Hughes seemed to have been her latest target but she needn't entertain any ideas there. She'd seen where Hughes was looking and it wasn't at Louie Anne Lee. And what a silly name *that* was! *"Louie Anne Lee!"*

'Ah, Mr Park,' greeted Lena Napier, complete with clerical collar, 'I've not seen you for some time. D'you know Captain Walker-West?' She made introductions. 'We've enjoyed a coffee with Mr Olde.'

Terry smiled weakly at the ex-army governor and Walker-West made the slightest of acknowledgements. Clearly the Captain saw someone like Park - with his loose sweater, tieless collar, brown and far-from-new slip-on shoes, and untidy hair - as an unworthy recruit to the officers' mess - definitely the type who'd let the Regiment down. Park, he thought, was probably one of those protesting semi-intellectual commies known to "march" through the city with their garish placards shrieking: *"Wha'd'we want? When d'we wan' it?"* Well, they'd get more than they bargained for from him whether they *"wan'ed it"* or not!

Proud, eighty-three-year-old Walter Walker-West stood tall and erect, with short, sparse darkish hair, a thin moustache, wore a light grey, dated suit, an immaculately folded handkerchief tucked neatly into the breast pocket, a small regimental badge perfectly centred on the lapel, regimental tie, expensive Oxford shoes and almost-new leather gloves. The gloves, Terry thought, were carried in lieu of a swagger stick. Captain Walter Walker-West was the very epitome of the regular army officer (retired). 'From one of the better outfits, y'know. Fine history. Brave record. Jolly good bunch of chaps. Credit to the Crown!'

How I loathe his sort, thought Terry, already incensed by the mere sight of the condescending Captain.

Adrian Olde hovered nervously. He eyed the left-leaning sociologist Park, the conservative-inclined Walker-West, closed his eyes, and prayed for peace. Lena, meanwhile, chattered on about *New Testament* readings for coming school assemblies.

But I don't suppose his type loves me, thought Terry. A London University social science graduate teaching humanities in some state-run comprehensive wouldn't be on the Captain's dinner party list. But, suppose he were on the interview panel! He shuddered.

Rev Lena Napier had now shaken Olde's hand and was escorting Walker-West to the foyer. Louie Anne stuck out her tongue at the photocopier as the Captain marched past. 'And I bet he's a randy old devil,' she whispered to Ingrid. 'Gives me the creeps!'

'Did you want a word, Mr Park?' asked Olde. 'Do come in.'

'It won't take a minute,' said Terry. He closed the door carefully as a precaution against four straining ears.

'I suppose it's about the new student teacher in your department?' Adrian Olde asked. 'I hear she had a problem in Year Nine. Nothing too serious, I hope? Never easy, Year Nine.'

'It's not about that, although I don't think she had that much of a problem Mr Olde, certainly none that needed bringing to your attention.' Terry was increasingly annoyed at the way stories were reported, distorted and spread. Why had a minor incident over the mildest of swear words been brought to the head teacher's notice?

'Good. And how about our own Miss Jones? Settling in? Going down well with the older years? Tackling enthralling topics?'

'Admirably: she's a valuable addition to the department.'

'Fine. No doubts about her then?'

'No, why?'

'Just that in their early years some teachers wonder whether they've chosen the right career. They find life harder than expected and perhaps have occasional misgivings. So, no worries on that score?'

Olde noted the slightest of hesitations.

'No, she's doing well.'

'Gets on with the staff? Made friends?'

'She's a popular colleague,' confirmed Terry.

Olde proceeded to address the window.

'Good. But tell me, going back to the two student teachers we have here from the university, how do you get on with their supervisor, Dr Mansfield, I think? Comes in fairly often, seems conscientious and pleasant? Dresses smartly and appropriately, a description which, I'm sad to say, would not apply to all her visiting male tutor-colleagues. And she's researching some rather unusual aspects of childhood education?'

Terry was becoming suspicious.

'Fine. I get on well with her,' he replied, 'she's a conscientious and competent supervisor and gives her students sound advice based on her own classroom experience.' He paused, Olde waited. 'She insists on high standards, assesses accurately and fairly, her qualifications are excellent, she has fresh ideas and makes good use of practical common sense based on her varied school teaching in both city and rural areas - all of which she is anxious to pass on to her students.'

Olde smiled a little, openly amused. 'Excellent,' he said, still smiling, 'excellent. But I wasn't seeking a testimonial!'

'No,' murmured Terry, colouring. 'Of course not.' Why the devil hadn't he just left it at: "Fine"?

'So, Mr Park, you seem to know Dr Mansfield well. Olde watched him carefully. Hadn't Park's response been altogether too fulsome?

But Terry was silent: he had said enough. He waited.

Olde asked, 'Are you teaching next period?'

'No.'

'Then sit down.'

Mr Olde did not sit down, but crossed to the window and closed, slightly, the blinds. He adjusted what looked like a framed family photograph which was standing alone on the sill. 'I understand Dr Mansfield – Susan Mansfield, I think? - is interested in alternative forms of education, including, perhaps, the gradual replacement of our traditional schools by a rather radical, individualistic approach, with a personal curriculum constructed for each child? It's certainly an unusual proposition she's investigating – most thoroughly, I'm sure - with the help, no doubt, of university facilities and, … and funds?'

'Yes. And she's published articles in that field.'

'Really? I must trace them.' Olde thought for a moment. 'She is a presentable woman: she would do well at conferences and seminars?'

'I'm sure she would.'

Olde waited.

'She has already presented papers in the USA,' said Terry.

Olde made to straighten a curtain that did not need straightening.

'Yes. I imagine she'd do well in North America. But it's interesting to meet someone actually working in that field. I have spoken to her about it – briefly, very briefly - and she's so affable. Even so she must have to strike a fine balance? She's walking, possibly, on something, shall we say, on something of a professional tightrope?'

'I'm not quite sure …'

'There may, perhaps, be a conflict of interests? On the one hand she is being paid to prepare, at public expense, impressionable young men and women in their very – very - early twenties for careers as schoolteachers, and, on the other hand, she is advocating the possible closure of the very schools in which those self-same students hope to teach and earn their living?' He hesitated before adding, 'is that not so?'

Terry became anxious. Why was he being asked all this? He wished he had developed the discussion of Jenny Jean Jones and her sex-primed topic. 'That's not necessarily the case,' he said warily, 'much of what she teaches her students – or on which she gives them guidance – is to do with the way children learn, when and what they learn, why they learn, and how they establish worthwhile relationships between each other and with their teachers.'

'Of course. I can see that. Much of what her students learn will be transferable to whatever system of teaching they later find themselves engaged in – whether in an ordinary school or elsewhere. That is a sound answer. And she is, I suppose, writing this up? Perhaps as a thesis? A new course? A paper? A book?'

'A book.'

'A book? Do you know when it will be available?'

'Early next year, I think.'

'I shall look forward to reading it.'

While he had been talking, Adrian Olde seemed to have revived. He appeared less tired and withdrawn. It was as if he had found their discussion stimulating, purposeful and pleasingly different from the humdrum pettiness and tedious administrative chores of so much of his routine schoolwork.

'Now,' he said sadly, having to return to the present time and place. 'You have something for me?'

'I wanted to give you this. I thought it would be better handed over personally.'

Terry held out the large, brown, official-looking envelope. 'It's, it's, rather confidential,' he added unnecessarily.

Olde took the envelope and from its thickness saw its contents were substantial. He looked at Terry quizzically.

'You're not leaving us? Not resigning? I do hope not!'

Now why, thought Terry Park to himself, does everyone think I'm resigning? What have people been saying?

'No, quite the opposite, Mr Olde,' he said aloud, trying to smile. 'It's an attempt to stay.'

Olde opened the envelope and recognised the contents instantly. 'Good heavens!' he said, 'good heavens!'

Then, as he sat down behind his desk with his back to the wide, deepsilled, curving window, which looked out onto the school's main entrance, he asked, not looking up, 'But shouldn't this have gone to the Chairperson, to Dr Napier?'

'I thought, first, you should see what I was proposing ...'

Olde cut Terry short. 'You said you're not teaching this period?'

'Yes.'

'Then please wait and let me read this through. Draw up your chair.' After reading the first half page he spoke through the inter-com: 'I'd like more coffee, Mrs Eastman, and a cup for Mr Park, please.'

'Really, I'd much rather Mrs Eastman didn't ...' began Terry.

'...see your application?' And, despite his tiredness, Adrian Olde managed a knowing smile and whispered, 'don't worry, she won't.'

Painfully slowly Olde read on. When he heard the expected knock on the door he slipped the application into a drawer and began to talk about the coming school sports day in late June and the need for better organisation than they had enjoyed the year before.

'I know the thunder, lightning, heavy rain, dark skies and rising wind caused considerable confusion,' he said, and flinched as he remembered the crowded, litter-strewn and saturated field, the flooded lower playground, the fleeing parents and the distressed governors, abandoned programmes, discarded ribbons, trailing tapes, upturned chairs, oozing mud, shrieking children and distraught, whistle-blowing staff.

Terry watched Mrs Eastman bend low to reach the coffee table, remove the crockery from Olde's earlier session, and replenish the tray. She took her time and guessed where Terry was peering. But once she had left, Olde, unusually, came straight to the point.

'Do you know what you're doing?'

'I'm sorry?' Terry, alarmed, thought his peeping had been noticed.

'Do you know what you're doing?' Olde waved the application.

'Oh, do you think I'm being impertinent applying ...'?

'Impertinent? Of course not. You'd be as good as any of the others and better than most, that's why I repeated my question.'

Terry stared at Mr Olde. The spark of pleasure he had shown when discussing Susan's radical research had gone. He was back to his drawn, highly-strung self. Terry felt grieved for the man; the job had affected his health. He guessed what was to come and the meaning behind his repeated, "Do you know what you're doing?" And he felt increasingly uneasy. He was unhappy with the game he and Susan were playing. Was he supposed to fool this man – pretend to be a serious contender for his job? Mislead him? Tell lies? Posture? Maintain some sort of mean pretence for weeks on end?

'I think you're an excellent teacher, Terry,' Olde said, and Terry noted that for the first time in many years Olde addressed him as "Terry". 'And you have every right to apply for headships or any other jobs in education. But,' and he leaned back until he was almost touching a low, two-drawer wooden filing cabinet on which a bowl of lanky and supposedly white hyacinths was standing perilously near its edge, 'I'm surprised at this.' He indicated the application. 'Surprised for two reasons.'

He paused again, choosing his words carefully. 'First, I'd gained the impression you had little time for the institution of head teacher – or "school leader" as it's sometimes known - that you felt the position was an anachronism and that today's teachers should be sufficiently professional to manage their school and their teaching by themselves. Is that not right?' But as Terry prepared to answer, Olde said: 'No, you can talk afterwards. But if that is your belief, I fail to see how you can apply conscientiously for a position you would prefer to see abolished. There is, I must say, a pertinent resemblance between your application here and Dr Mansfield's work in preparing youngsters to teach in schools she hopes will soon be history. Now, please, I don't mean that unkindly: I'm simply puzzled.'

'There is not necessarily a ...'

'Let me finish – and do drink your coffee.'

He did not know of, or had forgotten, Terry's preference for tea.

'The second reason, and on a personal note - the first reason was wholly impersonal, you understand - you've been able to see the sort of job this is - the one I have .You must have seen how stressful and demanding the work of a head teacher is today and I'm sure you'll have noticed the effect it can have on an incumbent. As an observant person you will be aware of the almost intractable problems facing a head teacher and often, I regret to say, of the little understanding of some of his staff and the paucity of the assistance some teachers give. So consider the matter carefully and ask if that is how you want to spend the next twenty years of your career. Consider – *twenty years*! And that's always supposing you can retire at sixty. Have you and your, your ... have you thought it through thoroughly?'

Olde had remembered Terry's divorce.

The phone rang in the secretary's next-door room. The call was not put through, but the head teacher waited. They could hear voices through the thin dividing wall but could not make out what was said. Terry was relieved at that.

'I'm not sure what to say,' he replied eventually. 'I have thought it through: I'd be a fool not to. And I appreciate a head's job is not easy. That's one reason why I think the post could and should be abandoned; it is unreasonable to lumber one teacher with such aggravation when there is no need for the role in the first place. And I, also, stress that is not intended personally.'

'How would you deal with our governor Captain Walker-West?' Again Olde rapped out the question. Again Terry was taken aback.

'I don't know him.'

'You saw him outside. Is he your type? How would you deal with people who are not your type? How would you deal with angry parents of excluded pupils? Or with Mr Collins of Teachers for Radical Action who kindly reminded me late last night of the legally binding regulations concerning my staff's limited obligations regarding cover for absent colleagues; or cope with a chief education officer who seems to forget that this school exists; or deal with a member of parliament who implies extra places for refused pupils can be manufactured out of thin air; or with the mother who thinks every moment of every day should be spent ensuring there is no bullying of her child when that very child is at the centre of much provocation; or with an impossible-to-replace scarce subject teacher who threatens to resign because her teaching timetable isn't quite what she wanted; or with the head of department who yearly complains about her textbook allowance; or with a politically-motivated governor who thinks every governors' meeting is a mini-parliament; or with the police inspector who claims he hasn't the officers to patrol the school to deter vandals; or with kitchen staff who insist Wal-Mart pay more than we do; or with cleaning personnel who say erasing graffiti in the boys' toilets isn't part of their job; or with the health and safety officer who refuses to believe adolescent boys have always pushed each other on staircases; or with the trouble-making lawyer whose objective is to earn a fat fee by winning a claim for injuries suffered by a disobedient girl during a gym lesson; or with insensitive inspectors who so upset a young teacher she cries and wants to leave; or with a delegation of irate parents who demand an extra school crossing guide at White's Corner; or the bus company manager who complains about our children's behaviour on his decrepit buses? But I could go on and ...'

'I appreciate what you say, Mr Olde.'

'But there is something else, something that is, in a way, far worse than all those things put together: the sense of isolation in this job. I mentioned how little you can rely on support from some staff, well, you can't *rely* on it at all. Sometimes you get it, and some teachers give magnificent support of course, and sometimes you don't, and that's what makes the job so trying - that ongoing uncertainty. It exacerbates the difficulties. For years I've longed to talk frankly about what's going on in this school and in the local authority and in education generally, but I've felt there's no one I could confide in. I've been let down doing that and, years ago, gave up trying. I admit readily that when leftist-inclined union leaders warn teachers about the dangers of "divide and rule" they're not far off the mark. There are divisions all through education, with groups and individuals vying for mutual or personal power or profit, a sort of slow continual jockeying for favoured positions in a callous, unnecessary, deliberately set up hierarchy. Often a head teacher can't even go home and talk about it because it's difficult for outsiders to comprehend what it's really like - even if a wife or husband is, or was, a teacher.'

Neatly he arranged the cups and saucers on the tray so that they were ready for collection. A spoon fell to the floor and he had to stoop awkwardly to pick it up. He looked old.

'It's sad that only now,' he said as he straightened and stretched a little, 'on the very verge of retiring, I feel I can take one of my own teachers into my confidence and say what I think.'

'That *is* sad,' said Terry, and, although he had reservations about some of Olde's observations, he spoke with conviction.

Both men were quiet. Olde had said all he had to say.

'Thank you for talking,' said Terry finally, 'and for your advice, and for speaking so openly and in confidence. I appreciate that.'

'And it *is* in confidence,' said Olde. 'It is given to help you, personally, make up your mind wisely. And, remember, this job isn't going to get easier. Nothing in today's society indicates a pending improvement in behaviour or an increase in personal responsibility or a tightening of self-discipline or a widening of respect. That trend will have painful carry-over effects on *all* our schools, even the famous, select, top ranking, fee-paying ones – yes, even them, *even them!*'

He paused, then added: 'and, I'm afraid, it will spread into other areas of life, in fact it is spreading already.'

He waited to judge the effect he was having. 'Less than an hour ago one of our governors, The Rev Lena Napier, our chairperson, was regretting that so much of childhood has been lost, that some of our colleagues in primary schools have classrooms full of supposedly sophisticated young adults: children who've grown up before their time. She said it's as if the innocent delights of childhood have been allowed – even encouraged by vested interests - to disappear. That's unhealthy.'

Terry nodded. He wanted to say that the people responsible should be sorted out and sorted fast, but Olde had changed course. The head teacher leaned over to lift the tray and then place it on his desk.

'But now,' he said, twisting one of the saucers round and round with the tip of a finger so that it made a rough, grating noise on the metal surface, 'I'll tell you something else, but this time it's relatively good news and will become common knowledge shortly. At their next meeting I shall ask the governors to agree a work-share to cover the maternity leave. It's far from an ideal situation because of the home circumstances of one of the ladies, but, as you'll discover if you become a head teacher, beggars can't be choosers.'

'I'm pleased that's solved, it was a problem for us all.'

'Not "solved", it's a compromise,' corrected Olde. 'Like so much in our lives, education is full of compromises. Are you a compromiser?'

Terry sat, his pink paper napkin still folded on his knee, staring alternately at Olde and then at the scene outside where a bus was being boarded by thirty eager children bound for the swimming pool. Bus journeys, swimming pools, changing rooms, stressed teachers, excited youngsters: more risks? Terry thought. A hunting field for lawyers?

'I don't think I'd be a good compromiser,' he said. 'In fact, I'm not sure I'd want to be. As I think you were suggesting, "to compromise" is not necessarily a worthy action. Perhaps there's been too great a willingness to compromise in education and in other areas?'

Olde gave a slow, gentle nod. It was a noncommittal nod: a nod of acknowledgement rather than agreement. 'Like people use the word "tolerance," Terry continued, 'as if tolerance were a virtue in itself. But it isn't. It depends on what it is that's being tolerated.'

'Yes. And does that apply to teaching children?' asked Olde.

'One hundred per cent, I should think.'

'I'm glad you put in the "I should think,"' smiled Olde. 'A hundred per cent might be extreme. The phrase rarely comes into a modern head teacher's language. Anyway,' he said after glancing at the square black and white wall clock and pushing the tea tray to the far end of his desk, 'I've a hundred documents to sort and,' with a smile, 'I'm one hundred per cent certain it's almost time for the next teaching period, and so,' he paused, papers in hand, 'would you like a few days to think over what I've said – consider it - then make up your mind?'

'But isn't the closing date tomorrow?'

'Leave the application with me. I'll put it safely away. You can take the weekend to consider. If you decide to apply, I will give your application today's date stamp to show it was submitted in good time. If you don't, you can have it back, shred it, and nobody need know. Just a little white lie.'

'That's kind of you, and I'm sorry to have added to your work.'

'Helping staff who contribute to the school is a task I enjoy.'

As he left the head teacher's office, and for the rest of the day, Terry was ashamed of the things he had thought and the things he had said about Adrian Olde. It left him not knowing what to do.

Then things got worse, because suddenly, as he locked his desk after afternoon school, a spasm of apprehension hit him. Had Olde in all that time got Susan's application in his in-tray? Is *that* why there were so many questions about her? If so, what must he have been thinking? And why did he think that he, Terry Park, would know so much about her? But he was being ridiculous. Susan couldn't have got her application in yet, and, even if she had, Mr Olde could never have covered up so effectively. He was too open, too ingenuous.

Nevertheless Terry needed reassurance before he went to bed. If the tiniest doubt remained he would not sleep. This tension and the need for total freedom from risk had become acute and he ascribed it partly to the spasmodic work on his novel, which absorbed nervous energy, partly to his interest in Susan's alternative education proposals, partly to Susan herself, and partly to his work at school, work which, despite his lengthy teaching experience, and contrary to popular belief, was becoming more demanding every year.

*

'I had to be quite sure,' he said to Susan on the phone. 'He seemed so interested in you and your research that it occurred to me, out of the blue, that he might have been quizzing me about you because he'd already received your application.'

'What if he had? What's wrong?' Susan seemed displeased. 'Why are you worrying? How *could* he have got my letter? It wasn't posted until this afternoon and it wasn't even sent to him – it went to the chairperson. So come on, there's something else on your mind?'

'What I've phoned about is what I've just told you.'

'And?'

He did not answer.

'And? Go on!'

'While I sat there with him I became increasingly uneasy. I thought we shouldn't be playing games.'

'Games?'

'Pretend games. Pretending we're serious contenders.'

'But we *are* serious contenders! We both want the job. Not "want" in the usual sense, maybe, but if I got it I'd make damn good use of it until the day I was thrown out. So would you.'

'OK, but even so I felt dishonest sitting there listening to him, with him being so helpful and open and my seeing how his job was getting him down. I felt I should have been more truthful. I think Olde's a kind man, and the pressure of the job isn't his fault, is it?'

'To some extent, it is. But that's beside the point now because he's on his way out. He can't hurt or be hurt much longer. So don't worry about him. What we've got to do is make sure everyone gains from his departure by exposing, even ridiculing, the whole rotten system, by making sure that people such as him and all the others, kind or otherwise, are not placed in similar situations in the future. Right?'

'Yes.'

'You don't sound too sure. Do you agree with that?'

'Yes.'

'Good,' said Susan.

'You mean you can't be sentimental when fighting a cause?'

'Exactly. And never forget that. There's no room for sentimentality in warfare. It's them or us, and it isn't going to be us! So now, lucky you, go to bed. I've a handout to put together: *Bertrand Russell and His Views on the Morality of Compulsory State Education.* Russell was opposed to schools as we understand them, so that should get my group going! And, for good measure, I'm ending the handout with Russell's, "The trouble with the world is that the stupid are cocksure and the intelligent full of doubt." How very true that is! So, good night, Mr Terry Park, and, remember, stop worrying. Oh, and Terry…'

'Yes?'

'Sweet dreams!'

But sweet dreams were not on the cards. Terry tried to read but could not concentrate. He played his favourite Mozart piano concerto but it did not offer its usual comfort. He switched to the radio for the ten o'clock news and became more depressed. Then he listened to what tomorrow's papers were headlining and, without exception, they led with the prediction that the coming general election would be held on Thursday, 2 May, the earliest possible date. While there was nothing official, such unanimous editorial agreement left little doubt.

And, for once in his life, Terry believed what the newspapers said.

Thursday 11 April.   An Internal Candidate

'I'm sorry, Mr Bennett, but there are no places. Each class has its full quota; indeed some have children over and above that.'

Ingrid Eastman eavesdropped on a conversation which had been going on for five minutes. Mr Bertram Bennett, a self-important supermarket manager recently promoted to regional duties in Outer Mansworth, was trying again to persuade Mr Olde to admit his son.

'I have had two similar requests from parents in the past month,' explained Olde patiently. 'I had to refuse both.'

With classes oversubscribed and threatening noises from TFRA, he had agreed that after Easter no more pupils would be enrolled until the new intake in September. With ongoing trouble over the suspension, the arrival of 'Bloody' Collins, the difficulties in finding temporary staff, and the displeasure of the governors and the CEO with his early retirement, Olde knew he had to face up to Mr Bennett. But Bennett, having heard that Olde was weak, would not yield.

'Yes, I appreciate you have a nephew here,' said Olde, 'and the next secondary school is five miles away and your wife doesn't drive, and this school has been recommended and you have an very important position locally and you know a councillor on the education committee, but there is no place.'

There were increasingly strong protests from Bennett.

'Yes, you're at liberty to take the matter to the Chairperson of Governors, the Chief Education Officer, your MP, and the Minister -

that is your inalienable right,' said Olde dejectedly. He had heard it all before. 'But I can only say again, Mr Bennett, there is no place.' There was a pause. 'Yes, you can, of course, demand a test case be made of this but I'm afraid it will not change the situation as far as I am concerned. I would need to be overruled by higher authority.'

He tapped a knuckle three times, slowly and deliberately, on the dividing wall as a signal to Ingrid Eastman. In thirty seconds she had knocked on Olde's door, put her head round, and said loudly, 'I'm sorry, Mr Olde, but the school nurse needs a word.'

Olde did not know whether callers suspected the ruse but he had ended many ticklish conversations in this way. However Mr Bennett was serious. Olde had met him and his non-driving wife and had categorised both Bennetts as "very high" on the Nuisance Parent Scale.

So, without his usual procrastination, he telephoned the Chief Education Officer's secretary and warned her of trouble and left the same message with Lena's newly recruited curate. While both Zing and Napier would be irritated, Olde knew they would have been forewarned. What Bennett did with his MP, or the Secretary of State, or even the Temporary Turkish Ambassador, was of little concern to him now and would be of less concern in four months' time. He was ready for coffee.

*

But Olde had forgotten *The Mansworth Evening Messenger and Times*. The editor was aware of parents' simmering anger at the overcrowding and of others' frustration at the school's lack of places and was not surprised when a Mr James Auberon Bennett asked whether the paper would be interested in *A Letter to the Editor*.

Hetty was on the reporters' late-morning turn and was told to check parental feeling about The Outer Mansworth Secondary School's admissions policy and the state of play with the head teacher vacancy. 'And sound out the grumpiest governors for their views, and,' the editor stressed, 'you won't have far to look. When you've done that, investigate stories of People's Patriotic Party big wigs being in town. That should stir things up! But watch what you write about the PPP; given only half a chance, they'll sue! I'll check your copy myself.'

Hetty was livid, but by three o'clock she had prised the bare bones of the Bennett admissions story from Ingrid, had spoken to an agitated Mrs Bennett, and then found another parent who had failed to get her son into the school but who, although upset, had refused Hetty a lengthier interview. Hetty had then spoken to a contact on the governing body who had 'no comment' on the 'possible' head teacher vacancy 'at the moment,' from which blatant evasiveness Hetty deduced a replacement for Olde *was* to be found, and to be found soon.

Hetty learned that the PPP was to rent an office near *The Messenger* and linked that to the likely election. Surely they can't be putting up a candidate here? But why else would they want a room? As an election base? Are we to get a bunch of them moving into Mansworth SW? But suppose we had a PPP man *and* a CSP man? That would make the old parties sit up and take real notice. *The Messenger* would have a field day. And so would I!

For once the so-hard-to-please editor seemed satisfied with Hetty's stories. She nearly smiled as Hetty left her paper-strewn office.

Then, only minutes later, the editor's subservient assistant poked his longhaired head round her door. 'You were spot on,' he shouted gleefully, pleased to be bringing good news for once, 'the general election's to be on Thursday, 2nd May. It's just come through – official - that's three weeks from today!'

'Right,' said the editor, 'all leave's cancelled. And make damn sure everyone knows - or you're out!'

*

'I checked it yesterday. It was obvious the general election was coming and I didn't want to waste time. You've nothing to lose. I can act as party agent for you, and a dozen students want to help. It will be their first general election and they're dead keen.'

Susan had cleared papers from her coffee table and was feeling in her briefcase for a paper-clipped bunch of forms. She began to spread them out, but Terry checked her.

'Don't jump the gun,' he said. 'There's lots to think about. I'm not signing anything yet. The election was only announced an hour ago and if you can't see problems, I can, such as getting nominations, time off school, a deposit, a credible policy, publicity, meeting rooms, type-setting, camera-ready art work, printing, posters, press releases, distribution, photographs, mail shots – and that's just to start with.'

Then he heard the whistle of the kettle and went to make tea.

Susan followed. 'I'll have tea, too,' she said. 'and fairly strong. I anticipated all your so-called problems and they're allowed for, even the five hundred pounds – half from you, half from me. I've got enough electors lined up as nominees; you don't need time off work though you'll take it if it's available; our policy is already there in the synopsis of your CSP novel; a colleague is adept with desk top publishing; initial publicity will be provided by Royal Mail with free delivery of our leaflet to every household in the constituency.'

'That's only ...'

'The beginning? Of course it is.'

'And my eligibility?'

'Eligibility? Come on, you're an adult aren't you? You're not a wig-wearing judge, an alien, a baron or count, a spy, a chief constable, an undischarged bankrupt, a convict, or a raving lunatic, are you?'

'Of course not.'

'Then away we go. Start practising smiles for television and the press photographers and for the sexy Hetty Hopkins men rave about! Pretend she's making eyes at you! Come on, smile! *Smile* for heaven's sake! And let's fill this lot out for our gallant Returning Officer.'

But Terry was still unsure. He wanted to be with her, close to her, stay with her, work with her, think with her, plan with her, but this was too much. 'Slow down a bit,' he said. 'Let's go through it again. How can I run for the headship of the school *and* for Parliament? I can't do both. People would think I really was a raving lunatic – and they'd be right.'

'Don't be so concerned about what people think. If you're going to be a politician you've got to grow a thick, thick, skin. Remember those politicians who've made a hopeless hash of their jobs but who stay on in the Commons or the Lords and then have the audacity to lambaste those who try to do better. They must have hides as tough as an old boar's backside.'

'I will ...'

'But if it's a conflict of interest you're worried about – head teacher or politician - then don't be. We need more head teachers to get into the world of politics – and they should be playing hell with what's happening to our schools. And who can do that better than a head teacher-cum-politician who knows what it's like to try to run a school these days? Put a few cats among the pigeons! Make the feathers fly!'

'I can see all that but ...'

'So what's the problem?'

'I feel uneasy. It's so much to take on.'

'All right, I can understand that, but stop wandering round like a lost soul – that won't help anyone. Pour the tea and then sit here and we'll talk it through. But, after that, we'll make a decision and make it this evening and, if we agree, we'll hand the election papers in tomorrow. Right? And no backtracking. Well?'

'No backtracking.'

'Sure?'

'Yes.'

'Excellent. Lots of good things can come out of this. First – and these are not in an order of importance – first, for once in our working lives we'll each be our own boss; second, we will be giving sixty thousand electors a real alternative, something really exciting; third, from all the responses we get you'll pile up honest, original, unadulterated material for your common sense novel, fourth, I'll be getting valuable public reaction to my teaching-children-without-schools proposals, whether that's favourable or unfavourable.'

'Are you saying … ?'

'Yes - that's my reward. A slice of *your* 'common sense' agenda will be *my* right to stress the common sense angle of giving to all parents, children and teachers, the option to decide what's best for them individually and as a team. Your common sense politics and my personalised tutoring system will run as one. That's the deal, and linking the two together is, in itself, simple common sense.'

'But the CSP isn't only about education, Susan. *It really isn't.* It's about all the obsolete institutions that divide and bedevil our country. '

'Nevertheless a lot of it *is* about education, and rightly so, for education affects millions, and a fully functioning democracy is dependent on it. So we start with education, then branch out. Agreed?'

Terry nodded, but he still had misgivings.

'Just think, we could be starting a new political era when MPs can't escape.responsibilities by claiming to be obeying their party whips. There'll be no party, there'll be no whips. And if we stress the right of citizens to take part in electronic voting on major issues we'll have furthered democracy immeasurably! We'll have made history, Terry, *made history*! My father would have loved a chance like this!'

'You thought a lot of your father?'

'With good cause. He was a sticker. He left school at fourteen, walked three miles to work every day, went to Workers' Educational Association classes, joined the *real* Labour Party, raked together the money to rent a tiny shop and buy stock, lived over it, helped Mum sell greengrocery until they'd enough cash – as well as twin daughters – to buy a better business and, by the standards of the day, finish up OK, proud of owing nobody a penny. No dodgy loans from greedy bankers for them!'

'And no politics?'

'No, not active politics, although Dad joined the Labour Party. But he told me his real wish had been to make genuine changes in society; he was very liberal in his way. But he was not a strong man and died at sixty-nine. But my mother's alive and well, still in Scunthorpe.'

'And they saw you and your sister through university.'

'With dire warnings about concentrating on our studies. They didn't want us to finish up selling cucumbers.'

'Nothing wrong with selling cucumbers?'

'Of course not, but they wanted us to get into a profession.'

'Which you did?'

'More or less!' she laughed. 'More or less! I kept my side of the bargain and was a good girl. But now I'm into radical education, and., if you're game, into radical politics. My father would have liked that.'

'So would my grandfather.'

'Of course he would, so come on, let's be brave, let's take a few risks. Let's both take a few risks. We'll take risks together, won't we?'

'Yes. Maybe,' said Terry. Momentarily he shared her exuberance, but his misgivings lingered. He still had doubts about the outcome. 'Susan, let's face it, let's admit it, we won't even keep our deposit.'

'What does that matter? Five hundred pounds between the two of us to do all I've said we'll do? It's incredible value and worth every penny. And think what a triumph it would be if we *did* retain our deposit and to do that all we need is five per cent of the votes cast.'

'That's nearly ...'

'Not nearly as difficult as you think. People are so cheesed off with the present set-up that only half of them voted last time, or rather they voted for the "Sod 'Em All Party" by staying at home. So, even if 30,000 turn out, which is unlikely, we need only 1,501 votes to get our money back. Then we can put up three fingers to the sceptics! So what's the problem? Well? Come on, we're almost there!'

He smiled, and she smiled back, knowing she had won the day.

'You're wonderful!' he said. 'Quite impractically wonderful!'

'I know I am,' she grinned. 'But just stick to "wonderful"! So, my dear friend, does that effusive praise of my feminine self mean we go ahead? Come on Terry,' she urged, 'will you be a candidate?'

But Terry had begun pacing again so Susan walked over to him and gripped his arms so that he had to turn, look at her, and stand still.

'Well?' She waited. 'Will you?'

He hesitated.

'Terry, *will you*?'

'Yes.'

'Good man! And you're wonderful, too!'

They hugged tightly for a long time. But while Terry was soon roused by the closeness of her body and its gradual merging with his own and by its tantalising warmth and seductive softness, and by her readiness to press herself firmly against him, she was excited by the political significance of what she had persuaded him to do. She knew she was right; the potential was immeasurable.

'Come on, then,' she said, slowly breaking away and tactfully ignoring the all too visible signs of his arousal, 'let's fill out the forms and then have a go at your election address. Yes?'

But Terry was quiet. Her withdrawal had pained him and he felt cut off from what really mattered to him. So damn the forms and the election address! Damn the fickle voters and the returning officer! Damn the media! Damn the election! Let them all go to Hell and stay there! He wanted her, and he wanted her here, and he wanted her now!

'Yes? Is that all right?'

He nodded, looked at her again, and then murmured 'Yes.'

'Quite sure? *Quite*?'

'Yes.'

'And that's got to be exciting hasn't it?'

'Yes,' replied Terry again. 'I suppose it has.'

Friday 12 April.   **A Man of Many Parts**

Adrian Olde had no interest in the general election. Yesterday's announcement had left him cold. He knew all three parties would put education high among their priorities, pump in more money, but make few significant and deep down improvements. His sole concern now was to get through the next three months. Ingrid Eastman thought he looked worse than he had done yesterday so she did not mention Hetty Hopkins' interest in Mr Bennett. Ingrid, having opened the morning's mail, knew there was enough melancholy news in that without adding a go-getting journalist's troublesome queries.

One of the teachers proposed for the maternity job-share now said she could not manage Tuesday afternoons. The company undertaking the leaking-roof repairs could not start until early May. A reference was required for one of the school's two impossible-to-replace physics teachers. The statement for the school bus repairs far exceeded the estimate. There was to be less pool time available for swimming lessons meaning timetable re-arrangements with many knock-on effects. Two experienced dinner ladies were leaving. The inspectors would visit Mrs Olive Sarah Graham and Miss Jenny Jean Jones on Tuesday 30 April and asked for Mr Olde's views on the two teachers' progress.

"Tuesday 30 April! The same day as the head teacher interviews!' Adrian Olde could hardly believe his misfortune - to have inquisitive inspectors prowling around while the place was packed with candidates, governors, education officers, scribes, tea makers, and the school's teaching timetable disrupted? No, it could not be done!

Olde sat bemused. Assembly had not gone well; Hull had complained about the state of the art block; Louie Anne Lee needed time off for dental work; two governors wished to see him about the exclusion; there were doubts about the playability of the tennis courts; the piano tuner was to retire. Olde sighed deeply before telling Ingrid he would be in Mrs Irving's room until break.

'And no interruptions, please,' he said.

He was surprised to find Terry Park sitting with the deputy head. Terry rose to leave but Olde stopped him. 'If you're free this period, stay, you might help with a few of these.' He waved the bundle of letters at Terry, took the easy chair Terry had vacated, and indicated that Terry should take a hard chair by the window. He asked Ursula to decide on the tennis courts and deal with Hull and the art block, mentioned the other items, then read out the inspectors' letter.

'What do we do?'

'Simple: they change dates,' declared Ursula. 'The interviews come first so there's nothing to discuss. The inspectors must be offered days that suit the school, not them. And,' she added, 'it would be better if neither Mrs Graham nor Miss Jones was told about their visit just yet.'

'Ah, yes, about Mrs Graham,' said Olde. 'I wonder what we...'

'Are you quite sure you want me to stay?' asked Terry. 'It might be unprofessional if you're to discuss Mrs Graham.'

'No, not at all,' stated Olde. 'You can be of help in a specific matter,

122

and whatever is said in here goes no further. So, please stay,' he said as Terry still seemed determined to leave. 'I need advice.'

Terry could think of none he could offer, but sat down.

'Mrs Graham needs our support and our care,' Olde said. 'Although she is intelligent and well qualified in her subject she is not, I am the first to confess, an outstandingly good teacher ...'

Briefly Ursula put her hands over her eyes, took them away again and then, as did Terry, turned to gaze out of the window where, in the Spring sunshine, a row of fine young chestnut trees was coming into leaf. Both teachers said nothing but thought plenty. Olde continued.

'I know what you're thinking, but there's good in us all and with Mrs Graham it may be taking longer than usual to show. And, I'm sure you will agree, some pupils have made her work difficult.'

'Mr Olde,' said Ursula turning to face him, 'Mrs Graham has been here long enough to display any virtues she might possess: none has appeared. Yes, she has difficult children, but so have sixty-six other teachers on the staff. Lucky is the teacher anywhere in the UK today who does not have difficult pupils, but most of those other teachers have not had riots in their classrooms, complaints from parents, very low assessments from inspectors, disgruntled cleaners, objections from teachers in adjoining rooms, unaccountable losses of materials, ill-thought out lessons, and piles of untidy, unmarked exercise books. They have not had such frequent and long absences, such a pathetic history of unpunctuality, such poor record keeping, and so many paltry excuses for not covering for indisposed colleagues. As I've said before, many times, she should not be a teacher and she should not be here. So, if you are asking me, let me make it clear, I will not speak for her. I will not! That woman should find another job.'

'*That woman?*' uttered Olde. 'Mrs Graham is both an individual and as much a human being as we are, and she is a person here in *our* school.'

'I think I should go,' interjected Terry. 'I feel I am not ...'

'Stay,' ordered Olde. His uncharacteristic insistence showed how upset he was. 'I want your advice on one issue, and then you can go. I want to know what union support Mrs Graham would get if the inspectors decided against her.' He waited. 'Mr Park?'

'I cannot say. I'm not in a position to ...'

'But you belong, I believe, to Teachers For Radical Action?'

'Yes.'

'So does Mrs Graham.'

'I did not know that.'

'She joined recently.'

Terry made no comment. For a while there was little sound apart from the hum of a large school in session. In the corridor a teacher talked firmly to a child, there was laughter from a nearby classroom, a mowing machine droned as it worked further away, a car hooted and sparrows squabbled in the chestnut trees while the glum occupants of Ursula's room gazed at each other until, eventually, Terry spoke.

'You think, because she's in TFRA, the union will support her?'

'That is what I would like to know.'

'But Mr Olde, I cannot speak for the TFRA.'

'You know Mr Collins?' asked Olde.

'Yes,' said Terry.

'Would Mr Collins recommend union support?'

'Mr Olde, you must ask Mr Collins that.'

'Would the union claim unfair dismissal?'

'Only if the dismissal *was* unfair.'

Again there was silence. Again Terry broke it.

'I'm sorry, but you know I cannot discuss Mrs Graham's work with you. However, just supposing – *supposing* - its quality is as poor as is described, *supposing* it is, then I doubt whether any professional association would support her retention as a practising, qualified, registered teacher responsible for the education and care of children.'

'I am much relieved,' said Olde. 'I feared a tribunal.'

'But they would want to know why Mrs Graham gained qualified teacher status in the first place and, if she was satisfactory then, what has happened since to put her in this ignominious position. They would want to know why her college passed her as a person suitable for work as a teacher, or, if the college was right to do that, what has happened subsequently to make her so weak that inspectors – for whom I have little time I might add - seek her removal.'

Olde's face was wan. Ursula felt compelled to speak.

'I have been in teaching for many years,' she said, 'and have seen teachers of such poor quality come into the profession that I've wondered how on earth they got in. Then I've been alarmed at how difficult it is to get rid of poor teachers once they are in post for it seems to me they can go on year after year, doing nothing for the children they are supposed to be teaching while becoming a drain on their colleagues and the other resources. I'm sure teacher training departments contain kind people who care for their students but I'm equally sure that at times some fail to face realities. They do not accept that by seeing into the profession a poor student they may be doing harm to children for many years to come. The needs of those children have priority over those of the teachers who fail to teach them. That is a clear process of putting the needs of the client first and is the essence of professionalism. Of that there is no doubt.'

'I see. And is that all, Mrs Irving?' asked Olde dejectedly.

Ursula paused. 'No,' she replied, 'it is not. I think it needs to be said that there is a duty, too, on the head teacher of the school in which such a particularly weak teacher is employed, to say, "enough is enough," and to do all he or she can to have that teacher struck off.'

'You are singularly outspoken.'

'You asked my opinion.'

Terry rose again but Olde waved him back impatiently.

'And what of her union? Is there no responsibility there? Where do the unions' priorities lie? Have they no obligations?'

Ursula did not answer.

Olde looked at Terry. 'Mr Park?'

'I've no time for any system which lets incompetent people become incompetent professionals who, whether they be teachers, vets, doctors, dentists, pharmacists, architects, engineers, pilots, lawyers or whatever else – people who then risk the well-being of their clients. It is immoral and, in terms of likely future difficulties, lacks common sense. The fact that the allegedly weak Mrs Graham was selected for teaching, allowed through her teaching course and then through her probationary year is *seemingly* disgraceful, however, matters like the working environment might have changed since she qualified. Also, I know of her background: she has a feeble husband, several children, irresponsible financial commitments and an inability to earn elsewhere what she is earning here. She would need to be a saint to admit her deficiencies and leave her job knowing the sacrifice that would entail - to herself and to her family.'

'That doesn't help one iota,' said Ursula aggressively, 'not one iota! Many pupils are still passing through *that woman's* hands: their needs come before her mortgage and her fancy holidays! So, what do we do? Or, more to the point, what does your friend Collins do?'

'If she's a member of TFRA she can ask for legal advice.'

'Dear God Almighty,' murmured Olde, closing his eyes.

'Mr Park, can't you speak to Mr Collins,' urged Ursula. 'Say we don't want inspectors assessing her here and reporting unfavourably?'

'*Here*? Is that what worries you – the school's reputation?'

'Not altogether,' said Ursula sharply, visibly riled, 'but wouldn't it be better for the woman to go voluntarily with a fairly clean slate – not wait until she's thrown out? Then, perhaps, she could get another job.'

'Another job? In teaching? So you don't mind if she goes and teaches some other school's pupils? Some other poor kids? Is that it?' censured Terry. 'Is it?' He, too, was exasperated. 'No: I'd rather the top brass here gave her such a rough ride that she left the profession of her own accord and left at top speed! That's their duty.'

Olde cringed. He was in uncharted waters. Ursula Irving bridled.

'Mr Park,' said Olde, and he spoke so quietly he could hardly be heard, 'we've so many problems here now that the last thing we want is disagreement among ourselves or trouble with the unions and all the subsequent publicity. So, please do what you can with Mr Collins.'

Ursula winced at the man's weakness: Olde, a senior head teacher, almost begging an assistant to help him out of a school problem which, if not wholly of his making, was one for him to resolve.

But Terry saw the anguish on the man's face. 'I'll see what I can do,' he said. 'But I hold out little hope.'

Nor did Ursula Irving.

There was a timid knock at the door. 'Not now, please,' called out Olde as if it were his office.

They sat in silence with Ursula wondering what she could do to end the session and get on with some work. But Olde did not seem anxious to go, nor, surprisingly, did Terry. As the clock could be heard marking off the seconds they sat listening to it as if noting its meticulous checking of time was the reason for their presence. Then Terry pulled his chair towards them, leaned forward, and spoke softly.

'Can I say something about another matter?' As well as speaking quietly he spoke hesitantly. He twisted in his chair as if not sure whom he should address: the uncertain head teacher or the determined deputy. 'It's, it's about the general election next month, on Thursday, May 2nd.'

'Oh that,' murmured Olde forlornly, 'more disruption.'

'I've, well, I've decided to stand as an independent candidate, and thought you two should be among the first to know.' Deliberately he turned each way to make sure both were following. 'There's not been time to be nominated officially, so I wonder if you would keep this confidential? That is until it's announced in the press?'

'Independent candidate?' echoed Olde.

'More or less, for the Common Sense Party. So far I'm its front - and only - runner.' Terry grinned sheepishly. He twiddled with the pen he had taken from his shirt's breast pocket and then put it back again. Now he did wish to leave – and soon.

'Well, well,' said Olde, 'fancy that. A man of many parts!'

'Good for you,' said Ursula, her face lightening, 'good for you!'

Both were relieved at the change of subject. Terry stood to leave.

'Good. Although,' and Ursula paused, 'do tell me this, and please, please don't be offended, Eddie Collins isn't behind this, is he?'

'Of course not,' said Olde before Terry could answer, 'Mr Collins is tied to the Equal Shares Party and the TFRA.' And then, with the faintest trace of a smile, he said, slowly, 'Mr Park's guiding light has been Dr Susan Mansfield, am I not right?'

Terry's face was the colour of the proverbial, but over ripe, beetroot.

'I thought so.' And then both head and deputy smiled before Olde crossed to Terry and shook his hand. He seemed to have a tear in his eye. 'Good for you! And, let me tell you, you'll get at least one vote!'

'Make it two!' But Ursula did not shake Terry's hand. In an action unprecedented in her years at the school she leaned and kissed him on the cheek. And that kiss, as both men noted, was no mere peck.

Mr Terrence Arthur Park, B.A., (London University, Honours), head of humanities, aspiring author, budding politician, was on top of the world for, as Olde had said, he was now "a man of many parts."

Saturday 13 April.   The Size of Classes

Adrian Olde, in school early, wrote a letter offering the inspectors another date. He fetched the personal files of Jenny Jean Jones and Olive Graham and updated them. The first update he recorded with enthusiasm, the second with trepidation. But he told no lies. Miss Jones had her work praised, Mrs Graham's weaknesses were fairly noted. Therein lay the irony: he was fairly sure from snippets picked up from staff that Miss Jones was unsure about staying in teaching whereas Mrs Graham, who had nothing like the same potential, wanted to stay for as long as she could. It was the old, old story.

He turned to his next problem: Mr Bennett. Classes were at their maximum and, looking again at the lists, he knew he could not let the Bennett boy in. To do so would lead to more problems on the staff and indignation on the part of parents previously refused. Changes must wait until September but as he was currently the man in command he would have to oversee, with the incumbent-elect, the compilation of next year's class lists. He considered his options.

An additional teacher in each of the five year-groups would solve the problem but would cost £150,000 in salaries and benefits and additional teaching resources. And all to admit four or five extra children? No one would listen to that and, anyway, the money was not there.

An agreement with teachers to increase each class size by one or two would suffice, but that was not on. He recoiled at the memories of meetings at which similar proposals had been put. Now, to make matters worse, there was this ghastly TFRA official - this agitating Collins. To be fair though, he knew the union man was on safe ground educationally, a class of thirty was more than enough for any teacher even if only a modicum of individual teaching was to be attempted.

He could try handing the matter to his deputy and say it would be good administrative experience and an invaluable lesson in tricky staff relationships, but he knew that the adamant Ursula Irving, who wanted no preparation for headship, would be unimpressed.

He could approach the Chief Education Officer and remind him of the authority's obligation to provide school places for all children, but knew the "don't-involve-me" Matthew Zing, M.A., Ph.D. (Cantab), would wheel out the 'no money' excuse and claim that, overall, the borough had no shortage of secondary school places; indeed, one school under threat of closure would welcome any newcomers.

He could claim illness. But although there were times when he felt distinctly off colour he knew that exaggerating his illnesses to avoid unpleasantness would be the coward's way out. He did not intend to end a professional life of forty-one years under a cloud of deceit.

He could place a notice in *The Messenger* to advise parents that the school was not what it once was and that they had best explore alternatives, but that, while true, was out of the question; it would be against his ingrained way of working. He had grown so used to saying to parents, "Ladies and Gentlemen, this is a fine school, a proud school, a happy school, a kind school, an exciting school ..." He cringed and closed his eyes. He could hear himself saying that with less and less conviction every term for the past seventy-five terms. But he could not change now. He must deny Mr. Bennett.

The excluded girl could be dealt with by offering home tuition for a few more months. Lena Napier had offered to visit the family and act as go-between with the Chief Education Officer. The chairperson could frighten the life out of the trouble-avoiding Matthew Zing by hinting at the difficulties brewing such as the rich mix of parental concerns, election-savvy governors, an inquisitive MP, angry unions and growing media interest. Knowing Zing, he guessed that would settle matters until September. He brightened at the thought of September. Then there came a knock on the door.

'Yes?'

'I'm off for a while, Sir, be back at twelve,' said Hull looking in. 'Shall I lock the outer doors, or will you be leaving soon?'

'Thank you, Mr Hull,' answered Olde with the glimmer of a smile, 'but I shall be not be here for long.' And he smiled again, briefly.

'Very good, Sir, I'll wait,' said Hull. Then he thought to himself, it's some time since I've seen the C.O. smiling. Reckon he's demob-happy! Then he frowned - but who will we get in his place?

Sunday 14 April.   **A Disappointing Island**

Susan pointed to the boathouse. 'They've got the boats out ready for the new season. While the university does not possess Oxbridge punts, if you're content with a common or garden rowboat, I'm game.'

Terry, too, was game.

After five hours hammering out an election address, designing roughs for CSP posters, drafting a press release, listing people who might make donations and others who might help with canvassing, both enthusiasts sought relaxation.

The six and a half acre, elongated, ninety-year-old man-made lake, with boathouse, a slender artificial sandy beach, water lilies, reeds, weeping willows, assorted fowl, nests, and a hutted island in its centre, was a feature of the university's main campus and, like the imposing gates and sweeping drive leading to Terry Park's school, appealed to prospective students and their proud parents. A proposal for a nine-foot high *Peter Pan* statue on the island to mark the coming Millennium had been turned down by an anxious Senate as it was feared Rag Week inebriates might adorn it unsuitably. Instead the money had been put to a refurbishment of the Student Union bar with a suitable plaque, and, as a sop to quizzical citizens, the acquisition of twelve expensively framed prints of prominent nineteenth century South Mansworth citizens. But that had been insufficient to prevent outbursts from teetotal taxpayers – all given headlines in *The Evening Messenger*. The jaded Vice-Chancellor had been heard to say: 'Damn it all, you can't bloody well win!' which had been deemed, by two university chaplains, to be most un-Vice-Chancellor-like.

'Where did you learn to row?' asked Susan, holding tightly to the seat ends and wedging her shoes against the rocking boat's sides.

'I didn't learn to row anywhere,' muttered Terry as the boat tilted and made another unsolicited turn. 'So don't take the micky.'

'If you mean, "take the piss", smiled Susan 'why not say so?'

'Because, Susan Mansfield, you're a lady and I need to show restraint.' He straightened the freshly varnished boat and then headed, in a passably straight line, to the tiny island.

'Show restraint? One of my nervous bosses showed little restraint yesterday when I took him my brand new ideas for student-led seminars, but sounded off yet again on how terribly concerned he was about what he calls my 'no-schools' research. He still hasn't grasped that I am not criticising teachers when I say we could make better use of the billions ploughed into education. And he thinks further publicity for my work will result in the university being outlawed by head teachers for teaching practice purposes as a payback for my "bringing their schools into disrepute" – as if it were some sort of Saturday afternoon sport.'

'Well, isn't it?' smiled Terry.

'Be serious!'

'He's the one who's serious! He needs the full co-operation of schools if he's to use them for your students to practise in year in, year out.'

She grimaced.

'Come on, Susan, if he couldn't place your students in schools you'd all be without jobs.' Then added, 'up the creek without a paddle!'

'I'd like to see him up this lot without a paddle,' she muttered as Terry lost stroke. The boat lurched, an oar splashed, and a long line of startled ducks and a pair of nesting moorhens rose in a wet, noisy protest.

'Sorry,' murmured Terry. 'I told you I was no good.'

She did not reply.

'Well, I'm a teacher, Susan, and I don't see your research in that negative light. Most teachers would welcome a radical change – especially if it meant greater freedom to practise. It's common sense,' he said with a smirk. 'The trouble with people in high places is that they're scared of upsetting the apple cart – or rocking the boat! "Let's keep things on an even keel," they say, followed by, "we're not doing too badly you know, not really." That fear and that sickening complacency underlies much that's wrong in schools – and in the UK as a whole.'

'Exactly. There have been few organisational changes in the school *system* since 1870,' said Susan, 'and I emphasise *system*. But officials daren't accept that. And that's true of MPs as well. And that's what we must stress in the next three weeks. But there'll be plenty of changes with the new Common Sense Party Member for Mansworth South-West in place! So, now, pull into the island, let's see what's there. And enough shop! No elections or schools for at least an hour!'

But it did not take that long to traverse the shoreline. The island's attractiveness from afar was unconfirmed by closer examination. The aging trees, stunted shrubs, patchy grass, crops of nettles, straggling brambles, scrawny thistles, remains of camp fires, broken beer crates, cans, bottles, and an abundance of other litter - some of a distinctly intimate nature - did nothing to redeem it. Even the wooden hut was in the final stages of collapse – and stank. The island was revolting.

The twisting path was wet where it went under low-branched trees and was only just wide enough for the couple to walk side by side. Before completing the circle, and as it neared the boat, the path ran close to the water's edge. Terry put his arm firmly round Susan's waist and drew her to him as if to keep her from slipping. Instantly he found the warm bodily contact exciting, and slowly, daringly, he tightened his hold, lowered his arm and tried to take her hand. But she eased away and slowly, but purposefully, took his hand and his arm and placed them at his side.

'I'm sorry,' he said softly, but she hardly heard him above the lap of the water. He raised his voice to make sure he was heard. 'I'm sorry,' he said again. 'I shouldn't have …'

'Don't be silly. Let's get back, there's nothing here to keep us. It's dreadful, disgraceful, disgusting. Cutting back on labour, I suppose.'

They returned to the boat and, after standing awhile to see that the ducks and moorhens had resumed their feeding, Terry held the rowboat steady as Susan stepped on board and then, before he sat down, pressed one of the oars hard against the bank and thrust the boat backwards into deeper water. Then it took him several minutes to swing it round and manoeuvre it onto a homeward course. In all that time he could think of nothing to say.

'Terry,' said Susan after a while, 'don't look so sad. Think about something else. Think about your common sense idea, or your job application, or your nomination, or your novel. And then tell me, sincerely, whether greater use of common sense, not just in education but in other areas of life, would improve things significantly?'

'I don't want to talk about that now, not now.'

'Yes you do, so tell me, will it?'

He shook his head.

'It won't?' she asked, pretending that was his answer.

'Of course it will. Why d'you think I'm a candidate? He looked at her. 'Don't *you* think it will?'

'Yes, and are we going to emphasise that ubiquity all through the manifesto, and into my alternative education scenario? Into both?'

'OK. If you like.' But he knew he had been gently rebuffed on the island and that had hurt. 'But *you* said "no more shop," remember?'

'That time's up and now I want to use every opportunity to push my proposals. And you must do the same about common sense and the new party.'

'If you like,' he said again. He turned towards the feeding ducks.

'No, not if *I* like, Terry! If *we* like!'

'You mean as opposed to the unrepresentative shower of politicians in power now? But that's already a theme of my novel. – or will be.'

She waited. The boat seemed to have a mind of its own and Terry took ages to correct its course.

'But your novel might not get published. And, if it did, might be read by very few people. A hundred? A thousand?' She was determined to continue the conversation although she knew she had upset him.

'You're really encouraging!'

'I'm realistic - using common sense!' She laughed as she tried to ease the tension while the boat rocked and then dipped noticeably. But she saw Terry was not laughing – there was no hint of a smile even, and she began to wonder whether she should have let him take her hand, keep his arm round her, hold her, and, perhaps, kiss? Should they have stayed on the island longer – should she have given way more? Or at least shown affection? Oh sod sex, she thought ferociously. Sod, sod, *sod* it! Why did sex have to get in the way of much more important things?

Terry concentrated on his rowing. He dipped the oars and pulled hard against the water. He barely glanced at Susan.

She became more thoughtful. She doubted whether sex had been the issue. Terry had wanted intimacy, certainly, but not sexual intimacy. He had wanted warmth, kindness, and a suggestion of closeness – a brief physical bond such as holding her hand or putting his arm around her waist and keeping it there – just for a few minutes. Down to earth sex in that unappealing environment would not have entered his mind. There had been no need for her to repel him. She had failed to offer him that closeness in relationships – that love, warmth, affection and concern - which formed the very mainstay of her alternative education proposals - for other people! She had been both thoughtless and unfeeling. But the moment had passed, she would have to press on.

'Terry, listen to me. I've been thinking.'

'So have I.'

'I've been thinking that you must turn your fictional CSP into a permanent body. Do less work on the novel and, after this election, do more on building a national party organisation using volunteers. It will be slow but it will be progress. It will get things moving!'

'Which is more than can be said of this damn boat!'

'Use the experience we get from this election as a foundation for a full-blown party. Then, at the next election you'll be in a strong ...'

'Susan, ever since we set out in this unmanageable boat you've been teasing me,' grumbled Terry. His wretchedness showed: his day had already been spoiled. 'You know that proposal is out of the question.'

'But is it?'

She could see how badly he had been hurt over something that was of far less significance to her. But she would not talk about that.

'Is it so far-fetched? Everything has to have a beginning. Someone has to start. Two hundred years ago there was no such thing as the Communist Party but within our own grandparents' time it became the most powerful political presence in the world and affected the lives of hundreds of millions of people.'

'Not a happy example.' His voice was one of disdain.

'Things went wrong. It wasn't necessarily the basic theory that was wrong, but the people who tried to put that theory into practice. But it shows what can grow from tiny beginnings.'

'Yes, but I'm no Trotsky or Lenin - or Stalin, thank God! I'm not even a Mikhail Sergeevich Gorbachov!'

'Yet you have some of Gorbachov's caring qualities,' she smiled.

'I doubt that.'

'All right, but look at the Labour Party if you want something nearer home. A hundred years ago it was a mere spot on the horizon. It was an outsider, an also ran, a bit of a laugh for the middle and upper classes – for both the Whigs and the Tories.'

He shrugged his shoulders.

But, while she could see he was in no mood to argue, she persisted, determined to make her point. 'It was. It was ignored. So don't you see, the Common Sense Party could start in the same way and make the same steady progress that the Labour Party made.'

'If you say so, but you're way over the top. Times have changed, and are still changing. And they're changing fast!'

'The speed of that change could help our cause.'

'It could. And it couldn't.'

Susan let that go and they sat quietly in the slowly moving boat until they reached the landing stage. Both remained thoughtful.

Then, to his surprise, Terry made a fair job of steadying and tying up the boat before he and Susan set off for the University Club.

'Bugger it,' he murmured to himself moodily as they walked up the hill, 'she's never had enough. She's already planning the election after next! And where will I be then? Where will she be then? Where the hell will *anyone* be then?'

Week Three

The new week brought no respite for Adrian Olde. Apart from the usual Monday morning crises the Chief Education Officer made known his displeasure at receiving enquiries from the local newspaper about the school, was annoyed about the rushing of the headship appointment, and concerned at the "utterly abysmal" response.

'It's been unduly hurried and suggests our schools are unattractive.'

That's one interpretation, Olde thought dejectedly, but his silence brought further criticism. Olde, being a compliant man, was one of the few head teachers with whom Zing could be assertive. Nevertheless, before ending the call, Zing had agreed to attend the hastily arranged preliminary meeting of the governing body's interview panel in the school library that same evening.

*

At eight o'clock precisely Hull brought in coffee and biscuits and took his time arranging the crockery. He saw Lena Napier without her dog collar; Dr. Matthew Zing whom he had once referred to as "The Big White Chief" but wondered whether that was now politically correct; Giles Townsend whom he did not know; Zoë Kennedy, a troublesome parent governor; Vic Sneade, whom he wouldn't trust with his grandmother's trinkets; the snooty live-in-the-past Captain Walter Walker-West whom he disliked, and that wealthy Hitler-like bastard Fergus Eastman whom he detested. He saw them gather round the periodicals table, reach eagerly for the coffee, then snaffle the biscuits. He heard Lena Napier give apologies for Adrian Olde, and Vic Sneade for Wendy Durrell, followed by Fergus Eastman's comment on the latter's poor attendance. Ursula Irving had declined her invitation. Hull noted that the air of animosity which often graced these meetings was already apparent and, as he closed the door, saw Sneade scowling at Walker-West while the Rev Lena Napier was introducing the six interview panel members to a clearly unimpressed Dr. Matthew Zing.

'Thank you,' said Zing. He did not repeat his view that six plus a chairperson was too large for an interview panel, but did say that the number and the quality of the applicants had disappointed him.

'When I became an education officer there would have been sixty people after a post like this!' he stated. 'How things have changed!'

'Why would that be, Dr. Zing?' asked Eastman provocatively.

Zing was taken aback, but before he could reply Lena Napier said, forestalling argument, 'perhaps we should look at what we have now, that's all we can do. So, you've details of eight "possibles" and we must select five or six for interview.'

'Was eight all we got?' asked Sneade.

'We got ten, but two withdrew last week,' replied Lena.

'Well, as far as I'm concerned,' said Vic Sneade bluntly, 'that leaves seven. You're keeping quiet about Park but you know he's a candidate for some daft Common Sod's Party ...'

'Common Sense Party,' corrected Wally Walker-West.

'He's a candidate for parliament, isn't he? snapped Sneade,' never mind his party! I used to think he was OK but now I'm not so sure. What does the man want to be: a teacher, or a headmaster, or a writer, or a politician, or some farting fishmonger?'

'I say...' protested Walker-West, while Zoe blanched at the image.

'Really, Mr Sneade,' said Lena, 'that was uncalled for. Besides, while you may question Mr Park's various ambitions, there would be terrible publicity if it were known we had rejected him because he chose to stand in our country's parliamentary election. And, with a general election likely soon, the timing could hardly be worse'

'Madam,' cried Walker-West, 'you're right on target!' He struggled to stay cool. 'We can't drum a man out because he's doing his duty!'

'Duty?' echoed Sneade.

'Yes, Sir, "*duty*"! Do I have to define it?'

'We're wasting our time again,' complained Zoë Kennedy, slowly recovering from thoughts of the fishmonger's exigencies.

'May I speak, Madam?' asked a hesitant Dr Matthew Zing.

Lena looked round and, as there were no objections, she nodded.

'I have been watching the political scene as well as the educational one,' Zing said, 'and there may, possibly, be a relevant, if tenuous, link. It could be that Mr Park who, I believe, is interested in radically different approaches to children's education – quite different from those in practice now, of course - is demonstrating that such changes can come about only if, at the same time, there are radical changes in our political system that will permit the emergence of political parties different from those in place today. Educational change and political change may, Mr Park might argue, be interdependent.'

'So two cheers for the Common Sense Party!' sneered Eastman.

'Thank you, Dr Zing,' said Lena, ignoring Eastman. 'That puts the matter well; we cannot sit comfortably in this library and ignore what is happening outside where politics are much to the fore.'

No one spoke.

'So, for the moment,' stressed Lena, 'we have *eight* applications. Please read them again and decide which to omit. All eight meet the governors' requirements: they have degrees and teaching certificates, possess or are studying for a head teacher qualification, are in our age range of thirty-five to fifty, have experience of responsible positions in schools, and, if we appoint with alacrity, can give their current employers statutory notice for a start here in September.'

'Yet all teachers have responsible positions in schools,' butted in Zoe 'The young teacher with thirty infants has far more responsibility and a far more responsible position than any of this lot.' She slapped a hand dismissively on her set of applications.

'Maybe, but I was referring to managerial responsibility....'

'This man Frederick Farthing, with some foreign degree in classics, he's not been in his job five minutes,' exclaimed Wally Walker-West.

'He gives explanations for wanting to move.'

'Well he needn't move here,' retorted Sneade. 'We've had too many fly-by-nights.'

'Mr Olde has been here since ...'

'Before him! Some of us can remember the shambles we had with all that signing on and signing off before Olde turned up.'

Captain Wally Walker-West snorted. He could barely disguise his contempt for Sneade. 'Mr Sneade need only put Farthing to one side as one who, in his humble opinion, is an unsuitable recruit.' Given half a chance he would have quick-marched this governor, this wretched Acting Unpaid Lance-Corporal Sneade, capless and beltless, into the guardroom to await a charge.

'And I'll eliminate Farthing,' said Giles Townsend. Several others nodded. Frederick Farthing could look elsewhere.

'I'm not happy about Susan Margaret Mansfield,' said Zoe. 'Do we want a university lecturer? Some of them are out of touch. And what's this research she's doing? What's "alternative education"? Sounds a bit – well, you know - a bit on the weird side to me.' Zoe looked to see if she had support. As no one spoke Lena replied to what was a frequently encountered Zoe Kennedy challenge.

'Personally, Mrs Kennedy, I think she *is* in touch. As you see, she visits students who are training to be teachers while they are practising in different schools in various districts – in primary and secondary.'

'Has she taught primary school kids?' asked Eastman scrutinising Susan's application.

'I don't think she has,' said Lena glancing at Susan's CV.

'So why's she supervising student teachers in primary schools?'

'That's not a question for the panel tonight. And anyway,' Lena countered hurriedly, suspecting she was on weak ground, 'she will be conversant with new developments – new ideas.'

'Huh!' retorted Eastman.

'And this research?' prompted Walker-West. 'I'm sceptical of research, can be a waste of time and money like some of the War Office non-starters that waste millions, and I, for one, don't know what this lot is about.' He was struggling to make sense of Susan's project-synopsis.

'I assume,' said Dr Matthew Zing, 'if I may contribute again?' he glanced at Lena, 'she may be advocating the education of children without recourse to the school as we have come to know it – the traditional school with its customary structure – that is its hierarchy, classroom organisation, working hours, three terms, set curriculum, teaching methods and testing. On the other hand her research may be comparing and evaluating the approaches of different deschoolers.'

'Deschoolers?' intervened Sneade. 'Who're they?'

'Educationalists who believe children benefit by being taught in a non-school environment,' explained Zing. 'Deschoolers would offer notions of alternative teaching, such as ways of teaching children at home or home-based teaching which is becoming increasingly popular. Or flexi-schooling, or individual or small-group tutoring, and so do away with the need for schools.'

'*Do away with the need for schools*? That's crazy. We don't want her – I'm damned if we do! So rule her out!'

'But I would not rule the lady out, Mr Sneade,' said Lena strongly. 'I would prefer to hear what she has to say by way of explanation and what else she has to offer.'

'No, she's out!' insisted Sneade. 'We'd be committing suicide if we considered crackpots like her! Deschoolers my flaming foot!' He looked round expecting support. 'And if we go and tell our children's parents we're thinking of scrapping the schools we'll need a new governing body as well as a new head teacher and a new CEO!'

'And police protection,' put in Zoë.

But Fergus Eastman appraised the attractive image Susan had clipped helpfully to her application. 'I'm with the Chair,' he leered, 'let's see what else she has to offer.'

'But she hasn't taught in a school classroom for years,' said Zoe.

'Well qualified for a headship, then,' bellowed Eastman.

'There are classrooms in universities ...' began Lena.

'You know what I mean.'

'That she's out of touch?'

'Yes,' said Walker-West.

'Well, I think you're wrong,' said Lena softly. 'It could be that the ones out of touch are the ones confined to schools. They're so absorbed with meeting the latest requirements and targets that they can't take in the whole picture of what's happening outside in the wider society and of how society's needs have changed. Whereas the ones in touch, who can see alternative ways of doing things, are the fortunate ones, such as Dr Mansfield, who can stand back and see the long-term changes a society must implement when considering how better to educate its children.'

'Ordinary teachers can't see the wood for the trees?' queried Zoe.

'More or less. And that's not their fault.'

'So whose fault is it?' demanded Sneade.

'Well it's certainly not Dr Mansfield's,' replied Lena abruptly.

'All right, let her stay in,' said Walker-West impatiently. 'But for Heaven's sake let's get on with it! I want to finish before lights-out.'

Susan's name went forward.

'So what about this man Park?' continued Walker-West, 'apart from his electioneering he's an insider. In the Regiment we liked to appoint our Commanding Officer. from outside – from outside Brigade even. Never keen on internal promotions; prefer a new man, fresh face.'

'Could cause splits on the staff,' agreed Eastman. He did not like the sound of Park's politics, and he'd heard the man was writing a book. Could be dangerous things, books. Hitler might have been right about books – burn the bloody books! 'The man's not even a deputy-head,' he said aloud, 'so what managerial experience has he got?'

'He's a head of department,' said Lena.

'They're all head of something or other these days,' complained Zoe. 'Things were better when you had only a head teacher and one teaching deputy. Then everyone got on with the teaching. After all, that's what they're paid for: the teaching. That's what it's supposed to be all about, isn't it, teaching the children?'

'If we're to interview six candidates,' argued Lena, trying to bring them to order without displaying too heavy a hand, 'Mr Park must stay in because we've all got doubts about Miss Gloria Underwood?'

'Doubts? She's hopeless,' rapped Sneade reading from his notes. 'She's thirty-six, been teaching twelve years, taught in seven schools, had only two years in secondary schools, went to teach in a college of further education – soon bounced out of that – has unexplained absences, writes a pathetic supporting letter, and still gives some retired and unknown college tutor as a referee. God, are we reduced to that? She's out. Out! "Out damned speck!"'

'*Spot.* Out damned *spot*,' said the CEO. 'But, yes, Mr Sneade, I agree, and, although I'm here as an observer and will not vote, I would feel uneasy if Miss Underwood's name went forward.'

'Then why's her name in here?' cried Zoe Kennedy.

'Because,' three or four members retorted in chorus, 'there's been such a poor response!'

'So that leaves Miss Joan Bates, Mr Paul Carter, Mr Kurt Rommal and Mrs Sonia Smith to add to Dr Susan Mansfield and Mr Terence Park,' summarised Lena Napier. 'Do we interview all six?'

'That's the idea, line them up,' said Walker-West, looking again at his watch and then at the list. 'Miss Bates seems reasonable and is already a deputy head; Mr Carter is head of a large science department and we don't often get applications from scientists; Mr Rommal is good on paper – head of a bigger sixth form than the one in this place; Dr Mansfield, well, maybe worth a try; Mr Park, OK, leave him in; and Mrs Smith, she's already a successful head teacher at a smaller secondary school near here so she's a safe bet. She'll do. Right?'

'Agreed,' said Eastman. 'Smith's got a good track record, sound CV, relevant experience, knows this area, fairly firm references, strong disciplinarian, the inspectors liked her.'

'Lucky to have her,' Zoe Kennedy added.

'Yes,' said Townsend and Sneade in unison. Then they both looked embarrassed because, holding directly opposite opinions politically, they hated to be seen in agreement on anything.

Lena Napier cast a quick look in the CEO's direction and he gave the slightest of acknowledgements from which Lena knew he was agreeable and seized her chance to close the meeting.

'Well,' she said, relieved, 'that's that! But we mustn't jump to conclusions. Several candidates look interesting and must be given a fair trial. So,' and she looked round, 'are we agreed that the names of these six be offered to the whole governing body for approval so that the six can be invited to interview here on Tuesday, 30 April, in the afternoon, at the school? Please show.'

She paused then all indicated agreement with the exception, of course, of Dr. Matthew Zing, who, as he had made clear, would not, as an official observer, cast a vote.

'And that they be invited to visit school in the morning, have sherry and lunch with us, and be interviewed in the library in the afternoon?'

'As long as the school's day isn't too disrupted,' said Zoe.

'I'm sure Mr Olde will see to that,' answered Lena.

Others were not so sure, but her proposal was passed unanimously.

For a time the panel members chatted to carefully chosen partners, glad to have come to a decision. Nobody mentioned the other divisive issues alive at the school but more than one hinted that, in view of the contentious nature of those problems, they might be put off long enough to allow the new head teacher to show his or, more likely, her, mettle in September? Of course they could! No problem there as long as they kept things ticking over nicely and remained quietly resolute.

'Hold the line!' ordered Captain Walter Walker-West (Rtd).

'Steady the Buffs!' Sneade sniggered.

Lena stood in the foyer talking to Zing.

'You're not happy about this, are you?' Lena asked.

'I am not. It is being rushed. The candidates should be interviewed more than once at different stages, assessed in various ways, set practical and taxing administrative exercises, given hypothetical problems and made to report on how they would resolve them. All the modern and tested interview procedures, which this lot have never even heard about, should be pursued. I repeat, it's being rushed. Disgracefully rushed.'

'Dr Zing, if we did all those things, and grilled the candidates for a week in a dark room and assessed all they'd done since the day they were born, would it make a scrap of difference? Would it improve the response we've had? What more would we learn? Wouldn't we still have to choose one person from this same shortlist? And, as we know already who that person's likely to be, wouldn't the whole thing be a needless, stressful and expensive nonsense?'

Zing shrugged his shoulders and said nothing.

Then, as they walked across the dimly lit car park Arthur Hull stood by the foyer doors, keys in hand, foot tapping, anxious to lock up before *The Standing Oak* closed and denied him his evening pint. The used coffee cups and few remaining biscuits could wait until morning.

Tuesday 16 April.   *HMS Pinafore*

Hetty had no difficulty getting the short list from Louie Anne Lee. Louie was certain Ingrid Eastman was passing information to her husband and, disliking them both, decided to do her share of leaking. It took little ingenuity on Hetty's part to see that Sonia Smith was firm favourite and that no sane bookie would offer odds of ten-to-one on!

Mrs Sonia Smith, Hetty discovered, was the essence of the well-in head teacher. She dressed smartly, did everything by the book, was smooth, knew the right people, attended significant courses, was seen at meaningful meetings, belonged to committees on which powerful people sat, worked teachers hard, used perks to divide and rule staff, was an inactive member of an insignificant professional association, knew the National Curriculum backwards, was prompt with test results and reports, curtsied to inspectors, flattered advisors, toyed with do-good politics, opposed gambling, abhorred tobacco, decried drink, and partook of rather than enjoyed highbrow vacations such as *A short appreciation of the early work of the Late Nineteenth Century Watercolour Artists of the Inner and Outer Hebrides* Few school leaders piled up as many Brownie points as Mrs Sonia Smith.

What might be against her were acrimonious divorces from two husbands who now lived far away. One was working in the prison service in New Zealand and the other was employed as an Afrikaans-speaking accountant in a mining company in South-West Africa. Both amassed air miles by putting distance between themselves and their ex-wife. Meanwhile, her school staff, as anxious to see her depart as others were to thwart her arrival, loathed Mrs Smith.

Hetty had then followed up several useful leads. She learned Sonia Smith had 'turned round' her school following unfavourable reports from a team of orthodox inspectors who had viewed the imaginative, arts-centred, creative, humane but statistically unquantifiable efforts of her predecessor with ill-disguised hostility. Although Mrs Smith was disliked as much by her governors as by her staff, her supposed 'saving' of the school had silenced her critics. She was safe.

*

In The University's Light Operatic Society's enthusiastic presentation of *HMS Pinafore* the striking likeness between the leading student's portrayal of W.S.Gilbert's First Lord of the Admiralty and the recently appointed Pro Vice-Chancellor was, of course, entirely co-incidental. The audience saw clear parallels between the administration of an antediluvian admiralty and a traditional university and frequented the bars before the performance, between the acts, and after the operetta ended. Although prices were high, the cash rolled in.

Terry and Susan were both on gins and tonics. Their iced drinks and a plastic bowl of peanuts were set on the low wall of a wide, seatless patio. For mid-April the night was warm.

Close to the gin drinkers, but unseen by them amid the gossiping throng, were a well-primed Captain Walter Walker-West, his quiet, less well-primed wife Winifred, and the Captain's older, austere, upright and teetotal spinster sister, Wilfreda Walker-West. The Captain's unmistakable voice carried far into the spring night. An outburst of laughter was followed by, 'Could easily be that damn school, you know, all that stuff we've seen in there! Swap a few sailors for a bunch of teachers and the dithering headmaster for the useless admiral, change a few words and some scenery and, Bob's your uncle, it's done! Damned farce the lot of it!'

He mopped his brow with an initialled, linen handkerchief before lowering his voice slightly as he said to his sober, elegantly dressed and unamused sister, 'You should just see the pathetic short list we've got for this head teacher chappie's post! Utter rabble! University researchers – one from this place – left-wingers, fellow travellers, trade unionists, amateur politicians, scribblers, wandering willies, yes-men and yes-women and God only knows what else. Useless shower!'

No one answered.

'D'you know, Wilfreda, and you, Winifred,' he said, 'I'd cancel this rotten interview parade and send the pitiful list of so-called applicants to the Ministry of Education or whatever it is they're called nowadays and say that if this is the best they can recruit they'd better get their fingers out and tell us what's gone wrong! The office-bound pen pushers earn enough!' Then, as they moved on the Captain's voice faded and Wilfreda's reply was inaudible.

Slowly the crowd thinned. Terry and Susan returned their glasses, folded their programmes, collected their coats, and made for Susan's flat. They had both enjoyed the operetta and taken heart from Wally Walker-West's remarks. If even the manly and conservative Captain was beginning to feel like that, things must be looking up.

Wednesday 17 April.   **An American Proposal**

Lena Napier read apologies from Adrian Olde, who was ill, and Ursula Irving, otherwise engaged, before the main governing body, with remarkably little dissent, ratified the short list of six. Concerns about internal promotions, CSP candidates and university researchers were quickly annulled when it was made clear that the excellent Mrs Sonia Smith was certain to be appointed. Her unblemished record and exceptional credentials satisfied everyone except Victor Sneade who claimed she was 'too good to be bloody true'. He was ignored.

One or two polite enquiries were made about Adrian Olde who, at lunchtime, had gone home unwell, and the meeting was breaking up when Mrs Sophie Johnson, a parent-governor, intervened.

Born in Austin, Texas, forty-one years ago, Sophie had two children at the school. She had been favourably impressed by what she had read of Dr Mansfield's research into alternative education and thought these governors unimaginative. She had not spoken earlier because, as a newcomer, she had not wanted to seem intrusive. Also, she guessed, the growing popularity of home-based education in the USA, if only because it was American, was unlikely to appeal to this insular group. But, to show the flag, she made a revolutionary suggestion.

'Would it help if we all met the candidates before the interviews?' she offered. 'In a sort of, well, a sort of casual, informal way?'

'Casual, informal?' queried Walker-West suspiciously.

Sophie did not make the mistake of beginning with 'In the USA we often ...' but said, cogently, 'yes, we could meet them in the evening before the interviews at a fairly free and easy social event. Nothing elaborate of course: cheese, crackers, cake, cookies, wine, fruit juice, coffee, quiet background music for an hour or so, just for a general chat.' A bored Sir Quentin Reynolds ceased his scrutiny of the library's list of recent acquisitions and said to Sophie. 'D'you know, Madam, that's the best idea I've heard all night!'

Seventy-four-year old Sir Quentin, who had been blessed with a nanny, governess, private tutor, an elite school and a leisurely three years at one of the better-known Cambridge colleges, sat on this governing body only as a penance. He felt the body was archaic in its attitudes to education and contained members he could not abide. Nevertheless he felt it his duty, as a conscientious conservative county councillor, to belong to numerous governing bodies of which this depressing example was the worst. Drawing on inherited wealth supplemented by fees as a company director on seven boards he gave freely of his time and money - particularly in supporting a charity aiding autistic children. For that work he had been knighted.

But, although a lifelong Conservative, Sir Quentin had moved to the left of his party and had almost resigned when two fellow county council members said they sympathised with many of the ideas of the ultra right-wing People's Patriotic Party and that they could well understand the support that up-and-coming party was getting. But the good knight disliked equally those vocal socialists on the council who were opposed instinctively and irresponsibly to authority of any kind at any time. The awful trade union activist Victor Sneade personified that breed. He saw Sneade as a hypocrite whose stick-in-the-mud ideas and opposition to industrial progress – or to any progress - made him one of the most reactionary people he had ever met.

'Who will pay?' Giles Townsend asked. 'How many free drinkers will turn up? Cash can't come from public funds. The press would have a field day: *School Knees-Up on the Council Tax!'*

Townsend gave strong but sly patronage to the PPP. Aged fifty-one, he was still in a middling position in his bank and unlikely to progress further. His intolerance of left-wingers and ethnic minorities was inherited from his equally intolerant: "Show the flag, send a Gunboat and Put a Shot Over the Bows" father. His intolerance had been strengthened by his belief that twice in as many years he had been bypassed for promotion because his cowardly bank bosses wished to curry Establishment favour by elevating two of its Asian employees. He thought both of those colleagues, one a woman much younger than he, had inferior career claims. His resentment had long festered.

'Will out-of-town candidates claim overnight expenses?'

The ever-observant Eastman had noted Giles Townsend's growing intolerance and had fed him, at cunningly calculated intervals, exaggerated stories of what was called positive discrimination. In his right-wing recruitment Eastman made profitable use of that controversial policy - imagined or otherwise. And he ridiculed what he saw as increasingly unpopular and discredited government support for political correctness. That philosophy could be doing its adherents more harm than good and the crafty Eastman intended to make the most of what he called "their crass short sightedness." But today, as he did occasionally, he pretended to distance himself from Townsend.

'Money spent on supermarket plonk will be chicken feed – mere peanuts - in this school's budget.'

'Do chickens eat peanuts?' queried Sneade.

'They do in this No-Man's-Land! Anything goes here!' exclaimed Walker-West. 'Pigs can fly till the cows come home if you ask me.'

No one did ask him, but Eastman repeated his support for the idea of a modest, non-flamboyant, ice-breaking social.

'So do I,' Mrs Wendy Durrell enthused. She was a good-looking, forty year old, casual member of the Tolerant Democrats, a part-time nurse, parish councillor, and, abandoned by her fly-fishing husband, the single mother of four children. 'I enjoy socials.'

'More than you do our governors' meetings,' Sneade muttered.

'And so do I,' echoed Mrs Nichola Murdoch. 'We should have more social events.' Mrs Murdoch was a receptionist in a doctors' practice – work she did for the interest, not the money. The wife of a well-heeled solicitor she was a room steward for the National Trust and an outspoken critic of teachers' claims to merit full professional status. She argued that compared with her husband's expertise, his onerous work schedule and his on-going responsibilities, teachers didn't know the meaning of competition or long hours or work-related stress.

But Sophie Johnson was delighted. Why had she hesitated? Clearly, given American help, the reticent British could be winkled out of their shells! Her grandmother had told her of how Uncle Sam had sent life-saving aid to Britain in the Second World War. Perhaps that effort could be revived tonight?

Lena Napier obtained a grudging approval for this unprecedented event. She thanked Sophie and added that she would like the teaching staff and older sixth-formers to be invited. While she sensed further misgivings at that, none was voiced. She got agreement that, subject to Mr Olde's concurrence, candidates would meet teachers and children during the afternoon prior to the social, and that that would be from 7.30 pm to 10 pm on Monday 29 April, in the school hall. Moderate amounts of reasonably priced wine would be served, responsibly of course, and Mr Hull would be in charge of decorations.

Thursday 18 April.   **The Nomination**

As Adrian Olde did not return to school Lena Napier decided, with deputy head Ursula Irving's none-too-enthusiastic support, to go ahead with the social without his by your leave and to include invitations with the letters being sent to the six short listed candidates.

With remarkable accord the two women worked out the programme and, following a courtesy call to Mr. Olde, copies were despatched by that observant couple, Mrs Ingrid Eastman and Miss Louie Anne Lee.

On the Monday candidates would sit with children and enjoy a school lunch, in the afternoon go with carefully selected teachers and classes to sit in on and take part in lessons and then meet for a staff room discussion over tea. Later there would be the social.

On the Tuesday candidates would be invited to school assembly and then split into two groups for formal tours of the school. Individual question-answering meetings with Lena Napier would follow mid-morning coffee in the staff room. Sherry with governors in the library would precede lunch in the school's domestic science wing. The six formal interviews, in the library, would run from 1.30 to 4.30.

All governors were sent details of a pre-interview meeting of the selection panel at 11.30 and of the full governing body *at 4.45 prompt* to approve, formally, the panel's choice of the new head teacher. There would then be time for the successful candidate to notify his or her current employer of his or her proposed resignation.

While Louie Anne Lee had little interest in these technicalities she wondered whether the whole of the auxiliary staff would receive an invitation to the social or whether Ingrid Eastman would be their sole representative. Louie Anne would love to see what her floozy boss would wear and whom she would chat up.

Ursula handed Terry his invitation and waved off his suggestion that

147

he was a mere makeweight. But, then, when he learned of the other candidates, he pretended, with a derisory laugh, to return it.

'Sonia Smith! That woman! Then I can forget it! It's cut and dried, Ursula. I'm only along for the ride!'

'Then *enjoy* the ride!' hissed Ursula, 'every damned minute of it!'

*

News of Terry's nomination as a general election candidate hit the staff room after school when Hull, as considerate as ever, left there *The Evening Messenger's* early edition. Its front-page headline read: "Local Teacher To Stand!" Hull, carefully wiping already wiped cupboards, loitered as the tired teachers trooped in.

Terry encountered congratulations, questions, disbelief, subservient bows, curtsies, salutes, touching of hats and several offers of a chair. He had requests for his autograph and for invitations to take Tea on The Terrace followed by Tours of the House, and permits for the Public Gallery at Prime Minister's Question Time.

Terry made light of it. This would be nothing to what he'd endure in the coming weeks: hecklers, smart Alecs, micky-takers, drunks, fools, bigots, perverts, anarchists, crackpots, the whole sorry bunch. Hull finished his cleaning, smiled, and moved on.

Terry disliked the photograph Hetty Hopkins had used and also her secondary headline, "Candid Candidate Calls for Common Sense." In one piece she had linked his Common Sense Party to what she had found out, none too accurately, of his calls for the reform of state schooling. But there was no mention of Susan Mansfield.

'Give over Mate! Not *more* school reforms! We've had one blasted reform after another,' an exasperated teacher cried. 'We've had a bellyful of reforms! Stuff your reforms where it hurts!'

'We've had no reforms that have changed the system,' retorted Terry Park. 'Yes, the changes we've had have been uncomfortable, frustrating and time-consuming, but they've been cosmetic and designed to get you so sick of so-called reform you that don't want any more. Wake up! Stand outside these school walls for once and see what's going on! Take in the big picture! Look at the whole city, county and country. The Establishment's taking you to the cleaners!'

The "bellyful" man shook his head vehemently; others drifted away not wanting to get involved in after-school arguments. Their stress-related exhaustion, as Terry well knew, helped to keep them to heel, all the spunk knocked out of them.

Terry read that the editor was making a page available daily for readers' letters on the election, and he could imagine what he would experience once Hetty linked him to Susan Mansfield and what would be described as her "Close-Our-Schools!" research. That brought him back to the head teacher post and how his application for that was likely to be received. His doubts grew about the wisdom of taking on both ventures at the same time. He must be out of his mind!

He winced when a departing maths teacher threw him an apparently casual remark, 'Watch it Terry, old bean, or you'll get two lots of the strong stuff dropped from on high: one from the governors and one from the politicians!' He smiled genially as he headed for home.

After more questioning from a few mildly interested staff Terry was exhausted. He refused Collins' phoned offer of a pint to talk things over but did listen to his diatribe about the electoral system.

'We need a benevolent dictator to push us into the next millennium, and your CSP crowd won't do that! It's too bloody respectable to get us anywhere useful in a hundred bloody years!'

But Susan's call thirty minutes later was encouraging. She told him his nomination was in order, that she had obtained two reasonable printing estimates, recruited eager helpers from among her students, finished a draft of the electoral address, gratefully taken office space and the use of a phone in a friend's centrally situated apartment, and received offers of donations from three colleagues.

'And remember what we agreed: you don't spend time preparing for the head teacher's job – nor do I. We'll manage that blindfolded. But we work like hell on the election. That's where the real rewards lie! So it's the general election we're going for, *both* of us!'

Friday 19 April.   **Chewing the Fat**

Olde, looking worse than ever, called a staff meeting to confirm what teachers already knew - his decision to retire - and to describe arrangements made for his replacement He gave the interview date and said short-listed candidates had been invited to a social at which teaching staff and Mrs Eastman would be most welcome.

Asked about candidates, Olde gave six thumbnail sketches. There was little reaction until he came to Sonia Smith when groans abounded. These, anticipated by Olde, were ignored.

He felt sure everyone would agree to Mr Park being relieved of his duties for the Monday and Tuesday of the interview week and that Mrs Irving should re-allocate his work.

Knowing Terry had several difficult classes, Mrs Graham asked if the English department would be involved in the reallocation. Most teachers realised she was afraid of being given an unruly class to cover and were unsympathetic. Olde said Mrs Irving would decide.

But her intervention prompted another from Daffyd Hughes.

'Has a decision been reached on the excluded girl?'

Interest rose.

'Not long-term, but she will not be returning immediately.'

'Will she be returning at all?' pressed Hughes.

Olde hesitated. 'The Local Authority is considering its options.'

'Such as?' asked Mrs Tipping.

'There are several. However I can say she will not be rejoining us this term. Further home-tuition is favoured.'

Olde sounded evasive. He had heard rumours that one day schools might be made wholly responsible for the long-term education of their excluded pupils. He hoped that day was at least three months away.

'But wouldn't it be better if she left school altogether?' asked Sarah Graham. 'She doesn't want to be in school and she's old enough to do a job. When my grandmother was fourteen she was already in work.'

'You know that, legally, that's out of the question,' stated Olde.

'There's too much that's "out of the question" in every walk of life,' pronounced Hughes. 'We should *question* what's out of the question!'

'She will be provided for without our staff being involved,' Olde said in little more than a whisper, disregarding Hughes. 'After all, that's what you wanted – the girl out.' His tired eyes turned to Terry.

'All right,' Terry said, shrugging his shoulders. 'All right.' He was conscious of the relief felt by his colleagues. 'That must suffice for now.' But he was aware of Olde's unease. Was he hiding something?

'And maybe,' Mrs Tipping suggested, 'at their interviews the six candidates could be asked how they would deal with this awful girl? Give them a pertinent and practical problem?'

'Sort the lions from the lambs?' laughed Hughes.

But he got no response. Attention was focussed on Olde. Although he gave what nearby staff thought was a faint smile, it was clear he felt wretched at what he viewed as his personal failure. 'Perhaps, but that is for others to decide,' was all he said.

Everyone seemed satisfied with the outcome except Ursula Irving. She knew that, deliberately or not, Olde was passing the problem to his successor and that his successor, being new to the school, would pass it on to her. That was no joke. The girl was being catered for outside school only until the end of this term and after that she had another two years of compulsory "education".

'If I could mention something else,' said Terry, glad to be changing the subject, 'you will remember I proposed a school mock election to coincide with the general election? We've always done that before and aroused interest, but in view of my own candidature for ...'

Olde cut in: '... you would not wish that to continue?'

'Precisely.'

'I would have been unhappy with the disruption anyway.' Olde paused. 'But I'm sure we all wish Mr Park well in both his ventures?'

The applause was more heartfelt than Terry expected.

'But should Terry get the headship *and* be voted into Parliament, we might need yet another head teacher!' smirked Hughes.

'Or he might manage both jobs at the same time?' queried another. 'A job-share? Shouldn't be too difficult?'

There was laughter and the banging of a spoon on a cracked saucer.

Olde coloured, and saw Ursula was losing patience.

'We'll cross that bridge if and when we get to it,' he said.

Even so, more than one teacher noticed that as he rose to leave Olde was in slightly better spirits than when the meeting began.

'He's on his way out,' Jenny Jean Jones murmured to a neighbour, 'I've only just started!'

*

'In your classroom,' said Dafydd Hughes to Terry at lunchtime, 'and you, Sheila, bring your sandwiches. Terry can boil his kettle.'

'This woman Smith isn't our only worry,' said Hughes as they settled down. 'What do you know about Paul Carter?'

'Only that he's head of science at Top Road Comprehensive.'

Top Road was the shining, inspector-favoured show school in North Mansworth to which all the county's important visitors were directed.

'He's a creep,' said Sheila. 'I've met him on courses. Ugh!'

'He's the creepiest creep that ever crept,' echoed Hughes. 'I'd rather have Sonia Smith any day or night, and no wisecracks!'

'We don't need "creep" three times. We know creeps creep.'

'Well, he's just the crappy creep they'd choose to creep round here.'

'It's him or Smith,' agreed Terry. 'God save us either way!'

Hughes had prised details of the six candidates from Louie Anne Lee who still made little secret of her fondness for him while Hughes, with eyes elsewhere, shamelessly used Louie Anne as an informer. He himself had checked on the two other candidates who, as well as Terry, were local teachers, but about the other outsider, a science master called Kurt Rommal, he had learned nothing.

'I know a bloke in Paul Carter's school,' Hughes said, 'and he filled me in. He says Carter's the ultimate "Yes Man" and useless with it. He's unpopular, got no ability, no ideas, no charisma, no conscience, always agrees with the bosses: "Sir, do please, let me lick your ..."'

'Congratulations!' said Sheila.

'What for?'

'Not one 'S' word!'

'This is not a sodding joke, Sheila!'

Terry laughed.

'And you needn't laugh, Pal. You've not got the slightest chance of getting the headship or of getting into Parliament. You're stuck here.'

'But I would vote for Terry Park on both counts,' said Sheila.

'You won't get the chance,' said Hughes. 'So it's possible we'll be stuck with Carter. And do you know he's a blackleg?'

'He is?'

'Thought that would wake you! Don't you remember the protest over class sizes at Top Road? The TFRA brought members out for just one afternoon? Well, Carter took the classes due to be taught by the strikers and the thick-skinned sod sneered when he was called a scab!'

Terry remembered the blacklegging and knew the authority had been shocked at the calling of only a token strike at their exhibition school, but he did not realise that the short-listed Carter was one of the blacklegs. He would check on that.

'And there's more than one governor here who'd soon vote for a blackleg,' he mused. 'How about Walker-West and Eastman?'

They agreed, ate, drank and were quiet.

'There's something else,' said Hughes eventually, 'Jenny Jones might have moved on come September. Another good one lost.'

'Why d'you think that?'

'Sheila dear, Dafydd is her confidant,' explained Terry. 'No secrets between that happy couple! I'm surprised he didn't invite her here.'

Sheila ignored that. 'She seems well settled to me.'

'*Seems* is the right word,' said Hughes. 'She puts on a brave face but she's struggling with some groups. Terry should know.'

'It's mainly the potty inspection that worries her,' said Terry. She wonders how she'll do and won't believe she's OK. She has no *real* trouble with her classes, she puts a lot into her preparation, and she's never talked to me about leaving.'

'She wouldn't, would she?' murmured Sheila.

'Usual story,' said Hughes with a shrug. 'Given time she could manage the teaching, it's all the other suffocating rubbish we get.'

'So what's she going to do?' asked Sheila.

'Why not ask her?' suggested Hughes. 'Have a woman to woman chat and find out, then let us know.'

'I will,' Sheila snapped. 'I should have talked to her before.' She hesitated, 'what fools we are to put up with it! We're letting Jenny and everyone else down, especially the children. We teachers let them all down when we refuse to stand up to the politicians – national and local - and say "enough" *and mean enough*! A fight to the finish would bring chaos in weeks and a clamour for settlement. Then we could start afresh, begin to act as real professionals, and help everyone.'

'And the benefits for children, parents, teachers and the country generally would continue for a century!' finished Hughes. 'Should have been done fifty years ago!'

Terry and Sheila both nodded. Too many timid teachers had let the profession lose status year after year after year and as each year had passed the position had become more and more difficult to rectify.

'So, Carter or Smith in, and Jenny Jean Jones out? Is that how it'll be?' asked Hughes. 'Keep in the bad, chuck out the good? "*Robin Hood, Robin Hood …*"' he sang loudly. 'So that's it? Is it?'

But he got no answer. There was no answer, and they knew it. So the despairing three packed up their litter and got ready for the afternoon school's three forty-minute slices of prescribed "education" with a two-minute breather between each slice.

Ingrid Eastman noted the general gloom on the staff and passed on the news to Fergus. Dear Fergus would be so pleased! He knew the PPP prospered on the widespread gloom and frustration that arose from all this pussy-footing around. It always had, it always would!

Modern Labour's MP for Mansworth South West was Dr Audrey Amy Anderson and she hated her monthly constituents' surgeries. She even disliked 'surgery' as it recalled too readily her years as a GP. She saw her stream of disgruntled constituents as a procession of NHS patients with their complaints, self-inflicted troubles, obsessions, demands for sick notes, or benefits, or cure-alls for every petty, harmless ailment.

Rumour had it that after leaving her fee-paying high school in a calm Canterbury suburb, Audrey, the only child of GPs, had gone to medical school and not encountered representatives of the whole social spectrum until initial training in an NHS hospital. Her first post had confirmed her fears and introduced her to "irresponsible, ignorant scroungers" at one end of the social spectrum and "well-heeled self-important patients" at the other - those who thought their self-inflated standing entitled them to special treatment. She disliked both groups and realised, too late, that her temperament did not suit contemporary, state-provided medicine. She toyed with the idea of becoming a ship's doctor as one old flame had done, but was warned off by her traditionalist parents. Then politics beckoned and, while preferable to medicine, that career left much to be desired. She was unsure what she wanted to do.

Today her mood was dark. She knew the general election would raise expectations, swell the ranks of moaners, mean she would have to beef up her public smile, kiss babies, congratulate mums – married or not - sympathise with everyone and be chary of uttering statements that might be quoted against her by trouble-making constituents who had little regard for the confidentiality of her surgery. Would she have fared better in the confessional as a Catholic priest? Perhaps not.

The morning had begun badly because, before her agent had primed her for the first session, the right-wing councillor, school governor, ex-army-officer and Tory club bore, Captain Walter Walker-West, (Retired), had arrived, uninvited, with a warning of skirmishes ahead.

'Now look here,' he had started, 'I know we're in different camps, but we'll both lose the battle if this CSP upstart gets dug in. People think politicians have jettisoned common sense and lost the voters' trust and this man Park – who's popular locally, you know - will play on that, pick up votes, and begin something big. We must be …'

'I'm not sure you should be here.'

'Just listen! *Neither* of us wants that! But this man is not only a

154

candidate for Parliament – he won't get anywhere this time – but he's up for the headship of the biggest school in the constituency. If he got it and improved it – which wouldn't be difficult - and claimed to have done it with nothing more than common sense, he'd be well positioned for a future general election. Think about it! The dear old British people want common sense: we politicians don't!'

'It's certainly a different angle.'

'It's sound tactics! And you'd better strengthen the guard because some trouble-making journalist is quizzing the other ranks about the large number of ministers of education there's been since the war.'

'Secretaries of State, actually …'

'Dozens! *She's* claiming there's no common sense in that either, no continuity, and that no government regards the top education posting as important. She says it's just a bridgehead for promotion to the higher ranks. That looks bad.'

'One MP can't do much about appointing ministers.'

'But a group could if it wanted to. And one more thing, briefly - because your waiting room looks like the sick parade before a winter route march - the appointment for this headship is being scandalously rushed and that gives the same impression: that it doesn't matter, that anything will do as long as someone's backside's on the seat. When planning's rushed the campaign goes wrong, with heavy casualties!'

Dr Anderson did not thank Walker-West for his visit. Nor was she pleased four hours later when the final constituent left after a lengthy diatribe on how "they" had refused her child benefit, income support, unemployment pay, supplementary this and that, rent and council tax relief, and other sources of state-provided aid. "Mrs Jackson next door gets the bleeding lot and as 'ad for years!" she had complained.

'Ten past two, and they'll have stopped serving lunches,' Anderson snapped. 'What a rotten, rotten, rotten morning!'

Her thin, worried-looking agent readily concurred He was by nature a cheerless man who knew that no sooner was one general election out of the way than he had to prepare for the next.

His depressed MP stood by the window as she pulled on her coat. Almost opposite her was the new fish and chip shop the planning permission for which had caused endless trouble when objections had been raised by nearby residents. But after a year of pleas from others who wanted a convenient takeaway she had agreed to approach some distant ministry or other. After further aggro with rowdy meetings, round robins, petitions, E-mails, phone calls, crude threats and barely-literate letters, the scheme got the go-ahead. Now the weary woman could view the litter, gaudy 'special offer' posters, anti-social double parking and groups of Walker-West's shirkers eating their chips from greasy wrappers many of which would end up in the already filthy gutter. She could smell, if she opened her window only slightly, the fishy, chippy, fatty fumes from the "restaurant" she herself had helped establish. She remembered her mother's words of wisdom, "make sure you *really want* what you ask for *before* you ask for it!" How true!

'They'll rustle up something at the Modern Labour Social Centre,' the agent said in despair. But he knew Anderson loathed the beer-smelling, smoke-filled centre, so he tried to change the subject.

'Problems from punters?' he asked as they reached his car.

'Two women came in – separately - worried about that school.'

The agent shuddered. 'Outer Mansworth Comp?'

'Of course. They were both fluent, thoughtful mothers not hell-bent on trouble. One, worried about bullying, said her boy doesn't want to go to school – he's twelve and it's the first time she's had this problem. She even quoted cases of child suicides in different parts of the country because of bullying in schools. The second claimed her children's education is blighted by the behaviour of a few others and that staff turnover's high because teachers are so fed up. And even worse, an influential group is starting a parents' petition for Downing Street to get the school's discipline tightened and disruptive pupils expelled.'

'Holy smoke! What a time to choose! Get any names?'

'Only in confidence. They also thought that – wait for it - what was wanted was more common sense. We're getting too much of this "common sense" caper. Anyway, why d'you ask about names?'

'I just wondered,' mused the agent. 'There's a potential teacher problem at that school if one particular girl is allowed back. "When she walks in, we walk out!" You know the kind of thing - everyone passing the buck – sabre rattling. But it's probably exaggerated.'

'Exaggerated? For Heaven's sake man, there's a general election in three weeks, my majority is 222, and there are enough parent-voters in that school alone to lose me my seat! How the hell can that be exaggerated? I'll tell you one thing, that school's getting me down – and why me? There's a head teacher with his posse of sheriff's deputies, a keep-out-of-trouble chief education officer and his army of clerks, a squabbling city council, a meddlesome churchy chairwoman, a bunch of useless governors, a here-today-and-gone-tomorrow inspectorate, and a government department sitting on its rear ends calculating their pensions. Why don't *they* sort it out? Why do I get parents moaning to me?'

The agent held his tongue. 'All right,' he said after jerky stop-starts at a well-used pedestrian crossing where non-car-owning walkers slowly and deliberately exercised their legal rights. 'I'll check it out on Monday.' Then, after another delay caused by a reversing milk float, he asked: 'What did Walker-West want?'

'Education. Same school. He's brassed off with it, too.'

'He is?'

The unhappy agent swung to avoid a child on a bicycle as rain began to fall. He switched on the windscreen wipers.

'He thinks the headship job's being rushed and he's worried about the potential of this Common Sense Party and this teacher Park's double candidature. He seems to think they're linked. Are they?'

'No. Well, not yet. Nothing proven. Park won't get either job, but he could make a start promoting CSP ideas that could catch on and be dangerous in future.'

'How d'you know he won't get the headship and build on that in the next five years? He could be the crafty, calculating type who knows exactly where he's going and how to get there. Why are you so sure?'

The agent accelerated as lights turned against him.

'Because it's going to Sonia Smith, head teacher at All Saints.'

'Is it that definite?' The MP persisted with her questioning. 'And slow down! The last thing we want now is a blasted ticket.'

'Yes, I know who's on the governors' appointing panel.'

'Who?'

'Your visitor, Captain Walter Walker-West, for one. He's over the top with the right-wingers, but he's still a Tory and sees the danger of the CSP. Then there's Zoë Kennedy, she's one of us and won't want Terry Park or the CSP for the same reason. Then Giles Townsend and Fergus Eastman, both nasty pieces of work - especially Eastman – he'd raise the flag for Attila the Hun – they're neither to be trusted but they won't want Park because he's too moderate. Victor Sneade, he's Modern Labour, or makes out he is; he might have supported Park once but he's probably upset by him going for both jobs – the usual union demarcation stuff: "one man, one job – all out brothers!" Mrs Wendy Durrell, a slapdash do-gooder who doesn't attend governors' meetings; she's supposed to be a Tolerant Democrat – so she's more likely to be tempted by Park's sloppy-soft ideas though she'll probably come round to our way of thinking in her own good time. So, Mr Terence Park might, if he's lucky, get just one vote.'

'And what about Lena Napier, the Church of England do-gooder? Hardly the Tory Party at Prayer, that one? Where does she fit in?'

'She's panel chairperson, but it's not a Church of England school. She'll only use her vote if there's a tie, which there won't be. They'll play safe and go for Good Girl Sonia.'

'Good girl?'

'Yes. Always does as she's told!'

Sunday 21 April.   The Manifesto

Unknown to Dr Anderson and her agent, both Terry Park and Dr Susan Mansfield spent half of Saturday and most of Sunday drafting the CSP manifesto. They had allowed twelve hours for the work after which, to Susan's annoyance, they were to have a late evening visit from Eddie Collins. Terry had said he wanted input from Collins who was a seasoned, no-frills, no-holds-barred campaigner, and, at the same time, wanted to inform him of union developments at the school. Clearly Collins, with more than enough on his plate, had been as reluctant to accept the invitation as Susan had been to give it.

'I don't like him,' Susan said. 'He's prejudiced, aggressive and foul-mouthed. I don't know why you put up with him.'

'Because I still prefer him to the believe-in-nothing, put-up-with-anything types who can't even be bothered to turn out to vote.'

'He ruins whatever case he's got with a level of crudity that makes people shy away from him *and* his politics.'

'He's committed. He has a cause and puts the cause before anything else, even before his ordinary job – before his teaching.'

'But he still takes the teaching salary? His priorities are cause first, teaching for cash second. Believe me, people such as him don't do teachers' reputations any good. He should pack in the teaching and get a fulltime job in a trade union.'

'You're too hard,' said Terry trying to put a stack of scribbled notes in some sort of order. 'He says what he thinks – and he's cheesed off with the equivocation we get from today's politicians. Besides, he's got experience, he can help us.'

'Help us? He can't even help himself! He thinks we're back in the days of the General Strike. Hasn't it occurred to him that society's moved on since 1926? Perhaps not as much as he wants – or as we want – but it's changed, and he's not the slightest idea of how to win support in that changed society, in fact he seems hell bent on getting people's backs up. He's not supporting his cause, he's ruining it. He's getting nowhere fast.'

'He's got the Equal Shares Party.'

'Precisely: and that's getting nowhere!'

'But you say the Common Sense Party is in a ...'

'The CSP is different. The CSP is not trying to change a society that no longer exists. The CSP is up with the times and wants to add to all the changes that have been made since the nineteen twenties, then to make more changes that are sensible, realistic and extensive. Changes which, once people know about them, will have popular appeal.'

'You didn't mention minimalisation.'

'Minimalisation? Where does that come in?'

'Collins introduced it weeks ago. Said huge organisations should be drastically cut down, and gave our huge prisons as an example. But you could go beyond huge prisons and look at how banks and hospitals and universities and supermarkets have grown bigger and bigger and less and less personal. Instead of a friendly cashier whom you speak to, you stick a plastic card in a hole in the wall, read words and numbers on a screen, and press buttons. Small shops where you knew the owner and talked to him or her can't compete any more; tiny churches, schools and theatres are closed as are small garages, railway stations and hospitals. The post office shuts 'uneconomic' branches which were a lifeline for many old people and lots of others without cars. You can go on and on. We need to use the 'minimalisation' theme repeatedly and we have to thank Collins for bringing it up.'

'I agree, it's important and would have appeal, but, as I said, I don't like Mr Eddie Bloody Collins.'

Terry was quiet.

'And I wish you hadn't asked him over.'

'Well, I have. So let's make the best of it.'

'I've no choice, have I? Or, as your too-vulgar friend would say, no *bloody* choice!'

With that she managed a wan smile, made coffee, settled to work, and agreed that the manifesto was to be simple in language, brief in content, radical in ideas, practical in policies and stress the notion of minimalisation - the smaller the better. Break up the big boys!

'Next, there's absolutely no point calling for common sense if we can't put together an easily-read manifesto in no more than one folded A4 sheet,' argued Susan, 'and it will keep down costs.'

But getting all their points into only 800 words was difficult. The temptation was to include too many proposals. But there was so much they wanted to say about the way society was managed and how that could be improved that argument ensued. In working towards a draft an item was included, excluded, and included again, while something initially thought important was relegated first to the "probables" then to the "possibles" and then to the recycle bin. As the evening progressed the patience of Terry and Susan wore thin despite three sherries each.

Eventually they decided the essential points would be called *The First Ten* and appear in all publicity. They read them through together:

1. National and local referenda on such issues as crime, policing, population, immigration, town planning. **2.** A single party state for 20 years to allow time for 'getting things done - people before party'. **3.** Modernisation of the legal profession, parliament, the monarchy and other outdated or elitist institutions. **4.** Disestablishment of the Church of England and support for a secular nation offering a humanist approach combined with religious freedom. **5.** Confrontation of contentious issues such as climate change, car usage, tobacco and alcohol consumption, private medicine and education. **6.** Development of people-centred professions in law, medicine, dentistry and accountancy. **7.** Drastic simplification of social benefits, and of income, council and inheritance taxes. **8.** Higher recruitment standards to - and the social elevation of - the teaching profession with trials of alternative education systems. **9.** A five-year plan to move a reduced and modernised government to centrally situated Birmingham – to be the UK's new capital city. **10.** Financial aid to local arts, and to home-based, locally recruiting football, hockey, cricket and similar clubs to develop community loyalty through pride in the teams' successes.

Education would have priority as all the others depended on it, but not education as practised now. Details of *The First Ten* would follow.

On major national issues there would be referenda with the electorate voting from home via Internet links. All households would, with government finance, have ultra-fast broadband connections.

For at least twenty years there would be no political parties. All representatives would vote on issues free of whips and in accordance with conscience and the wellbeing of their constituents. The "cabinet" would consist of those twenty representatives who secured the largest majorities in constituency elections. The First Minister would be elected by those twenty and would allocate ministerial duties.

All national and local institutions would be modernised. Obsolete parliamentary language, procedure and ritual would be abolished and privilege in education and 'the right to govern' attitude eliminated. Parliament would sit throughout the year for an eight-hour day, five days a week for forty-eight weeks a year in modern buildings. There would be 400 representatives with 20% of these standing for election each year – thus giving continuity of government and the abolition of the five-year cycle between elections and the removal of the governing party's advantage in deciding the election date. Members would vote electronically, in secret, from their seats. Ritualistic dress, language, titles, honours – including the honours system itself - and other antiquated, alienating and socially divisive procedures would go. Members would be prohibited from taking other paid employment.

All law courts would become warm, client-friendly meeting rooms clearly supporting the taxpaying citizens who financed them, with no eighteenth century, overdressed theatricals separating artificially and by fear the legal profession from the common people it would serve. Judges would be renamed legal advisors, be locally born, periodically elected, and responsible for and required to explain the advice they offered to a jury. Judges would be made aware of, and then constantly reminded of, the wider social conditions in which they worked. There would be a National Legal Service, (NLS), with offices or "surgeries" in each town; publicly trained and sensibly salaried lawyers would offer free legal aid and, where needed, legal defence, to all.

'We could argue this item should have come sooner,' said Terry as Susan looked up from the draft. The Law is in need of urgent reform.'

'Yes, we could have stressed that the legal system as it stands now is at a similar stage to that of medicine in the 1920s. Then only the wealthy could expect to see a specialist or get expensive medical treatment no matter what their illness, others, except perhaps those who had paid weekly into a hospital insurance plan, had to check their savings – if any - before they saw a doctor or took time off work for treatment. That changed when Labour's Aneurin Bevan brought in the NHS, paid doctors a state salary and provided treatment free at the point of delivery. Few people alive now can remember what the nineteen twenties and thirties were like so we should remind them and let them see that, to all intents and purposes the Law now – which should be the people's law – is similarly available only to the wise and wealthy because charges are so high and barristers so generously paid that legal redress is often far beyond the means of Joe or Josie Bloggs.'

'There's legal aid?'

'Oh come on, Susan, don't give me that! Have you read the terms of entitlement? Citizens shouldn't have to rely on means-tested legal aid – even when they are aware of it and know how to get it.'

'All right, but detail – such as you are giving now - is best kept for meetings, for answering questions on radio or television or in letters to the press – kept as further support for what we propose.'

'OK, but we must make the parallel – clearly and often.'

'Yes, but now let's get back to the draft.'

Within the National Legal Service – the NLS - each citizen would choose the solicitor on whose client list he or she wished to be placed. Mandatory, controlled and nationally subsidised fees would be charged for standard transactions - including house lets and sales and estate management. An individual's first will would be drawn up free of charge as part of the NLS so that no citizen would die intestate. When appropriate a general solicitor would refer a client to a salaried barrister who would not charge a fee to those referred - just as a GP refers a patient to a consultant in the NHS. The days of the legal system being too fearful, elite, remote, confusing or expensive for ordinary people would vanish as the existing inefficient, complex practices were swept aside to make way for a citizen-centred structure.

All religions would be free of state connections such as government, employment, education or the law, and would not influence policy or receive state aid or tax privileges Faith schools, if sections of the public wanted them, would have to be wholly self-supporting.

'And no bishops in the Lords?' murmured Terry.

'Not on your Nelly! But come on now, let's get finished.'

Representatives in the new capital, Birmingham, free of all party pressure, would introduce necessary and often unpopular - but fully explained - policies such as clearing roads of parked vehicles and imprisoning and banning for life those convicted of dangerous driving.

Nationally run services in education, law, accountancy, medicine, dentistry, would be provided. Professionals opting out of working in state services would repay all grants and other costs received from public funds for their training - plus accrued compounded interest.

Taxation would be simplified by a shift to a higher sales tax and a set 15% income tax for all, giving savings in administration. Redundant staff would, if willing and suitable, be re-trained for socially beneficial work. Governments would be severely limited in how much they could borrow.

Use of words that feed divisions in society would be prohibited in official publications. E.g. words describing how groups are paid such as salary, stipend, fee, pay, emolument, recompense, remuneration and wage. Work would be *work* – not vocation, profession, job, calling, situation, trade, pursuit, line, occupation, career, business or situation. *Workers* would be *paid* a *wage* and the wage of all *public workers*, including top-rankers, would be made *public* so people could see whether they were getting value for their taxes and complain if they were not.

Teaching would be reformed as a tutor-based service available to families and be elevated in training, status and pay but would accept increased responsibility and be answerable to parents for work done.

The nation's capital would be centrally situated in Birmingham and take advantage of that city's centrality and excellent transport links. National institutions would be moved from London over a five-year period and the disproportionate and costly importance of London, based as it is in the South East of England, would cease. Citizens in distant parts of the UK would appreciate that other places, apart from London, mattered, and thus feel more included in the nation's affairs.

Central government grants would support the growth of pride in local achievements, especially in sport, and the absurdity of a town or city fielding a team of which no player was locally born, or even a UK citizen, would end. This would help tackle social indifference.

These proposals would cover the inner pages of the folded A4 sheet. The front would highlight the CSP logo and slogan: *There's Sense in Common Sense – Vote for Terry Park!* and introduce, in one snappy sentence, the intention to press for *minimalisation* in those spheres of life where the ordinary voter was involved. The leaflet's back page would give party membership details, an application slip, and an appeal for volunteers and funds. Copies would go to all households in the constituency by free Royal Mail delivery. 80,000 copies would be printed. A limited number of the complete and more expensive thirty-two-page manifesto would go to serious enquirers and the media.

Collins arrived early to find Terry and Susan happy with their handiwork. But he was critical of their ten points saying four would be ample. 'People don't grasp ten points as an entity, they won't see what you're offering in terms of an easily assimilated package. You'll get ten seconds of their time if you're lucky and you've to get your basic message across in that. Select four points and hammer them home emphasising the common sense aspect of each.'

To Terry's disappointment Susan took Collins' side, but on seeing Terry's reaction, held back full support.

'All right,' she said tactfully, 'let's select four and put those at the top of the list then bring in the others as and when the time is right.'

'But all ten must go into the full 32 page manifesto,' argued Terry. 'It's fatal to run a campaign on too narrow a front. Already we've eliminated other topics we thought important – so we should keep in the ten that are left. Anyway, they're all inextricably linked.'

'Then you've got problems,' said Collins cursorily.

Terry shrugged his shoulders, unwilling to yield further and Collins did not press the matter. They talked on with Collins giving frank comments. Finally they agreed on the four dominant points that would head the list and feature in all press releases:

Referenda.   Single party state.   Simplification.   Education

Collins worried Terry further by his proposal that Terry should choose one of his candidatures and abandon the other. 'There'll be real negative feeling on this,' he said. 'People know you can't do both jobs – head teacher and MP - and think you're being greedy or bigheaded or stupid, or indecisive, or all bloody four.'

'No! If I withdrew from one now it would look like weakness. And it would bring opprobrium from those who have offered help in the abandoned job - and who would feel let down.'

'Rubbish! You're too bloody sensitive! What about the monarchy?'

'What about it?'

'Is it going to stay in your new society? A hereditary monarchy in your twenty-first century nation? Hell, Terry, how do you explain the common sense in that – your fine, new representatives bowing to a monarch?'

'I'm not bringing that in. You can forget that.'

'So you'll keep a hereditary monarchy? An unelected head of state?

Keep the Keeper of the Privy Purse and kings and queens, princes and princesses, ladies of the bedchamber?' Collins' indifference had given way to open frustration. 'You'll base your bloody manifesto on *Uncle Terry's Book of Fairy Stories*? You'll cart a glass slipper round the bloody constituency to see whose fancy foot fits it and give her – or him! – top job in a gingerbread parliament? Keep tiaras, dukes, duchesses and all that kindergarten crap? You'll march up the hill and march down again with the Grand old Duke of York for the *next* fifty bloody years? Where d'you think we live, Park? In some cobwebbed museum?'

His colour rose with his anger. Susan recoiled and looked away.

'I've no option,' said Terry. 'I'm not grasping nettles for the hell of it for you or anyone else. I'm not looking for trouble.'

'*Trouble*? Sod me! Politicians worth half their money can't avoid trouble! The poor souls who propose change anywhere at any time will find trouble! And if they don't someone will find it for them. For God's sake, wake up! Wake up and see all the dead wood choking the nation!'

'I'm not asleep, Collins! You saw what happened to Anderson: she nearly got strung up. People didn't see the difference between their MP criticising the monarchy as an institution and the Queen as an individual. They said the Queen was doing well. They weren't having Anderson holding forth about her – which she wasn't doing anyway.'

'Exactly! So you say the same: *institutions* will be criticised if they don't get up to date. You know that as well as I do, so just make it clear that you're after the institutions and not the individuals in them.'

'No. It's a non-starter. The monarchy's out.'

'And about time!'

'I mean it's out of our manifesto.'

'Scared?'

'Realistic.'

Collins grimaced. 'You really disappoint me, Park. But you'll get some tricky questions on the doorstep: there are Republicans at large! Beware of Republicans, they're not all in the USA! Be ready for them and have some convincing answers – if there are any! Now, what about land?'

'Land?'

'Do the sit-tight landowners keep their thousands of bloody acres while the population soars and ordinary workers haven't got room for a dog kennel or wheely bin? You can stuff that, mate.'

'We hadn't got as far as ...'

'Go on, stick it in! Over the first ten years land will be taken into public ownership; nobody will keep more than an acre. But for just one generation – the present one – the bloody landowner can stay on his patch as long as he gives free access to it and pays the government a fair rent – but after that it belongs to the state. No handing on huge swathes of grouse-shooting moorland to sons, daughters and maiden aunts till kingdom come. Bugger that, old pal! Shove it in your manifesto; tell the people the land will belong to them, they'll love it!'

Now Terry was really worried. While he agreed with almost all Collins was saying he could not go that far in his first manifesto.

'Perhaps later, in another election,' he murmured.

'How much later? 2084?'

'Maybe.'

Susan was uncertain. Collins confused her. They had done well until he arrived, but, she admitted, he was making relevant points. Even so, surely he could see that many of his suggested additions would get their CSP labelled a Born-Again Communist Party or a shady bunch of fellow travellers? Also, she thought, Collins made Terry seem wavering, weak, unsure of himself. Collins seemed to undermine him.

As if reading her mind, Collins said, 'And you mustn't appear nervous even if you've got the shits. Get that sorted out fast. Have at least one well-advertised public meeting. Don't be afraid of showing your face. Let them fire their bloody questions. Few will turn up, but that's their fault, you'll show you're available and not scared. Use a school hall – it'll be cheaper. Hire a colourful van with a loudspeaker – I'll drive you round. Get well in with someone on the *Messenger*. Make sure a reporter *and* a photographer go with you canvassing. Get it all in the news. Remember those four words: '*Vote for Terry Park*!' They've got to be heard and seen everywhere, and you can get them everywhere *and for free* if you're crafty and shameless enough!'

'I'm not sure about that' said Terry miserably. 'How many people know who I am – or care? It's the common sense angle we've got to stress, not my name. It's the *common sense* people want.'

'Nonsense! You're well known round here – or damn soon will be,' Collins chortled. 'Develop a high opinion of yourself. Don't belittle what you've done – you'll never make a politician if you do that! You've got to be a real big head and develop a bloody thick skin; be dropped in the shit and come up smiling. Right, Susan?'

Susan nodded forlornly.

'But use them both,' Collins pressed, use "Vote for Terry Park" *and*

"Vote for Common Sense." Make the buggers see they won't get one without the other. Happier with that?'

'Probably.'

'Good.' Collins grinned broadly and then looked round to make sure Susan had left the room to make tea.

'How about that Hopkins bint? You know her? She was at your school. Chat her up. She knows her way around, and she'd be worth having, too, but,' and he grinned again, 'watch out for her boyfriend!'

As Susan returned Collins looked at the camera-ready artwork strewn across the coffee table. 'What the hell's all that? Is that the best you can do? It's from the bloody Ark! And for God's sake, man, use a recent mug shot of your keen, confident, smiling self. Include photos of relieved constituents shaking hands with the candidate who's got the answers to all their problems – generate cheerfulness! Oh, come on, anything's better than those passport efforts.' He grimaced as he pointed to Terry's lifeless eyes looking straight ahead in photo-booth style. 'You can't use those! You really can't! You've got to be a tough, lively, sexy, man. Those could come from the 1944 election.'

'*Forty-five*,' Susan corrected, '1945, the year of the landslide Labour Victory. *1944* was the Butler Education Act – so called.'

'OK, 1945, when Churchill, the invincible war hero, was chucked out within weeks of victory!' retorted Collins. 'That shows what can happen in politics! Nothing's impossible. Nothing's certain! Nothing!'

'Thank you,' Susan said petulantly, 'but Anderson's not Churchill, Terry's not Attlee, and this is not 1945.'

'And another thing,' Collins continued ignoring her, 'going back to 1945, stress the wasted time that's elapsed. Stress that in fifty bloody years six hundred well-paid, supposedly intelligent MPs in a dozen ritual-riddled parliaments have been unable to come up with a simple, straightforward, cost-effective system of benefits, taxation, savings and pensions that the ordinary people can get to grips with. That's inexcusable failure. If people can't understand where their money's going and what it's being used for they get bloody resentful. They know that the more complicated the tax and benefits systems are, the more likelihood there is of mistakes being made and lucrative loopholes found. *Stress that!* Say that either the politicians are incapable fools – in which case they should make way for people who *are* capable – or they shun simplicity because so much money is made from their complicated set ups by accountants, lawyers, advisers, tax inspectors and other non-productive hangers-on. Emphasise the number of lawyers sitting in the Commons; rub that in. Put it in your manifesto. Voters will buy that in their thousands! They're aching, mate, *aching* for politicians they can trust, who speak their language, who live near where they live and who live as they live. They're longing for legislation that's simple and fair, for governments that are open and do what they promise when they bloody well promise it. Lay it on, man, lay it on thick and fast with a bloody great trowel!'

'Collins, *please*! We're not assaulting the whole establishment. That won't get us anywhere. Plans for change and progress have to be subtle.' But now Terry sounded jaded. 'We need to go carefully.'

'Bollocks! Sheer bloody useless crap! You've got to go all out. Politicians stick together to protect their tribal interests. You can never pick them off one by one, the rest rush in to protect the ones attacked.'

'Maybe, but I'd much rather concentrate on education,' said Terry, 'I'd rather make a start with that and stick to what I know something about, emphasise that since 1945 we've been moving in the wrong direction - away from small schools to bigger and bigger ones to the detriment of the child-parent-teacher relationship, and away from individuality at a time when, with the instability of families, it is reliable, long term, caring relationships that many children need above all else. Grades in silly tests are unimportant compared with love and affection, but you wouldn't think so looking at education today.'

'And their parents need ongoing help,' added Susan, 'and the way society's moving they'll need more and more help every year.'

'But you won't win elections on education. It's only one issue and not a top-ranker at that.'

'But it is! Seen alongside family help and care it's the vital issue,' insisted Terry. 'It supports all the others and it's Britain's last hope. This may sound corny, but education - and not the existing "schools type" education mind you - has to become the bedrock of society.'

Susan, agitated, shuffled papers, but, instead of supporting Terry, she turned towards Collins. 'Eddie Collins, I'm sure you mean well, and in much of what you say, you're right. After fifty years of two-party government most elements of life are less easy for ordinary people to comprehend than they've ever been, and disillusionment is rife.' She shrugged her shoulders. 'That said, you've more or less written off our two days' work. I agree we need to get to grips with the issues you raise, they're vital, but now we're both tired and we should have another go tomorrow, when we're fresh.'

Terry, also, suspected Collins was right, but he could see Susan had had enough, that she had been upset, and that upset him. He was not surprised when little of value emerged from the rest of the evening.

As Collins gave Terry a lift home he was unapologetic. 'What you've got is OK mate,' he conceded, 'but it has to be cut, to be made simple, unambiguous, given colour: it needs to vibrate! *'Vote for Terry Park!'* Plaster the bloody place with it, and with your *'Vote for Common Sense'* - use them both. People know you and like you, and they'll go for your common sense angle. That's what they'll go for: *you* and *it.*'

'You upset Susan.'

'Rubbish'.

'I say you did.'

'No, she just doesn't like me!' He paused at ill-lit road works. 'And she's not your sort either! She's not the warm, cuddly piece you need. She's a blue stocking! So what the hell are you playing at?'

'I'm not playing at anything,' snapped Terry. 'I'm trying to run for parliament and she's helping. And I'm not looking for a woman.' He paused. 'Not in that way.'

'Thank God for that! No hanky-panky in the press!'

'You suggested Hetty Hopkins.'

'Idiot! She *is* the press! She won't write anything against herself!' He hooted at an indecisive tabby cat. 'Anyway, when you do feel the jolly old urge, phone me. I've a few domestic types you can snuggle up to who'll keep their mouths shut if nothing else! No ice-cold, thesis-writing, university go-getters; just a bit of down-to-earth bed and board!' He laughed loudly as he stopped at Terry's house. 'Come on, old man, get your leg over! You don't have to be a married man to get a bit of the good old "How's your father!" And it would do you good, sort you out, get your priorities right!'

'Thanks. I was going to say, "thanks for nothing," but that would be unfair. Your political advice was valuable, even if it was over the top. But I don't want your bedding tips.'

'OK,' Eddie Collins chortled, 'and just think, Terry old boy, we didn't even start on the shambles at your school!'

'Not now,' groaned Terry. 'Have *some* common sense!'

'Point to you, mate! That'll keep. So keep your pecker up and *nothing else* until you're farting with the rest of the rake-it-in windbags on the back bloody benches!'

Week Four

The Silver Spoon

Giles Townsend was worried. Too often, he thought, he had sounded off at times when significant people were listening. He had become so incensed at what he saw as preferential treatment given to ethnic minority staff at the bank where he worked that, after a few drinks, he would voice his feelings stridently. At the long bar of the exclusive Mansworth South-West Gentlemen's Club he had been heartened to find recognisable, if quiet, support. But, alongside that, more than one member saw that when drink held sway Giles Townsend's discretion departed. To the Club Committee that was unacceptable.

'We no longer have free speech,' a well-oiled Giles had proclaimed in the crowded Club one Friday night. 'Our own politicians make laws to gag us! Whose side are they on? Go on, tell me that! Whose side are the publicly paid bastards on? All they answer to is the Race Relations Board, and the Equal Opportunities Board and the Equal Something Else Board, and they dreamed them up in the first place! Who's behind that leftist crowd in the media? Who controls it? I'll tell you, out-and-out Commies and their followers – crafty, bearded, longhaired do-gooders! And we pay for it. We pay to be shut up and then have to put up with the crap they churn out. We're bonkers!'

Some nodded and made sympathetic noises; they wanted to hear more. A few egged him on, just for the hell of it.

'Well said!' called one. 'You tell 'em, Giles. Sort the buggers out!'

'Nor do we get fair play. Too much goes to new arrivals – millions of pounds. They swarm in. But the overpaid politicians and liberal holy men and pontificating judges make sure they don't live anywhere near them! They'd soon change their tune if they did. "Not in my backyard," they'd shout: "not likely!" And where does this new bunch come in – this Common Sense Party lot? What would they do about it? Nothing! Have you read their manifesto? Damn short on the Common Market and the EU and crime and immigration and asylum seekers and what it means to be British. Same as all the other kid-glovers!'

'Perhaps we need extra workers,' murmured a usually self-effacing man thoughtfully as he sipped his lime-flavoured tonic water.

'Do we hell! We've over a million of our own unemployed – all paid to do sod all! Put *them* in the streets to clear the litter and stick *them* in the fields to pick the strawberries before you tell me we need more workers flooding in from God knows where!' He took another drink.

The self-effacing man blushed and wished he had not ventured an opinion. But Townsend felt better after letting off steam. 'My great-grandfather and grandfather fought for Britain in two world wars!' he claimed. 'And look at Britain now! What the hell did they fight for?'

He glared round. 'They fought because they were British and proud of it and they saw Britain was in danger. But today? Many people don't even know what it is to be British! They've had all their Britishness knocked out of them by traitorous lefties who shelter under the umbrella of political correctness and kneel before that faceless, overpaid, expense claiming bunch in Brussels. You wouldn't get me fighting. You can forget that! You can stuff that, mate! I'd go to prison first.'

'Well, he's safe on that one,' whispered one member, 'he knows he'd never be called up at his age: the silly sod must be fifty at least.'

'Millions thought they were fighting for freedom – including freedom of speech!' Giles continued, 'so what was all that about?'

He chose not to hear a quietly spoken man at the far end of the bar who tried to remind him that grandfathers and great-grandfathers of many of his despised 'new arrivals' had fought on Britain's side and taken hurt. Nor had he noticed two worried club committee members in serious conversation as they looked in his direction. They were getting too much of this from Townsend; the man got more bigoted by the day. But Fergus Eastman had noticed and cashed in slyly.

'I'll get you another pint,' he said after a long outburst about what the infuriated Giles had called "the drunken, gun-touting, knife-wielding, foul-mouthed yobos who rule Britain's city centres every night."

'I like what you say. Not many have the guts to speak up. They're scared or don't want to get involved! They shut up and leave it to someone else, anything for a quiet life. They see what happened to Powell and say it's useless to protest, the Establishment always wins.'

'Enoch Powell was brilliant,' said Giles. 'Should have been prime minister. He'd got British guts. One of the few in the whole decrepit lot. People trusted him – he was open and honest. But the scared bastards chucked him out! They weren't having him! Not him! Not good old Enoch! They'd have anybody, *anybody* but Enoch Powell!'

'Millions would have been happy to have had him as leader,' agreed

Fergus, handing over another pint. 'Thousands marched for Powell. And he had so many sacks of supporting letters the Royal Mail was swamped. We wouldn't be where we are today if we'd listened to The Gallant Right Honourable Enoch Powell, M.P. for Wolverhampton.'

Giles drank deeply and nodded, glad to have found a supporter.

'But something else to stress is the incompetence, shortsightedness and downright deceit of many politicians. They allowed millions into the UK and then became frightened at the implications of what they'd done when it was too late to do anything about it, so they made a virtue of necessity and told us a multi-cultural society was good for us and good for Britain and branded all who opposed it as reactionary or racist or fascist or all three. We must never let them get away with that!'

A few more meetings, a few more drinks, a few more stories, a few more outbursts, and a managerial final warning not to air his extreme political views so loudly or so often were enough to ease Townsend out of the Gentlemen's Club and, later, into the People's Patriotic Party. He had needed little bait and had hardly wriggled on Eastman's waiting line before being landed securely. He had donated a hefty initial sum to the PPP and then, annually, paid twice the usual subscription.

*

Now, years on, in the lounge bar of the upmarket *Silver Spoon Hotel* in Central Mansworth, Giles was less certain. He did not like the increasingly extreme policies of the People's Patriotic Party and he disliked intensely one of its leaders. Also, not being a man of limitless stamina, he began to wonder what would happen if the PPP became aggressive, violent and in constant conflict with the law. Where would the PPP be then? Where would *he* be then? And his wife? By that time he would not be angry with others getting promotion in the bank, he would be wondering whether he would keep the job he had already. Eastman was right: the Establishment always wins!

Eastman had invited Townsend to *The Silver Spoon* to meet two PPP leaders, but the austere couple, Jack and Gillian Cromford-White, both in their forties, had barely spoken since being introduced. They had left the provision of drinks and preliminary chat to Eastman. He had told Townsend that the pair ran a state-of-the-art printing business and that Jack, a tall, exceptionally thin man, also did part-time lecturing in a large technical college where a senior member of staff had strong PPP sympathies. Between them Cromford-White and his wife commissioned, edited, published, printed and distributed clever and deliberately restrained People's Patriotic Party pamphlets.

'Have these,' Jack Cromford-White had said handing over five eye-catching booklets. 'They'll give you an idea of what we do.'

They did indeed give an idea of what the couple did. They were from a low-priced but well-printed and colourful series: *Nationality Matters; Time to Start Counting; Britain on the Brink; How Long Will the Bomb Tick?* and *What About the Englishman?*

With trepidation Giles took them, murmuring thanks.

'We're working on a new title and wondered if you'd help?' Gillian Cromford-White, much more comfortably built than scrawny Jack, was expensively dressed, expertly coiffured, skilfully made-up and wore costly bi-focal glasses. The four rings on her left hand and the one on her right, her richly jewelled ear rings, fine necklace and bracelet, displayed wealth of an order Giles Townsend saw only on his bank's more prosperous clients. His apprehension grew by the minute.

Gillian handed Townsend the rough draft of a proposed new cover: "*So What's Happened to British Common Sense?*" Notes had been pencilled on the reverse side with some words highlighted in blue.

'There's a new party, founded by a group in this constituency,' she said. 'It has a candidate who's likely to stand at the general election, a secondary school teacher.'

'Park,' said her husband. 'Terence Park.' His thin pale face was as hard and ruthless-looking as any Townsend had seen in Cold War spy movies. 'About forty? Bit of a mixed-up left-winger? Fragmented but ambitious? You've met him?'

'Yes.'

'And spoken to him, often?'

'Occasionally.'

'You're a governor at his school?'

'As is Eastman, here,' murmured Giles nervously.

'We'd like to know what *you* think. *We* think he might be a bit of a problem. Someone to watch? To shadow? Same with his new party?'

Giles shivered. Where was this leading?

'Just take your time, Giles.' said Eastman consolingly. He had noted Townsend's apprehension. 'Any snippets will help. All in confidence, of course - no leaks here!' He tried to smile encouragingly but the Cromford-Whites didn't bother with reassurances.

Wretchedly Giles spoke about Park, separating fact from hearsay.

'Short-listed for a headship? Big school in a comfortable suburb?' Gillian's cold blue eyes narrowed, never losing contact with Giles'.

Increasingly nervous, Townsend described the school, its catchment area, and its problems. He told them of the short-listed candidates, of the discussions before the final selection was made, and of Terry's good standing as a teacher in Outer Mansworth and in previous jobs.

'Knows what he's doing, then? Smart chap?'

'Yes.'

'Not been eased out of anywhere?'

'No.'

'What's his degree?'

'Sociology, B.A. from London University.'

'London School of Economics? That place?'

'I don't think so.'

'Honours?'

'He got a First.'

'Did he? It hasn't got him far?'

'I don't think his face fits.'

'Good. And he's worked abroad we're told?'

'Yes.'

'For how long?'

'Several years – three or four, I think.'

'Doing what?'

'Lecturing. Teacher training. Wrote bits for newspapers.'

'Where?' asked Cromford-White.

'In Africa.'

'Can't you be more precise?'

'I'm not sure where. South Africa, I think.'

'You think?'

'Yes, it was. I'm pretty sure it was. Yes, South Africa.'

'During apartheid or after?'

'I'm not certain of that either. But probably during.'

'Can you find out?

'Maybe.'

Townsend looked at Fergus but Fergus Eastman looked away.

'Does he talk about it? Crow about how the blacks won?'

'Not that I'm aware of.'

'Glorify Mandela?'

'Don't think so.'

'Does he go back there?'

'No,' smirked Fergus. 'Not on a teacher's pay!'

'Money problems? Creditors after him? Bailiffs calling?'

'I didn't mean …'

'Never mind. We can enquire,' resumed Gillian with a smile that did nothing to calm Townsend's nerves. 'You work in a bank?'

'Yes.'

'Foreign section? Currency exchange?'

'Some of the time, but…'

'Does Park bank with you?'

'Yes, but I can't …'

'Changes money? US dollars, Euros, Swiss francs, Roubles?'

'Don't think so.'

'Find out, could be useful. What else? Married?'

'Divorced.'

'Any children? Access? Maintenance orders? Court appearances?' Gillian tapped the table, thoughtfully. 'Barristers' fees?'

'No. No fees. No children. Nothing like that.'

'Why was he divorced?'

'I don't know.'

'Another woman? Several women?'

'I haven't heard. I really don't know. I'm …'

'How about current girlfriends?'

'I'm not sure …'

'Try to be sure. We need you to be sure. Has he a girlfriend at present, locally, in this city perhaps or at his school – problems there?'

'I think he has a girl friend,' said Giles miserably.

'Think so?'

'Yes, I'd say: Yes. Yes, he has.'

'Not gay, then?' muttered Cromford-White quietly and, as Giles noted, with a tinge of disappointment. 'Tell us about the woman.'

'Bright, keen, about his age - on the short list for the headship, too.'

'Is she, by God? And well in with the CSP crowd?'

' I've been told she helps them.'

'What's her job?'

'University lecturer - here in Outer Mansworth.'

'University lecturer? Sounds promising! Well, go on!'

Townsend told them, unhappily, what he could about Susan. He knew something about her main work, had read her CV, her detailed application, her clever covering letter, her testimonials and references. He told them he had met her twice, briefly, in the company of Eastman and Park. The Cromford-Whites listened intently and showed interest, but still seemed dissatisfied.

'Nothing detrimental then?' asked Cromford-White, frowning. 'No hints of trouble? No brainwashing students, leading demos, strikes, supporting sit-ins? Not blacklisted anywhere, or known to the police?'

Giles shook his head determinedly.

'No dubious publications, for instance?'

Giles paused. 'She's writing a book – on education, I think.'

They had both noticed Giles' hesitation and pressed for more.

'*Think*?'

'Yes. Based on her own research,' Giles added.

'Oh, research,' said Gillian dismissively. 'Most of them are into research. Keeps them busy.'

'She's into alternative teaching. Plans nationwide changes.'

'Such as?'

'Wants rid of schools.'

'Does she Hell! Does she! Now, that's real revolutionary stuff?'

'I doubt it. Her university seems to be backing it.'

'That means nothing,' said Eastman butting in. 'That damn place is the same as many others, a real cesspool of rebellion! Anti-everything, pro-nothing. Bringing those head-in-the-clouds, irresponsible left-wing, underworked academics to heel must be our first priority.'

But Gillian Cromford-White's glance froze him out.

'Let's keep to the point. What are her politics? Communist? Out-and-out Red? Card carrying member? Problems with entry or exit visas, teaching contracts, work permits?'

'I doubt it,' Giles mumbled, 'she lectures abroad a fair bit.'

'Where?'

'Canada, USA.'

The Cromford-Whites looked displeased.

'We've people in place,' Eastman assured them, 'but they've come up with nothing yet.'

'Keep trying. There's no shortage of money for willing talkers.'

Giles trembled.

'But, really, we've no need to worry about her: she's getting nowhere,' insisted Eastman. 'We're confident of a local head teacher, Mrs Sonia Smith. No trouble there, a real yes-woman. She's certain to get it.'

'Well she has not got it yet and we won't be happy until she has.' Cromford-White's face was intimately close to Eastman's. 'Never count your chickens before they've hatched, Mr Eastman!'

'But she's no chicken ...' said Fergus half smiling, trying to lighten the atmosphere. But his effort was wasted.

'Keep trying Mr Eastman, and you, Mr Townsend. And if you find out anything, tell us. We'll feed it to interested bodies, anonymously, slowly, like a saline drip – drip by drip by drip. We want them both kept out – and kept out for a long time - of any possible sphere of influence. Kept right out. Not even a foot in the door.'

He paused. He could see they had doubts.

'Listen, both of you,' commanded Cromford-White, 'and take this in. This Common Sense Party, if it got off the ground, could cause us problems. Such a party - so different in nature from the three all-the-same, soft, tiptoeing, stand-for-nothing neo-liberal outfits we've got now - this CSP could provide the punters with a new and popular alternative – in other words the man in the street wouldn't get so brassed off with the existing shower that he felt he had to turn to us – to the PPP – he'd realise he *could* go to the CSP instead. So,' and he spoke slowly as if explaining things to two retarded infants, 'we might lose support, votes and money. Therefore we don't want any new party to get going, especially one with the sort of common sense, common man appeal that this one might whip up. We don't want it to get off the ground. They must get nowhere in this election or the next. We want them wiped out, fast. Fifty CSP votes would be fifty too many.'

Eastman listened diligently while Townsend squirmed uneasily.

Then there was the faintest flicker of a smile on Cromford-White's face as he continued. 'Gillian and I fly all over Europe and we're both interested in aborted takeoffs, we've had some. We need data that will scupper these two and abort their crackpot schemes before they leave the runway. Getting that data is your joint assignment. Don't say there isn't any to get because they're both the type who will have something hidden away that they don't want brought into the open - most people have – especially academics, or people who write books, or who travel and lecture or who do research. So do some research yourselves. There'll be something if you dig. Just dig and keep on digging!'

'Please don't look so anxious, Mr Townsend,' said Gillian Cromford-White. 'Digging for dirt is par for the course now. Everyone's at it: politicians, journalists, financiers. So we dig as well, and we dig deeply, and we dig and dig whether we like it or not!'

There was no need for them to stay longer and they made no effort at small talk. For Giles, who in the last exchange had been ignored, there was now even more to worry about. This whole PPP business had become a recurring, threatening, and long drawn out nightmare.

The frightening pair left, making no effort to pay for their drinks.

Fergus tried to appear unperturbed. 'You did well, Giles. They don't miss much, those two!' He seemed to accept the Cromford-Whites' intimidating attitude as normal. 'And you made a good impression. They're important people in the Party – we're lucky to get them here! So drink up! And cheer up! You could see they were pleased.'

But Giles had noted no such pleasure. Nor was he pleased himself for, until recently, he had enjoyed politics and looked forward to elections, but this next one was spoiled for him already.

Not only that but he felt sure all was not right with the head teacher appointment. It was being rushed and Eastman had been too keen to get him onto the selection panel. Why was that? Then there was the short listed Park and his fancy woman Mansfield, and Park's standing for parliament. Why had the Cromford-Whites been so interested in them? It was all too much and he wanted out. He would ask to come off the governors' selection panel; at least that would be a start and a relief. Next he could become less involved with the PPP itself.

'No chance, old chap,' Fergus said as they crossed the hotel lobby. Then, lowering his voice, 'you'll stay on the selection panel whether you want to or not, we might need your vote. Haven't you grasped that yet? We have to keep the old-style "do-gooders" and the "yes-men" up there in place until *we ourselves* are ready to get rid of them. *We* decide when they go because right now they're playing our game, consolidating our position, giving us time to plan, collect and recruit.'

He said nothing more until they were in the car park. 'We must keep the softies in position and encourage them to go on showing their limitless tolerance. We must let them continue to make their sickening excuses for doing nothing. We let them stuff their nauseating liberal views and give-away-other-people's-money-policies down people's throats until even the drowsy, 'do-nothing-now', 'let's-look-the-other-way', 'let's-not-get-too-involved', 'things-aren't-that-bad', and utterly pathetic British public has had enough and rebels. Then,' becoming as excited as he ever did, 'then, at exactly the right moment, we move in and we offer just the alternative people want, *and we win!* We take over, we throw out every leftish, soft-soap piece of legislation they've ever passed and,' he gloated, 'we throw out the wimps who passed it, the cringing civil servants who implemented it, and the unaccountable media editors who broadcast it. They're for the chop! We turf out all those gutless bastards who've let our country down. They'll answer to us, every sodding one of them – and it'll be years inside for some with unremitting hard labour – rock breaking and mail bag sewing - bread and water, and no parole – not a day off the sentence for any of them!'

He virtually snapped at the remote to unlock his car. 'Then we put our rules and laws into place until they're so strong nothing can shift them. Then you'll see the Great Britain of old rising again, showing the flag, freeing herself of fifty-five years of self-righteous, smug, sanctimonious, multiracial, multicultural, multifaith, neo-communist, politically correct cant!' He straightened one of the windscreen wipers and with venom flicked off the smattering of last autumn's crinkly leaves that had fallen from an overhanging branch. 'Then *we're* in charge, my friend, *we're* in charge: *forever*! They'll never get us out! They'll do what *we* want, when we want, how we want, and they'll do it *pronto*!'

He glared ferociously at Townsend and then grasped his hand and spoke heatedly right into the abject man's face. 'And that's not impossible, Giles, never think it is! It's happened before, in other countries, in our lifetime, on a big scale and it can happen again, and it can happen here! Believe me, even the British people will tolerate only so much, and then they'll rise, chuck out the stifling softies and bring the PPP into power! There are plenty of precedents. Plenty!'

Momentarily Townsend rallied. Eastman was right! He stood quite still, eyes half-closed. While listening to Eastman he had visualised the country he longed for: proud, strong, white, middle class, property-owning, prosperous, independent, responsible, patriotic, self- sufficient, law-abiding, and, most important, governed by men who were in command and brooked no nonsense – no more permissive bullshit from simpering lefties or their union-led brothers or their born-again bishops or their answerable-to-nobody, easy-going judges. That worthless shower would stand in the dock and beg for mercy. *Real men* would be in command! *That's* what he wanted. *That's* why he'd joined the People's Patriotic Party! *That's* what he'd get!'

But would he? Would the PPP deliver? Was the sort of nation he wanted the same as the PPP's nation? His doubts returned and grew. Was he being too naïve? Was there something different and sinister ahead?

Something hidden which the PPP was not revealing to its growing number of rank and file recruits? Was there something more than just "showing the flag?" And what flag? Whose flag? To whom would it be shown? And when? And where? And why? And how long would it fly? What if someone tried to pull it down, and did?

So, thoroughly confused, he shook hands half-heartedly with a watchful Eastman before walking to his car. He was in a quandary. Parts of this country were in a real mess, no doubt about that. Over fifty years of too-tolerant democracy, petty party politics, backbiting, compromise, indecision, the acceptance of anything and everything, spineless leadership, they had all brought *Great* Britain to her knees. It was that whole complex combination and interaction of often unidentifiable factors that had been the ongoing problem - the problem that had defeated loyal citizens and driven them to a crippling indifference. It had become difficult, almost impossible, to isolate the cause, to point the finger of blame, or hold any individual or group to account for repeated, expensive, dangerous, morale-lowering failures. It had been like fighting fog in a wet, never-ending winter. That was the crux of it, nobody was responsible. Nobody took the blame. Grossly incompetent leaders were handsomely rewarded while the man in the street paid the price. Spin won the day. Powerful people, often unelected, worked craftily but effectively in the background: unknown people who were never exposed to the glare of public scrutiny. That's when frustration became unbearable and public reaction threatening. But, as he knew well, it takes a long time for a volcano to reach eruption point but boy, oh boy, when it does! He remembered Mount St Helens in Washington State. What an example that had been! And how far her ash had spread!

But the People's Patriotic Party? The PPP? Did they have spin, too? Were *they* the answer? *Were* they? Certainly they were strong, different, clear-cut, determined. Yet still he had misgivings. But, if you couldn't vote for them, who could you vote for? Who'd make a real difference? Certainly not the tried and tired politicians for whom unthinking people voted but whom thinking people shunned. Those old parties had had their time – eighty years of it – and they had wasted it and injured Britain, maybe fatally. Certainly no party had the support of a majority of the electorate because public confidence had been so dissipated. Those old parties had been reduced to spin by the bucketful: reduced to smearing and sniping at the PPP and others who were "different". Were they, deliberately and despicably, raising fears, making people feel bad about joining the PPP? What was the ordinary voter to make of it all? Who was he to be believe – *anyone*?

He sat in his weekly-polished Mondeo, thinking. It wasn't just the PPP that bothered him. Why did Park's name keep coming up? The man was only a hard-up, middle-aged, low-ranking schoolteacher, a would-be novel-writer; a crackpot CSP candidate. He was nothing! But suppose his party made inroads like the Cromford-Whites feared? Suppose it offered an appealing and different approach from the main parties? What would happen if the CSP filled the vacuum instead of the PPP? More important, what would happen to the PPP if the CSP gained credence, grew, and took over?

Is that why the CSP man had to be frustrated? Be blocked from getting even this silly little head teacher's post in some ailing, provincial comprehensive school? Is that why he, Giles Townsend, was not permitted to leave the selection panel? When put like that it began to add up, as did Fergus Eastman's threats and the Cromford-Whites' icy commands.

'So you won't be leaving us,' Fergus had said loftily. 'Once in the PPP, old boy, you never leave! Nowhere to go! People know too much about you! You're stymied. It's the same with me. So, let's both stick around and finish the job. Then we can take on anything those shortsighted creeps throw at us. We'll both be OK then. Trust me, Giles, trust me!'

Tuesday 23 April.   **The Gentlemen's Club**

For much of Monday Susan had worked on the publicity leaflet so that when, at noon, 80,000 copies were delivered, she tore open the first packet and was delighted with the results. Before long volunteer students were stuffing some leaflets, together with press releases, into envelopes. Later, with Terry, she took the remainder to the Royal Mail sorting office. Their election campaign was under way!

*

And there was activity elsewhere. Zoe Kennedy, one of the Mod Lab school governors, talked to Vic Sneade, officially of the same party, about the need to deny Park both his ambitions. 'The CSP, if it caught on, would be a threat to Modern Labour,' she claimed.

'Cool it,' ordered Sneade. 'Park's getting nowhere. Smith's getting the job, and as for the election, the clown hasn't a hope in hell!'

'But I'm not so sure about Mrs Smith.' said Kennedy, 'I hear she's an unpopular martinet. And I don't trust her supporters, especially Mr Eastman. Believe me, Mr Sneade, I don't trust Mr Eastman at all!'

*

Similar doubts were being expressed at The Gentlemen's Club. Sir Quentin Reynolds was talking, reluctantly, to Capt Walter Walker-West.

'You seem very sure of this Smith lady?' Reynolds asked.

'Sure as you can be about a woman,' gibed Walker-West. 'But she's got no competition, it's a walk over. You can bet on it.'

'I don't bet.'

'O.K. But drink up.'

'And I hear the local MP's alarmed?'

'Another damn woman – I'd be glad to see the back of her!'

Sir Quentin frowned.

'Look, Reynolds,' said Captain Walker-West impatiently, 'why are you worrying? Although the big parties are getting steamed up about this common sense brigade at least they agree to close ranks and man the barricades! They can't afford to give ground. They think the rank and file might sense there's sense in common sense and start voting for it. Where'd we be then? Up the blasted creek!'

Creek? Wasn't it the heath that was blasted? Could Walker-West's Shakespeare be so shaky, even about the warmongering Macbeth?

'Yes,' Sir Quentin murmured, 'Close ranks. Man the barricades.'

Again the barman pretended not to hear and continued to polish already-polished glasses. The retired Captain's views and his ways of expressing them were not new to him and he didn't like them, nor, he guessed, did his companion. Sir Quentin, the barman thought, was different, he was a gentleman; he was quiet, considerate, and polite to staff, unlike Walker-West. But on the other hand Walker-West's Christmas tip was not to be sneezed at. You didn't upset Walker-West and his ilk lightly. You kept your mouth shut, kept your thoughts to yourself, served him his liquor, made sure you were well-turned out for the Christmas pay parade, stood to attention, saluted, said "Thank you, Captain, Sir," and pocketed his twenty-five quid.

'Park could be damn dangerous,' continued Walker-West. 'It's not so much that he's a threat, it's his allies in reserve. I've had patrols out and I'm pretty sure that Bolshevik "Bloody Collins" – how that name suits him - is one. Both belong to some new union, the, the ...'

'Teachers For Radical Action?'

'Exactly, the name says it all. "Teachers for Radical Action" my foot! Workshy shower the lot of them!' Wally Walker-West's blood pressure rose. He emptied his glass quickly.

'Fill it up,' he said to the barman, 'and another for Sir Quentin.' He motioned to the far end of the room. 'Bring them over there.'

He had indicated seats well away from the bar. 'But,' he concluded, sitting down before Sir Quentin had reached the table, 'don't you underrate Collins. That man doesn't give twopence what people think of him or what he does, and that's dangerous – it gives him strength. Never underestimate the enemy's firepower Reynolds, never do that!'

Sir Quentin promised not to underestimate the enemy's firepower, but smiled appreciatively at the barman as he arrived with the drinks.

Behind the modern knight's amiable smile lay a growing perplexity regarding his own political leanings. Just how far to the right would Today's Tories go, and would he go with them? There had to be a limit. But if his party didn't move to the right, how many would leave it altogether and move to fringe groups like the PPP? A few? A lot?

The rise of the PPP concerned him. He had noticed how Eastman operated and how he had recruited the disaffected Townsend. How many more would he get? The PPP's assault on irresolute, politically correct, multi-cultural, multi-faith, middle of the road governments - all afraid of offending anyone about anything either at home or abroad - had won the PPP support, at first clandestinely, but, more recently, openly. Yet, if the PPP argued that this tiny island needed a population-limitation policy, a policy it promised to implement as in its manifesto – a policy that was, it claimed, "regardless of colour, race or creed" who could deny it? To the average voter it was common sense, and that, of course, drew attention to this new party, the CSP.

Reflecting further, he had to admit there was no bedrock on which Britain's multi-racial, multi-faith society had been built. The need for such a bedrock, one of overwhelming public approval, had been ignored for decades as, in cavalier style, governments had imposed that greatly altered society on the indigenous population without consultation and without permitting the electorate to vote on such a nation-changing course. The arrogant fools had tried to build the foundations of their new society on shifting sands and the PPP was ensuring, as it had every right to do, that a nervous electorate was aware of all possible implications. And they were doing that thoroughly.

Wednesday 24 April.   **Learning Through Literature**

'Sophie!' cried Wendy Durrell. 'Just the person! But don't lose your place in the queue, I'll wait over there,' and she indicated one of the several post office windows that said "*Position Closed.*" Sophie Johnson edged towards the counter with packages for the USA. She hoped this would be the slowest part of their journey.

Wendy Durrell was a Tolerant Democrat of recent and uncertain persuasion. A robust, divorced woman of forty-four, she had four school-aged children and, despite that, worked part-time as a nurse. Disappointed by Today's Tories' record on the NHS and equally upset by Mod Lab's failure to address the needs of front line workers, she had, by default, become a Tol Dem. With no great enthusiasm she worked for the party in the free time she had and was voted onto the governing body of Outer Mansworth Comprehensive School. There she had met the extrovert American to whom she had taken a liking.

'Your idea for the governors' social evening is exciting.'

'No big deal,' answered Sophie. 'But I guess it will help the governors choose. You don't get much of an idea of what a guy's like when he sits in his best pants giving prepared replies to anticipated questions.'

The two women walked out chatting. 'But the social won't affect the outcome,' said Wendy. 'It's more or less fixed for this Mrs Sonia Smith to win, but I'd like to see her and the governors get a fright.'

'It's really so wrapped up?'

'Yes. But I shall vote for Terry Park!' Wendy said determinedly. 'I like him. Do you?'

'I don't know him, but if you're asking me to use what influence I've got, I'm sorry, I can't, because I'd go for another candidate, Susan Mansfield. I don't know her, either, but I like her work, it's real fresh and sooner or later *someone's* got to decide on what replaces schools. Nothing lasts forever, so it's not "if" schools go, but "when", and at least she's pitched in with ideas. She's brave.'

They walked on. 'But it's not all that simple. It's like our general election,' said Wendy, 'it's about tactical voting. Dr. Mansfield has no chance – I won't go into the reasons.'

'I can guess,' Sophie said quietly.

'So wavering governors should push for Park. Won't you help with that? Speak to some governors before the day?'

'Sure,' Sophie said smiling as she looked at huge Mod Lab posters on a hoarding. 'D'you know, Wendy, I just love your elections, and this "general" election's real neat. And, boy, is this some marginal! But, tell me, is voting always on Thursdays?'

'Yes.'

'Isn't that a workday?'

'Yes.'

'So where do people vote?'

'In town halls, libraries, community centres, schools....'

'Do schools close? Whole schools?'

'Some do, or parts of them.'

'To set up a few poll stands?'

'Yes.'

Sophie laughed. 'That doesn't say much for the importance of education? Isn't there a lot going for Saturday or Sunday voting?'

'We always vote on Thursdays.'

'Right. You always vote on Thursdays. She paused. 'Another thing, little use is made of school premises out of school hours. They seem to be closed and not used for more time than they're open. That's not economical? Couldn't they be open to the public more?'

Wendy smiled as if those were her views precisely. 'Yes, it's a disgraceful, appallingly inefficient use of expensive capital resources,' she said. 'And Mr Park must stress the lack of common sense in that.'

'But Dr Mansfield already uses that in her work. She'd retain some of the bigger redundant schools, alter them, and use them as community resource centres and keep them going all day, every day.'

'Even Christmas Day?'

'Why not? Millions in Britain don't make a big deal of Christmas.'

'I know,' said Wendy, not wanting an argument about Christmas. 'There's sense in what Dr Mansfield writes. Sound sense.'

They parted in the market place wishing each other well. Wendy made for the bus station thinking about five meals to get ready, three bills to pay, two uncut lawns, a stack of washing, and her youngest child's dental appointment at four-thirty-five. Sophie did little housework or gardening as she hired a maid and a gardener. Today, as usual, she headed for a restaurant to meet her husband for lunch.

She hardly noticed the other pedestrians as she walked along the pavement – strange word "pavement" – but then, she thought, so was "dual carriageway" and "hard shoulder," and the whole idea of traffic "roundabouts" whose weird left-hand-drive circulatory system had taken her days of nerve-wracking practice to master.

The British are like us in so many ways, she thought, yet they have some peculiar customs that make them different. Notable had been her introduction, as a parent-governor, to British schools. She could not understand all the fuss made about school uniforms – their wearing seemed contrary to claims that British schools championed individuality and drew out differences between children so that they could have their talents discovered and promoted. So why dress them the same? Why put girls in blazers, trousers, shirts and ties? That smacked of cross-dressing! She came to a "Zebra" crossing. *Zebra*! And it had once been called a *Belisha beacon*! Gee, what gives in the country?

Safe on the other side of the street, she mused more on uniforms. No wonder some girls rebelled, like the madam causing mayhem at the moment. Why should that girl – or any other - be made to wear such unattractive, unfeminine garb? When, cautiously, she had asked an English teacher friend about this she had been told it helped poorer parents who might be cajoled into clothing their daughters in the latest fashions, or prevent the discomfort of not-so-well-dressed children, or about having a pride in their school, or simply because plain, sensible 'uniform' dress, emphasised that school was a place for work.

But although she had kept quiet, Sophie Johnson wasn't buying that. She thought the rebel student – child? – teenager? - pupil? - scholar? – should win commendation as the defiant individualist who might, when an adult, do much to drag this old country into the modern age, like the rebellious and courageous Founding Fathers had done for America. Perhaps rank and file Britons needed their own War of Independence – to gain freedom from a restrictive, tradition-bound past? They needed rebels young and old to voice outrageous ideas and jolt people into thinking afresh: rebels brave enough to put their own jobs on the line in order to broadcast anti-establishment views?

But she'd better drop that way of thinking or she'd be States-bound without the option. Nor would she share her thoughts with her husband for he had to work with a British firm whose board of directors had more than its fair share of public school members. "*Public* school for *private* school?" And "*tradition*"? Did tradition bring lucrative orders and dollars? And "*prefect*"? When she first saw that she thought it was a misprint for "perfect", but no, some British schools had prefects – a title from Roman times? And what about "*house*" and "*house colours*?" Why did a school need houses - of whatever colour? Or *house masters*? And what were "*wall games*"? It was so strange.

*

When she heard Jenny Jean Jones had signed up with Teachers for Radical Action only weeks after joining the staff, Sheila Tipping thought Terry Park or Daffyd Hughes had influenced her, but now she was not so sure. Jenny had views of her own, views which lined up well with TFRA aims. Jenny was not afraid to voice her opinions and had been a regular attendee at union meetings. Certainly the loudmouthed 'Bloody' Collins would have been no attraction whatsoever.

She noticed that at first Jenny sampled school meals at lunchtime but that practice had been short-lived. Now she brought a roll, fruit and yoghurt, which she ate either in her own form room or in the staff room. Sheila thought she would ask the girl to join her for lunch and they could have a look at the language lab at the same time. Then she would try to find out what there was about Jenny's situation that might make her contemplate leaving.

Sheila enjoyed teaching. Working alone, apart from interesting French or German assistants, she was her own mistress. She had a speciality in short supply, an adequate language lab, pupils of above-average ability, and a healthy indifference to head teachers, inspectors, administrators, advisors and other nuisances. She made use of them only when she could see benefits arising for her pupils.

Frequently she contrasted her working situation with that of her husband who had moved recently from being a dental surgeon in the NHS to one in private practice. Although he now earned more he had to be both dentist and businessman and she knew he was not happy in that dual role. Apart from the worry of maintaining a viable business, that is keeping sufficient fee-paying patients, and the extra time given to administration, he had qualms of conscience. Should he be treating only those people who could afford his fees? And to what extent did he have a debt to society for the years of expensive training he had received? How, if at all, had his move affected his professional role? The notion of "professional role", in its sociological sense, interested Sheila.

One of the few subjects to appeal to her in her one-year Post-Graduate Certificate of Education teacher-training course had been an optional unit called the Sociology of Contemporary Education. One part of this had been the professional status of teachers. Were they, her sociology tutor had asked, "professional" at all? How in their current role did teachers rank against those classed as the "real" professions? The tutor had listed factors needed to elevate "job" to "profession."

The lecturer, an earnest Welshwoman, believed teachers should appreciate their own history and their current social standing and never aim to be mere "instructors" taking orders from other people. She tried to initiate discussion in her groups but little of value was forthcoming. Some students did not regard the study of professional status as relevant to what they were setting out to do in the average school classroom. They rated their "profession" on what they had seen of their own poorly paid teachers' struggles to keep going as they faced uninterested pupils on the one hand and government interference on the other. To them the social status their lecturer was describing was pie in the sky. It was OK for doctors and others to fight to maintain authority by means of their professional standing and to keep at bay government attempts to limit their freedom to practise, but teachers had given up that struggle long ago. And it was precisely that abandonment, the tutor had stressed, that had been a tragedy for the whole of society – not just for teachers. Until that was rectified and the job of teachers was elevated and their authority restored, many of the social problems faced by the country today would not only remain unresolved, they would get worse.

Sheila agreed. She came to realise that teachers' real opportunity to improve status and salaries had been in the late 1940s, 1950s and early 1960s when an acute shortage of teachers had given them the whip hand in bargaining. But a combination of different teachers' groups fighting each other, weak leadership from some unions, and a lingering wish to remain white-collared ladies and gentlemen rather than become workers who went on strike or worked to rule, meant they had, for fifteen years, thrown away golden opportunities for the advancement of the profession. Governments and local authorities had been unable to believe their luck when they found teachers accepting derisory salary increases of as little as forty pounds a year, working meekly with oversized classes, giving unpaid lunch time supervision and, in the face of all that, being willing to put in extra hours of voluntary overtime. A relieved Establishment had more or less praised those docile unions' executive bodies that had done so much of their work for them. Such unions had kept their members in order and told them, in true Victorian workhouse style, to be grateful for the occasional pittance tossed to them by the Workhouse Master. Long term the result had been a disaster for teachers and for the nation.

To the "real" professions the weak, marginalized, divided teaching force was a frightening example of what happened if you devalued yourself, partitioned your house, succumbed to political pressure, and fell for insidious blackmail such as: "you mustn't hurt the children." Yet the irony was that teachers' work underpinned the "real" professions who now stood so far ahead of them in pay and social estimation. That was depressing, and she had seen examples of it in one staff meeting after another when crucial, professional issues had been discussed desultorily or left for another day, while less important matters had aroused feelings and dominated proceedings.

Today, Jenny Jean Jones was a case in point. She was an intelligent, conscientious, thoughtful young woman who was, after only two terms' of teaching, showing signs of disillusionment. And now there was this rumour, emanating, Sheila suspected, from Dafydd Hughes, that Jenny was thinking of quitting. She wondered if she could help.

'I like teaching,' Jenny said. 'It is, after all, what I chose to do before I left school despite dire warnings. But in this school I find there's so little freedom to do what I want to do, and what I'd do best.'

'Go on,' Sheila urged.

'Well, I realise anyone teaching today has problems with young people who've been brought up in the kind of society we live in. The role models, expectations and values that exist out there often bear little relationship to those aimed at inside a school or to the values teachers would like to promote, and I know there are many reasons for that.'

'There are.'

'So in order to do worthwhile work today a teacher needs all her professional skills, all her powers of perception, all her imagination and ingenuity, all her ability to compromise when that's needed, all her talents in diplomacy, and all her expertise in manipulating a restrictive curriculum so that, to some extent at least, she ensures it meets as many of the needs of her pupils as possible.'

'Good gracious, that's quite a speech! It really is!'

'I've rehearsed it, deliberately. I've been trying to get things clear, to explain to myself - to set out what I've been thinking.'

'And you'd like to scrap the laid-down curriculum altogether.'

'A teacher in her first year can't do that.'

'Even though she'd like to?'

'Yes.'

'But aren't you doing that with your projects on sex-related topics? I hear that's going well with some difficult groups.'

'Who told you that?'

'Terry. And Dafydd Hughes.'

'Dafydd did?'

'He did.' Sheila finished her ham sandwich, polished a green, sour-looking apple, took a bite, and waited.

'It's easier to talk to Dafydd. He's not my boss.'

'I doubt if Terry Park sees himself as your "boss".'

'No, he's kind and perceptive. And, though there is some reference to social relationships in the official syllabus, I feel he's turned a blind eye to my ongoing sex-attitudes topic so as to keep me happy and the pupils quiet, and, anyway, there's a limit as to how far I can stretch that.'

'Is there?'

'I'm sure there is.'

'Well, I'm not. At my first secondary school I taught in the English department where the teaching was done solely through the medium of literature during the children's first three years – ages eleven to fourteen. All they needed for essential language development they found in the wide range of plays, poems and novels they read, wrote, acted in, enjoyed and discussed. They read some books together in class and others, chosen by children from an extensive, well-funded school library, were read individually. There was encouragement to use public libraries and to make personal purchases. Also, each class had a case of second-hand books from which children borrowed and to which they added. But the real value was the study of human life, relationships, social values and aspirations emanating from that rich reading. Of course the approach had to be altered as the restrictions of external exams approached – GCE 'O' levels in those days – which separated language from literature and required the study of a tiny number of so-called "set" books.'

'But …'

'If you added biography and autobiography to the fiction then the whole way of life of a society was represented in the reading and could be enhanced in a sensitively-led discussion. British and foreign literature, current and past, of many genres, became not only a school curriculum in itself, but an invaluable preparation for living as adults in our society. I taught part-time in that department and enjoyed it. It was satisfying for me and, I hope, enjoyable and of value to my pupils.'

'It must have been a very progressive school.'

'I suppose it was, but you need to be careful how you use that word, "progressive" and similarly the word "traditional'. When used thoughtlessly they can get people's backs up and blinker their vision. But, returning to your own classroom work today, don't you see a link between what that school was doing with literature and what you might be doing with the study of sex?'

'Extending its range?'

'Not only that, but making use of its almost unrivalled appeal and influence. You've got the real winner of a topic there because pupils are excited not only by the physical, thrilling and enjoyable aspects of the subject, although I'm sure that draws them in initially, but by the way sex permeates practically all aspects of their lives from their birth until well into their old age.'

Jenny listened thoughtfully. 'Old age?'

'Of course. But think about it in terms of the "traditional" school syllabus. There's sexual behaviour all through literature – novels, drama, verse; in art – painting, sculpture; in history - with changing attitudes and customs; in science – in biology with the reproductive process and the technology and medicine that allows birth control, safer childbirth, healthier babies, management of sexually transmitted diseases, which then allies itself to growth in the health sciences; in economics - with teenagers and women's higher education and their paid employment, spending power, choice, clout; in demography - with population growth, decline, movement; in music - the rhythm and emotion; in the complex realm of personal relationships; in history and social studies including the suffragettes, the press for women's liberation allied to the ability to limit family size and all the opportunities that that has offered; in attitudes to abortion and sexual licence and practices, the age of consent, the status of the genders in various religions at different times; in our shifting regard for single parents, marriage, monogamy, polygamy, celibacy, illegitimacy, homosexuality, masturbation, pornography, censorship, brothels, prostitution …'

'There's a whole year's work there.'

'Far, far more! Probably three if it was worked out carefully, and that's not allowing for the input from students. They would be encouraged to see all those studies as being directly relevant to their lives and their families' lives now and in the future, and there would need to be the study of other allied topics like sexual obsessions, rape and the abuse of women. In classes or small groups there would be brain-storming, unexpected asides, case studies, family trees, personal experiences, relationships, diversions, research, new books, films, reviews, reports, multimedia sources, the Internet ...'

'But the teacher would still be the key player?'

'Yes, but not in the orthodox "teacher" or "subject teacher" sense. And therein lies obstacle number one: I fear there would be resistance to any movement away from a subject-compartmentalised school organisation because of what would be seen by many as an attack on the status of subject teachers in secondary schools - linked to public indignation that the "old" subjects of their school years were being cast aside to make way for – of all things! – pure and simple sex!'

'Quite!' Jenny smiled. 'And there'd be other obstacles?'

'Oh yes: the usual vested interests. They abound and they're strong.'

Jenny thought for a moment. Her packed lunch was uneaten.

'But there would have to be implicit trust in the teacher so that she could work this out in a way that would best help the child?'

'Precisely,' replied Sheila. 'And such trust as that, like Terry Park's common sense, is in short supply, especially, perhaps, parental trust. And that's another major problem because to have such far-reaching trust would mean that teaching would need to be a true, full profession and no government would desire that. It would mean a great decline in central control of education The bulk of politicians would never tolerate such a loss of power no matter what party was in office.'

'Except The Common Sense Party?'

Now Sheila smiled. 'I agree: I have to, because all this is, in a way, a matter of plain, down-to-earth, irrefutable common sense. There is the obligation for teachers or tutors to find out what preparation for adult life their children need to have and for them to work out ways in which that preparation can best be effected. When they have done that those same teachers must have faith in themselves and be trusted by children and parents if they are to succeed. Trust is paramount.'

'But will those teachers be trusted by politicians?'

'What do you think?'

*

Such a politician, Dr Audrey Anderson, faced none of the household chores of her single mother constituent, Wendy Durrell: a domestic servant performed them for her. But the MP had other worries which increased when she received the Common Sense Party's campaign leaflet brought in by her condescending party agent.

'Not much in that,' he had said dismissively. 'Won't get them far.'

That was not the MP's conclusion after she had read the CSP list of objectives. Nor was she happy about the lack of foresight shown by her agent. He had been an inheritance of doubtful value but was, she had soon found out, a man well in with the party chairman.

There *is* a lot of common sense in this, she thought as she read the detail, and it could have a wider appeal than this ignoramus thinks. This 'minimalisation' factor itself could bring them hundreds of votes. She recalled complaints about the new Mansworth General Hospital being too big. The times she had heard: 'We get lost in it and wander round the corridors not knowing anybody. We knew where we were in the old one.' And, further, this Common Sense Party manifesto called for reform of archaic institutions that any mildly observant person had seen as essential for over eighty years..

She sat back for a while and recalled her early months as an MP. She had been nervous, afraid of doing the wrong thing or of saying the wrong words; unsure whether she could speak to this person or that, confused by the all-pervasive traditions, the precedents and protocol, the rigmarole, the strange hours of "sittings", made aware of the strength of party pressures, flustered by bells and lobbies, daunted by all the "Sirs", "Ladies", "Right Hons", "Gallant Members", and her connection with "The Other Place" and the bishops, law lords, barons, dukes, earls and one-time socialists who resided there comfortably and turned up when they wanted to - ermine-robed or not. And where did a marchioness or knight of the perishing bath fit in? Who wore wigs, cloaks or garters or sat on woolsacks in this day and age? She'd even heard that some wretched newcomer thought "ayes to the right, noes to the left" was a description of an aging countess's crinkly features! It had taken a month to discover what "talking-out a bill" meant and how wickedly time wasting that was. And as for the old, "I spy strangers!" that said it all! The "strangers" were mostly the tax paying, common people!

And she had thought how ridiculous and childish the age-old system was, if it could be called a system, and how it had hampered her. But like a new girl on her first day in high school she had tried to make sense of it and "do the right thing at the right time and be seen doing it." She had tried to do nothing that would make her look silly, or stand out embarrassingly from the obsequious crowd of novices, or risk being deselected by her constituency party, so she had tried not to rock a boat that was a century overdue at the breaker's yard.

But years later, here in her own constituency, was a fledgling party proposing a Modern Assembly free of Lords and Commons claptrap and the stultifying atmosphere in which the ancient Houses, ruled by precedent, languidly marked time. She could just hear these would-be CSP politicians claiming that no archaic decrees should impede, even for a moment, members working earnestly for the constituents who elected and paid them. And hear CSP members saying that 'the House' should be a welcoming place free of jargon, gibberish, posturing, ridiculous garb and petty procedures, but modern in its methods, language and outlook, readily understood by the voters and supportive of the members who worked there trying to voice the concerns of their constituents.

When she first entered Parliament she had thought how laughable the hidebound set up was and wanted to rebel. But she hadn't: she had fallen into line with all the other new, self-conscious boys and girls and accepted meekly and dutifully the preposterous protocol while she sat, often bored to tears, on the hard, green backbenches – just imagine, *benches*! What a cartload of eighteenth or nineteenth century tripe she had swallowed! And still did! She felt ashamed. She should have stood up and shouted: 'This is codswallop, an insult to every member here and every voter outside!' And if she had been thrown out, so what? The tabloids would have made front-page copy of it for weeks!

Because of this long-suppressed frustration she almost immediately and instinctively rallied to the CSP's side as would, she suspected, many others. The whole Westminster process was aged and, judging by the public's quinquennial lack of interest, already in terminal decline. Only a clean sweep of the whole discredited edifice would suffice if the needs of today's members and their constituents were to be met. Why, she thought, has it taken this CSP crowd to propose in their manifesto a way forward that should have been sought by those eager, numerous, all-powerful Labour MPs in 1945? And there had probably been, even in those days, some likeminded Liberals and Independents, and a smattering of Tories, who would have joined them in carrying out that mammoth, once and for all, spring clean.

Now, she admitted unhappily, because of the wretched party system, she would be cajoled into opposing those CSP ideas in which she believed, and mainly because those ideas had not been proposed by her own party leaders. And that thought made her turn again to the CSP leaflet: wasn't that "obey your party whips" stipulation something the CSP would scrap forthwith? Yes, she read, *it damn well was*!

*

At the same time, Susan Mansfield was taking a leisurely stroll round Outer Mansworth Comprehensive School accompanied by Terry Park. She had finished supervising her teaching practice students and Terry was giving her a conducted tour.

'You've only seen a few classrooms and the assembly hall as yet. There's much more to the school than that. Come on, let me show you the whole caboodle.'

'You know what I think about schools.'

'Yes, but this one is here and up and running. You can't simply ignore what already exists or the efforts teachers are making. And you'll be obliged to tell people what's going to happen to these school buildings while you get your personal tutor scheme going.'

'But I do that. Suitable schools will be refurbished as resource and community centres, some will be rural outposts for field studies or act as family holiday hostels and offer affordable accommodation, while those for which there is no educational purpose – however generously that is defined - will be sold off together with their valuable land to raise money for the new system's development. That will bring in hundreds of millions of pounds for financing the transformation.'

'All right, I was only joking! Now, there you have the first set of toilets, boys to the right, girls to the left. Here a stationery store, here a broom cupboard, here the school's main fuse boxes, and here the most important room of all, the teaching staff's kitchen.'

Arthur Hull watched them closely from his cubbyhole and thought it was an engaging sight. But Ingrid Eastman, from the internal window of her office, observed them, too. While the caretaker entertained further notions of a novel-like romance, Ingrid wondered about the political ethics of the detailed, personal tour being given to just one of the short listed applicants.

'That woman was getting an unfair advantage,' she told Arthur Hull later. 'Why should she get a private and lengthy inspection of the school escorted by a member of staff while the other candidates have to belt round in a bunch on the day itself?'

She would tell Fergus. He could store the information until such time as he could make good use of it, and that time, she smiled to herself, could be here pretty soon!

Thursday 25 April.   **Public Perception**

'*The Messenger* says you're the only CSP candidate in six hundred constituencies! Not much common sense in a one-man band?'

'Physician heal thyself?' voiced another student dismissively..

Terry Park's cause had not been helped by Miss Hetty Hopkins' imaginative journalism. While her material on the CSP seemed well intended, some was ambiguous and these students had interpreted it to suit themselves. Journalists should be more precise.

'Well, Terry?' said Susan, 'there's one to start with!'

Susan had rounded up a dozen of her postgraduate trainee teachers and seated them in a corner of the union bar. They were to give Terry as rough a ride as they could to help train him for doorstep canvassing, probing reporters, hecklers at rowdy meetings or troublemakers on the streets. The union's constant buzz replicated what Terry was likely to encounter elsewhere. The students' rewards were free drinks, within limits, and the opportunity to knock a tutor's friend.

'The CSP got off to a hurried start, is short of cash, and is running just one candidate to test the water. But the information we get about the support we attract will be worth the deposit.'

'Good answer,' said one girl. She liked the look of the candidate.

'But common sense to one voter isn't to another, is it? With world population doubling since 1960 and rising by 200,000 a day, you'd think mandatory and universal birth control would be common sense, but it could be offensive to some cultures,' said the girl's friend.

'True,' answered Terry, 'but the CSP will try, through education, to make those groups realise how unsustainable such trends are, how perilous their particular views might be, and seek to change them. But at first a tiny party like ours will have to concentrate on smaller areas where there is common cause, and push for progress in those'

'Such as?'

'Transport. Our roads are choked, pavements blocked, atmosphere polluted and accidents rife. Common sense says we move away from roads, end our car-controlled, car-saturated society, and maximise use of public transport and tax heavily private road users.'

'Old hat!' a heckler shouted. 'Heard it before!'

'And ban *for life* dangerous drivers. That's not "old hat". Common sense says we don't want such people driving. The CSP won't have them. Those drivers have had their chance and lost it. Controlling a car, bus, train, ship or plane is a life and death matter and we would treat it as such and make courts explain why they dish out sloppy sentences and let dangerous drivers back on *our* roads to endanger *our* citizens *again.* We need a wholesale change of attitude to vehicle use.'

'But what you'll find,' suggested a man whose immense bulk suggested he would encounter few discipline problems in schools, 'is that car users will make damn sure your sort never got elected.'

'*Your sort*?' Terry retorted angrily. 'What does that mean?'

'See! I riled him!' yelled the bull-like man.

'You rose to it!' Susan said, and Terry acknowledged his mistake.

'But you're right about banning,' conceded the heavyweight. 'Should have been done years ago. If you kill or injure on the road, and it's your fault, the state should make sure you *never, ever* drive again.'

'Banning a few drivers won't win you an election!'

'I didn't say it would,' answered Terry. 'And it's the CSP that would win the election, not me, and the party is as embryonic as its overall policy. You can't expect one candidate to come up with a national "cure-all" programme on his own in a few weeks.'

'If you haven't got things sorted out, mate, you shouldn't stand!'

Things went quiet. So far they were unfavourably impressed.

'OK then, why have school and college exams in summer?' The questioner was a thin, sallow-faced man who looked far from fit. 'It's hot and humid, it's the hay fever season, and it's holiday time.'

'Because it's always been done that way,' sneered the heavyweight.

'We'd change that' said Terry, 'and have major exams in spring. We'd examine all practices that are based on nothing but tradition like three term years, school hours and weeks, bank holidays, academic dress, legal mumbo jumbo, house conveyancing.'

'Get back to population. If you're so worried about too many people why not ban sex? That makes common sense! Couples shall not copulate, by order of the CSP, signed, *Terry Park, Sole Candidate!*'

There were laughs and cries of "Shame!" "Get Lost!" "Go Home!"

and this time Susan found it difficult to remain quiet. One heckler was an arrogant young man whom she disliked. On an initial school visit he had infuriated a struggling head teacher by suggesting, unasked and in his first week, three ways in which she could improve her difficult school. Then Susan remembered she had asked them to be tough.

'Thanks' said Terry with an ingratiating smile. 'Your interest is appreciated. Now I'll tell you what we'll do about justice.'

'Ah, no sex?' cried one young lady pretending to weep.

'Not tonight,' the arrogant man answered. 'It's justice for you!'

'I'll come to sex later, if that's what you want,' Terry countered.

There was an incredulous cry from the bar, 'how *does* he know?'

'But for now I want to stress that common sense says we don't need judges, barristers and court officials dressed up in fancy gear. If they need that gear to boost their egos and can't do their jobs without it they should say so – and get out and run a fish and chip shop.'

'And they'd burn the effing chips!' came from the bar.

'Nor do we need the ridiculous rituals of our old-fashioned courts,' went on Terry. 'Those courts, for which the public pays handsomely, are not there to boost the standing of the legal profession or protect it with a blatant self-perpetuating, self-serving Oxbridge "keep them out" mystique. Their Dickensian practices, "All rise!" and outdated terminology like inns of court, pupillage, articled clerks, tenancies, chambers, parcels, called to the bar ...'

From a different kind of bar came a beery, 'fire the bloody lot!'

'...taking silk and King's and Queen's council; they all intimidate, alienate, confuse and frustrate the public. Citizens who have not had a lawyer's privileged education become fearful of the very legal system which should be aiding them, compassionately, to live their lives sensibly, fully and safely. And then the sheer cost of becoming a precedent-obsessed lawyer makes progress in the profession difficult.'

'Even if you've been to Oxbridge to start off with,' added a man who'd been rejected by an unimpressed Oxford admissions tutor.

'Becoming a highly–paid barrister is nearly impossible for ordinary people. And many of the best-paid barristers' life-styles become so remote from those of common people they have difficulty empathising.'

'Same's true of a lot of judges,' said a student quietly.

'The answer's too long,' said an Asian woman thoughtfully.

'Not for a politician!' mocked the arrogant man. 'He's a born natural!'

'And you don't mention the CSP, yet you've got to plug that for all you're worth!' Susan added. She noted some uninvited students had joined her group, free drinks in hand, sensing fun.

Then, while Terry seemed lost for words, a new arrival leapt in.

'Who cares what judges wear if they get a kick out of it and pay for the gear. It keeps the cartoonists happy and gives us a laugh!'

'But they *don't* pay for it,' retorted Terry. 'It costs over ten thousand pounds to kit out a senior judge and the taxpayer foots the bill.'

'Ten thousand?' queried two students together, ' That could go to legal aid or pay poor student-lawyers' fees. My conscience wouldn't let taxpayers on a fifth of my salary pay for my unnecessary fancy garb.'

'You're very down on judges and their dress?' a girl said to Terry.

'I'm down on what that dress stands for and say the same of the absurd regalia of bishops, viscounts, lord lieutenants, masters of the roll, vice-chancellors, rear-admirals and,' he hesitated, 'toastmasters! Apart from anything else it is counter productive. Today everything should be done to draw in the common man, to get him fully engaged in the country's legal, political and educational systems, not put him off. '

The students seemed unsure. 'You're shocked? Well, listen to this. A top judge is treated so luxuriously it can cost a thousand pounds a night to accommodate him when he's sitting outside London!'

'While the poor sod he's trying lies in a prison cell!' cried a student in anger. 'That does do a lot for social cohesion!'

'You were supposed to be talking about justice,' put in another. 'What we question is the puzzlingly lenient sentences handed out to vicious criminals and road killers and the heavy-handedness shown to people whose offences are understandable but which probably involve taking property from those who've already got too much.'

'And why people are locked up for crimes they did not commit and years later released with their lives and families' lives in tatters and the original courts apparently unaccountable – and I say "apparently" advisedly because if that's how it *seems* to be to the general public then the damage, in terms of trust in the system, has been done.'

'The law doesn't bear examination as it stands today,' agreed one student. 'You're right to start with the law. Get that opened up, sorted out, brought up to date and simplified. Millions will back you.'

Terry followed up the support eagerly. 'Those judges whose courts wrongly imprisoned people will be summoned, if they're still around, to explain what went so wrong that families' lives were wrecked. Judges are highly paid public servants whom we are supposed to look up to, so it is only right, when their judgement seems strange or sentences seem out of proportion, that they are called on to explain their actions to the people who pay them and who rely on them for justice. Then they can be commended if they were right, or excused, reprimanded or fined if they were - perhaps understandably - wrong, with any money going to a distressed victim's compensation fund, or, if there was proven negligence, charged and tried. Some sentences have been imposed which have been seized on by the tabloids and infuriated the public, and have impaired the standing of the whole legal system. Judges *must* be more accountable. Further, moves will be made by the CSP for judges to be elected – yes *elected* – elected for set periods by the citizens of the district in which they were born and in which they will serve. In fact, I'd go further than that.'

He paused. The students were listening, interested.

'I'd have no judges as they are today. The jury, which, in reality, is already "the judge", will be renamed the "judicial body". The existing role of "judge in charge of the court" will disappear. He or she will become a legal advisor, plainly dressed, who will sit alongside and on the same floor level as the jury to give legal advice as and when the foreman – and what a class-conscious word that is! – let's say when the "jury spokesperson" asks for it. The jury will decide on sentences for the guilty based on ranges recommended by an elected parliament. Nobody in court will be more important than the jury spokesperson. The pitiful standing and bowing and "If it may please your Lordship or your Ladyship, or your Honour," and similar archaic, forelock-touching tommy-rot will become a titivating relic of our class-ridden past.'

There was silence for a moment. A few began to clap, then more.

'That was better. It was firm,' said the Asian girl, 'and made sense.'

'Common sense,' said Terry, 'just what the CSP stands for.'

'But the courts themselves are limited in what they can do. For instance they can't send people to prison if the prisons are full.'

'You're right,' said Terry, 'over 80,000 are in British gaols or police cells with more on remand, on bail, or probation or doing community service, or in youth custody. So what's gone wrong?'

'You tell us,' said the heavy man. 'You want our votes.'

'What's gone wrong is a debilitating weakness in the upbringing of our children: the insistence on separating the family from the nation's education service throughout childhood. The successful tackling of this sad country's enormous social problems such as crime, obesity, lethargy, smoking and drinking, can be done only at an individual level during childhood by parents working with and gaining immense support from skilled, knowledgeable personal tutors who know the children in their care individually and who can work with them and their parents closely and patiently over long periods of time.'

'And,' added Susan, 'by not seeing education in terms of old-fashioned schools which emphasise tests, examinations and careers rather than the opportunities - and problems - of life as a whole.'

'Then we'd need far fewer judges, court officials, police, warders, probation officers, magistrates, and we'd save money,' agreed the Asian girl. But another, sitting nearer to Terry, shook her head.

'That's all very well, but you won't be able to dispense with courts altogether, and, anyway, I don't think you're being fair.'

The speaker was a small, slim, dark-haired student who had been listening seriously while sipping her pineapple juice. 'My mother is a magistrate; she gives a lot of her time, unpaid, and takes her work to heart. She worries about cases, as do her colleagues and as, it may surprise you, do those in higher courts. They try to get things right. My mother's nightmare is finding people guilty who are innocent, ruining their reputations or sending them, wrongly, to prison. Because of that she's tempted to give the benefit of the doubt, or award community work or probation or a light sentence; then she's vilified by the media and, forgive me, by social psychologists, sociologists and criminologists cosily cocooned in their comfortable universities.'

She blushed, but Terry nodded encouragingly and she continued. 'Often the law is unclear, unhelpful, unwise, even unenforceable, and that's the fault of Parliament, not magistrates or judges. And, for all you know, some judges themselves, for many years, might have wanted to drag the courts into the modern age and throw their wigs in the trash can, but they've been powerless to do anything about it.'

'Which says it all!' laughed a well-primed and happy man. 'If even the establishment can't beat the establishment, who the hell can?'

The girl ignored him. 'My mother knows she and her colleagues seem to have low esteem in the public eye, but some of that is caused by the irresponsible coverage and over-simplification of high profile but complicated cases in the sensation-seeking popular press.'

'Very well said,' came from her equally slight companion.

'At times she isn't keen to go on with her court work. Where would we be, or would you be, if she and others – like the judges you single out for such criticism - all felt like that and resigned?'

'All right, and many will sympathise with you,' said Terry, 'but, as you suggest, much of the problem lies with public perception. Perception is everything. Once the idea is established that judges come from a top notch clique and are intimidating and remote, set apart from the rank and file, and by their dress and attitudes they tend to reinforce that perception, or that magistrates are out of touch, that the law is stupid or unfair, that many party-obedient MPs are ex-lawyers or have had an expensive, private education and that governments are incompetent, untrustworthy, concerned only with retaining power or promoting their own interests then,' he paused, 'then, once those *notions* are implanted they're almost impossible to shift unless a clean sweep is made of the whole *perceived* set-up.'

'But you're …'

'Let me finish. Because then, *even if those notions are untrue*,' he emphasised, 'they might as well *be* true as far as ordinary citizens are concerned. That's where the danger lies. Notions of that sort can lead to indifference, scorn, frustration or outright hostility and could bring a breakdown in our system of lawful government – such as it is. Fortunately that stage has not been reached, at least *not reached yet*.'

For the first time that night Terry's confidence grew.

'And your job? What public trust is there in teachers?'

At the sudden change of subject his newly found confidence evaporated like a shallow pond in a heat wave. Or *was* it a change?

'Why don't you tell us how your CPS crowd views education?' The speaker was a pale, bespectacled American with a drawling Southern accent. 'What *notions* have people got about that?'

Terry thought for what seemed an interminable time.

'Too slow, mate!' came from a voice at the side. 'Too slow.'

'I was trying to find words that would give a short but accurate answer to a wide-ranging, deep and complex question,' said Terry.

'You had plenty to say about wide-ranging, deep and complex legal matters. You found plenty of words for that!'

Heads nodded. The American waited. Terry turned to Susan.

'She won't rescue you!' mocked the arrogant man.

'Not tonight, darling! Not tonight!'

Drink was talking. Susan looked at her watch.

'My short answer is that CSP education policy would show how a contented life can be lived enjoyably using only a fraction of the world's resources we use now.'

'That's right,' said a boy whose ginger hair was shoulder length.

'We'd show, for instance, that the world consumes as much oil in six weeks now as it did in twelve months fifty years ago and ask, "will that trend finish and, if it doesn't, where will it lead?" Instead of encouraging children to expect more and more today and ever higher standards of living tomorrow, we'd change direction – show that we in the West already have more than enough for full, satisfying lives and that the other half of humanity lives on less than £1.50 a day.'

'*Two dollars*?' came from the American.

'Two dollars. We'd drive home the fact that if we continue to move in that direction we'll bring about a deserved calamity.'

'So you'd reduce expectations and put teaching for contentment in your manifesto?' asked the Asian girl.

'Yes, thank you,' said Terry smiling at her gratefully, 'that's it in a nutshell. That's it. Just three words, " *Teaching for Contentment*."'

'And you'd curb the supermarkets?'

'Supermarkets?'

'They tempt people to buy more and more – more than they need?'

'We'd look at them and the way they domineer markets and we'd make them employ all the shopkeepers and assistants they put out of business as a condition of getting planning approval for any expansion.'

'OK, but what about teaching?' came from an older student. 'D'you think you teachers do enough to defend children's right to learn freely?'

'I'm not quite sure what ...'

'Well, years ago, who'd have thought teachers would acquiesce to being told what to teach, when to teach it, who to teach it to, and have inspectors flitting round making sure they did it?'

'She means your infamous National Curriculum and the rest of the politically inspired fun and games,' explained the American.

'And,' the older student continued, 'whether we should assume that in future teachers will fade away so that lessons can be provided by a central government agency transmitting carefully selected and edited material directly to schools? The technology is already there.'

'Shades of *1984*' came from the bar. 'Have you read that?'

There was a laugh, but Susan sensed the students had had enough. Terry had learned a lot and the students had earned their drinks, so she moved round to thank them individually and was pleased to see that, as they drifted away, most were looking thoughtful.

'No real sparkle in that last piece. Needs some sexy bits. Get the low down on that Mansfield woman; she's having a lot to do with Park's party, and perhaps with him. I've heard she's been hanging round his school when they're both tied up with the head teacher job.'

'Well, she *is* short listed!'

'All the more reason to check her out!'

'I've checked. She's clear.'

'I'm told even the university's got doubts about her.'

'Well, we've got nothing on her!'

Hetty, tired of this daily criticism, was increasingly anxious to get another post even if it meant less money. She knew one of her earlier pieces, which had included prospective candidates' misdemeanours, had upset some readers, but it had generated lively correspondence. However this unyielding woman was never satisfied.

I bet Sonia Smith's no worse a boss than this, Hetty fumed.

'There's bound to be something, somewhere,' pressed the impatient editor. 'There'll be men sniffing. She's lively, with a good figure. There'll be men of sorts in that ivory tower where she works – there'll be some who are not past it. Try that! Then run something like: *Left-Wing Ivory Tower Woman Supports Local Teacher's Stand!*'

'That wouldn't raise a …'

'With a strong sub-head: *"Close All Our Local Schools!" Says Trendy Mansworth Lecturer.* Include a few negatives on her alternative education stuff. The Chief Education Officer's crowd don't like it, nor do the governors or head teachers. They say she's out of touch. As for parent-voters, just wait for *their* reaction when they're told their children won't be going to school any more! They'll throttle her with her own fancy tights! Go on, for Heaven's sake woman, you've got a wealth of material there! Be sure to link it to that CSP character, the teacher and parliamentary-candidate and novelist and God knows what else. Stir things up, but leave a bit for future issues.'

Hetty was irate. She stood for a while, tense.

'Well?' asked the editor. 'What's bugging you now?'

'I'm not sure about the angle.'

'Angle?'

'I've looked again at Dr Mansfield's work …'

The editor noted the "Dr" 'And?'

'I've looked at her ideas. She's cheesed off with the "One size fits all" kind of school curriculum. She wants children to have a choice, to have a personal tutor with a panel of other tutors working as a team, supported by community resource centres and educational, child-centred, Internet facilities. That could *appeal* to those parents who are fed up of mediocre, bully-prone, nine-to-four schools that are closed for three months every year. And you've heard today there's another report out on increased truancy and another on how many eleven-year-olds can't read or write properly when they leave primary school, or do simple maths. Slanting pieces at those things would grab parents.'

'Grab parents? Someone's been grabbing *you*!'

'They've not!'

'Yes they have! And what d'you know about parents? Or kids? Have you got kids? I have, and if some fancy Flossie from a university had the nerve to tell me that I didn't need a school for my kids and that I could bring them up using the Internet and assorted sites round town and a few trendy personal tutors like *Dr* Mansfield believe me, *Miss* Hopkins, I'd want her shut up, wrapped up and strung up - as would most struggling Mansworth working mums. So that's what *The Messenger's* angle is going to be on that one. Right?'

'Right.'

'Right.' The editor stood and waved a finger furiously. 'So let's get this straight. First, we print nothing, *nothing,* that's going to publicise this crank's so-called "academic research", nothing that would put it in a favourable light with a gullible public or help her get the headship of that damn school. Second, we print nothing that's going to promote the Common Sense Party or Park's barmy go-it-alone campaign. We stay with the majority of voters who want to keep their schools, keep their teachers and keep their three main parties. *Those voters are our readers.* That's what they want to read, that's what they're going to read! So push off and find something useful to write – right now!'

The editor did not sit down at her paper-strewn desk until minutes after Hetty Hopkins had left. Self-seeking, suspicious, far-sighted, scheming, and envious of her junior's youth and overflowing sex appeal, she could see the potential and the danger in both these stories, Susan Mansfield's and Terry Park's, so both had to be handled carefully and she would make damn sure Hetty Hopkins handled them in just that way.

What would we do if this CSP lot got a hold? What would there be to print if this country was run on common sense lines? There'd be no grumbles, no delays, no protests, no waste, no wayward politicians, no corruption, no incompetence, no opposition, no stupid decisions, no pathetic excuses for doing bugger all, and, before long, no *Mansworth Evening Messenger* either! Blast the lot of them!

Angrily she unfolded the previous day's paper to reveal a quarter page advertisement announcing a public meeting of the CSP and its candidate for Mansworth SW, Terry Arthur Park, at 7.30 pm on Saturday, 27 April, in Lower Mansworth Primary & Nursery School.

Silly bastard, she snorted, still fuming, who'll turn out on a cold Saturday night to hear him hold forth? But, to maintain an impression of impartiality, *The Messenger* would have to send someone to cover the meeting. More free publicity for the CSP! Damn Park and his party!

Trying to calm down, she pencilled a heavy moustache onto Terry's image, extended one of his ears, gave his mouth a turned-down look and shaded-in two front teeth. 'But I know one reporter who won't be covering his meeting,' she muttered. 'Not while I'm boss!'

Then her anger increased. That advert would draw readers to the CSP, but her paper had been bound to run it. And she had to admit that the carefully selected Collins-approved mug shot of a smiling Terry Park, before her additions, was appealing – quite appealing!

*

Dafydd Hughes had purloined the staff room copy of yesterday's *The Messenger and Times* and was showing it to Jenny Jean Jones after school. He pointed to the cheerful image of the CSP candidate.

'And they say the camera never lies!' he chortled.'

'That's unkind. I think it's pretty good of him and certainly not too flattering. And I suspect, Mr Hughes, there might be a tiny element of jealousy? Just a touch?'

'I'm not jealous of men's photographs, Miss Jones! Other attributes, perhaps, but not their phizogs!' They both laughed.

The secretaries' door was open and Louie Anne Lee, perched on her office stool, heard not only what they said but the tone in which it was said. If there was jealousy around it came not from Dafydd Hughes but from his ear-craning, nail-filing, low-ranking secretarial admirer.

'No,' Hughes continued, 'fooling apart, I fear Politician Park is on a hiding to nothing. Won't do his career any good either. He'll be lucky to get twenty votes and then he'll be seen as a crackpot – plenty of those in politics! Or he'll be seen by others as a man whose judgement is questionable, and that's putting it mildly.'

'So what made him stand?'

For once Hughes looked uncomfortable.

'I suppose I did, in a way – well, that is, me and a few others. We'd been drinking and fooling around and I challenged him to put up as a CSP candidate – in this marginal constituency. But I was only joking and micky-taking, and had no idea he'd take it seriously.'

'Well, he did.'

'Yes, he did, but it was his decision! And he could still pull out.'

'You know he won't do that – for all sorts of reasons.'

Hughes ignored that, and flipped over the paper's pages.

'Here it is, *The Showcase* at 7.15. '*Just Once More, My Darling.*' And it's adults only!' he grinned. ' Shall we give it a whirl?'

Jenny approved.

'OK, and we'll have a pint and a roll first – and I mean a cheese and tomato roll.'

'So do I,' agreed Jenny resolutely. 'So do I.'

Saturday 27 April.   **The Outsiders**

It was standard practice for the two school secretaries, alternately, to work on Saturday mornings. Today was Louie Anne Lee's turn and she had been relieved to see Hull go for his breakfast; she did not like the way he eyed her. But she welcomed such looks from Dafydd Hughes and Terry Park, and was pleased to see Terry crossing the foyer at the start of her stint. Almost, but not quite, he matched Dafydd in her order of male preferences and Dafydd, by the look of things, was losing interest in her. From the day Jenny Jean Jones joined the staff she had feared this might happen. But never mind, here was good old Terry to fill the gap.

'Bit of crafty photocopying on the side, Louie Anne,' he said.

'For the election?' she asked as she loaded paper into the copier. 'And you're really standing! Isn't that exciting? What if you get in! Would you still visit us in school as a real live MP? I bet you wouldn't speak to me after mixing with all those important people in London.'

'Of course I would!' He put a friendly arm round her. 'But don't get carried away, my chances of getting in are nil. This is a trial run.'

'Oh,' she said, a bit deflated. But then she perked up.

'*Try Something New!*' was the heading she read out as she picked up one of the campaign sheets. '*Don't Settle for What the Three Tired Old Parties Offer: Read What the CSP Will Do! Ten New Ideas to Start With and Many More to Come!*' Then, in bold, '**There's Sense in Common Sense: Vote for Park! Vote for Terry Park!**'

'The first bit's our slogan: '*There's Sense in Common Sense!*'

'We need common sense,' she said. 'How many are you doing?'

'Three hundred. Don't worry, I'll book it in when I've finished.'

' I didn't mean *that*! I meant what will you *do* with them?'

'Put them through letterboxes in a sample ten streets then follow up tomorrow to see if any householders want to talk to me.'

'Put one through my letterbox. I'll talk to you.'

'I don't know where you live.'

'You could find out! I'm on the electoral roll, just!' Then she said, seriously, 'I'd love to help you. I could do half the streets.'

'But you're working here.'

'Only 'til twelve, and I can nip off early. Mr Hull says Mrs Eastman often does if Mr Olde's not around.'

'I'm not sure it would ...'

'Please, I want to be part of it! I'd *love* to be part of it! I *will* be part of it! Off you go and make some coffee while I finish the copying.'

Terry hesitated, looked at her, smiled, then did as he was told.

'Terry,' Louie Anne said quietly as they drank coffee and ate ginger biscuits, 'Ingrid's been doing a lot of photocopying lately.'

'For the election?'

'No: for the head teacher appointment.' She lowered her voice further as she heard Hull returning. 'We did copies of all the data on all the candidates so that every governor could have a full set: the applications, references, records, CV's, confidential letters, notes of phone calls - the whole lot. She ran off more than we needed and the spares weren't shredded. I think she took them home for her horrible husband – I can't stand him!'

'But as a governor Mr Eastman would see them anyway.'

'He's got so-called friends everywhere. The extras could have been for them. Ingrid's been a bit odd lately, not at all talkative, can't make her out.' Louie Anne went quiet as she heard Hull returning.

'OK in here?' Hull asked, and then, 'All going well, Mr Park?'

'Spot on! No one else in? That's unusual?'

'Mr Collins came in earlier. Said he couldn't wait, was in a rush, but

208

left a note. I put it in your pigeon hole.'

Terry did not read Collins' note until later. It said, briefly, that he, Eddie Collins, had accepted the post of full time regional official with Teachers for Radical Action and that in October he would be moving to Birmingham Central Region with additional responsibilities - and opportunities. 'How's that for rapid promotion!' he had scrawled. 'So get your finger out, Park! Time *you* moved on!'

*

Louie Anne Lee did half the selected streets while Terry did the other and, apart from barking dogs, scurrying cats and twitching curtains, they seemed to evoke little interest. Then he took her for another coffee, of better quality, in *The King of Morocco*. There they saw that the early edition of Saturday's *Messenger and Times* carried an article recalling Mansworth South-West's General Election result of four and a half years before:

Modern Labour............................	13,888
Today's Tories	13,666
Tolerant Democrats	4,444
Council Tax Protest Group:	3,233
Bring Back Conscription:.............	*911
The Rhubarb-Rhubarb Party:	*5

(*Electorate*: 81,656),   (*Votes*: 36,147),   (*Spoilt Papers*: 747),
(*Turnout*:   44.6%),   (*Majority*:   222),   (**Lost deposits*: 2).

She described ill-tempered recounts, unseemly trouble after the declaration, and the tiny majority gained by the sitting member, Dr Audrey Anderson. Hetty then indicated that the re-organisation of constituency boundaries had reduced today's electorate to 78,787

She reported on Dr Anderson's creditable attendance in the House of Commons and mentioned her speeches on medical consultants' remuneration, traffic calming measures and constituents' concerns about some uses of National Lottery money. Hetty noted this record was above average for backbenchers and that Dr Anderson had been conscientious in holding monthly surgeries.

Hetty also commented on the number of spoilt papers, so large in fact that rumours of a movement towards a deliberate "spoil your paper" campaign by disaffected voters had won credence. But no group had claimed what could have been seen as a minor success.

'It will be different this time,' said Louie Anne Lee. 'You'll pick up those 'spoil-your-paper' people.'

But she did not know that for this coming election the vociferous local butcher, anti-vegetarian, pro-foxhunting, anti-supermarket stalwart Peter Perkins had founded an authentic paper-spoiling party. His original naming of it as: "Spoil Your Sodding Paper Party," was deemed inadmissible, and, after language to which the Returning Officer was unaccustomed, its title had been modified.

Then, although being of the same degree of disenchantment with party politics as the vote-spoilers, the long-standing Rhubarb-Rhubarb candidate, Humphrey Hugh Higginbotham, had dissociated himself from Perkins' campaign. He intended to run once more as a candidate in his own right. He had rejected suggestions that he rename his group: "The Up-Yours Party" and claimed he would win votes from an increasingly disconsolate electorate by staying with the well-established name of: "Rhubarb-Rhubarb".

Then Hetty had listed, alphabetically, the candidates, parties and policies for the coming general election:

Audrey Amy ANDERSON…	*Modern Labour Party.*
Christopher Cedric CLAY…	*Today's Tory Party.*
Dorothy DEVONPORT …	*Tolerant Democrats.*
Humphrey Hugh HIGGINBOTHAM	*Rhubarb-Rhubarb Party.*
Terence Arthur PARK … …	*Common Sense Party.*
Peter Ian PERKINS … …	*Spoil Your Paper Party.*
Sybil Olive SYLVESTER…	*Save Our Sparrows.*

As the three main party candidates were to be the subjects of full feature articles in later issues, Hetty had first interviewed the other hopefuls and written kind words about each. Hetty's jaundiced view of her editor and the paper's partisan political policies were beginning to influence her impartiality. Now she was hoping for the political sensation of all times with the election of little Sybil Olive Sylvester following her brave campaign to save the common house sparrow.

'Marvellous cause! Worthier than most of the others,' she muttered. 'but her case is hopeless in this land of unshakeable tradition'.

"Rhubarb-Rhubarb" Humphrey Higginbotham, the forty-four year old four times married man, father of four daughters, owner of four cash-laundries and four dry-cleaners, Hetty described as "a tribute to the nation, a wonderful example of that stalwart, enterprising British citizen not afraid to stand up and be counted." This last item was unfortunate because when Higginbotham's votes had been counted at the last election the teller had taken only five seconds to count them.

Peter Ian Perkins, or "Butcher Perkins" as his detractors knew him, had witnessed the bankruptcy of the business that had been in his family for four generations. The fifty-three year old knew the rise of vegetarianism had not helped him, nor had the ever-lasting acrimony about hunting with hounds which symbolised for him all that was wrong with this interfering Mod Lab society. But his real problem, the rise of the supermarkets, he tried to play down. Perkins had contempt for politicians who abandoned his kind and he manfully forked out a deposit to stand as one who could decry the whole, miserable, short sighted, grasping shower. Hetty, despite knowing she should be dispassionate, felt sorry for Higginbotham because she knew how much his centuries-old family business had meant to him and that it would never flourish again.

Eighty-two-year-old Sybil Sylvester was fascinating. When young she had been a hardworking member of the Royal Society for the Protection of Birds, and, after thirty years as a probation officer in downtown Leicester, had returned to her first love of registering, recording, feeding and protecting the British house sparrow. News from the RSPB that the species was in decline had upset her almost as much as the heart-rending human cases she had encountered in her professional life. In her address to voters she had written:

"A society that selfishly allows its environment to deteriorate to such an extent that its own friendly house sparrow is in decline is a society which is, *in itself*, in decline. Beware!"

'And three cheers for that,' Hetty said aloud..

Terry Park was different again. While Higginbotham, Perkins and Sylvester had no chance of winning, Park could be launching a party that might, in thirty years' time, rise to power. Then, while only seventy, Terry, as founder, might become Prime Minister. She could understand why her editor and other notables were keen to disparage his fledgling CSP. Yet, ironically, their transparent antagonism was in itself *for them* down-to-earth common sense! Her appreciative write-up would have to be carefully worded if it were not to be spiked.

*

At seven-thirty the assembly hall of The Lower Mansworth Primary and Nursery School contained only eight people: Terry, Susan and their scattered audience of four men and two women. The turnout was worse than either had feared, but they tried to be brave.

'Why don't we sit round as a group and talk about the CSP and what it might do?' Susan said. 'It would be less formal.'

They nodded and the younger of the two ladies said, 'I'm a teacher here. I could make coffee and tea, then we'd be even less formal?'

All agreed, and in three minutes Susan had introduced Terry and herself, and was asking for the names of the audience.

'Freddie Fields, I live near here and I'm a long-serving inspector with the Inland Revenue and in view of the unbelievable complexity, incomprehensibility, and absurdity of our ever-changing, time wasting tax rules, I thought the CSP sounded interesting – different – hopeful – reasonable – logical. But it's fifty years overdue!'

'John Andrews, retired. I was in business and I'm here because I'm so disappointed with the main parties that I'm prepared to listen to any reasonable alternative. I can't, in all conscience, support the People's Patriotic Party and so thought that if this CSP seemed OK I might use my vote for the first time in twenty years and vote for them.' He paused as if to say something else, but then decided against it.

The others nodded. Susan looked at the coffee lady.

'Norma Greene: Greene with an "e",' she smiled, 'as I said, I teach here. I've a class of nine-year-olds and, to be honest, I'm as interested in Dr Mansfield's education work as I am in the CSP and thought she might be willing to talk about it?'

'Try stopping her,' murmured Terry.

'Betty Bannister, community nurse. I work with older people in Southside Day Centre and, like Mr Andrews, I want to hear of ideas that could check red tap and stagnation and the high wages and golden handshakes given to the incompetent.'

Susan looked encouragingly at the hesitant man to her left.

'I've come to listen - to find out more about the party,' he said. 'I'm keen on all fresh thoughts and ideas. I was a commercial printer for forty years and I'm also retired. I'm Dick Nathan.'

212

'And?' Susan smiled encouragingly at the last person, a rather short, drably dressed man with grey, thinning hair who seemed much older than anyone else in the hall.

'Ernie Willis, reporter, *Mansworth Evening Messenger and Times.* I'm a freelance, really, but I get pre-set jobs when the paper's busy.'

He moved his chair further into the group, notepad on knee.

'Then please write something favourable,' said Terry, 'we need all the help we can get!'

Casually Ernie Willis surveyed the almost empty hall. By the look of tonight's turnout they needed more help than he could give.

'It's good you've all come,' Susan said. 'Can we use first names?'

'Christian names?' asked Betty Bannister.

The eight agreed to use Christian names. Freddy Fields started the discussion and within minutes Terry was fascinated.

'We could get millions of taxpayers who fill in ridiculous, worrying, time-consuming tax returns right out of the absurdly bureaucratic and complex system. Do you know it needs nearly ten thousand pages of rules and explanations to clarify our tax system? It's crazy. If politicians can't do better than that they should be out on their necks. Armies of tax clerks could be moved to socially valuable work and they themselves would be happier and healthier for the change.'

'How?'

'Treble VAT – at least - so that it's the spenders and not the earners who pay. Quadruple taxes on environmentally dangerous commodities and services like cars, trucks, planes, petrol, tobacco, alcohol, sugar, dogs, cats, pet food, fast food, gambling. That would make up for what is lost from millions of low earners who pay so little income tax it's hardly worth the cost of collecting. Simplify the system by having a single rate of income tax, no capital gains or inheritance taxes, and make up for those deficits by huge tax increases on bankers – especially foreign bankers - tax accountants, estate agents, lawyers, credit card companies, money lenders, advertisers, TV stations, and all resource-wasting, non-productive, non-useful businesses.'

Terry noticed the doubts on Betty Bannister's face.

'Then reduce the money wasted on bureaucracy. Simplify the social security set up by having a single, standard rate of survival assistance for claimants regardless of their other income or their expenditure and cut again the legislation, paper work and fraudulent claims of the crafty and reduce the loss of legitimate entitlements by those who can't understand what the hell it's all about, then you could scrap insulting, expensive means testing. People "on benefit", as we say, would be encouraged to cut their coat according to their cloth. Nanny State would fade away as citizens were encouraged to manage their own affairs using large doses of your party's much needed common sense. Tax refunds to charities would be scrapped. We'd do *anything* in fact, *literally anything,* to make the system *simple*: simple to understand, simple to collect, simple to enforce. Should have been done ages ago.'

Freddy Fields paused. 'And I must stress again, we'd free tens of thousands of intelligent, conscientious civil servants from an illogical bureaucratic treadmill so that their talents can be better used and then, after retraining, bring satisfaction into their own lives and help others by swelling the ranks of nurses, social workers, carers and others.'

'That's fantastic!' enthused Terry.

'The possibilities are endless,' murmured Susan as if thinking aloud. 'The really keen and suitable ones could be offered training as tutors and supplement the ex-teachers who'd be encouraged to return once a tutorial system is established.'

Ernie Willis made notes.

'But I've not finished,' continued Fields. 'Look at local government. Drastically reduce it by abolishing the collection of the hated council tax. Replace it by an annual *per capita* payment from the central government to each county council. How the council then used that money would be for their electorate to decide, but once spent they needn't go running back for more because there would *be* no more. Put massive fines on illegal, unsightly, dangerous vehicle parking, vandalism, pollutants and other threatening, nuisance-causing, noisy behaviour. That could raise billions. I can give more instances.'

But that was enough. The group argued heatedly.

'It wouldn't be allowed to work,' murmured Dick Nathan. 'Party politicians daren't put all that to the voters, they'd be massacred.'

'I'm not so sure,' murmured John Andrews.

'It could work,' said Susan, 'note I say *could* work, though, as you say, it wouldn't be *allowed* to work – in fact it would never be tried - like my proposals for education – they'll never be tried.'

'No, it wouldn't get off the ground,' said Betty Bannister. 'No one in authority wants to *listen* to proposals for sweeping changes in education or in any other walk of life. Take the House of Lords – and what an insulting name that is – of which there was talk of reform in 1911 – and it still sits and they still talk! But even where politicians have the intelligence or imagination to see possibilities they won't act because of self-interest, inertia, or fear.'

'Fear of not being re-elected?' asked Norma Green.

'Or of not being politically correct or of being unpopular.'

'That is the deadly weakness of a modern democracy. Politicians think in terms of only four or five years,' said Freddie Fields. 'There's no really long-term vision. The country needs a coalition government in power for twenty years. Then far-sighted plans could be worked out with decisive, groundbreaking starts made in vital areas. We might even agree on a sensible, manageable population size for this tiny country and do something to achieve it. Imagine, a crowded country like this doesn't have a population policy! It's incredible!'

'It isn't incredible – and that's the *real* tragedy!' said Nathan. 'And it's worse now because, even if politicians got some sort of policy knocked together, people suspect it wouldn't be implemented. There's no trust and without trust we're finished! Then even your twenty year period for recovery wouldn't be long enough.'

Nathan had decided, after all, that he would speak and edged his chair further into the circle. 'Look at the teaching of reading.'

'Reading?' asked Norma Greene as she refilled coffee cups.

'During my time as a printer I became interested in words such as: *knight* and *lamb*, *queue* and *cough*, *ought* and *laugh*, *fault, succeed, comb, seize, receipt, photograph, queue,* ... Customers got them wrong and children in school struggled '

'Still do,' muttered Ernie Willis, looking up.

'Exactly. My son had an awful time when he was starting to read,' continued Nathan. 'When my wife went to see the teachers they seemed to switch backwards and forwards from phonics to whole words to letter groups and now it seems they're still unsure. And it's starting again with our grandson. Where's the common sense in all that? Why fifty years to sort that out?'

Norma nodded sympathetically, and so did Ernie Willis.

'It goes deeper than that,' Nathan went on. 'Seventy years ago Bernard Shaw was trying to get common sense spelling introduced: *nite, lam, rong, cof, ort, laf, folt, sukseed, foto.* But the diehards weren't having that! Many youngsters' lives could have been transformed, but instead they were restricted. Children became discouraged by their own slow progress in reading and spelling yet they could have mastered both and then gone on to enjoy books and all those books have to offer. We let old language turn new people off current language. It's not only school methods we need to change, but the very words we teach.'

'And your own language is spot on when you use 'diehards', said Fields. 'Recently an MP spoke for 197 minutes so that some bill would be abandoned for "lack of time"! And our elected, privileged, complacent and highly paid representatives – that is the ones who bothered to turn up – just sat there and let him. They let an utter farce be made of *our* hard-won democracy. They forgot the struggle ordinary people had to win for them the right to sit in Parliament. They remain hidebound by ridiculous parliamentary procedures and conventions that should have been swept away a century ago, and they get so enmeshed in House protocol that an already alienated electorate either treats them with derision or fails to understand what the hell's going on. They see the House nine tenths empty during supposedly important televised debates. Members allow legislation to be passed to a second 'chamber': imagine, *chamber* in today's world! And a *chamber* largely unauthenticated by the electorate. At huge cost they drag members from overseas to make them vote in person in the House - just think of that in our exciting electronic age, an age of possibilities that has bypassed the brassbound members. Their insufferable arrogance as they pander to their selfish obsession with propriety and tradition is mind-boggling, and then they have the audacity to complain when millions of voters are indifferent to their inward-looking, fancy-dress, party-bound, whip-controlled antics. Good grief, if voters want an amateur pantomime they can get one at Christmas for five quid with the cash going to a worthwhile cause!'

'And the cast would be better looking,' grinned Willis.

They all grinned, there was no debating that, even in a democracy.

'So I'll vote for Terry Park!' ended Freddie Fields, sitting back.

'And me,' said John Andrews.

'But have you gone far enough?' asked Nathan.

'I'm not sure what you mean,' said Fields.

'I agree with your criticisms of our parliamentary system, but your lambasting it, admirably, let me add, will not get us very far. Those criticisms have been made before and ignored. Once members get elected to that anachronistic place they seem to lose their identity and become impotent. It's as if the magician's ornate mace casts its spell over them. They scurry to vote as the whips tell them, or sit quietly and uncomfortably on the benches so that after decades of that numb bum existence many a one who was a lively socialist with exciting ideas at eighteen becomes a knight, lady, lord, baroness or eighteenth earl at eighty, gives plenty of fee-earning after-dinner speeches and makes the most of the awarded title. Believe me, few are going to give that up because an embryonic Common Sense Party raises objections.'

'So?' muttered Fields.

'A new party, if it is to have any chance, has to propose something disparate. The electorate must be offered a real alternative which demonstrates how expensive, outdated and surplus to requirements our Parliament has become, and how people's interest in politics will never be revived under Westminster's lethargic, incomprehensible, part time London based way of working.'

'So?' repeated Fields. 'Go on.'

'The CSP should propose a model of government that replaces the parliamentary system now housed in The Palace of Westminster – just imagine a *Palace!* – the seat of our democracy is in a *Palace* which was until 1965 controlled – and wait for it - by the Lord Great Chamberlain! Good grief!' He looked ready to vomit and had to pause in his denunciation. 'That *palace* will become the NMABP – the National Museum of Ancient Bureaucratic Practices – with free entry on Boxing Day - and what the hell is *Boxing Day?* but ten pence at other times with half price for all pensioners over ninety-five who are on supplementary benefits. A few hapless lords who might not get a job anywhere else and so become a burden on the state can be paid the national minimum wage to serve as custodians of the artefacts, or salespersons in the museum's memorabilia shop selling replica coats of arms or colour photos of a clapped-out coronation coach or a busty baroness in full regalia, or be paid extra for describing to visitors the antics that took place when the palace was our so-called parliament. Such stories might brighten up tourists' visits and bring a few laughs!'

'Would those redundant lords get gratuities?'

'Maybe, from Americans – their dollars could go to the DLMBF.'

'What's that?'

'The Distressed Lords and Members' Benevolent Fund.'

'Will the public buy it?'

'Buy it? They'll queue for it! The British love queuing.'

'And they'll get a laugh!'

'Let me get this down,' begged Willis as the others chortled.

'At the same time the CSP will show it is a constructive body by putting forward plans for a new purpose-built, skilfully-designed ultra-modern government block in Birmingham. Then anything that's worth having from the old caboodle can be transferred to ....'

'Why Birmingham?' asked Betty Bannister.

'To get things moving. We'll invite ideas and vote on it – it could be Leeds or Sheffield – but for now we'll say Birmingham, our Second City, except it will be our First City - if you see what I mean.'

'But it needn't be any existing city,' Betty suggested. 'Why not build a new garden city in a beautiful centrally situated area – perhaps in Leicestershire or Rutland - a sort of independent capital territory like the Australians did with Canberra.'

'That's right, when they moved their Parliament from Melbourne,' added Terry. 'And I bet they had their share of doubters, even then, from the: "Oh-No-It-Can't-Be-Done" brigade.'

'All ideas can be considered and decided on by the people,' agreed Nathan. 'We'll invite ideas for the new buildings' construction from the public, we'll engage architects to implement them and invite tenders from contractors. The main assembly room will accommodate 400 representatives, with one secretary each, contain state-of-the-art electronic voting methods and have a huge public gallery. In the landscaped, always open-to-the-public gardens, will be libraries and restaurants. Representatives will work a forty-eight hour week with three weeks' holiday a year on a roster basis - so that there is never closure of the council. There will be no absurd protocol, no ornate dress, no Queen's Speech written on goatskin, no division bells and no whips to pressurise members - anyone doing that will be jailed for six months' hard for impeding democracy. Representatives will vote as constituents wish them to vote, and will be answerable only to them.'

'It would never be taken up.' murmured Betty Bannister.

'I disagree. Eventually the current characters, such as ministers, spin doctors, Right Honourables, Noble Lords and lackeys could not ignore it. Why? Because the CSP would put this plan to the public and, when the necessary money was raised – and you'd be surprised where it would come from because people are so sick of the present rigmarole – the required land would be bought and the building commenced. MPs would become 'National Representatives' or 'NRs'. They would cease to be "members of parliament" because that suggests – as it always has – that first and foremost they are 'members' – and everyone else is, by definition, excluded, even though their taxes pay the membership fees!

They would cease to be members of some distant time-warped place or club called – just imagine it in this day and age - The House of Commons. *Commons!* – it's derisory - the name says it all! Rather, each will represent the people in the constituency which he or she serves. Constituencies will be redrawn and new elections arranged.'

'Slow up,' Ernie Willis pleaded. 'There's so much to take in.'

'Far too much, said Betty Bannister, 'and it will be for most people.'

'But the two Houses – The Commons and The Lords - are pertinent – significant. They represent our divided society well: the ordinary people and the elite people,' said a sarcastic Freddie Fields. 'No?'

But Dick Nathan pressed on.

'The Commons would be renamed while the Lords would disappear. But, as I said, candidates would be independent, common sense candidates born in the area they represent. There'd be no contemptible dumping of some previously unseated party favourite on unwilling voters in a "safe" seat! Once elected, representatives would vote solely on what they thought best for their constituents. Their re-election would depend on that record and how much they had furthered common sense government. Their salaries would be set at the national average wage with fair, fully documented, expenses. Then they would know what it is like to live, as their constituents do, on a normal income with no add-ons, because no outside jobs would be allowed.'

'But, come on, this 'pretend' assembly of yours couldn't carry out any legislation? It wouldn't be allowed …' began Freddie Fields.

'No, it wouldn't have the power,' continued Betty Bannister.

'Let me finish. The CSP puts this proposal into its manifesto and promises to get the National Assembly – we'll call it that for now – up and running. It proposes that in that Assembly there will be an Executive Council elected by members to carry out the business required of it. While in office, Executive Council Members will be paid 50% more for their extra work and responsibility. Although, as you say, the representatives will have no statutory powers, they will meet regularly, discuss and vote on topical issues relevant to ordinary people, and will publish reports daily.'

Dick Nathan looked round to assess reaction. All were quiet. But Betty Bannister was looking down, again uncertain.

'Voters,' he said, 'can then compare those plain, modest, common sense activities with the strange expensive, longwinded nonsense of Westminster - that is when it deigns to sit and its members deign to attend. They'll begin to say "D'you know, the Birmingham way is the better way, we like it, it's common sense, it's true democracy! And then they'll say, "Why can't we have a *real* government like that? Why can't we do away with the time-wasting rowdies in London, that out-of-touch crowd that doesn't seem to know or care what ordinary people want or how they live? We don't need people who put themselves first, their party second and their constituents third.'

'That's unfair,' injected Betty Bannister. 'Not all MPs are like that at all! You can't bracket them all together.'

'Of course not. But it only needs well-targeted publicity about some and the damage is done.'

'All tarred with the same brush?' suggested Terry.

'Exactly,' Dick Nathan said. He paused, then went on, ' I know it's not fair on them but that's how it is. That's life. Anyway, people will want change. They'll say: 'Let's start again. Let's adopt the Birmingham model. It's for us to decide: after all, we're the voters and taxpayers. The Welsh and Scots have modern assemblies and are streets ahead of us.'

They were still listening. Willis was writing, furiously.

'Then,' explained Nathan, his excitement rising, 'over the years the demand would grow and grow until we have the People's Assembly in Birmingham not as an experiment but as the real thing. The Thames Talking Shop would pass away unmourned.'

'Float out to sea?'

'Or sink in the tide of public opinion.'

'Yes. There'd be no need for conflict, for a Second Civil War! That's how it would be done.' He sipped his now cold coffee.

'And make it clear there would be a wholesale review of the top civil service. Present occupants would not move automatically to Birmingham – not likely! There'd be rigorous assessment of their past performance, workload and pay. And there would be a review of how much power unelected senior civil servants would wield behind the scenes.'

'None,' murmured Norma, 'none at all.'

Dick Nathan paused, waiting for their response.

'Ye gods!' murmured Ernie Willis scribbling. 'There's red hot copy in this.' He could hardly wait to type it up.

Then Susan spoke. 'It's fantastic, awesome, amazing, wonderful, marvellous! It's a brilliant proposal! It would work its way into public favour in the same way as my alternatives for teaching children would eventually win the day as more and more parents saw how valuable the new approach was – and wanted it! There's an obvious parallel.'

'Stick to Dick's ideas,' pleaded Terry, 'one thing at a time.'

'They go together - his and mine,' insisted Susan sharply.

'You're dead right,' agreed Dick Nathan. 'One of the Assembly's first tasks would be to give a firm date for the reform of education. Next would come reconstitution of the legal system - starting with a free-on-demand national legal service and the periodic election of accountable, plain-clothed legal advisers for the courts.'

'A free legal service like the NHS?' asked Norma. 'To be called the National Legal Service? *The NLS*? With lawyers paid an annual salary from state funds, like teachers, nurses and doctors?'

'But some of that's already done and is in our manifesto. It is a key section ...'

'Yes, but it needs stressing again and again and again,' said Nathan. 'The law is the people's law and belongs to the people, it is for the protection of the people, it is paid for by the people and will be managed by the people. The present elitist carry-on is fearful, expensive, slow, misunderstood and often mistrusted. It will be made responsible for the ordering and wellbeing of a civilised society. No groups will be permitted to commandeer the law for themselves or to profit excessively from it.'

'All in all, what you are proposing,' Terry warned them quietly, 'is tantamount to a revolution.' He paused. ' Heads have rolled for less.'

'Indeed, and present-day head-hunters will be out in force chasing those who push such ideas! But always remember that, if their cause is good, the brave revolutionaries win in the end. Much good has come from revolution,' emphasised Dick Nathan. 'And only revolution, or fear of revolution – bloody or social or both - sees the reform or demise of a self-serving, deeply-entrenched Establishment.'

He checked to see he had their attention. They still seemed doubtful. Then he continued. 'Establishments never yield anything freely. The enfranchisement of women, a fundamental human right, took decades of speeches, meetings, strikes, demos, battles, imprisonments, force-feeding, heroines, and World War One disruption of work patterns to bring it about. It took all that to get the vote for women! Then it was given grudgingly and piecemeal. And remember such enfranchisement was within the last hundred years, not in Greek or Roman times!'

Susan was shaking her head. 'I agree with every word you say – but we can't put all that into our manifesto, not at this late stage.'

'Or at any other stage?' asked Nathan in a low voice.

'Maybe not.'

'Then I'm afraid you'll get nowhere. If you won't innovate and take risks your CSP will die, as will your own enthralling plans for the personal tutoring of children. But it's for you to choose, it really is. Now, I'm afraid, it's time for me to say that I've thoroughly enjoyed this discussion, and take my leave. It's so good and so unusual to meet enthusiastic people who have radical ideas and see far, far beyond our existing moribund society. So, as most current politicians seem unable or unwilling to give a lead, let the CSP step in and offer one – a thoroughgoing one. Then you'll get somewhere!'

'Behind bars,' murmured Betty Bannister.

'No, no, I don't think so,' Dick Nathan answered, smiling. 'In some ways things might be hopeful. I hear some MPs themselves are fed up with the Lords and Commons buffoonery, particularly some of the more recently elected women members. Try them, persuade them, and get some on board. You'd probably recruit a dozen to begin with.'

He hesitated, then continued, 'one final thought, why don't you give people some definite dates, some things to anticipate eagerly? Propose that if the CSP was returned it would, in its second year of office, name the 1st January as *National Common Sense Day*. From then on, each year, and on that day, one major common sense proposal or law would come into effect.'

They still seemed doubtful.

'A good one to start with would be reform of the penal system. Show that thousands are in jail who need not be here – the many non-violent convicts. The scandalous, counter-productive overcrowding in ninety percent of prisons could be remedied by building basic, army type camps for thousands of approved prisoners. Make them, the adult men and women, undergo a period of uniformed, supervised, strictly disciplined National Community Service which would cost us far less and get something useful done in return for their keep, with the understanding that transgressors would return immediately to an austere prison for the remainder of their sentences - where they would find life distinctly uncomfortable. That's real common sense. It cut costs, reduces the prison population and the need for so many prisons, helps society and helps the convicted persons by showing them trust and giving them something useful to do and to know that, partly through their efforts, they would be released into an improved society. That would be a wonderful start!'

His listeners nodded, so he went on, 'then could come measures like the move to Birmingham, referendum voting, alternative education, a ban on road parking, free public transport, a state-provided legal system, the election of chief constables and judges, simplified taxation, an easy to understand, standardised social security system. That dating would give you four years to make preparations, instigate the first reforms, then another year before you need to stand for re-election, that is if you want to continue with five years between elections.' He grinned. 'Perhaps make it ten? Or twenty?'

He smiled at each one of them in turn. 'And then emphasise that on January 1st each year, on *National Common Sense Day*, a new piece of common sense legislation would be initiated based on what people had asked for in the previous year and would be worked on throughout the ensuing year. Publish a five-year programme and keep to it. Offer something definite that people could look forward to and which would get them involved and lift their spirits. Make them think, give them hope! *Involve* them! Bring them back into our democracy. Make it a genuine democracy! Try it! You could be changing Britain for ever!'

Dick Nathan shook hands heartily with all seven people present, again smiled warmly, put on his jacket, adjusted the collar and put a crumpled note into Terry's hand. 'For the funds,' he said. He waved as he crossed the hall, and left. None of them saw him again.

They sat for a minute or more. Terry smoothed the note.'£50,' he whispered to Susan. She beamed.

'I'll go along with all that,' said Norma eventually. 'Every word.'

'And me,' murmured Freddie Fields who had seen the note passed.

'I want to think about it,' said Betty.

'Think about what?' questioned Norma impatiently.

'How much politicians can do on their own, even if they want to.'

'On their own?' queried Norma.

'He made no allowance for the powers of the international banks, corporations, oil companies, land owners, media moguls and lawyers to say nothing of Commonwealth, EU and USA governments.'

'Well,' asked Norma with marked irritation, 'so what?'

'They might be alarmed by a lot of his proposals, especially if the proposals were successful and looked like setting a precedent for their countries. They'd see that as a danger to be thwarted.'

'But we've surely not got to the point where we can't organise our own society and choose our own government?' said Terry.

'Haven't we?' replied Andrews. 'I'm not so sure about that.'

'And there's another thing,' continued Betty Bannister, 'he was *too* hurried, too impatient: wanted everything done at once.'

'He didn't. He said five years, just to begin with,' said Norma.

'And don't forget that the institutions needing his reforms are interlocked,' argued Susan persuasively, 'it's difficult to pick one and start with that while the others are still block the path. Everything has become such a complex interaction of interested parties, with such a range of diverse aims, and such rich incentives for a powerful few to retain the *status quo*, that change cannot be achieved piecemeal. I'd go further than him, I'd bring in a batch of reforms in the first five years.'

But Betty continued as though Susan had not spoken. 'And he was blinkered. He gave no credit to those politicians who sacrifice their time doing good. And not all old socialists slink through the back door of the House of Lords hoping their working class friends won't notice; some go reluctantly and others, who have much to offer, decline the invitation altogether because they cannot stomach the set up.'

'Which shows what a sickeningly senseless system it is,' said Terry.

'And some,' pressed Betty, 'are lifelong champions of ordinary people and give up their lives to that. And plenty of MPs could earn more money from their specialisms by working outside Westminster.'

'There'll always be laudable exceptions, but that does not invalidate his argument,' replied Terry. 'It's like saying we should keep the head teacher institution because most head teachers do their best and some work wonders. The point has to be stressed that it's the *system* that's faulty, not individual practitioners, then remind people of all the old class divisions that delay the growth of an inclusive, fairer society.'

'So he's put the cat among the pigeons,' murmured John Andrews.

'When it's too late for me to stay any longer.' said Freddie Fields, smiling. 'But I'll support you with a donation.'

'So will I,' said Andrews.

He reached for his wallet and took out notes. Betty Bannister, also rising to leave, was still uncertain and moved to speak to Susan as she began to straighten the chairs. There was little further discussion for, after Nathan's contribution, anything else would have been an anticlimax. But then, almost as an afterthought, John Andrews delved into his pocket and handed Terry a sealed brown envelope.

'I've just remembered,' he said. 'I was asked to give you this by a person who wants to be anonymous but who hopes it will help, and,' he continued, pointing to Terry good-naturedly, 'in case you get the wrong idea, it's *not* from me! This is my effort.' He handed over two twenty-pound notes.

Terry thanked him, slipped the money and the envelope into his jacket and helped tidy away the chairs and coffee cups. At the kitchen entrance Norma Greene approached him.

'I wanted to hear more about Susan's teaching plans,' she said, 'and remind her that there's a lot of stress among children now. With some it becomes a full-blown depression and it's partly due to the strain the system puts on them – tests, grades and the whole raft of ever-rising expectations.' She paused, but Susan was still engaged. 'We seem to be taking years of childhood away from some pupils. I wanted her to put that in her work and to point out its importance. I don't think she makes enough of it. A so-called education system that makes children mentally ill is a national disgrace and a fundamental attack on those children's human rights and a cause of anxiety for their parents. It is indefensible.' She hesitated. 'And many people are guilty by default.'

Terry nodded. 'I wouldn't dream of defending it.'

'But never mind that for now,' said Norma cheering up, 'what we heard tonight was fascinating, in fact exciting, it did me good and I'll be voting for you and sending a cheque and so will Betty. But,' she whispered, 'we don't want everyone to know that, not just yet.'

And that will be par for the course, thought Terry sadly: "Here's some money - but please don't publicise my name."

The tiny audience drifted away satisfied with the meeting, but Ernie Willis waited, and, seeing Terry otherwise engaged, and Susan parting from Betty Bannister, he stepped over to her before Norma could intervene. 'I've put my notepad away, Dr Mansfield,' he smiled, 'I'm no longer a reporter: I'm just me! Can I have a word?'

'Of course.'

'I've read some of your material on alternative education and I'm more than just "interested". It's got a lot going for it. So could I do a piece about it sometime soon? It would not be *Messenger* generated or edited. I'd make a readable feature article of it with a photo and something about you personally: twelve hundred words attributed to me, and you'd see the script before submission.'

'That would be good.'

'I'll phone. I'd better move now and write up tonight's effort: it's terrific stuff! And good luck with *both* your projects!'

The caretaker shuffled as the clock showed a minute to nine, but that last minute had been paid for. Norma and her friend had gone and there was just time for Terry to open the envelope.

'Good grief!' he shouted. 'Look at this!'

There was a single sheet of paper with, "I trust this helps the cause!" written boldly on it and, attached by a paper clip, was a banker's order for £10,000 in favour of *The Common Sense Party*.

'Fantastic, terrific!' murmured Terry. 'Amazing! I can't believe it! Who the devil can have sent it? *£10,000*? And no strings?'

Susan took the order and examined it. 'Incredible!' she said.

'The CSP can have its own current account! It has come of age!'

He gave Susan a kiss on the cheek and promptly she turned her other cheek. 'And one for this side!' she ordered indicating the spot 'No discrimination in the CSP: both cheeks treated fairly!'

She smiled as he held her shoulders and obliged eagerly with a deeper, lingering kiss. She felt its warm imprint for several seconds. Then, when Terry had thanked the "I've seen it all before" caretaker and slipped the fifty and twenty-pound notes into the envelope, she told him about Ernie Willis and his proposed article. Terry was delighted. They'd had a good meeting, encouragement, exciting ideas, well over £10,000, and promises of free publicity! Wonderful!

Sunday 28 April.   **A Personal Rejection**

The euphoria created by the banker's order faded as Sunday wore on. The response to their morning's canvassing ranged from cool to icy and, after three hours of largely futile door-knocking, Susan and Terry were ready for a rest at their rendezvous, *The King of Morocco*.

'I'm shattered: I only want a sandwich,' said Terry.

'They don't do sandwiches on Sundays, only full meals. Have a turkey salad and I'll have the same. Order them with the drinks.'

Terry returned with beer and red wine. 'They don't do salads either, just traditional Sunday lunches, and they're not serving those yet.'

'Damn!' murmured Susan. 'OK, so we'll sit a bit then go back to my place. I can do some tuna rolls. And for Pete's sake liven up! I've trudged round too and I'm no more joyful with what I discovered.'

'It's not just that …'

'Keep it till later. I'm taking the weight off my feet and appreciating my drink. I might have another! You do the same.'

But she did not have another and later in her apartment as they ate, with little enjoyment, she saw how low Terry was.

'You start,' Susan said. 'How did you get on?'

'Awful,' he said gloomily. 'Most doors were not answered. Some people were suspicious. One old boy peeked over his door chain to see my ID and as I hadn't any said he'd call the police.'

'Did he?'

'I didn't wait! But what a state of affairs! A few said they'd decided already, lots said they weren't voting. The times I heard, "Won't make no difference, mate!" Only one said she'd read our leaflet and that it had some good ideas but we wouldn't get anywhere. She said the current set up was crazy as it discouraged initiative and that in a recent general election many MPs were elected on a minority vote – that is less than half their registered constituents voted for them so that huge numbers are represented by members they did not support. She said that was farcical. He paused. 'But one encounter was frightening.'

'Go on,' prompted Susan.

'There was this huge, hard-muscled, shaven-headed, tattooed man of fifty-plus wearing trainers, scruffy jeans and a sweaty vest. He said he didn't know how I had the bloody cheek to bang on his door to talk about voting. He'd been voting for thirty...' Terry hesitated, 'for thirty *something* years – he used the 'f' word quite often - and voting hadn't made a blind bit of difference. He said people were never asked to vote on what mattered. They'd never been asked to vote on crime or the effing EU and Brussels ruled the roost, nor on immigration and whole areas had been taken over – just forced on people. What sort of free country was that? "Go on," he shouted wild-eyed, and I thought he was going to thump me, "*you* tell *me*! You're the bloody politician! There's only one lot I'll vote for – and the wife, the kids, my Dad, uncles, brothers, sisters, the bookie and the bloke next door and his tart of a wife – and that's the PPP! Get it? The effing PPP! So shove off mate!"

'When I said the People's Patriotic Party wasn't standing here he yelled: "That's why I'm not voting, you silly sod!" He said he'd rather rip his voting paper into little bits and shove them up his fat MP's farting arse piece by tiny piece.'

Susan smiled. 'But surely, Terry,' she said soothingly, 'if his MP had to break wind at all forcefully such tiny bits would be blown out again?

He'd get his own back?'

'OK!' Terry nearly grinned. 'OK. But I was shattered'.

'You weren't ready for Mr Shove-Off-Mate?'

'Not to be yelled at as crudely as that.'

'And you've not mixed with people like that?'

'Have you?'

'More than you, it seems. So what next?'

'For a time he calmed down and went on about how voters had to choose a party, not people. He said he'd vote for Today's Tories but that would mean supporting pot-bellied foxhunters and their yelping hounds. He kept saying people had to vote for a load of things they didn't want in order to vote for one they did.'

'And he has a point,' retorted Susan. 'Didn't you tell him we'd have nationwide referenda on important single issues so that people could vote on each one separately and make their voice heard?'

She slipped off her shoes and curled up on the settee massaging her toes. She had not expected such dire despondency so soon. Was Terry merely an armchair politician, a theoretical sociologist?'

'No chance. He slammed the door on me. Honestly, Susan, he just seemed so sick of politicians he didn't want to hear anything from any of them, and he's not alone! That's the really depressing point; the old parties have messed everything up so much that all politicians are seen in the same light, and that includes us. That's what's so hard to take. So what do we do? If we can't get our ideas listened to, where do we go? How will radical change, *or any change*, come about? It's hopeless!'

'Is it? You haven't asked me about my morning.'

'Don't tell me it was better!'

'Worse: a really grim mixture of rudeness, antagonism, indifference, suspicion, prejudice, disbelief and ignorance. Two didn't even know a general election was imminent! Imagine that! And right-wing bigotry flaunted – right out in the open. It won't be long before it's respectable.'

Terry cringed.

'But I don't get morbid. It's an experience I value. I'm learning.'

'Good for you.'

'And I didn't know Mansworth had so many rabid dogs eager to tear me apart. I'm sure one house had six hungry Alsatians leaping round on the other side of the door scratching the paint and making a din!'

'They probably thought you were a *real* politician!'

'I learned a lot from an elderly woman who told me her life story.

She'd retired from teaching to work for a travel agent. She'd become less of a professional teacher and more of an instructor putting over material other people chose for her in ways and at times they wanted the curriculum "delivered". She said she hated that word "delivered", she was neither a midwife nor a milkman.. She said her idea of *true* education couldn't be measured by inspectors in a few days, it takes months of enlightened study to discern and evaluate the gradual changes in development that enable young people to live rich and full lives. She said itinerant officials with checklists hadn't a hope of doing that and, while they personally hadn't set up the system, they should recognise what was happening and return, voluntarily, to the classroom. I let her talk on, then, after complaining about indiscipline and teachers becoming managers, she said something that shook me.'

'Well?'

'She said schools as such were now difficult to justify. Some were too cumbersome and, despite teachers' best intentions, struggled to be places of caring, loving education. Their curriculum was prescribed, teachers shackled, testing excessive and politicians prominent. I tried to speak but she was in full stride. In her niece's village, she said, four families had joined together to educate their eleven children and had pooled funds to pay an experienced teacher for three hours on Saturday mornings to advise on work-projects for the next week and to teach the whole group - aged five to twelve - for two of those hours. For the rest of the week - and they didn't keep to school hours - they progressed by sharing ideas and allocating themselves teaching tasks and supervision. They enjoyed joint learning experiences by using TV, radio, film, Internet, libraries, galleries, colleges, museums, department stores, train stations, parks and other venues where genuine learning could take place free of charge.'

'But that's your line! She'd read your stuff!'

'She hadn't, that's the whole point. I asked her. She hadn't heard of my work or me. I tried to tell her about my coming book, but she said you didn't need to write books, just get out there and get on with it and use intelligence, imagination, love, and a bit of common sense.'

'Common sense? Didn't you tell her about ...'

'About the CSP? I started to, but she said she'd read the leaflet and that we hadn't a hope and she'd be wasting her vote by voting for us. She wouldn't be voting for anyone. Then she closed the door as if she was suddenly tired of talking, and that was it.'

'Didn't she see that your work and the CSP slot together?'

'If she did she didn't say so.'

Terry twisted his coffee mug first this way, then that, until suddenly he stood up, shifted Susan's feet along the sofa, and sat down close beside her. She edged away, but only slightly. For a while he was quiet, deeply thoughtful, then he turned and looked directly at her.

'Susan,' he said, 'Susan, let's pack it in. Let's quit! They don't want us and we don't want them, and we don't *need* them. And with the CSP, let's face it, we haven't even started the hare let alone caught it.'

He went to take her hand, but she withdrew gently. Her face was expressionless.

'Let *us* decide what we want to do with our lives,' he urged, 'instead of allowing others to dictate to us whether they be politicians, lawyers, accountants, administrators, head teachers, advisors, examiners, inspectors, vice-chancellors or any of the rest of the shower.'

Susan stared in astonishment, but this time Terry was not going to be put off. He clenched his own hands.

'Shall we?' he pleaded, 'come on Susan, let's do our own thing and to hell with the lot of them! Let's be like those fine village families the woman talked about who taught their own children. They'd got the answer, and they'd got initiative, foresight, perseverance and guts.'

'Terry,' Susan cried, amazed at this turn of events. 'This is only the first half-day of a three-week campaign! We've hardly started.' Then she laughed: 'and anyway we haven't any children to teach.' She slid away from him and returned her feet to the floor.

'We could have.'

'Could have? What *are* you saying?' She leaned back and stared at him. His face was flushed, but he was deadly serious.

'We could have children,' he said quietly, ' you and I. And we could live together, be partners, or colleagues, or friends, or get married, or whatever arrangement you wanted. And have children, one, two, three – you're still young enough.'

'Well, thank you for that! So I become a mother and abandon all I've been working on? Just like that? Be a multiple mum?'

'Yes! We'd both go on with those parts of our work we wanted to go on with: the parts that *mean* something, because that's the essence of it, don't you see? It would be *our* time, *our* choice, *our* work.'

'And I'd live with you, or you with me? Starting when, tonight?'

'Don't make light of it.' Now it was Terry's turn to slide away, rejected. 'I really like you, Susan, very, very much, far more than you can ever guess. And it's becoming much more than 'like', very much more.' He moved back towards her.

'No!' Susan said emphatically. 'Sit there, sit right there, and answer me honestly. Is this some form of fooling around, or some delirium brought on by your experiences this morning?'

Terry did not answer at first, then he said, 'it's neither.'

'Neither? You *are* serious? But you haven't even hinted at this! I don't know what to say, I really don't.'

'But I've felt like this for a long time, and I did hint at it, on that wretched island. Didn't you notice that? Yes, of course you did. You must have done, you stepped away, and you moved my arm. I simply haven't said anything since then because of that. I've been too scared.'

'Scared? Don't be ridiculous. And why bring all this out now, with all we've got on, especially all *you've* got on?'

'I've just said. I don't want to "go on" any more. It's futile.'

'So you'll marry me instead? Is that it?'

'I didn't mean it like that. You mustn't think that. I never, never, *never* meant it like that.' His despondency was complete and they sat in silence for several minutes until he said, 'You twist my words.'

Susan turned to him and this time unclenched his hands and held them tightly between hers. She looked at him closely. 'All right, I believe you are sincere, but if you're not, and if you're having me on, I'll never forgive you. *Never*. Do you understand that?'

He nodded.

She moved closer as if she wanted him to hear even though she lowered her voice. 'Terry, listen, I am fond of you, very fond. That's one reason I've joined up with you on the CSP initiative even though career wise it won't help me one little bit. But that's only one reason. I also believe yours is a vital cause. And, yes, while I'm fond of you – and I am - I'm not in love with you, whatever that means. To be frank, I take it that "being in love," means that one person cannot live fully without the other; that happiness and completeness or fulfilment in life cannot be achieved if those two people live apart. But, and I'm truly, truly sorry, I do not feel like that about you. In other words – and I don't want to upset you - I'm not "in love" with you, and you must understand that my work, my ambitions, and, for me, a satisfying life can be achieved without one particular man at my side, and without children of my own. I'm sorry it has to be like that, I truly am, but, with me, it does. That's it.'

'I see.'

'But do you?' she said in an undertone. '*Do* you see? Because when I said I did not need a man to further my life and work, I did not mean that I never need a man for support, companionship, friendship and plain, outright physical sex. I have deep, womanly urges that need satisfying and I've been with men for that and, I hope, given equal pleasure and satisfaction to them. I know I tried.'

Terry recoiled. He slid away pulling his hands from hers. He hung his head.

'Susan, you say you don't want to upset me and then in the next breath you tell me about other men you've been to bed with and let me picture what went on.' His lips pressed tightly together until they whitened. She waited.

'You let me imagine them making love to you, feeling you, kissing you, stroking you, touching every intimate part of you and, after all that, you say you don't want to *upset* me? I don't want to hear any more. I *don't*. I just want to go, and want to go now. To finish with everything.'

Susan placed a hand forcefully on his shoulder.

'Sit still. What I am saying is that I take a different view of sexual relationships from you, as I do, no doubt, with my views on girls' education and women's rights. Those views have grown up with me and become part of me. They are not better or worse than yours, but *different*. I cannot contemplate marriage as a "till death do us part" institution. I think that is too restrictive for intelligent, curious, sociable, healthy, educated people. Sex is not only for procreation, it's for enjoyment, relief, ego bolstering and deep companionship, in which giving to the other and taking from the other is crucial. It must never be seen as a once and for all union, a binding together, an inescapable life sentence. It must never be commandeered for narrow, self-serving purposes by church, state, or law. It must never tie together in misery two people who no longer respect one another. Social institutions which try to do that I hold in utter, utter … *utter*, contempt.'

Terry had no reply. Her words had cut him. He felt an overall hopelessness. He had been a soft, ingenuous fool.

'You're a lovely man,' she said, 'and, as I feel now, I could sleep with you night after night, and be as close, as passionate, as inventive, as you or I could be. I really could! You can have me, love me, hold me hour after hour, but you cannot possess me, exclusively, as a lifelong wife or as a permanent lover. I don't want that. I don't need that. I can't stand the thought of that. I won't have that. Never.'

Terry shook his head. But the primitive force of her words had excited him, his desire to take her was almost irresistible, but he could not stay with her and at the same time suffer the pain of the images that would never go away: images of her lying contentedly in the arms of the man who had just loved her, or of the one who had gone before, or of those who would certainly follow.

Yet Susan persisted, determined to make matters clear beyond all possible doubt. 'I know it is distressing and not what you wanted to hear, but while you were with me I would love you in the sense that I would love to feel you hard against me, but there would be no commitment to an 'as long as we shall live' relationship. None. Think about it, and, please, please, try not to think ill of me.' She paused. 'But no,' she said as Terry started to reply, 'I asked you to think about it. Sit there and try to take in what I said, fairly. And, believe me, I don't often, in fact I've never, spoken to a man in this way before. You are the first, if that's any comfort.'

Terry raised his head slightly, but would not look at her. Susan put out a hand and touched his chin and slowly, gently, turned his head until he was forced to face her.

'Do you still want to leave?' she whispered. As she waited she smiled kindly. 'Do you?

'I'm not sure. I don't know. I don't know what I want, or what I think I want, or even what I damn well think! I don't. Really I don't.'

'Let me help. I would like you to stay tonight to sleep with me.' She snuggled up to him, her scent alluring, and the gentle pressure of her body undeniable. 'I want you and need you to stay. Will you?'

'You don't have to ask, do you? You don't! You'll get it your own way in the end – you women always do – every time, every time!'

'Do we?'

'Yes. And you don't need to ask that, either.' He almost shouted at her he was so distraught. She saw he was almost in tears.

'I do,' she said quietly. 'I do need to ask that question, and I do need an answer.' She was unyielding. 'So tell me, give me an answer.'

'All right. Yes! Yes! *Yes*! Is that enough? Why the hell do you need to ask, Susan, why? Why, when you know damn well what the answer's going to be? Why?'

'Because I don't take you or anyone else for granted. And I'm glad, really, really glad, to get that answer. We're agreed. Tonight, and all night.' She swept his hair from his forehead and, with her hand still in

233

place, kissed him lightly on the lips. Then, almost immediately, she retreated sharply and swung into work mode. 'Now, we've £10,000 to spend, or do we trace the donor and send it back?'

'No.'

'So that means we've real work to do, a campaign to run, your head teacher interview to prepare, or is that for the chop, too?'

'No.'

'Then I'm going to cook a superb dinner and you're going out for two bottles of decent wine – no stinting – and, slowly, we're going to drink it all, and talk and talk and talk and exchange confidences and then,' she paused to see that he was listening fully, 'we're going to go to bed and are going to make love to each other and I'm going - we're going - to enjoy every marvellous, magical minute of it and then we're going to sleep till morning, tired - but content. Does that seem OK?' She smiled, teasingly, 'does that make a commendable bill of fare for the revolutionary prospective parliamentary candidate and the radical headmaster elect? Does it?''

'For heaven's sake, Susan what do you think? What do you damn well think? But don't let's wait, I can't wait, I really can't; let's go to bed now, please!'

As he took her in his arms she closed with him willingly and knowingly, her breasts pressed against him. The sensation, for Terry, was indescribably fine. His eyes closed and, furtively, Susan watched his changing expressions of joy. His hands wandered over her and he felt her incredible softness and warmth, her fullness, her wholesome maturity. Inexplicably her body seemed so firm and yet so pliant. Sexually it was superb, it was at the pinnacle of enticement. He would have this wonderful woman, if only for one night, while she was in her sexual prime. Whatever else she said he knew that for a brief time she would be his and no one else's, and in return he would give the whole of himself to her and try his utmost to make it memorable for them both. After that he would have something magnificent to recall: something that could never be taken away - by anyone.

'Ten thousand pounds,' she whispered gleefully as she eased herself from his hold and adjusted her blouse and smoothed her rumpled skirt, 'and that's not my fee, Mr Park, It's what we've got to spend – and to spend wisely! So, come on, for, like Disney's seven dwarfs, it's "heigh ho, heigh ho, and off to work we go!" Time to make a start! A start on sorting out the Establishment!'

Week Five

Monday 29 April.   **The Social Evening**

Monday was crunch day for the parentally renowned educational establishment of Outer Mansworth Comprehensive School (Mixed). It began with a telephone call to Adrian Olde from a hesitant and barely audible Giles Townsend to say he could not attend tomorrow's head teacher interviews, as his wife was ill and must not be left alone. He apologised, asked Olde to pass on the news, and rang off.

Townsend had begun to regret his involvement with the People's Patriotic Party. His wife had been unhappy from the start although, like many others, she agreed with some of the party's demands which, she argued, were given inadequate attention elsewhere. But some PPP policies worried her and her husband's membership and outspoken views had lost her several timorous friends. Her concern was that the party was extreme while she was a woman of more moderate, yet firm, right wing views. She accepted Giles' point that the PPP had put up candidates in local elections with success and that membership was growing, but she could never see it winning a general election and wondered what its strategies would be after repeated failure.

Most worrying of all she could see that, despite his efforts to hide it, Giles was stressed. She guessed he felt trapped within a group that would not release him easily and knew that for weeks he had slept badly. Now, she had been told, he was concerned that having been cajoled onto the interview panel he would be seen as a devout party member sitting alongside and voting with the neo-fascist, well-heeled Eastman, and she thought Eastman was one of the nastiest pieces of work she had met in the whole of Outer Mansworth. Then, after a frightening Sunday in which Giles had paced the house saying he was snared and would lose his job at the bank, she had persuaded him to leave the interview panel. That, she thought, would show a modicum of independence and begin his gradual rejection of party pressure.

*

Also worried, but for different reasons, was Mrs Sonia Smith. Under orders from Zing she had accepted the invitation for interview but since then had been hearing about the medley of problems at Olde's school. Clearly what had been one of the best schools in the county had deteriorated markedly and she could see only too well what lay in store for the incumbent. Did she want that?

Her anxiety grew when she heard rumours that she was the favourite candidate. Increasingly she was inclined to look round the pleasantly sited, sensibly sized and manageable school she ran already. She saw the obsequiousness of her well-trained staff, the support of the "anxious-for-their-children-to-succeed" parents, the subservient nature of the pupils, and the generous support of the powers that be. She would be a fool to throw all that away for Olde's mess of pottage. She did not need the increase in salary nor want the additional stress the job would bring; she had been stupid to let her name go forward. Now, she imagined, very few had applied and she could understand the governors' unprecedented rush to make an early appointment.

Mainly because of this she had, several times in the past week, been on the point of withdrawing. She had hesitated because if she did so her high standing in the eyes of the local education chief, who regarded her as the least troublesome of his head teachers, would take a tumble. Also, she would be choosing the coward's way out of a predicament that was of her own making. But the weekend had been trying and her few remaining friends had urged her to withdraw. Yet still she hesitated: could she pull out at only twenty-four hours' notice?

Then, after taking her smooth as clockwork assembly, talking to the agree-with-anything teachers who were trying to keep well in, congratulating smartly-dressed children who tried hard and brought their work for her to admire, checking minor problems in the mail with her ever-efficient secretary, walking round the school's spotless buildings and litter-free grounds with her compliant caretaker, and recalling the inspectors' glowing report, she made up her mind: she would stay. If that meant being in people's bad books and no further promotion, so be it. It was her life and, contentedly, she could see out her time here.

She phoned Mr Olde's secretary who seemed to be a somewhat familiar, gossipy woman and checked the name and telephone number of the school's Chairperson of Governors.

*

For poor Giles Townsend matters were less straightforward. Fergus Eastman got news of his proposed withdrawal long before the other governors because Ingrid, who had listened-in to Townsend's call to Olde, made sure of that. Fergus was in action instantly. While his lunchtime visit to Townsend's house was clearly unwelcome he was able to see that Mrs Townsend was not ill. Ten minutes later, after a no-holds-barred conversation in which Townsend was told how unfortunate it would be if his more salacious outbursts reached the bank's senior managers, the wretched governor had called Lena to say that for a few hours his wife would be able to manage by herself.

'Good man,' said Eastman listening, 'we might need your vote.'

'But another thing worries me,' said the miserable Giles quietly lest his all-too-alert wife should hear, 'which, if it should come to light, I shall deny ever telling you, *come what may!* Do you understand that, Eastman? *Come what may,* so don't think what I'm going to tell you can be used against this Park, but this morning someone opened a current account in the name of The Common Sense Party in the sum of £10,000.'

'Ten thousand quid? Where did that come from?'

'Keep your voice down for God's sake!' Giles was now beside himself with fear at the mere thought of what he was doing, 'and, remember, if word gets out I'll swear on oath it did not come from me regardless of the consequences. D'you really get that, Eastman?'

'Yes. So where did it come from? Who's tipping up that money?'

'There's no telling. It was a banker's order – untraceable as far as I personally am concerned. But I'm pretty sure I've seen the depositor before. I think she's one of tomorrow's candidates.'

'*She*? Susan Mansfield?'

'That was the name.'

'*Mansfield*? You're sure?'

'As sure as I can be.'

'That's really worth knowing! Just think for a minute Townsend, it's not you who should be heaving your guts up, but that flighty Mansfield and her bolshie boyfriend. They're both in this together and they're getting thousands of pounds and, whatever you say I can or can't do, the money still comes from undisclosed sources! Not only that, but have you read their CSP manifesto? The changes they propose are so radical and cut across so many sensitive areas they're going to upset a hell of a lot of people and a hell of a lot of groups – high up people and merciless, ruthless, stop-at-nothing groups. Cromford-White was making that point last night. "Let them stew in their own juice," he said, "let the pair of them simmer slowly for a very long time!"'

'He did?' Townsend's voice exuded fear.

'He did. He said that in many quarters the Common Sense Party's manifesto would be seen as the work of dangerous, subversive insurrectionists out to wreck this country's prospects and that we should therefore back-pedal and give them time to dig their own graves.'

'And save us the trouble?' murmured Townsend, slightly relieved.

'Exactly. The powers that be have ways of sorting out upstarts like Park. He'll soon wish he'd never even started his new party!'

'But he's done nothing wrong, Eastman. It's a free country. We've got free speech. Anyone can put forward ideas or start a new party.'

'Nothing wrong legally, but d'you think the power-loving party leaders, affluent lawyers, top educationists, wealthy industrialists and comfortably-off civil servants are going to sit on their arses doing bugger-all while he shouts his mouth off and spreads nasty notions that might hurt their lifestyle? And don't give me that "free speech" crap either, not in the UK today!'

But Giles was unconvinced. 'We don't live in a dictatorship. In this country you can't be fined or jailed for having ideas or expressing thoughts or even for setting up some way-out party. Well ... not yet.'

'There's no need for jails! The Establishment has its own ways of dealing with the Parks and Mansfields of this world. The pair won't know who's targeting them, how it's done, or what's hit them: they'll sink in shit. Quietly, behind the scenes, our Mr Park will be dumped - not dumped in jail, but in no-man's land and left to rot. He can go on yelling his crazy ideas until he slips slowly into a filthy, muddy, crater of his own making and he'll pull that university trollop in with him and nobody will hear their shrieks because nobody will want to! They'll both sink without trace - and good riddance! But, best of all, Townsend, nobody will be able to prove a thing! Cromford-White was adamant on that – and he knows what he's talking about.'

But, while Fergus Eastman beamed contentedly at colourful visions of the floundering couple, Giles Townsend remained a deeply worried man.

*

The Reverend Dr Lena Napier was irate. Never had her curate known her so ill disposed. Hurriedly the trembling man found urgent work in the team's most distant church.

Lena had spent almost an hour informing exasperated governors of Townsend's coming absence, only to learn that he *was*, after all, to attend

238

the interviews. So she began phoning again to say that a last minute replacement was unnecessary.

As soon as Lena had finished that task, which fitted uncomfortably with her other Monday morning duties, Mrs Sonia Smith telephoned to ask if she could visit over an important issue. When asked if it could wait Mrs Smith explained briefly what it was about and was told, in no uncertain terms, to come to the rectory.

For five minutes Lena Napier forgot her Christian pledge to be an understanding, compassionate and supportive listener.

'At this stage, Mrs Smith, only one day before the interviews, you decide to withdraw from the selection process? Here we have a large school serving a thousand children and their parents in urgent need of a head teacher, and you –and I make no bones about it – you, the favoured candidate, say you do not wish to proceed?' She paused as if to regain breath. 'Mrs Smith, that is indeed, as you suggest, "unfortunate", and I would ask you to reconsider while you are here and while knowledge of the matter is confined to me. Let me leave you to consider.'

'No, I have already considered and I have considered carefully: I am not an irresponsible person. I have decided the position is definitely not for me.'

'*Not for you*? Then in the Lord's good name, who *is* it for? You applied, you are the right age, you have the experience, the references, the qualifications, the esteem of the authorities, so Madam, I find your withdrawal unacceptable and I ask you to sit for a while – for as long as you like in fact - and think again!' Lena again made as if to leave.

'No. Please, don't go!' Now the head mistress's tone was of one giving an order, and although Lena bridled, she sat down.

'I am sorry, Dr Napier, but I have made up my mind. Further, while I appreciate your position, I think it better to speak now than to attend for interview and decline the post should it be offered. That is not how I operate. And that would only present you with further difficulties because, as things stand, the Governors have a day to reflect on whether to appoint from the remaining candidates or to re-advertise.'

At this Lena's patience was wearing wafer thin. 'Mrs Smith, I don't need reminding of the governors' duties and options, whereas you don't seem to recognise the repercussions of your action.'

'Are you suggesting …'?

'I am suggesting nothing. I am *telling* you that your actions will have consequences far beyond one afternoon's interviews.'

'So it's a threat?'

'Certainly not,' said Lena hastily, 'although I see it has occurred to you that you will be doing your career no good at all. What I mean is that it harms a school immeasurably when a professional person of your current standing withdraws so belatedly her application for its headship. Our detractors, of whom there are enough already, will trade on that and begin to ask awkward - if irrelevant - questions about the attractiveness of the school. So, *please,* think again.'

'There is no point in my thinking again.'

'Your withdrawal is final?'

'It is.'

'Very well.'

Neither woman spoke until Lena Napier said, coldly, 'Then, as a busy person yourself, you will realise that I, too, have much to do.'

'Then please don't let *me* delay you. I will let myself out.'

'There is no need for that, Mrs Smith. I shall see you to the door, willingly.'

*

The promotion-conscious Chief Education Officer, Dr. Matthew Zing, could not contain his anger. He promised action with an alacrity Lena had not seen before. He asked her not to inform other governors of Sonia Smith's withdrawal but to leave matters to him.

Half an hour later he phoned back. He had been unable to persuade Mrs Smith to change her mind and he wanted a meeting with Lena. He, too, was invited to the rectory.

'You need to advise the governors of this,' was Zing's opening remark, 'and, if you are agreeable, do that by phone today. Yes?'

'Yes.'

'Good. Ask, first, whether the governors want to interview the remaining candidates or to cancel, re-advertise, and broaden the field.'

'There's no hope of broadening the field, Dr Zing. And if we cancel now we shall have to phone one candidate immediately to prevent his leaving home to get here for 1.30. For another candidate I imagine that is already too late.'

'Too late? They're getting here today?'

'Were you not sent a programme? Candidates are invited to see the school this afternoon and attend a social event this evening.'

'Of course. Yes. But what a bloody mess!'

Lena was silent, her eyes lowered.

'I do beg your pardon: I forget myself. But I am worried.'

'So am I.'

'Of course. All the governors will be displeased, while the local press will love it, especially that damned reporter, Hetty, Hetty.....'

'Hopkins?' offered Lena. 'And is she "damned,"so young?'

'Of course not. I forget myself again. But it becomes clear that the better option is for you to proceed with the published programme and continue as if nothing has happened.'

Lena gazed at him in disbelief.

'As if nothing has happened? What are you saying? Here is a school already on the downward path, the dead cert candidate we all relied on has withdrawn, the PPP seems to be in on the act, the TFRA are agitating, the local press is aroused, we have five dubious make-weight candidates on a short list of five and no time to fill the gap. And you say we go on, Dr Zing, as if nothing has happened?'

'Yes, Madam, because you have no choice. If you are going to interview tomorrow you must interview these five and, let's say, you try to *pretend* nothing has happened. So, please, let's review the five: let's review their pros and cons. They may not all be that bad.'

Lena was appalled. Had the world gone mad?

'They may not be all that bad?' she repeated. 'They are the same set you so gloomily cast doubt upon at the initial meeting when you claimed that in your early days there would have been sixty applicants for a post like this! Don't you remember that?'

'Of course I do, and, if I remember correctly, you said, "Perhaps we should have a look at what we have now, that's all we can do." So, shall we do just that?'

Lena Napier almost growled her reply. 'All right, Dr Zing, but you start: it's your idea.'

'Right, but first let me apologise for my abruptness.' He paused. Lena nodded. 'So, Miss Joan Bates, a deputy head. Her advantages: some managerial experience, age 36, a bit young but just within the agreed range, good on discipline, her school has an excellent inspectors' report, does everything by the book. Disadvantages: unmarried, poor degree, little further study or additional professional training, no head teacher experience to offer this very large school, strange hobbies for a woman - motor cycling and mushroom growing - minor niggles in two of her references. So, what do you say: D+ moving towards C-?'

'I fail to see why being unmarried is held against her.'

'I simply feel it is better for a head teacher to have brought up children of her own, and would say the same of a bachelor applicant.'

'I don't go along with that, but the little I've heard about her doesn't impress me either. So, yes, a D+.'

'Paul Carter. Head of Department. Advantages: right age, several children, steady marriage, lower second in physics, distinction in his PGCE, sound teaching record, unusual and useful to have a scientist as head of one of our schools. Disadvantages: no head or deputy head teacher experience. So, C+ or B-?' asked Zing. 'Even a straight B?'

'Lower than that: the lack of leadership experience drops him to C or less. He's not popular at his school, always tries to be well in with authority and never questions anything. Just imagine that in education today, Dr Zing, a teacher who never questions anything! It beggars belief! It really does! And yet the man has an older sister who's the opposite: thoughtful, well liked, creative, considerate …'

'You're not interviewing his older sister.'

'Pity. Anyway, with the unpopularity I have been told about, Mr Carter gets a C without the plus.'

'Dr. Napier,' said Zing wearily, '*your* governing body put him on the short list; it wasn't my doing. I agree with some of what you say, but a head teacher doesn't have to be popular, that's not what he's paid for. Carter is a straightforward, traditional, law-abiding teacher. He has no interest in trouble-making teachers' unions, is non-controversial and highly unlikely to cause problems. In today's dire circumstances who could possibly ask for more? So I'd stick to C+. I'd even go to B- or B, but let's say, C+. Is Paul Carter still a C+?'

Lena nodded. 'And is Kurt Rommal a C+?' she asked.

'Good gracious, no! Even though he's head of a large sixth form, that cannot be seen as whole school management experience – it's different, it's particular, in fact could be seen as a drawback as it may mean he's little experience of younger pupils – pupils who will always be in the majority. Also, I had a quiet word about him with a trusted colleague who works in Rommal's own county, it seems Rommal's something of a radical protester who goes on marches – mounted police, dogs, shouting, banners, slogans, ill-clad women trudging along with infants in push chairs – things like that! Some of his sixth formers go up to university as if they're still in the rioting Sixties or striking Seventies. I can't think why on earth the man's short listed.'

'Two governors were insistent.'

'I can guess which! And, apparently, this Rommal runs on a short fuse; there was some scuffle with a government advisor recently and an outrageous dispute with a nervous young lab assistant who resigned that very day. He seems to be thoroughly frustrated in his current post. He's not a serious candidate? E or E+ for him, surely?'

'Far too low, and tens of thousands of teachers are "frustrated in their current posts," Dr Zing. But, I have to agree, he doesn't seem entirely suitable so have your E+ or, perhaps, D-.'

'Very well, D-. Next, Dr. Susan Mansfield. University lecturer. She wouldn't be *my* choice at all.'

'Dr Zing,' said Lena with growing impatience, 'we did not have queues of suitable candidates stretching twice round the Town Hall eager to be head teacher of Outer Mansworth Comprehensive School from whom we could select the perfect short-list with ample reserves ready to hand. One-day common sense might rule again and someone might ask why that is, but until that magical moment arrives, let's get on with what we've got. So, Dr. Mansfield: her positives first.'

'That's just it, I see only negatives,' murmured Zing.

'Then let me begin. Dr Mansfield has been a head teacher even though temporarily and for a very short while and some time ago. Academically she is outstanding. By disposition she is pleasant yet authoritative, well-organised, conscientious, visits schools of different types in the course of her work and insists on high standards from her trainee student teachers. I feel she would head a school competently and allow no nonsense. Her professor writes well of her.'

'Professor? That moves me not!' answered Zing. 'He could be as bizarre as she is or wants rid of her. And from what I've heard of her research she doesn't even support the existence of schools! So how can she manage a school if those are her beliefs? It would be farcical! A Gilbertian joke! And it's ages since she *taught* in a school.'

'Is that a drawback?'

'What do you think?'

'I think the onlooker sees most of the game and sees how the whole team should play, even the need for a different manager or tactics.'

'Please! You know that in the old days she wouldn't have got a look in with any down-to-earth LEA. She's a straight D for me.'

'Never! She has more interesting ideas than three of the others put together, and some of her ideas are finding favour. There's growing support for integrating home and school in education and for lowering barriers that don't help child, parent or teacher but instead encourage schools to emphasise uncertain academic and employment skills instead of the personal, emotional and social. After all, how important are work skills – skills which may be outdated in a few years' time - compared with the pupils' ongoing, lifelong, personal needs?'

'Isn't that the line of the next candidate? But he calls it "common sense." Aren't weird ideas his forte, too?'

'He has others.'

'Very well,' said Zing forlornly. 'Let's look at him. But first, what grade does Dr Mansfield get? I'll go up to 'D+'.

'No, no, *no*! C+.'

'Much too high! Let's say C-.'

'C,' Lena demanded. 'Nothing below C. I insist.' She folded her arms.

Zing nodded wearily before he moved on. 'All right then, C. Now, Park. Advantages: right age, good degree – though in sociology, a questionable subject by all accounts - good references, has worked abroad – I wonder what he did there? Knows this school, though that could be an advantage or a disadvantage, sound teaching experience, well regarded by staff and, maybe, by parents.'

'And pupils.'

'And pupils. Has a modicum of leadership experience; recently got a passable though very far from scintillating inspectors' assessment. Disadvantages: no headship or deputy headship experience, unhappy marriage background, highly active politically …'

'That's a disadvantage?'

'*Yes*,' said the CEO, showing irritation, 'doubly so; he's trade union minded - and with the TFRA to boot - and he has this CSP agenda on the go which will upset many governors and parents.'

'Perhaps.'

'Much more than "perhaps"! And by standing as a candidate in the general election he gives the impression he doesn't know whether he wants to be a head teacher or a politician.'

'Can't he be both?'

'Good Heavens, no! The politics would soon take over: I've seen it happen. He'd become a politically-minded, outspoken, campaigning head teacher – a truly frightening species!' Zing shuddered at the very thought and closed his eyes tightly. 'No, no! He gets a straight 'D'. However, as you will recall, I'm merely here as an advisor.'

'Again, much too low a grade. I insist on C at the very lowest.' Lena paused, but met no opposition, 'so go on, where does that leave us?'

'With Paul Carter. He should win with an unblemished C+.'

Now it was Lena's turn to close her eyes.

'So,' pressed the anxious CEO determined to tie things up to suit himself, 'first, I suggest – *suggest*, mind you – that you continue with the interviews tomorrow and, second, that you push, or persuade, I should say, the governors into accepting Paul Carter as the new head of Outer Mansworth Comprehensive School. How does that seem?'

Lena's head sank. Paul Patrick Carter wins with a C+. So, large schools were appointing top people on a C+. Where was the sense in that? And how much had they discussed the candidates' kindness, patience and compassion, their ability to help the many children growing up in troubling times often with little or no family or church support? Not at all! She was ready to give up hope, but giving up hope was a sin.

'Yes, all right then, it's Mr Carter,' she said sadly. 'I've little option, have I? Although,' and she paused for a while before saying softly, 'I never thought things would come to this.'

'Lena,' said Matthew Zing consolingly, 'neither did I!'

*

The social evening was nothing to write home about. It started late and was over by ten. Hull had strung up a few faded flags left over from a long forgotten coronation, while his poorly inflated red, white and blue balloons were failing to hold the little air they had. Adorning one wall was a faded picture of the Queen hung between crossed Union Jacks while poorly framed black and white photographs of past soccer teams and one of a netball team had been hung, askew, to Her Majesty's left. Ursula had drawn the line at tinsel and, although unhappy about the four plant pots containing flowerless shrubs placed equidistantly across the stage, decided she would not risk upsetting Hull by asking for a rearrangement. The dusty, creased, uneven and partially opened curtains revealed untidily assembled electronic gear used for amplifying unrecognisable music at fund-raising discos. The result was that the half-hearted effort to brighten a dreary school hall had left it looking like a dreary school hall.

The supermarket's red and white wine proved marginally more popular than the same store's crisps, sandwiches, sausage rolls and mini-pork pies, while the too-slim laboratory technician's choice of music and its high volume were to few people's liking. She, a plain, unsociable young woman, was indignant when asked to turn down the sound and obliged by lowering it to such an extent that it was barely audible even above hushed voices in a thinly-peopled room.

Governors, teaching staff, and the five watchful candidates kept themselves to themselves only occasionally, and warily, stepping forward to peep at the name tabs of guests from alien camps before, in most cases, backing, smilingly, away.

Terry, who wished to appear acceptably informal, wore top grade trainers, brand new jeans and a pale yellow tee shirt bearing the emblem "*I Love Arizona!*" He tried to be jolly and introduce people to each other but achieved only half-hearted integration. Although he spoke but briefly to Dafydd Hughes and Jenny Jean Jones he had time to see that Hughes had a full glass of wine and wondered how he had managed that as the glasses being carried round on tin trays were barely half full. But two halves make a whole, he thought to himself. Jenny Jones was drinking pineapple juice, no doubt the canny girl wanted to keep her wits about her if she was to spend an evening with Hughes.

Susan, in a well-cut, perfectly fitting olive-green trouser suit, helped with conversation as did Ingrid, whose short, clinging, light, tight skirt and skimpy blouse on her ample torso left little to the imagination of men like Vic Sneade or the craning-from-afar Hull, or any randy voyeur below the age of ninety-nine. Erotic dreams abounded and warmed the viewers' innards – which was more than could be said of the red wine which had not been given time to breathe or the unchilled white which had a disappointingly low alcohol content. The barn like hall was cool and even the hot-blooded Ingrid wished she had left less flesh on display.

Almost unnoticed the lab assistant turned off the music as an unenthusiastic Adrian Olde emerged from his corner to greet his guests.

'We must thank our American friend for this happy event, and thank staff and pupils who have worked so hard on its practical aspects.' He looked round, 'and Mr Hull, of course, for his zealous contribution. As always, it is pleasant to see our governors ...' he nodded vaguely to Victor Sneade who had made no effort to dress for the occasion and was now on his third glass of red wine, 'and give a most hearty welcome to our principal guests - the candidates who will, we hope, enjoy themselves ahead of tomorrow's shared ordeal.'

There was a barely discernable ripple of polite laughter and some faint supporting smiles from those who did not dislike Olde excessively. The head teacher glanced at his notes, as in morning assembly, and, without his usual "There are a few announcements before the final hymn ..." gave apologies from Dr Zing, Mrs Durrell, and, unthinkingly, from one of the six candidates, Mrs Smith.

News of Mrs Smith's non-attendance was of no surprise as Ursula had informed the staff and the governors had been telephoned. What was a surprise was, 'But I'm here, Mr Olde!' coming from Wendy Durrell. 'I'm sorry, I should have told you I *could* come after all.'

'Never mind, it's good to see you,' said the startled Olde. 'Our Chairperson, Dr Napier, has had a very busy day but, happily, will be joining us shortly.' Olde gratefully accepted the wine offered by his senior secretary and sat down knowing he had few similar obligatory, meaningless speeches to make before his retirement.

'Ah, Mr Carter, welcome to Outer Mansworth!' said Fergus Eastman. 'Let me introduce Mr Giles Townsend, a fellow governor.'

The thinly moustached Carter, the most formally attired man in the hall, correct even to his college tie and a folded silk handkerchief peeping from his dark blue blazer's breast pocket, shook hands limply.

During the evening the rimless-spectacled Carter talked confidently, correctly and effortlessly. Skilfully he selected from his repertoire of correct phrases those he thought each listener would like to hear. He was smooth, quiescent and conventional, he ate little, drank less, and bowed slightly as Eastman and Townsend took their leave.

'Good God, what a creep!' spluttered Townsend spilling white wine on Hull's polished floor. 'God save us from creeps!'

'Shut up! He's just the man we want,' snapped Eastman. 'He'll keep things ticking over and keep Park out. Then Park will get so cheesed off with having Carter as head teacher he'll move away of his own accord. Haven't you grasped yet that we need to keep in place the bland, tolerant, liberal, well-behaved do-gooders? They'll do our work for us by getting the average man so pissed off that in sheer desperation he'll go for extreme parties like ours. So we *both* vote for Carter! Got it?'

Giles nodded glumly. He "got it". He would vote for Carter.

'Ah, Dr Mansfield, please meet Nichola Murdoch.' Sophie Johnson paused while the women shook hands, 'and Wendy Durrell.' There was another pause. 'With me, they are both on the school's governing body.' The four chatted and a jovial sixth-form waitress, who, thoughtfully, had sampled the wine to make sure it was fit for the governors' palates, cheerfully topped up their glasses. Then Wendy asked Susan about her work. 'I'm intrigued to know what will replace the school system…'

'*Might* replace,' corrected Nichola.

'*Will* replace schools, Nichola. All systems have their time and then wither and die. Remember how long we put up with pounds, shillings and pence? But that stupid system went in the end – despite the diehards' dire warnings, as did ounces, and Fahrenheit, and feet and inches. Just think, 1760 yards to a mile! Can you believe it? Or sixteen ounces to a pound and 112 pounds to a hundredweight! Just crazy! But they're all gone now. And the school system, as is evident already, will be no exception to the process of remorseless, ongoing, institutional change…'

'Dr Mansfield,' interrupted Wendy, 'how would your plan work?'

For nearly five minutes Susan outlined her scheme, emphasising its potential for individual, caring education through the provision of personal tutors, parental involvement and bespoke study programmes. As she spoke, earnestly and clearly, the group was joined, unnoticed, by Sir Quentin Reynolds. He listened intently.

'While that sounds wonderful,' said Wendy, 'the practicalities kill it. While I admit it's feasible, it wouldn't be acceptable to parents. I'm a single Mum – and not by choice!' she laughed, 'and I need the schools. I have to know where my four children are while I'm at work – I'm a part-time nurse - and there must be millions like me who need the schools and their teachers on a regular, year long, dependable basis.'

'As child-minders?' asked Sophie.

'No, not altogether, although I think …'

'But I've long seen teachers as child-minders,' said the expensively dressed Nichola Murdoch contemptuously. Even for this undemanding occasion she wore something new. 'Too many are overpaid, and as for being professionals, like architects or surveyors well, really …'

'Although I can't go along with the whole scheme,' interceded Sir Quentin diplomatically, 'I do think Dr Mansfield's idea of a personal tutor for each child, with the tutor changing every two years during the child's ten years of elementary schooling,' and he noticed Susan flinch at "elementary" and "schooling", 'and having those five tutors belong to a tutor-panel known to and supported by parents, is right on the ball. So is her laudable proposal for always-open community resource centres offering immediate help to needy families - that's on the ball, too.'

He paused. 'I speak from my own experience of private tutors,' he went on, 'they were excellent and I gained much from them. I would like to see all children offered a private, personal and particularised education with a good, supportive friend at their shoulder – one who is supportive of parents, too. I'm all for it. It is desperately needed.' He beamed at Dr Mansfield.

'Ah, Dr Napier's arrived,' said Wendy. 'She does look tired. I'll have a word with her.'

Wendy left the group talking among themselves. She was pleased Sir Quentin had intervened so positively. He was a modest man of immense generosity and kindness and, usually, a man of few words; he must have been impressed to talk to Susan like that.

Sir Quentin Reynolds, who had disliked intensely having Greater Mansworth's ring road named after him, stayed alongside Susan as the others circulated. 'I'm pleased you're on the short list,' he said. 'And as I'm not privileged to be on the interview panel tomorrow, I can speak, somewhat paradoxically perhaps, as both an interested and disinterested governor.' He smiled. Susan liked him.

'What Mrs Durrell, the nurse, said about so many parents needing schools as care centres for their children is, sadly, true,' he continued, 'with the result that altogether too much is expected of schools, and a school's functions become enigmatic. And, at the same time, I'm afraid far too much is being removed from the area of family responsibility and passed on to schools. We are, perhaps, not too far from the practice of some regimes where children are handed over to the state at birth and see little of their parents from that time onwards.'

'Surely that's taking things too far …?'

'Please, let me finish. That policy would alter drastically the structure of society as we know it and, in my view would alter it for the worse. I realise your alternative plan has merit on both social and educational grounds, but I think you should counter the "Mrs Durrell type" opposition with a severe warning of how parents' reliance on our obsolete school-based system has unappreciated dangers.'

'There are many.'

'One of which lies in herding children together for long periods so that they are, for five days a week, in close contact with each other. Can that be healthy in any way? I think not. And, with such numbers, it becomes impossible for teachers to note all that is going on and so the school provides, free of charge and readily to hand, opportunities for bullies, thieves, drug-pushers and similar unwanted types to do their dirty work. The large school is tailor-made for such villains, so, not only is it paid for by us today, but it lays up unhappiness and expense for the future. You should emphasise those dangers, they have to be faced. Now,' and he touched Susan's arm as if confidentially, 'I ought,' he glanced at the names on his list, 'to meet Messrs Rommal and Carter.'

Susan was left standing alone in the rapidly filling hall. There had been a surge of late arrivals most of whom headed for the jolly wine waiters and the supermarket buffet. But what, she thought, should she make of Sir Quentin Reynolds' intervention? Did he fully support her ideas? Was a nod as good as a wink? *Verb sap?*

She watched her supporter-cum-advisor cross the floor, skilfully avoiding a boy carrying an overloaded tray. Sir Quentin had spoken fairly and made sensible points. As she stood in the throng she let her thoughts run. Was the wealthy Sir Quentin also an ardent supporter of common sense? An ally of those who offered radical solutions to debilitating problems? Her thoughts raced away. Sir Quentin was generous to good causes; could that have run to ten thousand pounds?

Sir Quentin had, politely, buttonholed the solidly built Kurt Rommal and his assessment of Rommal soon rose. He liked his outspokenness, his enthusiasm for science as an exciting, thought-provoking school subject and his willingness to be critical of what he had seen of science teaching in several schools. His obvious self-confidence, and the way he spoke earnestly of his sixth formers as responsible students rather than wayward youngsters encouraged Sir Quentin to listen.

'It is vital to address the needs of different age groups in schools more markedly than we do,' explained Rommal, 'and, where possible, reduce the size of those groups even if it means fewer hours a week of direct, in-school supervision. I sometimes look at classes which give teachers most trouble and think that, taken in groups of three or four, the young people in those classes would not cause such dire problems. There is something intrinsically different in the reactions we get from, and the relationships possible with, a party of three and a crowd of thirty.' He tapped his glass emphatically. His shirtsleeves were too long for his jacket; a broad, engraved gold ring adorned one finger. 'When people reply to that sarcastically by saying: "What's new?" I say: "Well, if you know it already, why don't you do something about it? For heaven's sake, just try - *try* something different!"'

Rommal paused. 'Many of these youngsters would be better off, Sir Quentin, having a teacher to themselves for just two or three hours a week than they are spending over twenty-five hours in a classroom in an unwilling, conscripted group of thirty with a teacher who hasn't a chance and knows it! But I'm putting this badly ...'

'I think you're putting it well. Go on.'

'This insistence on continuing in the same old way when there's so much better on offer makes me angry, and at times it shows. But it's children's lives we're dealing with, not new shades of lipstick. Yet there's probably more money for research into cosmetics than there is for exploring alternative ways of teaching children. I'm not saying *no* money's going into education, it's flooding in by the billion.'

'Just as it floods into the National Health Service or the Police Force with equally questionable results, perhaps?'

'Perhaps, but I don't know so much about those. But in schools money alone is not the answer, especially if it's spent on the wrong things by people who don't know what's needed.'

' So what is the answer?'

'Ah! Now you're asking! You definitely won't like this, but first politicians have to get out and stay out of areas they know next to nothing about.' He paused, noting a change in the music; who the devil had given that miserable girl *The White Cliffs of Dover* followed by *There'll Always be an England*?' What sort of place was this? Would the national anthem terminate the proceedings with everyone leaping to attention? He'd already seen one Colonel Blimp character who'd jump to his feet, salute the flag, and open fire on escaping dissenters.

'Second,' Rommal went on, recovering and speaking loudly above the din, 'there must be a massive movement towards greater family responsibility; and third, and you won't like this either, a willingness on the part of teachers to form one trade union in order to use their combined muscle and experience to knock some sense into the whole field of education from nursery schools to universities. It's common sense that's lacking more than money. And money won't buy common sense – rather the opposite – it gets in the way. "Just shove in another million to keep the reformers and deschoolers at bay."' Rommal went to take a sip from his glass forgetting it was empty.

Sir Quentin stood perusing Rommal. 'You're wrong about me, Mr Rommal, I do like what you say, or most of it.' He hesitated, 'and I imagine, you'll be interested in a fellow candidate's attempts to get common sense onto the national map?'

'If you mean Terry Park, he hasn't a chance. His CSP is a non-starter; few will vote for him. He and his friends are wasting precious time, energy and money that could be put into persuading one of the main parties, one with some punch, to look at new ideas. The old Labour Party might have done that once, but not any more; this Mod Lab lot is as hidebound as the others and their record on humanitarian, individualised education is appalling. They're test and target mad.'

He stared at Sir Quentin as a tall and attractive waitress refilled the good knight's glass. He held out his own and, for the first time, smiled. And, as Sir Quentin observed, the girl smiled back, pertly.

'And, you Sir, are you on the Board tomorrow? If so, I might as well go home!'

'No, I'm not on the governors' interview panel but I am interested in ideas - even if there's little likelihood of their coming to fruition. Ideas, however strange, are a nation's lifeblood, they must never be suppressed – never. Now Mr Rommal, it's been good to talk to you although I'm sad to see you so pessimistic about the CSP. If common sense cannot get a foothold in its own right I fear for the future.' Then he offered his hand which Kurt Rommal was pleased to shake.

'And nice to talk to you,' he returned. 'Now, I'd better be a good candidate and see the other governors.' He walked towards Snead.

Sir Quentin sought Carter and that was his worst move of the night. After two minutes he sought escape, hoping against hope he'd be rescued from this bland "I-must-be-so-nice-to-everyone" creature. In desperation he looked for Terry Park to whom he had not yet spoken, but Park was engaged. Then he saw Susan standing alone looking depressed after talking to Fergus Eastman and Giles Townsend.

'Ah, I see Dr Mansfield's free,' Sir Quentin said to Carter, 'do please excuse me, I need a word,' and, tersely and out of character, he left Paul Carter in full flow. But in the crowd of merry drinkers the insensitive Carter didn't even notice he'd gone.

'I wondered,' Sir Quentin began as an excuse for speaking to Susan a second time, 'whether you see a connection between your own proposals for a personalised schooling - or rather non-schooling,' he corrected himself, 'and Mr Park's ideas for a new political party based on the promotion of common sense? The thought intrigues me.'

Susan saw where he'd come from: any port in a storm!

'The CSP?' she asked innocently, 'yes, although I understand it won't be a party in the traditional sense. It will be a coalition of numerous groups of individuals answerable to no party whip.'

'But the points you made earlier were based, in my interpretation of them, on common sense, on a common sense that has been lacking in the school system for decades? Am I right?'

'Yes. But the CSP isn't concerned solely with education, although I would like to think that a party, any party, would take up my own proposals. But the traditional parties are afraid of upsetting those vested interests keen on maintaining education's *status quo.*'

'Vested interests?'

'Publishers, booksellers, stationers, printers, photographers, administrators, advisers, inspectors, secretaries, nurses, consultants, insurers, contractors, high fence builders, grounds men, dinner ladies, alarm system fitters, cleaners, suppliers, computer dealers, bus companies, caterers, outfitters, unions…'

'Unions? Teachers' own unions?'

'Yes.'

'Are they vested interests?'

'It's a dubious area, I admit,' said Susan, 'but existing unions have their own traditions and their histories, hierarchies, fulltime staffs, pension funds, investments, properties, reputations, conferences, journals, web sites and various sacred cows. Would they be prepared to give them up and see head-office and regional jobs lost to a single, all-embracing professional association of personal tutors - the new "teachers"? I'm not optimistic.'

'But you have a greater problem than that, an inescapable problem that you'd be forced to deal with. Are we not, in this country, cluttered with bricks and mortar schools, as we are with bricks and mortar hospitals, prisons, town halls, churches? What *do* we do with them? They're a nightmare to maintain, as antiquated as the stagecoach, as unfitted for current purpose as our massive cathedrals are for the tiny congregations they usually attract. But they are all *there,* physically *there,* and we don't have the money for their wholesale replacement. Probably we don't have enough money to knock them down and cart away the rubble. So, what do we do with those old school buildings?'

Susan could have answered by talking of time scales and gradual replacement of buildings or the keeping and converting of some for use as youth hostels and social centres, of prime land that could be sold to raise cash for future educational purposes, but she was tired and in no frame of mind for further, energy-taxing argument.

Nor was Sir Quentin. He talked politely but he too felt tired. This lady's ideas were fresh and positive but wasn't she being unrealistic? Who would listen to her or read her books or take the trouble to find out what could be done? Probably nobody. It was sad, very sad. But he would go now, his car and his chauffeur would be waiting.

And so the social ended. The indifferent wine was drunk by 9.20, the unexciting food consumed by 9.30, the ghastly music silenced by 9.40, and the five weary candidates had been scrutinised, questioned and appraised by 9.50. A hinting Hull hovered - for now that Ingrid had left he was ready to lock up. Adrian Olde, like Sir Quentin, had already gone. And also gone, Terry noticed, were Hughes and Jenny Jean Jones, but he had not seen them slip out. Other guests, also anxious to leave, proffered thanks to Ursula Irving and The Reverend Dr. Lena Napier. In those few hours people had learned much about each other - personalities had been assessed and score cards marked.

As they walked to the university campus both Terry and Susan were content. They had given good impressions of themselves to several governors and made fair cases for their current trains of thought. Susan described Sir Quentin's encouragement.

'I feel sure, after talking to him, that's where the £10,000 came from,' she said. 'It would be in keeping with what he was saying tonight and he's rich enough to make a donation like that.'

Although not certain, Terry was inclined to agree.

'And something else happened today,' Susan said. 'That freelance reporter, Ernie Willis, who was at our public meeting, phoned to say he wanted to interview me for an article. It was urgent because if it was put off it would stand no chance of publication before the election and he wanted to marry my "no schools" ideas with the CSP.'

'Did you see him?'

'Yes. He thinks he can place the piece with a national paper the day after next - and before the election. He's got connections. He was with one of the London tabloids, *The Daily Dawn Crier,* for eight years.'

'D'you trust him?'

'Yes. He promised to read me a draft over the phone tomorrow.'

'But that's our interview day!'

'He'll call before I leave home. He's well up on school matters and raised an issue I've not thought about enough. He says schools have become so standardised – sanitised - was his word, by different centralised government edicts that the creative, eccentric, nonconformist teachers - oddities - if you like, who had interesting, even outrageous, thoughts and strange ways of teaching and grabbing children's attention, the ones who were inspirational, have all but disappeared. In their own way, he argued, they were the cream - the very people who got children thinking, wanting to do things, go places, question the powers that be, delve into politics, demonstrate, debate, seek off-course reading and writing. They were the real radical gems, he said, but they'd run a mile from schools as they are now.'

'*Run*? Terry exploded. Most wouldn't be admitted in the first place and those that were would be out again – smartly! They've gone, those old provocative, stimulating people, gone forever, and they're a real loss! Your bloke's right, we must use that idea, we must stress that converse thinkers are unpopular with the set-in-their-ways authorities – and with the old parties - Mod Lab, Today's Tories, or Tol Dems.'

'And the same's true of universities in my experience. Political correctness, regimentation, expansion, targets, quotas, dilution and pot-hunting are eating their way into bodies that should be inspiring the nation with new thoughts, new ways of doing things – radical or not. I told my dear boss we'd soon have more faculty meetings than we have student seminars. He spluttered, but really argue about the....'

'He works freelance, doesn't he, your journalist friend? What's his background? Was he a teacher? He seems clued up?'

'No, I asked him that. He said lots of people of his age – I think he's well over seventy - talk about their school days and the teachers who most influenced them, and said the "way-outs" are always mentioned, and not just for a laugh. Adults recognise the effect those unusual teachers had so that later, when people like Ernie Willis look back and evaluate their own school days, they are grateful to them. That's what's so sad. What will our current pupils think when, in forty years time, they look back on their years at school? Who and what will they remember? Will anyone or anything stand out? *Anything*? But come on, let's cheer up; we can sink a quick one before they close. You can get the gins and tonics while I nip to the loo and fix my hair!'

Tuesday 30 April.   **Five Interviews**

Lena Napier could hardly believe how trouble-free the morning had been. The full governing body had accepted, unenthusiastically it is true, the interview arrangements and the likelihood of Paul Carter becoming their new head teacher. Only Sir Quentin, who had, with Sophie Johnson, suggested more consideration be given to Rommal and Mansfield, expressed any doubts while the ever-watchful Eastman, realising things were already going his way, and not wanting to tangle with Sir Quentin, had quietly let that pass.

The candidates' tours of the school progressed without incident. Two, including Susan, were shown round by Ursula Irving, and three, including Terry, by Adrian Olde. Then the tour leaders changed places and, after a further tour during which Kurt Rommal appeared critical of laboratory provision, the two groups united for a question and answer session. It was not until then that Susan found time to talk to Terry.

'Ernie Willis's script was first rate. At first I thought there was too much on my work and too little on the Common Sense Party, but he said the balance was OK and that he'd have to re-write the whole piece to change it significantly, then he'd miss the deadline.'

'Good grief, Susan, if *you* thought there was too much on your stuff it *must* have been one-sided!'

'Don't look a gift horse in the mouth. The paper's circulation is a million – probably two million read it - and we're not paying a penny. Anyway, the CSP *did* feature. He said it was the first new idea in party politics for fifty years and had great potential. So try to be a happy candidate and let's see what the governors are offering in the library. Come on, this way. Ah! Just look there!' She stretched her neck. 'There's dry sherry – and good stuff, too - I recognise the label! I'll go first!'

The pre-lunch gathering was as enjoyable as such occasions can be and, like Susan, everyone was relieved to find the sherry was better than the wine offered at the social. Rev Lena Napier saw Paul Carter standing on his own, and, not having met him, approached. She soon discovered how little she had missed and was eager to pass him on to Eastman. Minutes later Eastman, reaching desperately for a second sherry, moved him to the repulsive left-winger Sneade. 'Let's see what Sneade makes of him,' he said to Townsend as he downed half a glass in one gulp, 'he'll be even less polite.'

Lunch saw no problems. Diplomatic seating ensured no politically opposed governors faced each other, while the candidates, all of slender appetite, were interspersed. The Reverend Lena Napier said grace.

Coffee was taken in the staff room but, as afternoon school was set to start and finish early, only a few teachers remained. Dafydd Hughes, as he passed, whispered, 'right shower you've got here, Terry, Old Boy! You're mad to get mixed up with them. May they have mercy on you!'

'I appreciate your good wishes, Mr Hughes,' Terry replied loudly as Hughes left. 'But please, don't let me keep you from your classes!'

Lena was glad to see Hughes leave. She had still not made up her mind about him - musically talented as he was. And she was unhappy to see the disdainful Walker-West in serious conversation with the scheming Eastman and the mediocrity Townsend: all three were on the selection panel. She would have been even less pleased if she had overheard the Captain's Orders of the Day.

'Right. You've both met Carter,' the gallant man said, 'and seen that he's a bootlicker, but that's not the point. He's the only one acceptable to the governors because they've all got something against the others and I want Carter appointed to keep that CSP blighter out. I suppose you want Carter in for different reasons but that doesn't matter. Together we will almost make a majority so we give Carter an easy ride - no awkward questions. Then, if the blighter doesn't make himself too objectionable, he might recruit Durrell and Kennedy because they're probably under orders not to back the CSP either. Right?'

'Right,' Fergus said as he poked Giles fiercely.

'Right,' agreed Giles. He was anxious to get the afternoon over.

'But be as hard as you like on that university female – *and* Park!'

The Captain looked round the room: what a spineless bunch of layabouts! Clackety-clack women, overweight men! *Men?* Useless in combat! A month's drill with the RSM would sort them out and I'd take the passing out parade. "Eyes right, eyes front … *as you were!*"'

People saw the Captain smiling to himself, moustache twitching, hands rubbing together. Poor old fellow they thought, still fighting WW2! Or, not too sure of their recent European history, or any other history, the youngest present wondered if it might be WW1?

Coffee over, the interview panel withdrew to the library and the candidates were shown to the school's stark medical room. It had, with the addition of five hard chairs, a rickety mug-ringed coffee table, and outdated but still unread copies of *The Outer Mansworth Monthly Magazine of the Local Industrial Development Society (free to members),* been turned into a temporary waiting room. Well-worn medical equipment was available to any who might wish to check height and weight - but not blood pressure. The room, being close to the library where the interviews were to be held, was a convenient station and would save the panel's time and the interview secretary's legs as each candidate was called to the fray.

'There'll be tea, coffee and biscuits later,' Ursula announced. 'We'd rather you didn't smoke, but do feel free to stroll outside. I'm told you will be called alphabetically so, allowing half an hour for each, you can calculate the timing.'

She smiled, and, while looking at them sitting there so nervously, told herself again she had done right in opting out of the headship stakes. 'Good luck!' she said as she closed the door on the poker-faced group of two women and three men. And she meant it!

*

'Do sit down, Miss Bates. I think you've met everyone here except Dr Zing, our Chief Education Officer? Dr Zing has been invited to join us and we value his presence.'

The governors nodded as Lena Napier turned towards the CEO who managed to lower his face and give, as his lips parted slightly, what might pass on a sunny day for a CEO's welcoming smile.

'The others you met last night. Starting on your left, from Dr Zing, we have Mr Giles Townsend and Captain Walter Walker-West. On your right, Mr Fergus Eastman, Mrs Zoe Kennedy, Mr Victor Sneade and Mrs Wendy Durrell. The gentleman on your extreme left is Mr Wright from the Local Education Authority who will take minutes. They all invite you to join an open and friendly discussion on how a large school like this might best be managed.'

'Thank you.'

Miss Bates was plainly attired. Her thick, dark-brown hair was swept back into a tight bun. She sat flagpole straight while the long skirt of her pale blue suit showed less leg than a fully draped Victorian piano. Miss Bates did not use makeup or wear jewellery, and nor did the girls at her school, indeed it was rumoured, according to a sniggering Sneade, that they still wore broad brimmed hats, shapeless gymslips and navy blue knickers.

The lady confirmed that her qualifications and experience were, indeed, exactly as stated on her immaculately completed application form and that she was, without any possibility of doubt, Miss Joan Audrey Margaret Bates, born near Leatherhead in the UK, principal deputy head teacher of Paradise Road Extension Secondary School for Girls. She confirmed her early 1970's 'A' level results, told them why she wanted the job, not mentioning the pay, related how her school won its salutary, well-publicised inspectors' report, explained why she was keen for girls to play soccer, and agreed with Wally Walker-West that if the older ones followed her own pursuit of motorcycle riding it might 'toughen 'em up a bit and give 'em some road sense.'

'Should they live long enough,' murmured Mrs Kennedy.

'You're a disciplinarian, Miss Bates?' continued the Captain.

The lady was cautious. 'All young people should be well behaved.'

The panel nodded in unison: all young people should be well behaved.

'And develop self-discipline.'

Nine heads nodded again. And, looking at Miss Bates, there were few doubts that the good lady's own self-discipline set a fine example.

'Thank you, Miss Bates,' said Lena after less than the allocated thirty minutes. 'The governors appreciate your attendance.'

Again the heads nodded: they did appreciate her attendance and they appreciated even more this masculine lady's early departure.

*

However, after only three minutes of Mr Carter, they were ready to recall Miss Bates: 'all is forgiven, Miss Bates! *Please* come back!'

There was nothing with which Paul Carter disagreed. Nothing could remove the simpering smile from his face. Nothing nonplussed him. He was adept at appearing to support two sides at once as he balanced on a rickety fence, at smoothing his way out of blatant contradictions of earlier insipid answers to what he had seen as controversial, risk-ridden questions. He anticipated craftily and rode out effortlessly all attempts to make him commit himself to anything. He claimed long experience in all methods of teaching mathematics and astronomy.

'So how d'you link astronomy with your multifaith religion and your willingness to include it in the multicultural, all-inclusive, tolerant, warm, pupil-centred, hospitable, family-friendly, community-conscious school you've told us about?' asked a near-vomiting Sneade.

Carter responded coolly, yet promptly.

'I would, of course, enlist the help and heed the advice of my wise and widely experienced governors, the knowledgeable officers of the local education authority plus those of the Department in Whitehall, the views of local church leaders and of diverse social and voluntary groups. We would all work together and, with close and appropriate consultation and subsequent discernment of our children's primary needs, and, given adequate time, understanding, patience and tolerance, embrace all means of furthering their immediate and future well-being.'

'What about exclusions? Would you throw out the troublemakers?'

Mr Carter referred Mr Sneade to the Government's carefully laid-down guidelines on permanent exclusion, its desire to see the minimal use made of such a step, the need for local education authorities to provide alternative and adequate educational facilities, the philosophy behind pupil referral units, the need for head teachers to try all available routes prior to expulsion, and the Government's wish to see excluded children's early re-instatement in mainstream schooling having, of course, all due regard for the interests of the other pupils, the school's teaching and auxiliary staff, and the needs of the community.'

'You'd go by the book?'

'The law gives me little choice,' smiled the unflappable man.

The Chief Education Officer gazed disbelievingly at his minimal notes as the candidate said he had no questions to put to the panel.

'Well, thank you, Mr Carter,' Lena said, and the panel watched in awe the calm and blessed departure of, in Sneade's words, 'A modern day Houdini!'

'Could any question floor him?' asked Wendy Durrell, wincing.

'No, he's too adept at dodging every issue,' said Zoe Kennedy scathingly, 'and, like fools, we let him, for over twenty minutes!'

*

'Dr Mansfield,' said Lena early in Susan's interview. 'I'm sure the panel would like to hear about your research into the alternative forms of childhood education mentioned in your application.'

'Is that relevant?' interrupted Wendy Durrell.

'Could we let Dr Mansfield to indicate relevance?'

With a visibly bad grace, Wendy Durrell concurred.

'I'd be glad to do that, of course,' said Susan cautiously, 'because it could be that the panel has detected a paradox. Why should I seek to be head teacher of a school like this when I question the very future of such schools? If I were on the panel I would ask the same question.'

'So how would you answer it?' snapped Sneade.

'To begin with by saying that much of my research has been both misunderstood and incorrectly reported ...'

'Oh, I'm so sorry to hear...' began Zoe.

'Never mind all that. D'you want schools to stay?' rapped Sneade. "Yes, or No?" We've had too many dodgy answers this afternoon.'

'Not from you, of course,' placated Lena Napier hurriedly.

'I regret that,' said Susan sympathetically. 'But I shall not be evasive. Briefly, I believe the type of state school instituted in the 1870's and 80's – whose basic structure and purpose is still with us today - is no longer appropriate to the needs of contemporary children or their parents or the needs of our complex, confusing society. Increasingly we are confronted with the institution's adverse effects because that outmoded model can now do more harm than good. '

'Schools do harm?' questioned Fergus Eastman.

'Yes, *harm*. Have you, for instance, any idea of what it is like to be bullied and afraid to seek help lest you invite further vicious attention? To be a nervous child forced to go to school even though he dreads the experience – perhaps one of the five per cent who at some time stammer or stutter? To have to give up fascinating, enjoyable ways of learning at home in order to study laboriously topics of little interest or relevance to him in a school under teachers not chosen by him? To attend a place he hates and where someone he dislikes might teach him for a year? To be thrust into the company of those who can never be his friends, to be lonely in a crowd? Further, and this is vital, there is no longer any need for such compulsion or for an 1870's "one size fits all" school-based approach. There are now kinder, more effective alternatives available undreamed of by our forefathers.'

'Yet, despite all that, *you still want to run a school,* Madam?' retorted Walker-West triumphantly. He beamed at those around him as if expecting applause for his killing thrust.

'Yes, because my proposals for tutor-based teaching, with each child having a personal study programme supported by large well-staffed local community resource centres will take years to develop. The changes I propose will be voluntary, spasmodic and gradual, and depend largely on parental support for their progression.'

'So?' encouraged Zoe Kennedy.

'So for up to twenty years there will be, unfortunately in my opinion, many traditional schools still in operation.'

'Aren't you aware, Dr. Mansfield,' began an unsmiling Eastman, 'that over a hundred million children in the world get no schooling at all? That their parents would be delighted to be able to send their children to the very schools you're so keen to scrap?'

'That maybe, but there's no need to begin that unfortunate hundred million children's education by forcing on them our own old school-based system – a system which is already outdated. You wouldn't say we should help developing countries build a present day transport system by sending them our old canal barges, row boats, clippers, cart horses, stage coaches, airships, antiquated coal-fired steam engines and ...'

'That's no answer!'

'And we should not assume that because children in the developing world don't go to school they don't get an education. That would be insufferable Western arrogance. Those children learn from their families, elders, peers and traditions, and they learn by being free to explore their environment, safely, in their own time. That makes for a natural, valuable childhood education which British and American children have been almost forced to forego for years.'

'You astound me,' muttered Eastman shrugging his shoulders.

'It makes good sense,' said Zoe.

'Anyway, as I said,' continued Susan ignoring Eastman's remark while turning to Zoe, 'the demise of schools here in the UK will take many years. There will be no overnight switch.'

'I'm delighted to hear that,' murmured Wendy.

'Meanwhile, if I were a head teacher, I would continue my research in the front line, as it were. I would not allow myself to be imprisoned in an office. I would get myself and everyone else out of the school as often as I could, as far as I could, and for as long as I could, and so help the teachers minimise the damage schools can do to children.'

'First "harm", now "damage". Those words insult every teacher in the system,' exclaimed Sneade. 'Do you really mean them?' He glared at Susan. 'If so I don't know how you have the nerve to come here ...'

'Thank you, Mr Sneade, thank you,' said Lena Napier, 'but do let Dr Mansfield continue.'

Sneade half rose, paused, coloured markedly, looked as though he would rebel, but gave way.

'Dr Mansfield,' said Wendy quietly, 'many children are proud of their school and enjoy attending it, and their parents are satisfied with what is offered and they support the school in a host of ways. Some might be "old boys" or "old girls" of their own school and, through associations which they join voluntarily and keenly and then generously subscribe to, keep in touch with former teachers and the friends they made. Where does "harm" and "damage" come into that scenario?'

'But, Mrs Durrell, is that scenario enjoyed by all children, by all parents, in all schools? Are all schools like those you describe?

'No, but you are not ...'

'So what of children who have to attend those *other* schools?' With difficulty Susan had managed to hold back: 'Don't *they* matter?'

Wendy Durrell was silent.

'It is sad,' went on Susan, 'that proposals for change are seen as an attack on people currently practising in schools and on the good work many do. If everyone saw things in that way we would be unwilling to advocate any change, at any time, in any place, for any reason'

'You will have read John Clare's poetry?' asked Lena quietly.

'A great deal of it.'

'Then you could, perhaps, quote in your work his lovely lines,

> "And little footpaths sweet to see
> Go seeking sweeter places still."

They seem apposite to your argument. We should never give up seeking to improve matters even if they are good to start with.'

'Thank you.' Susan smiled at her appreciatively. 'That is true.'

'So do go on,' Lena prompted. Matthew Zing watched intently.

'Well,' Susan paused, 'we have to ask why we "school" children at all? Why? Why do we keep them there for eleven years? Why? Think about it: *compulsory* attendance for *eleven years*! What is it all about? Why spend billions on state education? What do we expect to get from it? Why, after all that expenditure, do so many children resent having to attend school and, if they can, leave promptly at sixteen unable to read or write properly? Why do so many play truant? Why? Can we justify compulsory attendance? Isn't the very need for compulsion and the laws that support it the ultimate give away? Why do we ...'

'We're supposed to be asking the questions,' interrupted Eastman sharply. 'You're supposed to be answering them.'

'Which I will try to do, and I repeat *try*,' responded Susan coolly. 'But we have to ask the more fundamental question: what sort of world will our children be living in when they grow up and how do we persuade all parents to co-operate in preparing them for it?'

'And then?' came a three-voice chorus.

'We must help them – parents and children - to prepare for it and to do that we have to look to the methods available now and those which will be available in the future, rather than mourn the passing of the methods of the past. If we are unable or unwilling to do that we should abandon the struggle and hand everything to the politicians, the media, the international corporations, the bureaucrats, or simply join those poor simple folk who are unable to see beyond a national lottery or the worthless promises of governments or the supposed hereafter of the mullahs, bishops, and rabbis or the false euphoria of the inebriated but desperate souls who succumb every night to some conglomerate's overpriced beer.'

There was silence as well as nods of approval. Finally Eastman, nervously aware that Susan was gaining support, spoke up.

'So now, Madam, if we could come down to earth for a moment,' he said, and waved dismissively as Susan began to demur, 'we have right here, where we are met, a school of a thousand young people. It has to be organised, managed, paid for and made to work for two hundred days a year for the good of the majority who attend it and to their parents' satisfaction, and it has to be safe. So, in providing for children's safety and to give parents reassurance, what would you do, as the on-the-spot, unable to pass-the-buck head teacher, to protect those children from, I hope, the few dangerous, aggressive, disruptive pupils who daily cause problems out of all proportion to their number?'

'He means would you chuck them out?' Snead interceded.

'I dislike the words you use,' retorted Susan.

'Never mind my words,' rasped Sneade. 'You tell us what you think of exclusion. What would you do with the current case that's worrying the governors right here at this school *now*?'

'Dr Mansfield cannot be asked about a specific case' warned Lena.

'Then she can answer generally.'

'My answer is simple. Under my alternative system there would be no schools so the matter of expulsion from them would not arise. Expulsion would become both a thing of the past and a practical impossibility.'

The panel gaped at her. Again Eastman was first to recover.

'That's too easy! What happens until your scheme gets going?'

'I would exhaust all the measures proposed in existing legislation. There, are, I suppose, some mildly acceptable provisions there. But if all that failed and after I had done all I could to persuade the child to change, I would seek transfer to the Pupil Referral Unit and tell the child that he had not been forgotten by the school and therefore had not been fully expelled and that he would be visited at the PRU by myself and other teachers known to him, that a school liaison teacher would visit his parents, and that we would get him to see that as soon as his behaviour improved and he was no longer a threat or distraction to others he would be welcomed back at this, or rather, his, school. He would not have been "chucked out" or, to use an equally objectionable phrase one sometimes hears, "*left to rot!* "' She almost glared at Sneade, and Sneade glared back. But he had no answer.

'I like that reply,' said Zoe. 'It does you credit.'

Dr Zing and Mr Wright both scribbled away, but no one spoke until Wendy Durrell said, 'Before this we were discussing your alternative, no-school, individual-tuition scheme. Can we go back to that, because I've no doubt that to you, Dr Mansfield, what you propose is common sense? First, all children are different, therefore, second, they should have individual study programmes geared to their needs, and third, they should be aided by parents, personal tutors and resource centres, and fourth, any new system should facilitate that approach.'

'I'm pleased you see it linked like that.'

'I don't. I see it linked directly to the Common Sense Party's agenda for the coming general election...'

'She can't make comments like that!' objected Zoë heatedly. 'She's trying to get the candidate to talk about her politics. Politics and religion are taboo!' Zoë Kennedy bridled.

'Not in private schools or church schools.' said Wendy.

'You know this is not a private or church school!' exclaimed Zoe.

Lena glanced at Zing, but he would not catch her eye.

'Madam Chairman,' said Susan dispassionately, 'I am not worried by the lady's question. I am happy to answer it.'

Again Lena looked, fleetingly, at the CEO. She interpreted the faintest movement of his shoulders as a sign of indifference.

'Very well,' said Lena. 'But, Dr Mansfield, please answer only if you choose to do so. If you do not, we will, and entirely without detriment to your case,' she stressed, 'proceed to the next question.'

Before Susan could begin, Eastman had interceded. 'Whatever we think of Dr Mansfield's anti-schooling ideas,' he said, 'she hasn't a hope in hell, if you'll excuse the expression, Madam, of getting them into nationwide operation by herself. She would need the support of a political party willing to include her extraordinary proposals in its manifesto. There's only one party likely to do that, and that's this new Common Sense Party, and that hasn't a hope in hell either. That needs pointing out now so that we know where we stand. Mrs Durrell's introduction of the CSP was timely, permissible and relevant. The candidate's strange - and, if I may say so - unworkable scheme and the

CSP's implausible manifesto, go together like stillborn twins.'

'Well, Dr Mansfield?' Lena was furious at being told by Eastman, of all people, what was and was not permissible, but she showed restraint. 'And remember, you do not have to answer.'

The CEO raised his eyes slightly to observe Susan's response.

'I admit, no, not admit, I *accept,* that my long-term programme is based on common sense. There are many areas where common sense is at a premium and education is one of the prime examples. Instances where common sense is lacking are illustrated in my university work and will appear in more detail in my new book. I will never apologise for supporting the revival of common sense.'

'Nor should you,' murmured Lena, and waited to see if there were objections to the Chair venturing so stark an opinion. None came.

However Matthew Zing then spoke, softly, deliberately and almost confidentially as if anxious to indicate that he was not an accredited participant but merely an interested observer offering the occasional helpful remark. He joined the match as if he were a spin bowler brought on after the high-speed merchants had retired to the outfield exhausted.

'Should we not be wary of relying on what is, perhaps, that rather nebulous notion called, popularly, "common sense"?' he questioned quietly. 'The word "common" could be defined in terms of "routine, regular, customary, conventional, prevailing, accepted."'

'"Run of the mill?"' Wendy Durrell added, or '"commonplace"'?

'"Or humdrum?"' offered Eastman gleefully. Quickly he changed his mind about objecting to Matthew Zing's intervention.

'In which case,' continued Dr Zing, 'the meaning of the word "common" in "common sense" could be seen as one different from that attributed to it by Dr Mansfield?'

'Or as seen by the CSP,' murmured Wendy thoughtfully.

'But you must forgive me,' said Zing with a rare, almost full smile, 'I so enjoy playing with words - like completing crossword puzzles – it's a weakness of mine. My home is full of dictionaries and Mrs Zing and I both delight in long sessions of Scrabble. We play often.'

And how that must rouse the loving couple, Susan thought, how very exciting! She chose to see that as an end to Zing's thesaurus exercise, but they would have to watch the use others made of the word "common".

But Zing leaned forward: he had not finished. 'Common sense, to a philosopher, is seen as a concept based on the idea that what we see, or smell, or hear, or feel is the reality with which, or in which, or on which, we live and work. It has a strong element of appealing simplicity. But we cannot allow such a concept – a naïve concept, perhaps – to dictate how we behave – how we order our lives. Think, if we looked around us we would see that the world is flat, or that the sun circles the earth, or that the moon itself emits light, or that the air we breathe is not there because it's invisible, or that this school, or Mansworth or Britain, is at the centre of the universe. We would make some awful mistakes if we assumed all those things were true and then, because of those assumptions, acted upon them. Now, wouldn't we?'

'That makes a good debating point,' answered Susan. 'Ideas – good, bad, workable or unworkable need to be considered – indeed they are vital. Ideas must never be dismissed out of hand and we must also remember,' she smiled, 'that ideas which seem preposterous today may be appreciated and adopted in twenty years' time. I know, too, that you could quote Descartes: "Common sense is the most widely distributed commodity in the world, for everyone thinks himself so well endowed with it." But I would question that, too.'

Zing nodded, but said nothing.

'But now I, too, want to deal with new ideas and I know how hard it is to get them considered in the UK. I've seen many able colleagues move to North America for that very reason. I would, therefore, embrace any party prepared to give my plan a try. I agree that the Common Sense Party, with "sense" here meaning "astute, judicious, practical or pragmatic," is, perhaps, the only party at present likely to give my work a second glance, but that party, because it stands for something new in a hidebound society, is, I agree, unlikely to win elections. British people stick to the tried and tired old parties of the past and, unwittingly, aid their nation in its continuing decline.'

'Madam, you seem to have a very low opinion of Britain and the British people!' grumbled Wally Walker-West. 'There's far too much "running down of Old England" from you university people. You bite the hand that feeds you.'

'On the contrary, I believe there's immense talent in Britain, quite as much as in any other country and more than in most. It's the use to which the talent is put and the lack of encouragement it's given to develop to the full that raises questions. But I'm not, that is ...' Susan wavered, dissatisfied with her answer. Zing's intervention had been disconcerting.

'Yes, go on, go on,' prompted Eastman, hoping to trip her up.

'That is, I'm not anti-schooling. We are, as one governor said last night, and just as many other developed nations are, saddled with old schools. Thousands of children are in them, just as thousands of people are in our old houses, old hospitals, old prisons and old army barracks, so, for the immediate future we are obliged to do what can with them. Therefore, if I were head teacher, I would do my best for the children here now. At the same time I would find succour in the knowledge that the school will, eventually, be replaced by a kinder, more understanding, more personal and worthier system.'

'You'd work at your plan from within our school?' asked Zoe.

'With your salary paid for by the school?' murmured Wendy.

'Rather than work from within the university?' added Eastman.

'Or by writing books?' asked Townsend.

'Some sort of fifth column?' growled Sneade.

'It won't affect the outcome,' stated Wally Walker-West knowingly. 'She's starting a major battle from a weak position. Can't win, got too big an army against her and she'll be out-manoeuvred. Fatal tactics.'

'Dr. Mansfield,' said Wendy Durrell before Susan could reply. 'I see you have no children of your own?'

'Madam Chairperson, that is another unacceptable question, this time about the candidate's personal life,' objected Zoe.

'I have no children,' said Susan before the Chair could intervene.

'Well, I have four,' said Wendy. 'I'm divorced, and, as I told you last night, I work as a nurse. Frankly, if you closed your "old" schools I would have to give up my worthy work with sick people in your "old" hospitals in order to teach my own children in my "old" home. Such teaching would be work for which I, personally, have limited resources, for which I have not been trained, and for which I have little enthusiasm. The quality of life for my children, my patients and myself would then be lower than it is now because of your, and I must say this to you, your ill-considered notions. When Mr Eastman says your plans have no chance of being widely implemented and the Captain says you can't win, I'm not only relieved, I'm elated.'

She sat back as if she had said her piece. But then she spoke again.

'This will upset you,' she said to Susan, 'but one day you may find what I have said is helpful. Unless you and your high-flying academic sympathisers face up to the impracticality, unpopularity and dangers posed by your bizarre ideas you will get nowhere, will deserve to get nowhere, and, I hope, will get nowhere. As you see,' and she managed a smile as if offering some consolation, 'I believe in plain speaking. Well,' she paused again, 'here's some more: I shall not vote for you.'

'Mrs Durrell! That is a most improper statement and you should withdraw it! We will have it expunged from the minutes,' Lena said to Mr Wright, the flustered, scribbling clerk.

'I, too, like plain speaking,' Susan said warmly. 'I can assure Mrs Durrell I have heard her argument put in various ways fifty times. Not only is her point outdated, it is weak and inconclusive. If we continue to confuse the teaching role of a school with its childcare role we shall get all the uncertainty, frustration, indiscipline, buck-passing, low standards and poor morale we endure throughout the education service today. I do not believe those two roles can be merged within one institution. They simply do not work together.'

'You would separate the roles: childcare and teaching?' asked Zoe.

'Precisely.'

'But role-separation was not in the plan you outlined earlier, or, as far as I recollect, in your application for this job or in the work you have published,' pressed Eastman, chancing a guess with the last item.

'I have changed my mind.'

'In the last few minutes?' scoffed Walker-West. 'Retreat already?'

'No, Sir, in the last few months!' Susan showed real irritation for the first time. 'I have changed my mind - with regret - because I thought, and still think, that the personal tutor and individual tuition model is ideal. But we do not live in an ideal world.'

'You can say that again!' Townsend muttered miserably.

'And so I have been working on amendments to my original proposals, but they are at a tentative stage.'

'We'd still like to hear them,' said Wendy, with no trace of sarcasm.

'I say, look here,' said Walker-West. 'Is this the place to get …?'

'What *is* the place?' intervened Susan. 'What *is* the place to hear of new ideas? Is there one? If so, tell me, Sir. I'd love to know.'

Walker-West did not reply, but stared at her as if seeing her afresh. This woman is quick, tough, impertinent, intelligent and overbearing, he thought. Much too dangerous a combination! She'd make one of those damned female officers the army signs up nowadays. Imagine *her* in the Regiment!' He paled at the thought and gripped his chair seat.

'There are other candidates,' murmured Eastman meaningfully, looking first at his watch, then at the library clock and then at Lena. He was uneasy, and, anyway, he thought, Mansfield had had her time.

'But we would like to hear more. Are three minutes enough?' asked

Lena. She was taking no further instructions from Eastman.

'Yes.'

'Then please go ahead.'

Susan thought for a moment. Very well, she said to herself, in for a penny, in for a pound.

'It is true,' she answered, 'that many parents want, for whatever reason, to be free of the need to care for their children.'

'I resent that, I really, really, do,' protested Wendy. 'I really do!'

'Dr. Mansfield, do continue,' said Lena.

'It would take too long to go into all the reasons, suffice to say some reasons are worthy, some less so. Please ...' and she almost begged as Eastman began to protest, 'let me go on. Whatever the reasons there is clearly a desire for children to be looked after during the day by people other than their parents. Many parents enrol grandparents or seek a reliable childcare service. In that case childcare centres, not schools, should provide that service. The two must be separated once and for all. Childcare centres, where children are protected, occupied and given informal learning experiences by means of appropriate stories, radio, television, toys, games, and where they are fed, washed, exercised, rested, protected, brush their teeth – such centres do not need highly qualified teachers, to run them...'

'I say ...' began Walker-West again.

'Any more than patients need skilled doctors to do those things for them in hospitals. My amended proposal, therefore, is that those children whose parents demand it be entrusted to approved child minders operating in some of the old school buildings we have now - adapted as necessary - and that those schools be renamed childcare centres and offer partial or total care to children aged from two to thirteen inclusive from 7a.m. to 7p.m. in three four-hour sessions for which parents will be charged a fee per session. Most parents would be using the centres because they are out at work so they could pay from their earnings. But mere payment would not ensure acceptance: the parents would have to ensure that the child behaved responsibly.'

' I'll buy that last bit!' murmured Wendy.

'Then,' continued Susan, 'from our existing teaching force the keen and able teachers, equally carefully selected, would be retained and retrained and then offered professional teaching contracts and go on to practise in separate non-school, non childcare premises, with small groups of children – never more than twenty. Children would often be taught individually or in twos or threes at the tutor's discretion – and would cover the literacy, numeracy and other areas, like literature, drama, film, music and art - necessary for living a contented life in the coming 21st century. While the children would seldom meet as a full group of twenty, that size, with other groups linking up with it occasionally, would provide opportunities for activities such as plays, concerts, choirs, and sports. The children would be there because they wanted to be there and would remain in those groups as long as they or their parents wished - provided they studied seriously. They would not be admitted to a tutor group until parents signed to say they agreed to those terms and acknowledged that they were using an expensive service which the state was no longer required, legally, to provide.'

'The Holy Mother of Jesus, it's less workable than her other ideas!'

'Perhaps, Mr Eastman, we could allow Dr Mansfield to end without blasphemous interventions?' objected Lena Napier colouring.

'For those parents,' continued Susan before Eastman could retort, 'who require childcare above all else, that will be provided. However, the tutoring element, the really skilled and expensive part, will be there for parents who see that the education service has more to offer than the provision of free-for-all, day-long, baby sitting.'

'I didn't come here to listen to this!' bawled Sneade, half rising.

'I'm sorry you feel that way,' said Susan, 'but not surprised.'

'What d'you mean?'

'Well, let me say what *would* have surprised me would have been the panel's acceptance of my ideas, or even, I regret to say, a willingness to consider them constructively and impartially.'

'Then you will not be disappointed,' said Lena. She despaired at Susan's increasingly antagonistic attitude; she seemed intent on professional suicide. 'However, this panel is composed of intelligent individuals who can think for themselves and more than one may be inclined to consider your ideas, strange as that may seem to you.'

Susan fidgeted. The governors had galled her. She had gone too far.

'Dr Mansfield,' said Zing quietly, 'before you leave, could you put, in one sentence, precisely what your plan would do for education?'

'Yes, of course, just let me think for a moment.' Susan paused, then said as calmly as she could. 'My proposals would restore, for the first thirteen years of their lives, all children's right to a simple, carefree childhood by freeing them of the compulsions, restrictions and pressures of current school attendance so that, alone or with small groups of other children and the trusting help of a personal tutor – and, hopefully, their parents – they could pursue, safely and enjoyably, in all innocence, a range of interests of relevance to them at their age, particularly those in the arts, by using fully the exciting teaching and learning facilities that the next millennium will offer.'

Zing studied her thoughtfully, but wrote nothing down. 'That is quite a sentence - and quite a prospect!' he said, smiling. 'It really is.'

'Whose side's that bugger on?' whispered Eastman to Townsend.

'I'm afraid,' said Susan, 'we've got the school curriculum upside down and that single fact is having devastating effects on society. The basic subjects or basic areas should not be the English, maths, history, science and geography of old, but an ongoing introduction to a range of leisure activities that will interest, involve and satisfy young people and which will stay with them – in an adult form, of course – for many years. They need to have an aim in life and be able to see that their education fosters that aim.'

'And what will happen ...' started Wendy Durrell.

'So that what we now call "the basic subjects" would not be so, but would become available to children and young people as and when required, that is when those youngsters could see a need for them ...'

'Ye gods!' Walker-West ejaculated. 'This must never be!'

'Just as book production can now be done on demand as and when a purchaser wants a copy and not printed in thousands in the old-fashioned way in the hope that some might sell to someone some day, so, in education, we introduce units or modules of maths and English on demand and do the same for other traditional subjects at the time when a student asks for them because he wants them as an interest in themselves or needs them to further his ambitions. What we now label basic subjects will become add-ons in the way that chess and soccer and art, drama and music are add-ons now. As with books, developing technology will supply produced-on-demand educational basics which will be variable, attractive, constantly updated and made available to anyone, anytime, anywhere.'

'A revolution!' stormed Walker-West rising from his seat, 'a dangerous revolution that will carry our poor old country to chaos!'

'Well, society will certainly be in chaos if we fail to raise our children in a way that shows them that life can be enjoyable and rewarding without the mad, undignified, competitive, push-each-other-out-of-the-way scramble that it has become today. That, Sir, is where the real danger lies.' Susan paused, but no governor spoke. Walker-West sat down, shook his head, and was astounded yet again.

'Anyway,' Susan concluded, 'I hope that's made things clearer.'

'It has. You summed up well, Dr Mansfield,' said Lena. She, too, paused, then said: 'Are there any questions you wish to ask us?'

'No. But let me say one more thing. If we accepted that one teacher could relate well to twenty children, in small groups, knowing them, caring for them, loving them, interesting them and teaching them what she thought was best for them as individuals, then the other thousands of *non-teaching* employees in today's over-manned education industry – and I emphasise *non-teaching* - could be dismissed. With those huge savings we could reduce that tutor to child ratio, offer tutors better resources, and, in terms of children's happiness and the wider social good, do far better than at present *and* with the same amount of money. That is common sense. All I have said is common sense, with or without the CSP. Now, Madam, can I thank the governors for inviting me here? I have been delighted to attend and to talk about my ideas.'

Susan's long interview was over. There was silence as, with dignity and with head held high, she walked from the library.

*

'Right, let's get one thing clear ...' started Sneade almost before Susan had closed the door, 'we're not obliged to appoint anyone today and bugger me if we're going to ...'

'Appoint her!' finished Eastman. 'Definitely, definitely, not!'

'And we're definitely running behind schedule,' said Lena as calmly as she could, 'so, as we *all* agreed, ladies and gentlemen, we'll discuss Dr Mansfield's application along with the others at the end.'

'*Doctor* Mansfield? That woman's no doctor!' reviled Vic Sneade. 'I wouldn't have her examine me!'

'Oh, I don't know,' smiled Walker-West as his rarely used imagination flickered into life.

'Please,' said Lena. '*Please*!' And she glared at the nervous clerk as she rapped out, 'Now, Mr Wright, we'll see Mr Park!'

'Park? Not another crank,' groaned Walker-West, his smile quickly fading. 'We'll get more bullshit from him. Where do they find them?'

*

Terry managed a quick word with Susan. 'How was it? OK?'

'Yes. Lively, stimulating, enjoyable, bad-tempered and worthwhile. And they're shaken - aghast. Just what we wanted.'

'But you won't get the job?'

'You can bet a hundred to one on that!'

'No takers! And you can put even higher odds on me! Ah,' he said, seeing Mr Wright. 'An unhappy Herald! Don't the angels sing today?'

*

Only two minutes into Terry's interview controversy rose.

'We've heard much about the need for common sense in schools,' began Sneade. 'What are your views?'

'There's a need for common sense everywhere, not just in schools.'

''Stick to schools,' insisted Sneade. 'Like this one here.'

'But as I teach in this school, it might be ...'

'All the better!' Sneade retorted, close to an insolent grin. 'You can give us actual examples of how common sense could help to improve this place - and that shouldn't be difficult.'

Terry paused.

'Well? How about it?' Sneade's patience had worn tissue thin and his offensiveness leapt from him unchecked.

Terry could see he was being goaded, and, although he thought he had prepared himself adequately for forthright questions, the sneering way in which Sneade spoke and his taunting, toothy grin, galled him. He hadn't liked this pushy man in *The King of Morocco* and he liked him even less in here. He almost rose to the bait.

'Common sense in schools would tell us to pay far more to those who teach than to those who don't. It would warn teachers against taking orders or advice from those so-called "superiors" who have no teaching qualifications or experience, no notion of the damage disruptive behaviour can do, no professional skills, no knowledge of classroom stress, no in-service training, no idea of how to cope when faced with poor or inadequate resources, no enduring commitment to or liking of children, no breadth of reading, no long term views on the needs of society, no imagination, no humour, no proposals to improve their qualifications, no resilience, no sense of ... '

'Would you say you were a negative man, Mr Park?' cut in the teasing Eastman. 'A pessimistic man who looks for all the things he has not got rather than those he has?'

'I know that if thirty-five children are put into a room built for thirty

274

something has to give; that if a school administrator is paid more than a classroom practitioner there's resentment and that the wrong message is given; that if unruly pupils are kept in a school against the advice of those who teach them then other children lose out while nothing is gained, that if lawyers pocket hefty fees by suing schools then worthy extra-mural social and sporting activities cease, that if publicity-seeking politicians interfere continually in teachers' work then that work will suffer, that the government's so-called league tables are so meaningless they'd be a joke if they didn't do so much harm, that we waste time and upset children and teachers by testing things that don't matter, that debating is non-stop so that things like streaming and non-streaming rise and fall in favour like tides on Brighton beach. With *all* these things common sense has been thrown out.'

'Onto pebbly sand?' queried Wendy Durrell.

Terry smiled sadly.

'Now look here, Park, if you're made …'

'*Mr* Park.' murmured Lena correcting the Captain.

'If you're appointed to this headship would you try to put all these things right in your first year?' Walker-West's contempt for this insubordinate, low-ranking interviewee was apparent. He'd have the man run out of the Mess pretty damn sharp.

'Of course not. No one person could hope to right all those wrongs in one year, or in two or three; they've been building up for fifty.'

'And not tackled?'

'And not tackled.'

'But a strong trade union would tackle them?'

'The operative word is strong, Mr Eastman. Teachers have never had a single, strong trade union. That's why they're in such a mess now and for that, by and large, they've only themselves to blame.'

'So teachers, too, lack common sense?' Wendy asked, softly.

'In their attitude to trade unionism, yes,' said Terry.

'But unions are not beyond reproach,' said the CEO quietly.

'No, they're not, but nevertheless they're the teachers' only hope.'

'Are they?' queried Eastman. 'By ordering strikes? Running closed shops? He paused. 'Posting pickets, going slow, working to rule, like dockers, railwaymen, postmen and car workers do - or used to do?'

'Yes, if other routes are exhausted.'

'Yet you have little time for those "other routes," Mr Park?'

'I don't follow you.'

'Let me quote from an article you wrote in a teachers' journal some four years ago. "Governments and education authorities can survive indefinitely meetings, letters, petitions, enquiries, pleas, lobbying, banners, posters and peaceful demonstrations, so there must come a time when *inevitably*," your word, Mr Park, "*inevitably* the only thing that will make entrenched employers move an inch or yield a penny is when schools are closed, parents are howling loud and long, and ballot boxes beckon."'

'Where …'

'Where did I get that from? I have friends! But the question is, Mr Park, did you write it and, if so, is it still your view?'

'I did, and it is.'

'So you would write the same today?'

'No.'

'No?'

'No.' Terry defied the governors. 'I would put it more strongly.'

Now it was not only Mr Wright who was scribbling feverishly.

'*Mr* Park,' said Wendy Durrell, 'let's suppose your own union, Teachers for Radical Action, kindly allows one school to remain open long enough for you to tell us why a child attends that school in the first place. Or tell us why a child comes to this school, or to your school if you become its head teacher.'

'Believe me, Madam, I don't wish to be argumentative, but I cannot accept "*your*" school. It would not be *my* school. The school is publicly owned, its teachers publicly paid, other resources publicly provided. It doesn't enhance relationships if an elegantly dressed and pompous head teacher calls it 'my' school, 'my' pupils, 'my' staff, 'my' governors, 'my' parents. A school belongs to all connected with it – those who teach in it and study in it and those who pay for it.'

'You're playing with words, Mr Park: you know what I mean. Why does a child come to, let's say, to *this* school, each morning?'

Terry saw the danger. He remembered their long session with Susan and guessed her "replace schools" views had upset them. Probably, even after a hundred and twenty-five years of state schooling, there'd been disagreement on what the hell a school was for!

'I was not playing with words, I was making a serious point about something that is insufficiently understood but, to take your question, there are many reasons why children attend school: to learn to work with others, learn about others and learn about themselves, to sample activities some of which may be enjoyed for a lifetime, to realise that great wealth is not needed for happiness, to value healthy lifestyles, to recognise that the world's resources are finite, that our notions of race, nations and cultures are dated, to learn basic skills – and civility.'

'I see patriotism's left out of your list, Mr Park,' interceded Walker-West indignantly. 'Patriotism's not important to you, eh?'

'Only if it implies pride in one's country because of the good things that country has done and the ways in which it has helped the rest of the world, but if patriotism means a British soldier has to obey an order to stick a bayonet in a German' soldier's belly and twist it when it's in there – a fellow human being who's someone's husband, son, brother or father – a complete stranger to him, then patriotism isn't a word in my vocabulary and I would like it expunged from everybody else's.'

Walker-West stared in disbelief. 'Good God, man, you'd have a front line soldier disobey the lawful command of his officer?'

'No, I would not. But I would ask who appointed his officer in the first place and why they did. For instance, did his men elect him?'

'*Elect him, Sir?* That's scandalous! You'll advocate mutiny next!'

'I will not, but I do ask how many lives would have been spared if some really high-ups in the First World War had been elected by their subordinates. Thousands, millions? And on both sides? Anyway, I'm afraid yours is the response I expect from people suspicious of change, the people unwilling to accept that if our society is to be modernised and all its people included in it and made to feel important players, made to feel that they matter, that they are listened to, then nothing – *nothing* - should be seen as sacrosanct – even your patriotism.'

Wally Walker-West blurted out: 'Rubbish, Sir! Absolute, damnable rubbish. You and your kind want to turn our society upside down, don't you? *Don't* you, Sir? Turn it upside down!'

'No,' said Terry wearily. 'Just tilt it a bit.'

'Until it topples, falls and breaks into tiny pieces,' slipped in Mrs Durrell. 'Until it's broken beyond repair.'

'Exactly, Madam,' cried Walker-West. 'Exactly! Until everything of value and that we've defended for centuries is thrown away and gone forever. Until every tradition's scrapped, every convention abandoned, every courtesy cast off, every duty ridiculed, every custom jettisoned, every law broken, every shred of respect discarded, every...' But he was lost for words. His face became a dangerous shade of crimson.

'And I see you said nothing at all about children learning to read,' noted Eastman undemonstratively. 'Isn't that important?'

'Certainly, it has to be encouraged day in, day out. Our children will probably get far more from the good literature they read than from anything else in the school curriculum. But it's the *good* literature that's important and the problem is that many children live in a non-literature environment. We should not assume that all their homes are book-laden. On the contrary, some homes are book-bare and children from those homes require all the help they can get in choosing suitable books whether from bookshops, libraries, market stalls or anywhere else. They need individual help in starting a reading habit which will last them a lifetime. And that's where personal tutors, working closely with children and families over the long term, become invaluable.'

'I see,' said Fergus Eastman craftily, 'and I'm sure we'd agree with you heartily, yet, less than three years ago, Mr Park, you wrote, in a respected journal, and to the consternation of many, that teachers need not or indeed *should* not persist with the teaching of reading?'

Terry remembered the article; it had caused mayhem for months.

'That is different. I wrote that if by age thirteen, after eight years of dedicated teaching, a child still hadn't mastered the art of reading then, in some cases, the school should relent and find another activity that the child could pursue usefully and successfully so that he or she did not risk leaving school later with nothing but a sense of failure. I wrote that if a pupil left school aged sixteen despondent, knowing only of his own inadequacy in what others saw as a crucial area of life, then that was destructive of the child's self-esteem and dangerous for society. I argued that, for those many children, eleven years of compulsory and expensive state education had been a scandalous, wasteful, inhumane process. I explained my thinking.'

'That teachers should give up?' summarised Eastman bitingly.

'No, but that in those circumstances they should change objectives.'

'Nevertheless, give up on reading?'

'If you want to put it so simply, and in those circumstances, yes.'

Eastman nodded. His fellow governors were quiet. After a lengthy pause, Terry said, 'But going back to the original question ...'

'Leaving out reading,' murmured Wendy Durrell.

'Giving up on reading,' stressed Walker-West. 'Surrendering!'

'And to sum up,' continued Terry, ignoring them, 'a school helps to prepare children for the different roles they will assume after their formal education has ceased.'

'Not then, to be looked after?' queried Wendy thoughtfully.

'Looked after?'

'When parents are at work, or tired of looking after him or her? Isn't that a reason why a child comes to your – to *the* – school, Mr Park?'

Apart from the sound of the clerk's pen on paper and the bottom-shuffling Captain's chair creaking, there was silence. Then bells could be heard ringing, doors banging, windows closing, a teacher shouting, children calling, and the undeniable sounds of a scuffle nearby. Two ice cream vans chimed in competition, seagulls squabbled, a bin lid clattered, a dog barked and another replied from far away. A whistle was blown, a car hooted, brakes screeched, scooters were revved. A guitar was strummed, a few girls sang and a football hit a library window. It was going home time.

'I would not accept that,' said Terry.

'Why not?' asked Zoe Kennedy.

'I would not accept that willingly, only as a *fait accompli* because I have no choice. But as I was asked if I was a negative person, I would see that as a negative reason on the parents' part for using schools.'

'You prefer a clear separation of the two roles: the teaching role and the childcare role? Would you see that as common sense?'

'And common sense must be much in your mind?' queried Sneade.

'And much in the news?' mused Eastman. 'Everyday, everywhere? We can't get away from common sense.'

'Common sense needs to be with us everyday, everywhere. That is indisputable. Common sense is not transient or ephemeral or to be used as and when we like, or avoided when it doesn't suit us.'

'But as an ardent trade unionist and a university-trained sociologist, Mr Park, you will know that if a large part of a teacher's time is spent as mere custodian that fact could detract from her professional role or her "perceived social status" if you prefer?' Wendy was tenacious. 'After all, millions of untrained people care for children worldwide every day. It can hardly be recognised as professional work in the sociological meaning of professional? So I ask you, again, would it not be best to disentangle the caring role from the teaching role? That is the amateur from the professional? The unskilled from the skilled? The unpaid from the paid? Would not *that* be common sense?'

'And there's such a need for common sense!' goaded Eastman.

'A great need.' He would not let Eastman draw him now. 'But...'

'Yes?' insisted Eastman, determined to get a reply.

'Having millions of amateurs caring for children worldwide is nothing to be proud of and not a legitimate reason for maintaining the *status quo*. Raising children is a skilled, important task that should not be underestimated. Rather than have the education service - such as it is - take children away from their homes so that their parents then work more or less in isolation from them and see little of them, education should be linked, no, *inextricably intertwined*, with home and parents to give reliable support, encouragement and sympathy in our crazy world. The two go together in the upbringing of a child.'

'Could we, perhaps, change the direction of our questions?' Lena Napier asked hesitantly.

'Why?' snapped Sneade.

'Yes, why?' asked Eastman, and, when Eastman's heel hit his ankle, the wretched Townsend nodded furiously.

'Thank you, but I've no wish to change the subject, Chairperson,' persisted Eastman. 'We have here a legal responsibility to appoint a suitable head teacher and it is widely known that Mr Park proposes to stand as a parliamentary candidate for the CSP. Yet he seems reluctant to say to what extent this 'common sense' of his would be used in the administration of our school. Now, Mr Park, why the hesitation?'

Terry floundered. He had tried hard to explain, but these governors, Sneade, Eastman, the pathetic sabre-rattling Walker-West and the probing Durrell, seemed determined to discredit him. Had they done the same with Susan? But, no, she had emerged smiling.

'Would your CSP ideas stay within this school?' pressed Eastman. 'We do need to know. For instance would you abolish BST?'

'British Summer Time? Yes, it's confusing, expensive, makes no sense and doesn't add a minute to the day.' But he was startled as the panel, perusing notes, fired questions at him. Who had put them up to this?

'And you'd scrap bank holidays?'

'Yes. They're disruptive, obsolete, cost millions ...'

'Have 100 minutes in an hour and ten hours in a day?'

'Yes, much simpler – make time metric.'

'Ban drunken drivers for life with no exceptions?'

'Yes, not to do so is criminally irresponsible. And further ...'

'Prohibit parking on pavements and on all busy roads?'

'Yes. It is dangerous, unsightly and not what the roads are for.'

'Raise the minimum driving age first to eighteen, then nineteen?'

'Yes, and eventually to twenty, then twenty-one and ...'

'Introduce ten-yearly driving tests for everybody?'

'Yes. And make them difficult and include an intelligence test.'

'Pour funds into noise abatement measures?'

'Yes. Deny production permits for noisy vehicles, machinery …'

'Reinstate really hefty dog licence fees and introduce cat licences?'

'Yes.'

'Ban the public sale of fireworks, even on November the Fifth?'

'Yes.'

'Make all tipping illegal?'

'Yes, the first sort's ugly and unhygienic, the second's demeaning.'

'Make Birmingham the nation's capital?'

'Yes. It's central, has space, and excellent transport links. '

'And downgrade London's importance?

'Yes – show people that other places matter as well as London.'

'Have a modern, purpose built assembly instead of Westminster?

'Yes, in Birmingham.'

'Introduce proportional representation?

'Yes.'

'Make full use of national referenda on all major issues?'

'Yes.'

'Make school attendance voluntary?'

'Yes.'

'Abandon religious assemblies in state funded schools and withdraw all state funding from faith schools?'

'Yes.'

'Close fee-paying public schools and scrap university fees?'

'Yes.'

'Abolish the House of Lords?'

'Yes.'

'Have your new national assembly in Birmingham sit all year round and work for five eight-hour days for forty-eight weeks?'

'Yes.'

'Reduce MPs' salaries to the national average wage, regulate their expenses, and ban them from having any other paid work?'

'Yes.'

'And do the same with the MEPs? Your so-called "fat cats"?'

'Yes.'

'Scrap the honours system in its entirety?'

'Yes.'

'Enrol everyone in a fee-free, state-supported Legal Service?'

'Yes.'

'Modernise and humanise the courts – make them people-friendly?'

'Yes.'

'Elect locally born magistrates and judges every four years?'

'Yes.'

'Make all non-violent criminals work usefully in the community?'

'Yes.'

'Build more community resource, social and education centres?'

'Yes.'

'Ascertain an optimum population size for the UK and then have a population-control policy including immigration and emigration?'

'Yes.'

'Have a hefty obesity tax on unhealthy, fattening foods?'

'Yes.'

'Enforce a metered water supply to every household?'

'Yes.'

'Allow euthanasia?'

'Yes.'

'Legalise properly- regulated and licensed public brothels?'

'Yes.'

'Simplify, drastically, all state taxes, allowances and benefits?'

'Yes.'

'Move school and university exams from summer to winter?'

'Yes, if we still have exams.'

'Teach parents how to do their childrearing job?'

'Yes, but I can't accept the …'

'Expel their most troublesome offspring?'

'Yes, but not put as crudely as that.' Terry faltered. Now most of the questions were coming from the odious Eastman.

'Allow parents to take their children on holiday in term time?'

'Yes, if we still have terms, but …'

'Withdraw from Europe?' snapped Sneade.

'Yes, with an option to return when common sense prevails.'

'Which would be?' demanded Eastman.

'When the absurd common agriculture policy's scrapped, when the exorbitant administration costs are quartered, when the size of the Assembly is halved, when the ridiculous and money-wasting trekking from one parliament to another is abandoned …'

But Terry faltered again, beaten, dispirited. Now five of them were smiling at him in a sickening "We've got you" manner and he knew they were throwing his whole CSP manifesto back at him derisively, prompted, no doubt, by the ferreting, wife-aided Eastman. He knew now they would never in a month of Sundays have him as their head teacher or school leader or whatever else they wanted to call the job. Bloody Collins had been right, dead right! So you can stuff your stinking job, he thought, and stuff yourselves at the same time. Then, abandoning discretion, he ended, 'and when the Bullies of Brussels let us eat straight or bent bananas or any bananas we like!'

'Bananas?' exploded Walker-West. 'Look here, Madam Chairman, I've had enough of this. Don't let's beat about the bush. In the Regiment we called a spade a spade and got on with it, so, with your permission, I'll put a straight question to *Mr* Park: Mr Park, if you had to choose between being a CSP member of your Assembly in Birmingham or head of this school here in Mansworth, which would it be?' He waited. ' Well? Come on man! Speak up! Let's be knowing!'

Tension was high. They could have been electing the first President of the United States. Terry studied each governor in turn and was unimpressed by what he saw. Dafydd Hughes, as well as Eddie Collins, had been right to say they were a shower, a consummate shower. He was a fool to have tangled and now wanted out.

'Well?' pressed Wally Walker-West, 'which would it be?'

'To be a Member of the new National Assembly in Birmingham.'

'Right, I have no more questions,' said the self-satisfied Captain with a lip-curling smirk. He leaned back contentedly and straightened, deliberately and proudly, his regimental tie.

And there were no further questions from anyone else. Likewise, the candidate, Terry Arthur Park, B.A. (Hons), had none to ask of them.

*

Kurt Rommal had had a raw deal. As the last candidate to be called he had languished for two hours in the cell-like waiting room with the obnoxious Carter. Other candidates had relieved the monotony with strolls outside or the exchange of hilarious stories of incompetently managed, money-wasting, patronising, 'no-decision-made', clearly-rigged, politically-biased, expenses-begrudged, interviews. Carter had related no such stories.

Then, when Kurt Rommal's long wait was over, an ill-disposed panel confronted him. They barely listened to his answers to their inane questions. Clearly they had been upset by earlier exchanges and were indifferent to their final, head-of-sixth form applicant. His frustration became all too apparent when, after less than fifteen minutes, the Chairperson thanked him for his attendance. Rommal, never a patient man, yielded to temper.

'Isn't it customary,' he rasped, 'for the candidate to be asked if he has questions to put to the panel?'

'Yes. Yes, it is. Of course it is. You are quite right. Mr Rommal, I do apologise. Please ask your questions,' said Lena.

'Why is one candidate given forty minutes to present her case and another thirty-five while I get...' he studied his watch, 'fourteen?'

'That's not your business,' said Eastman.

'Why?' countered Rommal.

'Because how we conduct our interviews is our concern!'

'There's a well-known procedure ...' began Rommal.

'Not here there isn't,' snapped Sneade. 'In this city we do our thing in our way in our time. That's what we do here.'

'There's a ...'

'Besides, nobody made you apply.'

'You invited me.'

'You didn't have to accept,' retorted Eastman.

'But *you called me*!' persisted Rommal. 'I make enquiries, travel three hundred miles round trip, stay overnight, attend a sorry social, prepare my case, write letters, fill in your ridiculous forms about my school exams of thirty years ago, photocopy testimonials, ask busy people for references, am shown round a school that's not a patch on the one I work in now, miss teaching my exam classes for two whole days, wait hours with some chinless wonder in an airless waiting room that needs reporting to Health and Safety, and then face you lot for barely fourteen minutes!'

'You've said enough, Sir!' ejaculated Wally Walker-West.

'I've hardly started! First, I object to the way these interviews are being conducted, second, I object ...'

'Object all you like,' shouted Sneade, 'object till the sodding cows come home - it won't make no difference! And don't bother to collect your expenses if that's how you feel!'

'You're refusing expenses?' asked Rommal, incredulously.

'Mr Rommal,' said Lena, 'you should not get so upset by what is, after all, hardly your concern.'

'Is it not? Well, let me suggest, Chairman …'

'Chairperson!' corrected Wendy.

'Chairperson, that this whole thing was fixed at last night's juvenile knees-up of a social in a dingy school hall with a few tatty flags left over from some pre-war Empire Day Parade dangling over the sausage rolls, when what a candidate wore and how he spoke, the way he twiddled his less-than-half-filled plastic glass of special-offer supermarket plonk, and whom he sucked up to and for how long, were the chief determinants of who gets this rotten job.'

'Well, you won't get it for one!' bellowed Sneade pointing to Rommal. 'So, so, you can piss off! Go on! Piss off now!'

'Mr Sneade!' implored an alarmed Lena Napier, 'you must not …'

'Sneade?'snorted Rommal, '*Sneade*? I'll remember that name – it reminds me of something else that has a nasty sound.'

'You insolent bastard,' yelled Sneade moving round the table, his face flushed, his shoulders hunched, his fists clenched, his feet flexed, his desire for a fight to the finish unmistakeable. 'And your name reminds *me* of someone else – some goose-stepping Jerry – some big-headed general with an iron bloody cross who got his flaming arse kicked from one side of the forest to the other!'

'*Forest?*' shouted an indignant Walker-West, '*desert*, man, *desert*.'

'Gentlemen, gentlemen …' begged Lena, 'please …'

'*Gentlemen*?' roared Wally Walker-West this time rising to his feet. '*Gentlemen*? They're not gentlemen, Madam, they're idle, trade union, trouble-making, card-carrying Bolsheviks, both of them!'

Now, ignoring Kurt Rommal, the enraged Sneade swept round as if to aim a punch at the arrogant, insufferable and long-despised Captain Walter Walker-West (Retired). But Wendy Durrell, who had thrust herself bravely between them, stopped him. 'Sit down, and grow up, both of you,' she hissed. 'Sit down, and sit down *now*!'

Reluctantly, and slowly, the two men moved apart, scowling.

'And you look like some anti-union, Tory Party sponger!' Rommal retorted as he wagged a finger at Walker-West. 'Live off a private income, do you? Live off the workers? Well, you idle wanker, you'll be hearing from my *workers'* union.'

'That communist outfit? Teachers for Revolution?'

'Teachers for Radical Action - to give it its correct name! And they've got lawyers who'll sort your type out in five minutes flat!' He looked round: 'and the rest of you will be hearing from them, too. This shambles is a distortion of democracy and a waste of public money! It needs maximum publicity in the tabloids with positions, names, addresses, photographs, and it'll get them!'

He frowned ferociously at the collar-fingering Lena and then at the wilting secretary. 'Scribble that in your useless notes,' he shouted at the wretched Wright, 'every word! Go on, get writing, and I'll check you've done it and if you haven't you'll wallow in shit for a week'

He took a few steps back from his chair and pointed a finger at each panel member in turn to make sure each knew he or she was included in his final tirade: 'And I'll bet fifty quid not one of you is a teacher. That not one of you knows what it's like to stand in front of thirty-five kids who don't want to be there and then try to do something that might be marginally useful with them for hour after hour, day after day, month after month, year after year!'

He glowered at them, red faced, but, with a supreme effort, managed to lower his voice.

'And yet you have the audacity to sit there appointing a head teacher to a school like this! I don't know how you have the nerve. Yet there are fifty teachers here in this building right now who could tell you what was needed, and they'd make a better job of doing things than you would if you sat there 'til Christmas Day. But no one asks them, do they? Do they hell! This whole thing, from beginning to end is one great big, pathetic fiasco, a farce!'

He clenched his fist, glared one last time at Sneade, strode out, collected his brief-case, ignored the other astounded candidates, grabbed a handful of waiting-room biscuits, used the staff toilet, didn't flush it, emptied the soap dispenser, pocketed a wad of paper towels, combed his hair, cold-shouldered the startled secretaries, refused to acknowledge Hull's valediction, shoved open the doors, and left. The last the school heard of him was the furious revving of his motorcar engine followed by a series of bangs from its aging exhaust.

Mr Rommal was going home.

*

'Well,' said Zoë Kennedy as the noise died away. 'Well?'

For the first time since the school was opened there was smoking in the library. The stunned panel sat in silence.

'Well? What do we *do*?' repeated Zoe. 'Sit here all night?'

286

They turned to the Chair.

'I will write to Mr Rommal to apologise and say how overwrought we were by our earlier duties,' said The Rev. Dr. Lena Napier. 'It will be done today.'

'It will not,' said Eastman. 'You will write to Rommal to say his application has been unsuccessful and that while the Governors were appalled by his unprofessional conduct, they will, in the wider interests of the school, not be instigating proceedings and that they will accept his claim for standard, essential, *minimal*, fully receipted, expenses. And,' he added, 'use second class mail.'

The proposal was approved and minuted by the quivering Wright.

'Perhaps, now, we can get back to the headship,' said Wendy Durrell. 'And for God's sake let's appoint someone today because I'm not, let me repeat, *not*, going through this pantomime again.'

'Nor me,' Zoe Kennedy quickly agreed.

'OK. We'll use an elimination process,' Eastman began, 'Then we appoint the last one left in.' Townsend nodded agreement energetically.

'Like musical chairs,' scoffed Sneade.

Lena was apathetic. 'Very well, do as you wish.' She was more than willing to give up the chairmanship, or chairwomanship, or whatever else they wanted to name it, there and then.

'Good,' said Eastman. 'So who votes for Joan Bates?'

No one voted for Joan Bates. Faces whitened at the thought.

'Carter?'

Kennedy, Townsend and Walker-West voted for Carter.

'Dr. Mansfield?'

'If there is a tie, I will vote for her,' Lena offered.

'Park?'

'I liked him. At least he has fresh thoughts,' said Wendy Durrell.

'But do you *vote* for him?' asked Eastman.

'Very well, yes! I will vote for Terry Park!'

'Right. Now, just for the record, let's make sure there's nobody for Rommal,' cautioned Eastman.

There was nobody for Rommal.

'What about you, Eastman?' demanded Walker-West. 'What about your vote?'

'Carter,' said Eastman, 'I'll go for Carter. And that settles it!'

'Does it hell!' Sneade shouted. 'I haven't voted!'

'There's four for Carter,' Eastman said before Lena could take over. 'It makes no difference what you do.'

'Oh yes it does! I move the suspension of standing orders. We readvertise. I put it that we bring in a different set of applicants. I propose that we re-advertise and send this rotten bunch packing.' Contemptuously he swept his papers to one side. 'Stuff the lot!'

The governors looked at one another, puzzled. What was "the suspension of standing orders"? Giles Townsend was about to raise his hand but something held him back. He was beginning to feel sick.

'Well?' ranted Sneade. 'Say something! Do we re-advertise?'

Mr Wright trembled again. He was running out of paper.

'Mr Sneade,' said Lena trying to regain her composure and her authority. 'You can see no governor wants a rerun of this performance and no one wants this school to be without a head teacher for the next six months. Nobody thinks that by re-advertising we will attract a stronger field, in fact if word gets round that we cannot make an appointment today everyone will suspect the worst and steer clear of our school altogether. I beseech the governors, therefore, I really do, to make an appointment now, that is...' and jadedly she looked at the library clock showing twenty-five minutes past four, 'within the next quarter of an hour. Think carefully.' She waited. No one demurred. Then she said: 'First, who wants to appoint today?'

Slowly two hands were raised.

'Against?'

Two hands were raised.

'Abstentions?'

Two more hands were raised.

'Then my casting vote goes with the first two,' Lena said quickly before anyone could object. 'So we appoint today. Get it down, then!' she said to the dithering Wright, 'we appoint today.'

Wright scribbled. His reading glasses had misted over again. He would resign tomorrow.

'So, let's try again, and, in view of what has occurred with the unhappy Mr Rommal, is our choice restricted to Miss Bates, Mr Carter, Dr Mansfield and Mr Park?'

'I'll tell you this, I leave right now if Mansfield is appointed at any time,' said Eastman. 'Appointing an anti-schooler would make us a joke and complete the debacle we've had today.'

Wally Walker-West and Townsend said they would do the same.

'Nevertheless, her name must remain on the list. So it's Miss Bates, Mr

Carter, Dr Mansfield or Mr Park?' asked Lena.

Eastman waited.

'Is there still no one for Miss Bates?' she asked.

'No takers,' said Eastman.

'Which leaves Mr Carter, Dr Mansfield or Mr Park.'

'Park doesn't even want the job,' said Walker-West emphatically. 'He said so.' The others nodded. 'He's too political and too bound up with the Mansfield woman. And he's on the school staff – an insider.'

'Not much going for Park, then,' concluded Eastman cheerfully.

'Will anyone vote for Mr Park?' asked Lena.

Wendy Durrell said: 'Yes, I will still vote for Mr Park.'

'Mr Carter?' Lena asked. She was becoming increasingly uneasy.

Three hands went up: Eastman, Townsend and Walker-West. Lena looked round hoping desperately they would not appoint Carter. There were still two votes left and her own. She waited.

'I'll vote for Mansfield,' said Vic Sneade loudly but grudgingly. He ignored the looks of surprise; let them think what they liked, he refused to go along with Eastman's choice, whatever it was, and he knew Mansfield was out of the running anyway.

'Reluctantly, I'll still go for Carter,' said Zoe Kennedy at last. 'What's the alternative? There's too much against Mansfield and Park.'

'Four for Mr Carter?' said Lena softly, sadly. 'Four does it?'

They all nodded gloomily. Four did it.

'Shall we call him in?'

'Yes. Get the exercise over,' ordered Walker-West. 'Run him in.'

Mr Wright departed to fetch the victorious Carter while the library clock measured the passing of precious time. Paul Herbert Carter did not run in, but walked in serenely, bowed slightly, smiled nauseously, sat down confidently, and accepted the post.

The panel's job was done.

'Do accept our congratulations, Mr Carter,' said The Rev Dr. Lena Napier, attempting a weak professional smile, 'on becoming the head teacher of Outer Mansworth Comprehensive School. I'm sure all the governors will wish you well in your new post.'

But her smile quickly faded. Never had she offered congratulations with such heinous insincerity. Tonight, as she kneeled, she would pray for the Lord's forgiveness, and also for His blessing on Mr Carter.

But even if he had detected such insincerity, Mr Carter didn't mind.

*

'Don't worry about it,' whispered Louie Anne Lee, 'you wouldn't have wanted that rotten job anyway would you?' She hesitated. ' But, but ... I didn't like the look of Mr Carter.'

'That's just it,' said Terry, 'nobody did, it's insane. Nobody wanted him yet we've got him!' He thought for a moment. 'D'you know, at present this school isn't that bad. The fact that it's got troublemakers on the staff such as politicians and trade unionists gives it character and keeps it from being a complete government-devised sweat shop. But under Carter it will be just one more innocuous, bland, inward-looking school. It will seek praise from the inspectors for sticking to the National Curriculum and will try to gain local glory with really wonderful exam results for a few of its top pupils.'

Louie Anne nodded. While collecting cups, saucers, plates, unused serviettes and unread magazines from the waiting room she had seen Terry sitting there hunched and depressed. Her heart had gone out to him. How could she help? She so wanted to help!

*

Meanwhile the triumphant Carter had phoned his school and finalised administrative matters with Lena and the CEO. Apart from Terry, all the other candidates had gone home while a few governors stood in the foyer looking despondent. Without enthusiasm the governing body as a whole had ratified Carter's appointment just before the deadline, glad that the business was over and that a new head teacher would be in place for September. But only one member seemed really pleased.

'So that's settled!' chortled Eastman gleefully. 'We've done it, and with excellent timing! We'll have a new bum on the seat in September.'

'Wrong bloody word again,' snarled the nearby Sneade. 'Tell the truth for once, Eastman. Go on, *say it* man: we'll have an utter *arsehole*!'

But this brief intellectual exchange in Outer Mansfield's seat of learning went unheard by the occupants of the nearby waiting room.

*

'This will cheer you up,' said Louie Anne later as Terry prepared to leave. She handed him the *Messenger* folded back to show the Collins-approved, CSP advertisement: the first big spend from their £10,000. It stood out starkly: "*Vote for the Common Sense Man!"* and, also prominent was: '*Vote for Park and his Common Sense Party!'*

'Nobody can miss that! And there's a good write-up,' Louie Anne said

290

eagerly, turning to another page. 'That's far more important than Carter and his awful job.' She waited, expectantly, 'well, *isn't* it?'

'Yes, I suppose it is!'

First Terry read the write-up and then turned to view the advert. 'Yes, it is, of course it is! Thank you, Louie Anne!'

He leaned over and kissed her lightly on the forehead. She smiled, so he touched her cheek as he looked at her closely: she was a beautiful girl, and so genuine.

'Ooo! I've never been kissed by a Member of Parliament before,' she said smiling, 'and I like it!' Louie Anne beamed with pleasure.

She looked at Terry admiringly and, only half jokingly, whispered in his ear, 'One day, Mr Park, we might cuddle up cosily on the backbenches out of sight of Mr Speaker! Imagine that!'

Terry could imagine nothing less likely.

Wednesday 1 May.   **The Aftermath**

If Tuesday was a day of disappointment, Wednesday was one of hope. With keen students Susan canvassed all morning while Terry stayed in the temporary CSP office. He dealt with callers, gave interviews to friendly reporters and took a phone-in on Radio Mansworth's popular programme, *Your Very Own Chatty Hour!*

The full-page display had worked well. Hetty's editor, inundated with controversial letters, phone calls, fax messages and E-mails, was forced to leave Hetty to her own devices and Hetty was making the most of it by giving the CSP subtle but favourable publicity.

The students walked ahead of Susan asking householders if they would like to talk to the CPS agent. With those who did, about one in twenty, Susan's canvassing tactic was to show the newspaper's half-page spread and ask whether the constituent had seen it. She was pleasantly surprised by the number who had, and, with those whose responses were good, she went through the manifesto, noted comments, and sought support; increasingly this was promised. More common sense in politics and less political correctness was what most voters wanted and what, to date, they had not got.

The radio phone-in – also boosted by the advert - lifted Terry's spirits greatly. An amiable presenter smoothed the way and gave more time to callers supporting Terry than to the few who were opposed.

Early visitors to the CSP office applauded his efforts. They took piles of leaflets for distribution and eye-catching posters for window display. One supporter showed Terry a crumpled copy of that morning's *Daily Dawn Crier*, the popular national newspaper.

'D'you know this Willis guy?' the young campaigner asked.

'I met him at a meeting. He's a journalist - a freelance.'

'He's done you proud. You can nick some quotes, though there's more about some woman's no-schools teaching scheme than the CSP.'

Terry's eyes swept over the headline, but he made no comment.

'Smashing photo of the woman as well – real good looker – local lecturer - researching at the university. D'you know her?'

'Yes, I know her,' Terry murmured, 'I know her well.'

At mid-day they changed places - except that Susan spoke on the commercial radio. Despite a lethargic presenter she explained CSP aspirations fully. 'Britain must have more common sense,' she stressed. But one caller was irate, 'Never mind common sense, tell us how you'll get rid of political correctness. It's stifled this once fine country and the people in it, and you politicians have let it happen without a whimper!'

They turned out in the evening to visit shopping malls, pubs, and bus and train stations. While most people did not want to know, some listened encouragingly. Both Terry and Susan thought it was a pity time was so short because another week, free of the head teacher interviews, would have made a big difference. Readers' letters to *The Messenger* praised their efforts and a popular city councillor, fed up with the three main parties, urged readers to vote for Terry Park and common sense. They tried telephone cold calling but got nowhere so they went out again distributing their remaining leaflets. At least, they told themselves, they'd tried.

*

Things were less rosy at Terry's school. The few teachers who could contemplate living without their teachers' salary were contemplating, those whose teaching subjects were in demand were viewing the field, those whose subjects were ten a penny were listing people who might pull strings, those near retirement age were checking pensions, those who had toyed with jobs outside teaching were broadening their horizons, and those with minor disabilities were wondering whether kind doctors would support their early retirement on health grounds. Those who enjoyed none of these possible exits set pupils work to do, sat by their classroom windows and gazed at a cold, bleak Paul Carter dominated landscape. For them the time passed slowly.

'I met a bloke who sold up and hitch-hiked across America,' said Dafydd at break. 'Said he couldn't give a damn, got odd jobs – illegally - had a wonderful time! Met up with five tarts in five states!'

'And came back with the pox?' a colleague queried.

'Some women make more in one night than I get in a week,' said Sheila picking up the theme. "And tax free, my dear, *tax free*!"'

'A head teacher near here cashed in his lump sum, opened a small prep school and works happily with children who want to learn and whose parents want them to learn,' said Ursula, 'and I've heard of another who makes a stress-free living coaching carefully selected pupils and who accompanies a super rich family on holiday every summer: Rome last year, Paris the year before, Casablanca yet to come!'

Similar grass is greener on the other side stories followed, but Jenny wondered whether people outside teaching thought the grass had a richer hue on the teachers' side of the fence.

However no one was surprised when Ingrid Eastman announced that Mr Olde was indisposed and would not be in today.

'Nor tomorrow,' Ursula thought gloomily.

The day wore on with the image of Carter darkening it by the hour. At four the school was deserted. The library was closed, no pupils were in detention, choir and orchestra practices were cancelled, both secretaries took advantage of the head teacher's absence and went home, the groundsman sidled off, Hull mooched in the betting shop, the cleaners drank tea, and the school's tomcat dozed in the boiler room. The scene was set for September.

Thursday 2 May.   **The General Election**

The turnout for the general election was the worst on record despite warm, sunny weather. Agents despaired, candidates hung their heads, bored poll officials twiddled their thumbs or knitted, voters ignored appeals, canvassers gave up, the media reported apathy, relieved returning officers anticipated a quick count; be home by midnight?

Undeterred by this ubiquitous indifference, Terry had made use of his last day of authorised absence from school to stand in streets, address passers-by from a loudspeaker van, talk to people outside shops and knock on more doors. It was the remarkable response to one door-knocking that raised Terry's spirits. In a pleasant Victorian villa an elderly lady, well dressed, said how interested she had been in the CSP manifesto and how it gave hope to her and the country.

'But why are you so timorous?' she had asked. 'You need to attract attention by pushing forward really radical policies that will make people see they can prosper only by adopting revolutionary strategies.'

'What would you propose?' asked Terry. 'We already ...'

'Let me finish,' she said as she placed a hand on the door as if to steady herself. 'Violent criminals, drug dealers, people traffickers and so-called road rage murderers need to be imprisoned on a secure, basically equipped, remote island because, put simply, they are not wanted here. Strongly-fenced camps – patrolled by hungry hounds - should be built on windswept moors for vandals - camps which they can vandalise to their hearts' content provided they are made to live in what they've vandalised. Proportional representation is a century overdue. Taxation and benefits systems even simpler than the ones you suggest are vital, and access to low-cost legal services essential. Instead of the dysfunctional society we're getting now, show what Britain *could* be like - a streamlined, 21st century republic owned *by* - and governed *by* and *for* - its people. Give electors a *real* vision, a *real* alternative, *real* hope! Let them see what life *might* be like if the ancient and stultifying institutions were swept aside once and for all.'

'Madam, that's just what ...'

'You'll get nowhere with weak, half-hearted programmes. People are detached from politics. Nothing short of a gigantic, *really* gigantic, shock wave will revive interest. Really shake them; be strong, courageous, ruthless. Remember, young man, faint heart ne'er won fair lady!'

'Amazing!' Terry said. 'But I don't think people ...'

'Don't tell me, Mr Park, you don't think people would accept it?'

'Exactly.'

'Then try them! You've nothing to lose because they won't accept what's on offer now. They've had enough and don't care, and because of that you'll find they won't even listen to you or anyone else; that will be your greatest problem. Believe me, I should know.'

'You should know?' Terry looked at her intently.

'I ran as an independent in two general elections. Hemmings was my maiden name, Heather Hemmings, and I stood for The Fair Play Party. I was its only member! I lost my deposit twice, but that wasn't what upset me, what upset me was the willingness of people to embrace mediocrity and be bamboozled into thinking they had an electoral choice. They hadn't, and they've had no real choice since the letdowns of the post-war Labour government.' She paused again as if to regain her breath. 'Do you want to hear any more?'

Terry nodded keenly.

'The 1945 Labour government, with its massive majority and a war worn electorate aching for change, took the wrong road.'

'It did?'

'Yes, what was needed then, and what that government had the strongest-ever mandate to provide, was a firm basis for an egalitarian, inclusive society where birth, school, dress, class, elitism, snobbery, tradition, ritual, ceremony, uniform, regalia, wealth, station, privilege, accent, and all the other evil, socially divisive and dangerous features *had no place*. Those pre-war insulting absurdities could have been rooted out, broken up, and burned on a public bonfire. To do that they needed to close the public schools, open up the old universities so they admitted students on an ability-only basis, reform the Civil Service from top to bottom, institute a hefty wealth tax, scrap the honours system and the House of Lords, and revolutionise the slow, inefficient, unreliable, expensive, all-pals-together legal system. The sheer force of popular feeling in 1945 at the end of that awful Second World War was such that their reforms could not have been blocked. Feeling was strong - we even had two communist MPs to prove it! The old pre-war ruling, incompetent, uncaring, arrogant few could have been sent packing on one-way economy tickets to South America.'

Her face was flushed and alive.

'Such cauterisation would have been painful and needed courage to complete, but it could have been done! Men and women who had fought fascism for over five years would have stood no truck, once back in their own country, from obstructive right-wingers. But that socialist government chose to nationalise this and that, make a start on the social services and spend billions rearming against the socialist USSR. So the roots of the old system remained and we now know how deep they were for they were able to cling to life and then sprout again when the threat was past. Those ultra-blues had been able to dig themselves in and, throughout six years of Labour government, were permitted to keep, and pay to use, their treasured private schools, their private doctors and dentists, their land, and their accountants and lawyers. Once they saw the direction the party was taking and realised there wasn't the money for both massive rearmament *and* broad social reconstruction, and saw that the Americans weren't going to prop up a socialist government, they knew all they had to do was wait. And they had to wait only six years until Attlee's Labour Government, invincible in 1945, collapsed, bankrupt, in 1951. Winston Churchill was back! Jubilantly the Tories could resume their privileged ways of life. They were again at the helm. The common people had been denied; a once-in-a-lifetime chance was gone. In 1945 Labour had plans for a marvellous edifice, but failed to provide firm foundations.'

'It set up a wonderful health service.'

'Did it?'

Terry was nonplussed.

'Think about that,' she said, 'think of all the people today who choose not to use the NHS – and are allowed not to use it.'

Terry didn't answer.

'At the birth of the NHS some doctors were allowed to choose private practice - as did some dentists and teachers. They opted out of what was a marvellous opportunity to serve ordinary people. Since then there's been no real choice for most citizens, just a pretence of choice. If you've got money you've got a choice between state and private; but no money - no choice! The same in education. And there's no choice in politics either, nothing that radical or disillusioned people can vote for except the far right or the far left, and now it's the far right that's leading. But, if you got your CSP organised there *might* be another choice, but not with your timid agenda.'

'We thought we'd go cautiously, a step at a time.'

'Like other new parties that have disappeared without trace.'

'I see what you mean,' said Terry. 'I really do, and I'm grateful. You're like a breath of fresh air. There's so much to think about.'

'Well, don't think too long! You'll be surprised how many will vote for you if they're inspired and see you mean business and see a way out of this political morass. Then you can build on that.' She made as if to close the door and Terry turned away, but she called him back.

'Here's something else to put in your charter. Demand a National Publishing House – a NPH - one that's state subsidised but not state controlled. One that will publish low-demand books that have exciting ideas and fresh thoughts but minority appeal and low sales. Too many big commercial publishers opted out of that long ago and now fail the thinking, reading, public. Some don't read the work submitted to them, or even consider that sent in by "unknown" authors, and that's disgraceful. They're too dominated by political correctness, wily accountants, takeover bids and undue concern for the powers that be. They churn out shallow "celebrity" titles "linked to the movie." That drains money from the total sum that's available for book purchase. Put that in!' She paused. 'But wait there ...' and moved into the house.

And you could say the same about TV, thought Terry. What could have been a top notch tool for social improvement and a readily accessible educational opportunity for the whole population had been lost to moronic adverts for tinned cat food, polluting cars, cheap booze and skin cancer causing holidays on the sun-drenched beaches of Morocco or the swimming pools of Timbuktu, anything for a quick buck. The teaching opportunity of the century had been lost.

Heather Hemmings returned with a creased, brown envelope. 'Take this. Read it when you get home. It's a letter I wrote to the press before a general election thirty-five years ago. I shan't need it now.'

Before a surprised Terry could thank her, the elderly constituent had disappeared behind her front door. He heard her fix the chain.

*

'Read it out then,' Susan said later in her kitchen, 'while I work.'

"Dear Editor,

I have studied the manifestos of the main parties and have seldom been less inspired. Not one offers voters something radically different from what has been trotted out before.

What Britain needs is a batch of fresh ideas proposed by people who, having future generations in mind, think imaginatively and make proposals which, while they may seem extreme today, have viability and potential for the years ahead.

Look at just one reform which would have most politicians scoffing because they (a) haven't the imagination to think up such revolutionary ideas themselves or (b) are frightened of upsetting their party leaders or (c) envisage so many problems they won't even give the idea a second thought"'

'Or all three,' murmured Susan.

"My suggestion is that each accredited citizen be given, weekly and tax free, sufficient basic income to enable him or her to survive on: i.e. enough to buy *essential* food, clothing and heating and to pay rent for *basic* accommodation, plus free health, education, old age care, *and that would be all!*

Anything a citizen wanted above those basics would need to be earned - with taxes paid at a rate sufficient to finance my proposal. Then the expensive, complex system of state allowances would be scrapped with enormous savings in manpower and the elimination of fraud. The only exceptions would be extra funds for those certified medically unable to work, and the parents of young children who chose not to take outside employment because they wished to home-educate. Such simplicity, which could be carried into all walks of life, would let citizens know exactly where they stood and realise that the welfare state was there to help in genuinely – and *only* in genuinely – difficult times.

I suggest, Sir that if a party came up with ideas like these there would be a resurgence of interest in politics.

Yours sincerely, Heather Hemmings."

Below was pencilled: "*Sent to six newspapers - but never published.*"

'I'm not surprised,' cried Terry, 'it's over the top! It's just a far-fetched version of what Dick Nathan was advocating at our meeting.'

Dismissively he returned the letter to its envelope and then to his pocket. 'We can't propose anything like that – the country could never afford it and we'd make a laughing stock of the CSP from Day One.'

'But don't you see,' said Susan impatiently, 'that's her whole point. We need to put forward such extraordinary – outlandish - ideas that people are shocked, made to think, made to see there *are* alternatives, made to ask questions, made to contrast what we've got now with what might be, made to ask why we're in the mess we're in given the fantastic resources we have to hand, made to see there are other ways of doing things that should be catapulted into mainstream thinking.'

'But we can't do what she …'

'There you are you see, even you: "*we can't!*" And you haven't even given her idea a chance. Had *you* thought of her "sufficient basic income for everyone" idea? Had you?'

'No.'

'Well think about it now! Because although you reacted negatively, her idea has now been planted in your mind. Gradually you'll start to think:

"Well, I'm not sure, but yes, I *can* see advantages, it *could* be worked on, even if it doesn't finish up exactly as she proposes, and it *does* solve many problems – and it *would* help lots of people. There's no harm in *considering* it? Then you'd say: 'Yes, maybe we *should* give it a *try* – just for a while." And, Mr Park, you won't be the only one to think that way. Before long it will be on the popular agenda, and *that's* what the Establishment fears - too many people beginning to question, to consider, to see alternatives, to agitate, to get involved. It doesn't like alien thoughts being fed into the minds of common people.'

'Like scrapping our schools!' Terry smiled dryly.

'Exactly. But you needn't say it with such derision.'

'Sorry, but you ruffled my feathers. Anyway, the idea of paying everyone in the country a living wage, no matter how basic, is mad'

'It's not. It's an idea worth thinking about. It would close down huge tax, pensions and benefits sections of the civil service, save billions, and make a few government ministers redundant as well.'

'Another reason why it won't happen!'

Susan shook her head; her task was going to be harder than she thought. Even Terry's response to that woman's original way of thinking had been one of customary British pessimism, "It can't be done."

'All right, let's leave it there because what matters tonight is what happens in the Town Hall. So put a move on, finish your meal, get your jacket, pin on your rosette, and let's move. I don't want to miss a second of this. I can't wait for those votes to be counted. We're going to be OK. We're going to do well. I feel it in my bones, I really do!'

It was not until they had walked for some time that she realised Terry had been asking her a question.

'Susan, just listen for a minute. Listen! Do you think *she* sent the £10,000? She *was* the Fair Play Party after all. Maybe she saw that as the forerunner of The Common Sense Party and wanted to help?'

'Perhaps, but several people might have sent it and you know what my guess is on that, and we're telling nobody. But that's not top priority now so cheer up and speed up. Let's see how fit you are!'

*

The dismal assembly room within the Town Hall was less crowded than they expected although familiar faces abounded. Scrutinisers scrutinised, counters counted, policemen patrolled, candidates eyed the growing lines of votes, agents fretted, reporters reported, attendants emptied bins of plastic coffee cups and crunched up sandwich wrappers, while a plump and lethargic Lord Mayor fiddled forlornly with his heavy chain of office.

'They've finished,' hissed Dr Audrey Anderson the Mod Lab candidate. But they hadn't. She fingered the notes for her speech of acceptance and - God forbid that she would ever need them – her words of begrudged congratulations for the wholly unworthy winner should she lose. But the phone numbers of four shipping lines that cruised in far waters and employed ships' doctors had been noted in her diary.

Today's Tory Party candidate, Chris Clay, was hopeful: he was the only one with realistic expectations. A majority of 222 was beatable and his followers had worked hard, but with limited success, to get the voters out. There may be recounts, but he could weather those and they would make the loathsome Anderson sweat profusely.

Dorothy Devonport, for the Tolerant Democrats, had given up. Too many canvassed voters had castigated her for being on the side of the wrongdoer, the scrounger, the wastrel, the cheat and the vandal, and told her that tolerance was a virtue only if it supported society's hardworking, law-abiding citizens. Were the halcyon days of the unthinking do-gooder soon to be part of English social history?

However Humphrey Higginbotham of The Rhubarb, Rhubarb Party, who had arrived in the hall carrying ten lengthy sticks of rhubarb each with a heavy, broad, far-reaching and still wet leaf, had been delighted with his reception on doorsteps. Tributes had abounded and support had escalated. Clearly Britain's future lay in rhubarb!

Terry sat with Susan at the back of the room nervously watching all that was going on, while Hetty Hopkins, seeking exclusives, circulated as she tried to grill the seven candidates. Her Great Hulk grumbled and wandered like a disorientated grizzly bear between the Town Hall and *The King's Head,* but Hetty knew he would be good to have around in case of late-night fisticuffs.

'You're doing well,' Hetty told Terry, deliberately ignoring Susan. 'Your votes are piling up and we've had hundreds of enquiries following your advert! Can I have your initial reaction to the exit polls …?

But Susan, unimpressed by a bulging blouse and short skirt, saw her off: 'The candidate will issue a press statement as soon as the result is declared. Thank you for your interest.'

Peter Perkins was ecstatic. He needed no Hetty Hopkins to tell him his "Spoil Your Paper" campaign had been a triumph. Tray after tray after tray of spoiled papers was being filled. His supporters had been asked not to vote for him but to put a heavy 'X' from one corner to the other on the ballot paper, and that they had done. But a pompous official had annoyed Perkins when he said, 'No Sir, you cannot see the spoilt papers to read the remarks written on them, and also, Sir,' the man had hinted darkly, 'some of the comments are so disgusting that the city police are perusing sections of the Obscene Publications Acts, as amended…'

The candidate, in his imagination, gave a two-fingered salute.

As a second recount was announced it was clear that Mansworth's house sparrows had not flown very high. While the elderly Sybil Sylvester knew that two neighbours, three twice-removed cousins, the Methodist minister's mother, the pet-shop owner and his gullible daughter, and she herself had voted to save the struggling bird, there had been little doorstep encouragement during her tireless weeks of canvassing. One forthright voter had said the crackpot candidate could stuff her sparrows, present their effigies to the natural history museum and then clean their filthy muck off her bedroom windows. Another, tipsy, had assured her that his tomcat's greatest pleasure in life was to pounce every sparrow in sight!

Tension was running high and the Returning Officer soon forgot about an early night. Dejectedly he announced another recount.

Bystanders listening-in on their radios to already-declared results learned that the two main parties were neck and neck. Mansworth South-West was to be no exception.

There was another false alarm when the Returning Officer looked as though he was about to ascend the podium with his thin, grey-suited minion in tow, but then changed his mind. For the anxious Dr Audrey Anderson a hasty visit to the Ladies' had been required, but, before she could emerge, only partly relieved, the Returning Officer had conferred yet again with party agents and approached the microphone with deadly intent.

'As the Returning Officer for the constituency of' Mansworth South West…' the important man began, 'I hereby declare that the number of votes cast for each candidate …' he scrutinised his paper in the poor light, ' for each candidate are as follows.'

Unnoticed, and for the first time in forty-four and a half years, the Bachelor of Medicine, Audrey Amy Anderson, M.P., mother of two, general practitioner and politician, emerged from the Ladies' with unwashed hands.

There was silence in the Town Hall. Then, as if for good measure, the Returning Officer repeated: '...are as follows:

Audrey Amy Anderson:	(*Modern Labour*)	8,123
Christopher Cedric Clay:	(*Today's Tories*)	8,124
Dorothy May Devonport	(*Tolerant Democrats*)	*999
Humphrey Higginbotham	(*Rhubarb-Rhubarb Alliance*)	*262
Terence Arthur Park:	(*Common Sense Party*)	4,001
Peter Ian Perkins:	(*Spoil Your Paper Party*)	*1
Sybil Sylvester:	(*Save Our House Sparrows*)	*9

Spoilt papers: 6,532.   *Electorate: 78,787.*   **Lost deposits: 4.*
Turnout: (including spoilt papers): 28,051 (35.6%).

The silence did not last. Roars of applause, slow hand-clapping, boos, stamping of feet, jeers, chants, cheers, cries of '*shame, get lost',* and vulgar whistling filled the packed hall after each announcement. With alacrity, vigour and only half-hidden pleasure, the patrolling police ejected would-be firework throwers and other likely troublemakers.

Peter Ian Perkins grabbed the microphone shouting, 'The six and a half thousand spoilt papers show the utter contempt people feel for politicians.' But, despite loud cries of "*hear, hear*!" and "*let him speak!*" he was dragged from the stage by the combined force of a policeman, a hefty official and an incredulous Audrey Anderson. Her face was a ghastly white as she realised she had lost by one vote.

Sybil Sylvester's result was greeted by a drunken rendering of *Bye Bye Blackbird* from a rapidly growing, chair-tipping, brawling, bawling and drunken element. The police cells would be full tonight.

Eastman turned to Townsend: 'Good. Let the yobbos break the place up, the result's marvellous for us. It means there'll be no radical change, we'll get the same ineffectual shower in office as before but with a different label. The Cromford-Whites will be pleased.' Then he paused. 'The only fly in the ointment is Park's vote.' He scowled darkly for a moment but then said, on a happier note, 'but we've got time, Townsend, time to stifle Park and his lecturing mistress!'

But his lackey Giles Townsend was not happy and any mention of the Cromford-Whites still terrified him. He had never got over their visit.

There was more raucous shouting from outside as other results were relayed, but Susan ignored it. She was over the moon.

'Terry, Terry darling, don't you realise? We've done it: we've easily got our five per cent and kept our deposit! Lovely, lovely, lovely Terry' and she hugged him and kissed him as, lightning-like, Hetty Hopkins thrust her tired photographer towards them. His ceiling-bounced flash would give tomorrow's *Messenger & Times* readers an intimate close-up of the interlocked couple.

'There'll be another recount,' spluttered Terry, breathless in Susan's body-merging grip. 'They'll never, never concede on one vote!'

But they did. Christopher Cedric Clay of Today's Tories accepted the result eagerly and acknowledged the honour bestowed on him by the perceptive voters of Mansworth South-West, while hundreds hissed and then began *Land of Hope and Glory* even though others were halfway through *Rule Britannia!* Terry, after his few words at the microphone, got cheers that excelled any afforded the other also-rans. Susan joined him as he left the stage, her face a mixture of joy and relief. They hugged again and more press cameras clicked.

'Never,' scrawled Hetty Hopkins, 'has a winning candidate been so coldly received, or losers such as Perkins and Park been so loudly applauded. Mansworth voters showed they are weary of the old parties. They either voted for common sense or showed their disillusionment with our antiquated system by either abstaining completely or by spoiling ballot papers in hundreds and thousands.'

Exhausted and fed up, her editor let it pass.

Friday   3 May.   **Repercussions**

It was too late in the morning for Terry to go to bed so he dozed in an armchair until the radio roused him with more election results. There was to be a hung parliament. While each party had gained fewer votes than in the previous election all were claiming a *splendid* Victory! He frowned when he heard that the PPP had won five seats and come close in ten others, but switched off in disgust when the commentator tried to play down the PPP progress. That's just it, Terry thought, shove it under the carpet, close your eyes, look the other way, shrug it off, pretend it hasn't happened, and may Heaven help us all!

Later he was too tired to appreciate fully the congratulations he received at school, but did note that Ingrid was smug. The sweet-scented

Louie Anne Lee ignored Ingrid and gave Terry a close hug, which, had the surroundings been more propitious and his own energy more abundant, he would have prolonged with pleasure.

Genuinely delighted, Adrian Olde congratulated him, as did Ursula Irving. 'So people really did vote for Terry Park!' said Olde. 'It was a remarkable feat with your one-man stand.' Then he smiled, 'with a one-man and one-woman stand! So now, if you work hard and build up your party, and get Perkins to persuade his paper-spoilers to join you, you'll be in with a real chance.' Olde looked out of his window to watch another swimming-pool bus unload its noisy charges. 'That's a better prospect than the headship of this school.'

Or any other, thought Terry.

Congratulations continued throughout the lunch hour. Newspapers were glanced at and speculation made on what the new government would do for teachers. 'Not much,' was the consensus. But widely accepted was the fact that Terry had done well. 'Now it all depends,' said one sceptic, 'on how big a mess this new lot makes. If it's shambolic enough people will turn to your CSP in hordes.'

Terry had doubts, the disillusioned hordes might turn to the PPP?

One unsmiling person was Dafydd Hughes. He waited until the celebratory noises had subsided and teachers had dispersed to decide what to do with their classes until the end of Friday school, before he moved to sit with Terry.

'Well done Mate, you proved me wrong - and lots of others as well.'

'Thanks,' Terry replied, 'thanks. But you look frazzled round the edges. Were you up all night, too?'

'No. It's not that, it's about Jenny. She bothers me.'

'*Bothers* you? Come on, I haven't seen you taking evasive action.'

'I haven't, and I won't, not if I have anything to do with it. But she's definitely thinking of packing it all in. Of getting out.'

'Out of here?'

'Out of teaching – altogether.'

'She's told you that?'

'Yes, and I'm sure she'd have told you before long, so don't hold that against her.

'Come on! You know me better than that!'

'Sorry – but she wants to give private tutoring a whirl. She wants to set up her own learning and teaching groups, starting with about four groups, but with never more than three or four children with her at any one time, and then tutor them in topics that interest them - ones they come up with themselves. She thinks she can make a go of it.'

'Financially?'

'And professionally.'

'You're sure of this?'

'Yes. She reckons she could live on less than she earns here and would be happier doing something she enjoys and that children want to do and which their parents support.' He hesitated. 'She says it's no use hanging round waiting for that to happen in this God-forsaken dump so she might as well shove off and have a bash on her own.'

'She put it like that?'

'No,' Hughes smiled weakly, 'but that's what she meant.'

Terry had difficulty taking it in. 'When was this?'

'Last week.'

'I see. Another good one going.' Terry paused, shook his head, and then turned to Hughes. 'Look, Dafydd, I'm sorry, but this really is a lousy time. I'm knackered, I really am. Get me a coffee – no make it a tea if there's one left in the pot – there's just time.'

Afternoon school was five minutes away and Terry had hoped for a quick snooze. Now there was this.

'Thanks,' he said as Hughes returned. 'But can't this wait?'

'No. I've put off telling you because of the headship interviews and the general election; I thought you'd got enough on your plate.'

'You'd have been right.'

'And it's now Friday and I wanted a word before the weekend to tell you what she's been thinking. She's a serious girl at heart and doesn't like what she sees here or many of the things she hears or reads about education elsewhere. So she wants out.'

'She shouldn't believe all she hears and reads, you know that.'

'If a tenth is true it's enough - and *you* know *that*! She wants out.'

'And you don't want her out?'

'No.'

'Why?'

'Oh for God's sake, man, can't you guess? And besides that, I don't think she'll make a go of it. She's studied home schooling and the eminent people who've written about alternative education in one form or another and she's picked up some fancy ideas. She's got a long list of celebrated people who never went to any school and say they're glad they didn't.'

'Like the anthropologist Margaret Mead? Her grandmother wanted her to have an education so she kept her out of school!' mused Terry. 'Or John Kirkbride: "That children do not come to school by choice is another terrible indictment of our whole educational system."'

' I'd buy that! How many of these do you know?'

'Scores. I can lend you a book.'

'Don't bother. But what about Jenny?'

'That's up to her, isn't it? You can only point out the snags, tell her not to rush things, be supportive, and leave it at that.'

Hughes did not reply.

'Come on now, Dafydd, that's all you can do. You're not her keeper.'

Still Hughes was silent. Terry had never seen him so dejected.

'OK,' he conceded, 'I'll talk to her. I'll point out a few problems. But I won't put her off completely as she might be on to something good and I'm not having her coming back in a few years saying "You told me not to." So I won't *tell* her anything. In fact, on thinking about it, I wouldn't mind having a go at it myself. But, honestly, I'm not up to seeing her now. I'm not. Won't early next week do?'

'Of course it will, and thanks.' Hughes rose to leave. 'You're a good bloke, Terry, I won't forget this.' He held out his hand. 'And you did well, really well - both of you! Got far more votes than I expected. But there's the bell! So on your feet, Park! More "education."'

Terry, too, had heard the bell. He had half expected a call from Susan during the lunch break, but none had come. There was no call after school either. Terry put it down to fatigue after the headship interviews and the three weeks of electioneering.

At home, after a snack, he fell fast asleep. Eventually, wakened by the phone, he staggered to his feet, but was too late. He checked 1471, recognised Susan's number, and called back.

'I rang earlier,' she said, 'twice, but got no reply. I was going to suggest meeting at *The King of Morocco*, but it's late now and I've too much to do. Meet me there for coffee in the morning, about eleven.'

'But it's only half past nine,' Terry protested.

'Too late for me. I'm shattered. I'll see you tomorrow.'

'Come on, Susan!' pleaded Terry, now wide awake, 'don't be like that, we did well. Even Olde was impressed, and Hughes. They all were - well, nearly all. It was a wonderful result: you said so yourself. And we kept our deposit. Just one quick drink to celebrate?'

'Not tonight, Terry, I'll see you tomorrow. We can talk then.'

Terry could not imagine what was so urgent she couldn't meet him for half an hour. But he, too, was "shattered" and after a beer and then another with a tot of whisky to help it down, he rolled into bed and slept until nine-thirty next morning.

Saturday   4 May.   **A New Dawn**

'No, I just want a black coffee, please. Really!'

'Coffee in a pub?' Terry expostulated. 'Since when …'

'Get me a coffee,' said Susan heading for the window seat. The pub was nearly empty. 'But you have what you want.'

Terry sensed something was wrong. He ignored the barman's leer as he ordered coffee.

'I'm not having a real drink,' Susan said, 'because I'm driving this afternoon and tiredness, alcohol and driving are lethal.'

'Driving? Where to?'

'Birmingham?'

'*Birmingham*? Haven't you had enough for this week?'

'More than enough, but I've got to forget that and get there today. That's what I wanted to talk to you about last night when you didn't answer. You see, and I know you won't like this, Terry, but I've got a research post, with a leading team, a high-powered team, in a principal and progressive university in Portland in Oregon. It's an incredible chance, not to be missed. The enthusiasm, the drive, the resources, the sheer get-up-and-go philosophy, are unbelievable.'

'Oregon? Good God, Susan, that's five thousand miles away!'

'Six. But listen, Terry, listen while I explain. Please! Listen! This has been more or less fixed for months. I could have gone before Easter, but put it off, mainly for your sake.'

'For my sake? *My* sake? Come on, Susan, you've been headhunted! The Yanks were after you and made it worth your while to go! Right?'

'No, not exactly.' She paused. 'I was going to tell you weeks ago, but first the headship and then the general election came up and I chickened out. I knew it would upset you.'

'*Upset me*? Of course it would upset me! The States? Hell, Susan, Oregon? On the Pacific coast isn't it? On the far side? Not even the Portland in Maine?'

'And it would have put you off doing your best for both positions. I didn't want to harm your chances for the headship ...'

'Damn the headship! And the election! I lost both.'

'Please, Terry, please hear me out. I could never have turned this job down. Not only is there the research work but a Chicago publisher is almost certain to take my book and the American market's enormous. I don't think it would ever be published here – no one would even look at it. I have to be over there. I can't work from this distance, and there isn't the same money here. Those four things all go together: enthusiasm, research, publication, finance: they do. They really *do*. And the chance won't come again, it can't, it just can't'

'This is the last straw, Susan, it really is. What am I going to do?'

'You'll manage, you will. You *will*! Believe me! Now, go and get another drink, please, and get me one as well, but a small one.'

'Bugger the drinks!'

'Terry, I've tried, I really have tried and tried and tried and tried to make it clear to you that I like you, that I'm very fond of you, that I enjoy your company, that I think you've got terrific talent ...'

'Thanks!'

'But I've also made it clear, Terry, and you must admit I have, that I'll never be a one-man woman. Never. That's just not me.'

Terry shut his eyes as if that would stop him from hearing her.

'But I could see you were different from the other men; different and better. You have the imagination, ideas and plans that this poor, outdated country needs if it is to survive. And I'm not embellishing it.'

'But you're...'

'Patronising? No, I'm not. Nor am I enhancing your ability, nor am I exaggerating this country's plight because if it doesn't modernise its institutions soon it's in real trouble. The signs are all there. But that will be its own fault. That list the ninety-year-old woman gave you on the doorstep was spot-on. We should have been braver and included all her proposals in the manifesto and a few more besides.'

'It was too late. And ... anyway, forget the election, that's past.'

'I will not forget it, and nor will you, because there will be other elections.' She looked at him piercingly, demanding his attention.

'I could see how difficult it was going to be for you to give me up, *which you've got to do*.' She emphasised each word in repeater-rifle fashion and held up her hand as Terry prepared to protest again, 'I wanted you to have something to help with that. Well, now you've got it.

You've got the chance to build a new party, a party based on common sense, a party free of tie-me-down, all-the-same, outdated politics, free of self-important privately-educated elites, free of the nauseous propaganda churned out by tribes of do-gooders and the contemptuous cohorts of the politically correct. Then there are the lefties, the neo-fascists, the traditionalists, the social climbers, the Westminster conventionalists, the-live-in-the-past nobility, the bewigged sit-on-high judiciary – all stifling this poor country as they have for the past sixty or seventy years while other nations have forged ahead. But – just listen a minute - you can be in at the beginning of change, in fact you *are* at the beginning of change. Change *has* begun. The thousands of votes for you, the thousands of spoilt papers, the thousands who stayed away, all showed people are browned off - they've had enough. This is the chance you've wanted.'

'I wanted you.'

'I'm sorry, I know that, but …'

'How long are you going to be away?'

'I'm not coming back. I'm leaving this country for good. A small feeder or test unit is to be based in Birmingham UK, but I'm to be in the main USA team along with two others from England.'

'Two men?'

'Perhaps. I don't know. But there's no other special man in the frame if that's what you mean. And you must stop thinking like that,' she urged. 'I'm not indispensable. There are women out there who are much better for you than I am. Much, much, much better. There really are. They would love you as I never could.'

Terry shook his head. 'I'd settle for whatever love you could give me. That would do.'

'You will find a woman who will love you without limits.'

'But will I love her?' He shook his head again. 'I don't think so. Not as I've come to love you.' He took her hand and held it tightly. 'I would have taken whatever you could give me, no matter how little, and I'd have been happy with that, quite, quite happy.'

Susan did not reply. She looked down at the pub's old table, at its scratched, stained surface, her now unwanted coffee, his half-finished beer, an array of mats, an empty ashtray, a solitary peanut missed by the early morning cleaners, his bunch of keys, her heavy purse, a wilting carnation in a mass-produced and slightly-chipped vase, a fly that looked as if it would land on the peanut, but changed its mind and flew away.

'I'm sorry,' she said. 'But that's how it is. That's how it's got to be. It has, truly. So let's go now. Please, Terry, please, let's go.'

He did not answer, but sat holding her hand.

'I don't want to go.'

'You've got to.' She waited. 'And I've got to.'

'No, you haven't got to. You want to.'

'Yes,' she said quietly. 'Yes, if I'm honest, I want to leave England. I've had enough, too.'

'That's what Jenny Jones said about teaching. She's had enough.'

'That doesn't surprise me.'

Terry picked up his glass with one hand but did not drink. He tilted the glass, to and fro, to and fro, and with each tilt the unwanted beer almost went over the rim, but not quite. Then he set the glass down and stared at her for a long time. She said nothing.

'Don't lose contact, not altogether,' he said at last, knowing he was beaten. 'Write. Let me know how you're getting on. Will you?'

She was silent. She looked away.

'Will you?'

'Yes.'

And with that, reluctantly and very slowly, he let go of her hand.

'But,' she continued, 'only on two, no, three conditions...'

'No conditions.'

'Yes. Just listen. First you promise not to sit around waiting for me, just hoping and hoping and hoping, because it's not going to happen. That's hard, but it has to be said. Second, if I write to tell you about my work, you will write to tell me how the CSP is progressing – how it's growing - and what you're doing to push it forward. Third, you will press on with your novel, finish it, and send me a signed copy when it's published. Is that agreed?'

'Is it important?'

'Yes, it is, very important. So, is it agreed? Truly?'

'It has to be,' Terry nodded, 'what other option have I?'

'To find someone else'

Terry shook his head.

'Yes, to find someone else: a lovely woman. Perhaps someone much younger than I am, someone who wants to be married, to be a wife, to have a home and children – lots of children and grandchildren. Love her, Terry, treasure her, be warm and kind and gentle to her, respect her, and the rest will follow. You'll see.'

She stood up, patted his hand, then his forehead, but did not kiss him.

She collected her purse, hesitated, turned, and walked away. She did not look back as she let the door swing to behind her.

Terry sat, flat beer beside him, shattered. Nothing mattered now. Nothing. He could replace his drink easily, but didn't make the effort. "To find someone else!" Just like that! "Find someone else!" Where? In some sleazy dance hall or strip joint? Some singles' over-forties, final-fling all-inclusive holiday on the Costa Bloody Brava? Or in some God forsaken adult education class, *Basketwork for Beginners*, run by some frumpy spinster in tweeds? Good grief! What a sodding laugh it was! "Find someone else!" Just like that!

He sat and sat for a long time, gazing at nothing.

'Oregon!' he kept saying to himself, 'Oregon!' He knew nothing about Oregon except that it was a million miles from Mansworth.

'And how much are they paying her?' he muttered. 'A hell of a lot! That's the trouble with the Yanks; if they want something they move in, pay up, get it, and move on to their next target. So damn the lot of them, every one, all three hundred million!'

*

'Terry? *Terry*? Are you all right?'

For a moment Louie Anne Lee stood in front of him before she perched, gingerly, on the edge of Susan's chair. 'Are you all right?' she repeated. 'Has she gone?'

'Louie Anne!' said Terry, surprised. 'What are you doing here?'

'I'm asking if you're all right and whether your friend's gone.'

'Yes,' said Terry, 'my friend's gone.'

'And are you all right? Are you? Because you don't look all right.'

'I'll be fine in a minute. How did you know we were here?'

'I didn't. I saw you through the window – from the street. You both looked unhappy. Then you were here, later, by yourself, still unhappy, so I came in to find out why. That's all.' She spoke affectionately. 'Honestly. There was nothing else. Not really.'

Terry looked at her while she sat looking back at him curiously, her head slightly to one side, still perching where Susan had sat.

She was a beautiful young woman, he thought, so slender, so simply dressed, so little make-up, so kind, so pleasant, so concerned, so keen, so unassuming, with such lovely, long, thick hair which she now wore loosely - unlike at school - so that it reached well below her shoulders.

'Are you here on your own?' Terry asked.

'Yes. I'm supposed to be Saturday morning shopping.'

'Shopping?' he repeated quietly. 'I see.'

'Yes. I've bought two sleeveless tops, nice ones, perfect fit, quite reasonable, too, in the Marks and Spencer sale.'

'For your holiday?'

'Maybe, I've nothing booked, though, not yet.'

They sat quietly.

'Two sleeveless tops, he repeated, 'In a sale. Right.'

She waited.

'Right,' he said again. 'That's good, very good.' Then, quite out of the blue, he asked, 'how old are you, Louie Anne?'

She smiled and, inexperienced as she was, seized what she saw as her chance.

'Old enough to have a drink.'

Terry smiled, his first smile for a very long time. 'Of course. I'm sorry. What will you …'

'A sweet white wine.'

'A large glass?'

'Please.'

She slid onto Susan's chair and watched him cross to the bar. He was a marvellous man. She'd fancied him for such a long time, and, if she were truthful, she'd fancied him more than that wandering Welshman. Younger men did not match Terry Park, yet she had been unable to do anything but watch because that university woman was out of her league. She could never compete with Susan Mansfield's degrees, books, papers, assignments, theses, journals, programmes, lectures, seminars, tutorials, conferences, postgraduate students, professors, readers, vice-chancellors, bibliographies, research: the whole vast, complex, closed and unexplored world of an established university. And the woman probably had other experience too, and plenty of it.

She waited, and then smiled as he returned.

'There you are, a large glass,' said Terry. 'And a beer for me and crisps for us both.' The crisps were in a white, plastic bowl taken from the bar. 'Cheese and onion.'

'Thank you,' Louie Anne murmured. 'I like cheese and onion.' She helped herself, delicately, taking one crisp at a time.

'Will she be back soon, your friend?'

As she asked she turned away from him and sipped her wine. It was refreshingly cool, and sweet.

'Susan? No, Susan's not coming back.'

'Not coming back?'

'No.'

'Not at all?'

'Not at all.'

'And that's why you're looking so miserable?'

'Am I looking miserable?'

'You are. Of course you are. You know you are: down and out, beaten, abandoned. So can't I help? Please? Help just a little?'

It seemed ages before Terry answered. Then he leaned towards her and put a hand gently over one of hers. Subconsciously he pressed his thumb lightly against the underside of her wrist and then began to move it slowly in tiny semi-circles backwards and forwards. 'How old *are* you, Louie Anne?' he asked again.

The pub was unusually quiet for a Saturday morning. A couple were chatting at the bar, an elderly man tut-tutted as he read *The Telegraph* editorial, there was no music, and no one was sitting near them.

'Nineteen. Nineteen years, eleven months, three weeks and four days. My birthday's on Wednesday.'

'Half my age.'

'Does that matter?' she asked softly, not shifting her hand, but slowly moving the other one closer to his. 'Does it?'

Terry laughed quietly as the tips of his fingers took over from his thumb and he began to massage first the smooth, warm skin on the back of her hand, and then that – much warmer - beyond her wrist. But there was nothing subconscious in Louie Anne Lee's cautious repositioning of her arm on the table as she edged her other hand, slowly, towards his. This time he did notice.

'Do you know, Louie Anne Lee,' he said, 'I don't think it does! Come to think of it, not much matters at all, does it? So drink up and I'll fetch us another. And would you like a bite to eat?'

'Oh yes, I'd love that,' she said eagerly, 'I'd just love that!'
